SANDRA BROWN

DEADLINE

First published in the United States of America in 2013 by Grand Central Publishing
A division of Hachette Book Group, Inc.
First published in Great Britain in 2013 by Hodder & Stoughton
An Hachette UK company

1

A CIP catalogue record for this title is
available from the British Library.

Trade paperback ISBN 978 1 444 73216 0
Ebook ISBN 978 1 444 73889 6

Printed and bound in Great Britain by Clays Ltd, St Ives plc

Hodder & Stoughton policy is to use papers that are natural,
renewable and recyclable products and made from wood grown in sustainable
forests. The logging and manufacturing processes are expected to conform to
the environmental regulations of the country of origin.

Hodder & Stoughton Ltd
338 Euston Road
London NW1 3BH

www.hodder.co.uk

DEADLINE

Prologue

Golden Branch, Oregon—1976

The first hail of bullets was fired from the house shortly after daybreak at six fifty-seven.

The gunfire erupted in response to the surrender demand issued by a team of law enforcement agents.

It was a gloomy morning. The sky was heavily overcast and there was dense fog. Despite the limited visibility, one of the fugitives inside the house got off a lucky shot that took out a deputy US marshal whom everybody called Turk.

Gary Headly had met the marshal only the day before, shortly after the law enforcement team comprising ATF and FBI agents, sheriff's deputies, and US marshals met for the first time to discuss the operation. They'd been congregated around a map of the area known as Golden Branch, reviewing obstacles they might encounter. Headly remembered another marshal saying, "Hey, Turk, grab me a Coke while you're over there, will ya?"

Headly didn't learn Turk's actual name until later, much later, when they were mopping up. The bullet struck half an inch above his Kevlar vest, tearing out most of his throat. He dropped without uttering a sound, dead before landing in the pile of wet leaves at his feet. There was nothing Headly could do for him except offer up a brief prayer and remain behind cover. To move was to invite death or injury, because once the gunfire started, the open windows of the house spat bullets relentlessly.

The Rangers of Righteousness had an inexhaustible arsenal. Or so it seemed that wet and dreary morning. The second casualty was a red-headed, twenty-four-year-old deputy sheriff. A puff of his breath in the cold air gave away his position. Six shots were fired. Five found the target. Any one of three would have killed him.

The team had planned to take the group by surprise, serve their arrest warrants for a long list of felonies, and take them into custody, engaging in a firefight only if necessary. But the vehemence with which they were fired upon indicated that the criminals had taken a fight-to-the-death stance.

After all, they had nothing to lose except their lives. Capture meant imprisonment for life or the death penalty for each of the seven members of the domestic-terrorist group. Collectively the six men and one woman had chalked up twelve murders and millions of dollars' worth of destruction, most of it inflicted on federal government buildings or military installations. Despite the religious overtone of their name, they weren't faith-based fanatics but rather wholly without conscience or constraint. Over the relatively short period of two years, they had made themselves notorious, a scourge to law enforcement agencies at every level.

Other such groups imitated the Rangers, but none had achieved their level of effectiveness. In the criminal community, they were revered for their audacity and unmatched violence. To many who harbored antigovernment sentiments, they had become folk heroes. They were sheltered and provided with weapons and ammunition, as well as with leaked, classified information. This underground support allowed them to strike hard and fast and then to disappear and remain well hidden while they planned their next assault. In communiqués sent to newspapers and television networks, they'd vowed never to be taken alive.

It had been a stroke of sheer luck that had brought the law down on them in Golden Branch.

One of their arms suppliers, who was well known to the authorities for his criminal history, had been placed under surveillance for suspicion of an arms deal unrelated to the Rangers of Righteousness. He had made three trips to the abandoned house in Golden Branch over the course of that many weeks. A telephoto lens had caught him talking to a man later identified as Carl Wingert, leader of the Rangers.

When this was reported to the FBI, ATF, and US Marshals Service, the agencies immediately sent personnel, who continued to monitor the illegal weapons dealer. Upon his return from a visit to Golden Branch, he was arrested.

It took three days of persuasion, but under advice of counsel he made a deal with the authorities and gave up what he knew about the people holed up inside the abandoned house. He'd only met with Carl Wingert. He couldn't—or wouldn't—say who else was sequestered with Wingert or how long they planned to harbor there.

Fearing that if they didn't move swiftly, they'd miss their opportunity to capture one of the FBI's Most Wanted, the federal agents enlisted help from the local authorities, who also had outstanding warrants for members of the group. The team was assembled and the operation planned.

But it became immediately obvious to each member of the team that Wingert's band had meant what they'd said about choosing death over capture. The Rangers of Righteousness wanted to secure their place in history. There would be no laying down of arms, no hands raised in peaceful surrender.

The lawmen were pinned down behind trees or vehicles, and

all were vulnerable. Even a flicker of motion drew gunfire, and members of the Rangers had proven themselves to be excellent shots.

The resident agent in charge, Emerson, radioed the operations post, requesting that a helicopter be sent to provide them air cover, but that idea was nixed because of the inclement weather.

Special Ops teams from local, state, and federal agencies were mobilized, but they would be driving to Golden Branch, and the roads weren't ideal even in good weather. The team were told to stand by and to fire only in self-defense, while men in safe, warm offices debated changing the rules of engagement to include using deadly force.

"They're playing pattycake because one of them is a woman," Emerson groused to Headly. "And God forbid we violate these killers' civil rights. Nobody admires or respects us, you know."

Headly, the rookie of the team, wisely held his own counsel.

"We're feds, and even before Watergate, *government* had become a dirty word. The whole damn country is going to hell in a handbasket, and we're out here freezing our balls off, waiting for some bureaucrat to tell us it's okay to blast these murdering thugs to hell and back."

Emerson had a military background and a decidedly hawkish viewpoint, but nobody, especially not he, wanted a bloodbath that morning.

Nobody got what they wanted.

While the reinforcements were still en route, the Rangers amped up their firepower. An ATF agent took a bullet in the thigh, and, from the way it was bleeding, it was feared his femoral artery had suffered damage, the extent of which was unknown, but on any scale it was a life-threatening wound.

Emerson reported this with a spate of obscenities about their being picked off one by effing one unless…

He was given the authorization to engage. With their assault rifles and one submachine gun—in the hands of the wounded ATF agent—they went on the offensive. The barrage lasted for seven minutes.

Return fire from the house decreased, then became sporadic. Emerson ordered a cease-fire. They waited.

Suddenly, bleeding from several wounds including a head wound, a man charged through the front door, screaming invectives and spraying rounds from his own submachine gun. It was a suicidal move, and he knew it. His reason for doing it would soon become apparent.

When the agents ceased firing, and their ears stopped ringing, they realized that the house had fallen eerily silent except for a loose shutter that clapped against an exterior wall whenever the wind caught it.

After a tense sixty seconds, Emerson said, "I'm going in." He levered himself up into a crouch as he replaced his spent clip magazine with a fresh one.

Headly did the same. "I'm with you."

Other team members stayed in place. After checking to see that their guns were loaded with fresh magazines, Emerson crept from behind his cover and began running toward the house. Headly, with his heart tightly lodged in his throat, followed.

They ran past the body sprawled on the wet earth, took the steps up to the sagging porch, then stood on either side of the gaping doorway, weapons raised. They waited, listening. Hearing nothing, Emerson hitched his head and Headly barged in.

Bodies. Blood on every surface, the stench of it strong. Nothing was moving.

"Clear," he shouted and stepped over a body on his way into an adjacent room, a bedroom with only a ratty mattress on the floor. In the center of it, the ticking was still wet with a nasty stain.

In less than sixty seconds from the time Headly had breached the door, they confirmed that five people were dead. Four bodies were found inside the house. The fifth was the man who'd died in the yard. They were visually identified as known members of the Rangers of Righteousness.

Conspicuously missing from the body count were Carl Wingert and his lover, Flora Stimel, the only woman of the group. There was no sign of the two of them except for a trail of blood leading away from the back of the house into the dense woods, where tire tracks were found in the undergrowth. They had managed to escape, probably because their mortally wounded confederate had sacrificed himself, taking fire at the front of the house while they sneaked out the back.

Emergency and official vehicles quickly converged on the area. With them came the inevitable news vans, which were halted a mile away at the turnoff from the main road. The house and the area immediately surrounding it were sealed off so evidence could be collected, photos and measurements taken, and diagrams drawn before the bodies were removed.

Those involved realized that a thorough investigation of the incident would follow. Every action they'd taken would have to be explained and justified, not only to their superiors but also to a cynical and judgmental public.

Soon the derelict house was filled with people, each doing a specialized job. Headly found himself back in the bedroom, standing beside the coroner, who was sniffing at the stain on the soiled mattress. To Headly, it appeared that someone had peed in addition to bleeding profusely. "Urine?"

The coroner shook his head. "I believe it's amniotic fluid."

Headly thought surely he'd misheard him. "Amniotic fluid? Are you saying that Floral Stimel—"

"Gave birth."

Chapter 1

Present day

What's with the hair?"

"That's how you greet a man returning from war? Nice to see you, too, Harriet."

Dawson Scott resented her summons—no other word for it—and made his resentment plain as he took a seat, then sank down into a bona fide slouch. He propped one ankle on the opposite knee, clasped his hands over his concave stomach, and yawned, knowing full well that his attitude would crawl all over her.

It did.

She removed her jeweled reading glasses and dropped them onto the desk. Its polished surface symbolized her new status as "boss." His boss.

"I've seen soldiers who just returned from Afghanistan. None looked like something a cat threw up." She gave him a scathing once-over, taking in his three-day scruff and long hair, which, since his time out of the country, had grown well past his collar.

He placed his hand over his heart. "Ouch. And here I was about to tell you how good you look. You're carrying those extra ten pounds really well."

She glowered but didn't say anything.

Twiddling his thumbs, literally, he took a long, slow survey of the corner office, his gaze pausing to appreciate the panoramic view through the wide windows. By craning his neck just a bit, he could see Old Glory hanging limp atop the capitol dome. Coming back to her, he remarked, "Nice office."

"Thank you."

"Who'd you blow?"

Under her breath, she cursed him. He'd heard her say those words out loud. He'd heard her shout them down the length of the conference table during editorial meetings when someone disagreed with her. Apparently with her new position came a certain restraint, which he immediately made his personal goal to crack.

"You just can't stand it, can you?" she said, gloating smile in place. "Deal with it, Dawson. I'm above you now."

He shuddered. "God spare me an image of that."

Her eyes shot daggers, but she obviously had a speech prepared, and even his insulting wisecracks weren't going to rob her of the pleasure of delivering it. "I have editorial control now. Full editorial control. Which means that I have the authority to approve, amend, or decline any story ideas you submit. I also have the authority to assign you stories if you don't come up with your own. Which you haven't. Not for the two weeks since you've been back in the States."

"I've been using up accumulated vacation days. The time off was approved."

"By my predecessor."

"Before you took his place."

"I didn't *take* anything," she said tightly. "I earned this position."

Dawson raised one shoulder. "Whatever, Harriet."

But his indifference was phony. The recent corporate shakeup had measured a ten on the Richter scale of his professional future. He'd received an e-mail from a colleague before the official blanket notification went out to all *NewsFront* employees, and even the distance between Washington and Kabul hadn't been enough to buffer the bad news. A corporate asshole, somebody's nephew, who knew slim to none about news-magazine publishing, or news in general for that matter, had named Harriet Plummer as editor-in-chief, effective immediately.

She was a disastrous choice for the position, first because she was more corporate animal than journalist. On any given tough editorial call, her top priority would be to protect the magazine against possible lawsuits. Stories addressing controversial topics would be watered down or canned altogether. Which, in Dawson's opinion, amounted to editorial castration.

Secondly, she was a card-carrying ball breaker who had no leadership qualities. She harbored a scornful dislike for people in general, an even stronger antipathy toward the male of the species, and big-time loathing for Dawson Scott in particular. As humbly as possible, he recognized that her animosity was largely based on jealousy of his talent and the respect it had earned him among his colleagues at *NewsFront* and beyond.

But on the day she was appointed editor-in-chief, the source of her hostility had ceased to matter. It was there, it was robust, it was enduring, and she was now in charge. That sucked. Nothing could be worse.

Or so he'd thought.

She said, "I'm sending you to Idaho."

"What for?"

"Blind balloonists."

"Excuse me?"

She pushed a file folder across the desk toward him. "Our researchers have done the heavy lifting for you. You can acquaint yourself with the program on the flight out there."

"Give me a hint."

"Some group of do-gooders started taking blind people up in hot-air balloons and showing them the ropes. So to speak."

The cheeky add-on didn't get a smile out of Dawson, who kept his expression impassive. Leaving the folder where it lay, he asked, "And this is hard news?"

She smiled sweetly. Or tried. On her face, coyness didn't quite work. "To the blind balloonists it is."

Her smugness made him want to vault the desk and wrap both hands around her neck. Instead, he mentally counted to ten and looked away from her, toward the windows. Four stories below, the broad avenues of Washington, DC, baked under a midday sun.

"Despite your belittling description of the program," he said, "I'm sure it's worthy of national notice."

"Yet I sense a marked lack of enthusiasm on your part."

"It's not my kind of story."

"You're not up to it?"

An invisible gauntlet landed on her desk alongside the untouched file. "I come up with my own stories, Harriet. You know that."

"So come up with one." She folded her arms over her wide bosom. "Let me see that reputed genius of yours at work. I want to witness in action the writer everyone knows and loves, who's hailed as always taking a fresh approach, who writes with rare insight, who lays bare for his readers the soul of the story." She gave it a count of five. "Well?"

With as much equanimity as possible, he unclenched his teeth and said, "I still have vacation days. At least a week's worth."

"You've had two weeks off already."

"Not long enough."

"Why's that?"

"I just returned from a war zone."

"No one forced you to stay over there. You could have come home at any time."

"There were too many good stories to tell."

"Whom do you think you're kidding?" she scoffed. "You

wanted to dress up and play soldier, and you did. For three quarters of a year. On the magazine's nickel. If you hadn't come home on your own when you did, I, as incoming editor-in-chief, was going to haul your ass back."

"Careful, Harriet. Along with your dark roots, your envy is showing."

"Envy?"

"Nothing you wrote was ever short-listed for a Pulitzer."

"But you've yet to be nominated for one, ergo you've never been awarded one, so big fucking deal about those rumors, which you probably started yourself. Now, I've got other things to do that are much more important." She arched a penciled eyebrow. "That is, unless you want to turn in your key to the men's restroom here and now, in which case I'm more than happy to call Bookkeeping and request your severance check."

She paused for several seconds, and when he didn't move, she continued. "No? Then your butt is in seat eighteen-A on a flight to Boise tomorrow morning." She slapped an airline ticket on top of the research folder. "Regional jet."

Dawson pulled to the curb in front of the neat Georgetown townhouse and cut his car's engine. Raising his hips, he fished a small bottle of pills from the pocket of his jeans, shook out a tablet, and swallowed it with a gulp from the bottle of water in the console cup holder. After recapping the pill bottle and returning it to his pocket, he flipped down the sun visor and checked his reflection in the mirror.

He did look like something a cat threw up. A very sick cat.

But there was nothing to be done about it. He'd been sorting through all the mail that had piled up on his desk, when he got Headly's text: *Get over here. Now.* Headly wasn't that imperative unless something was up.

Dawson had left the remainder of his mail unopened, and here he was.

He got out and made his way up the flower-lined brick walk. Eva Headly answered the doorbell. "Hello, gorgeous." He reached across the threshold and pulled her into a hug.

A former Miss North Carolina, Eva Headly had aged admirably well. Now in her early sixties, she retained not only her beauty and shapeliness but also her dry wit and natural charm. She hugged him back, hard, then squirmed out of the embrace and slapped him none too gently on the shoulder.

"Don't 'gorgeous' me," she said, rounding off the *r* to sound soft. "I'm mad at you. It's been two weeks since you got back. Why are you just now getting around to seeing us?" Her expression was laced with concern as she took him in from head to toe. "You're as thin as a rail. Didn't they feed you over there?"

"Nothing like your Brunswick stew. And they've never heard of banana pudding."

She motioned him into the foyer, saying, "That's what I missed most while you were gone."

"What?" he asked.

"Your b.s."

He grinned, cupped her face between his hands, and kissed her on the forehead. "I missed you, too." Then he released her and tilted his head in the direction of the den. Lowering his voice, he asked, "Is he getting used to the idea yet?"

She matched his confidential tone. "Not even close. He's been—"

"I can hear the two of you whispering, you know. I'm not deaf." The gruff shout came from the den.

Eva mouthed, "Be afraid."

Dawson winked at her, then walked down the hallway in the direction of the den, where Gary Headly was waiting for him. When Dawson stepped into the familiar room, he felt an achy tug of nostalgia. Countless memories had been made here. He'd raced his Matchbox cars on the parquet floor, his mother warning him not to leave them for someone to trip over. His dad and Headly had patiently taught him how to play chess with the set on the table in the corner. Sitting with him on the sofa, Eva had coached him on how to win the attention of his sixth-grade crush. For the first time since leaving Afghanistan, he felt like he'd arrived home.

The Headlys were his godparents and had forged a bond with him on the day he was christened. They'd taken to heart their pledge to assume guardianship of their best friends' son should the need ever arise. When his mom and dad were killed together in an auto accident while he was in college, even though he was legally an adult, his relationship with the Headlys had taken on even greater significance.

Headly was wearing a parental scowl of disapproval as he took in Dawson's appearance. He was considerably shorter than Dawson's six feet four inches, but he exuded confidence and authority. He still had all his hair, which was barely threaded with strands of gray. A daily three-mile run and Eva's careful supervision of his diet had kept him trim. Most sixty-five-year-old men would covet the figure he cut.

He said, "By the looks of you, it was a tough war."

"You could say," Dawson replied. "I just had a skirmish with Harriet and barely survived it."

As Dawson took the offered seat, Headly said, "I was referring to Afghanistan."

"It was tough, yeah, but Harriet makes the Taliban look like pranksters."

"How about a drink?"

Dawson covered his slight hesitation by consulting his wristwatch. "It's a little early."

"Five o'clock somewhere. And anyway, this is a special occasion. The prodigal has returned."

Dawson caught the slight rebuke. "Sorry I haven't gotten over here sooner. I've had a lot to catch up on. Still do. But your text had a ring of urgency."

"Did it?" At the built-in bar, Headly poured shots of bourbon into two glasses. He handed one of them to Dawson, then sat down facing him. He raised his glass in a toast before sipping from it. "I'm drinking more these days."

"It's good for you."

"Stress reliever?"

"So they say."

"Maybe," Headly mumbled. "At least it gives me something to look forward to each day."

"You've got plenty to look forward to."

"Yeah. Old age and dying."

"Better not let Eva hear you talking like that."

Headly grumbled something unintelligible into his tumbler as he took another sip.

Dawson said, "Don't be so negative. Give yourself time to adjust. It's been less than a month."

"Twenty-five days."

"And counting, obviously." Dawson sipped the liquor. He wanted to chug it.

"Hard to come to a dead stop after being in the Bureau all of my adult life."

Nodding sympathetically, Dawson felt the warmth of the bourbon curling through his gut, settling his nerves, which the pill hadn't yet had time to do. "Your retirement doesn't become official until . . . when?"

"Four more weeks."

"You had that much vacation time saved up?"

"Yep. And I'd have just as soon sacrificed it and stayed on the job for as long as possible."

"Use this time as a period of adjustment between your demanding career and a life of leisure."

"Leisure," he said morosely. "Soon as my retirement is official, Eva's got us booked on a two-week cruise. Alaska."

"Sounds nice."

"I'd rather someone pull out my fingernails with pliers."

"It won't be that bad."

"Easy to say when you don't have to go. Eva's ordered me a prescription of Viagra to take along."

"Hmm. She wants you to make up for all the nights you couldn't come home?"

"Something like that."

"What's the downside? Knock yourself out." Dawson raised his glass.

Headly acknowledged the toast and, after a moment, asked, "So, how'd it go with Dragon Lady?"

Dawson told him about the meeting and the story Harriet had assigned him.

"Blind balloonists?"

Dawson shrugged.

Headly leaned against the back cushion of his chair and studied him for an uncomfortable length of time.

Irritated by the scrutiny, Dawson said, "What? You got a comment about my hair, too?"

"I'm more concerned about what's going on inside your head than what's growing out of it. What's the matter with you?"

"Nothing."

Headly just looked at him, not having to say anything.

Dawson left his chair and moved to the window, flipping open the shutters and looking out onto the well-manicured patch of lawn. "I talked to Sarah when I passed through London."

The Headlys's daughter was older than he, but, while growing up, the two families had spent so much time together that they'd been much like brother and sister, grudgingly caring about each other. She and her husband lived in England, where they worked for an international bank.

"She told us you'd 'passed through' without staying long enough to go see them."

"Flight schedule didn't allow time."

Headly harrumphed as if he didn't accept that as a plausible excuse to forgo a visit. And it wasn't.

"Begonias are thriving."

"They're impatiens."

"Oh. How's the—"

"I asked you a question," Headly said with annoyance. "What's the problem? And don't tell me 'nothing.'"

"I'm fine."

"Like hell you are. I watched a zombie movie on TV last night. You'd fit right in."

Dawson sighed over his godfather's tenacity. He didn't turn around, but he propped his shoulder against the window frame. "I'm tired is all. Spend nine months in Afghanistan—trust me, it'll wear you out. Hostile terrain. Temperature extremes. Bugs that bite. No booze. No women except for the service members, and hooking up with one of them is tricky. A good way for both partners to get into some seriously deep shit. Hardly makes getting laid worth the hassle."

"You've had time since you got back to find an obliging lady."

"Ah, but there's a problem with that." He closed the shutters, turned around, and grinned. "You got the last great girl."

The levity fell flat. The worry line between Headly's thick eyebrows didn't relax.

Dropping the pretense, Dawson returned to the chair, spread his knees, and stared at the floor.

Headly asked, "Are you sleeping?"

"It's getting better."

"In other words, you're not."

Dawson raised his head and said testily, "It's getting better. It's not easy jumping back into the thick of things, returning to an ordinary schedule."

"Okay. I'll buy that. What else?"

Dawson pushed back his hair. "This Harriet thing. She's gonna make my life miserable."

"Only if you let her."

"She's sending me to Idaho, for chrissake."

"What have you got against Idaho?"

"Not a damn thing. Nor do I have anything against the vision-impaired. Or hot-air balloonists. But it's not my story. It's not even my *kind* of story. So forgive me if I'm finding it a little hard to work up any enthusiasm for it."

"Think you could work up some for a better story?"

Headly hadn't asked that casually. There was substance behind the question. So, in spite of his dejection, Dawson felt a tingle of anticipation. Because Headly hadn't been only his godfather and lifelong good friend, he'd also been his invaluable and unnamed source within the Federal Bureau of Investigation.

Taking his silence for interest, Headly continued. "Savannah, Georgia, and its environs. Marine Captain Jeremy Wesson, a decorated war veteran, one tour in Iraq, two in Afghanistan. After returning from his last deployment, he retired from the corps, and, by all accounts, went off the rails.

"Fifteen months ago, give or take, he got tangled up in a messy affair with a married woman, one Darlene Strong. Husband Willard caught them, and it didn't end well for the illicit lovers. Willard Strong goes on trial for murder the day after tomorrow. Chatham County Courthouse. You should be there to cover the trial."

Dawson was already shaking his head.

"Why not?" Headly asked.

"Summertime in Savannah."

"Look at your calendar. As of today, it's September."

"Still, no thank you. It's hot down there. Humid. I'd rather go to Idaho. Besides, crime isn't my specialty. And frankly, I've had enough of the military for a while. I don't want to write about a dead Marine. I've been doing that for the past nine months.

"In fact, maybe Harriet's assignment is a blessing in disguise. That feel-good story may be just the tonic I need. Something hopeful. Positive. Uplifting. No severed limbs, or blood-soaked fatigues, or flag-draped caskets involved."

"I haven't told you the hook."

Sourly, Dawson asked, "What's the hook?"

"Police obtained Wesson's semen off Darlene's clothing. This, of course, to help make the prosecutor's case against the cuckolded husband, Willard."

"Okay."

"So the RANC in Savannah is a Bureau buddy of mine, former New Yorker, big baseball fan named Cecil Knutz."

" 'Rank'?"

"Resident Agent in Charge. Top dog in the resident agency there."

"Okay."

"Anyway, Knutz saw the report from CODIS. Wesson's DNA got a hit, a match."

"He was already in the system?"

"He was. Has been for a while, in fact."

Headly paused to take a sip of his drink. Realizing that was a tactic used to build suspense, Dawson said, "I'm on pins and needles."

He set down his glass and leaned toward Dawson. "Captain Jeremy Wesson's DNA matched that which we retrieved off a baby blanket found inside the Golden Branch house."

That wasn't a mere hook. It was a grappling hook that found purchase in the center of Dawson's chest. Dumbfounded, he stared at Headly.

Headly said, "Before you ask, there's no possibility of mistake. The match was ninety-nine-point-nine-and-down-to-the-nth-degree identical. In other words, the recently obtained sample and the one from 1976 came from one and the same individual. We got Flora's DNA that day, too. We know she mothered the child whose DNA was on the baby blanket. And Jeremy Wesson's age fits. Indisputably, he was Flora and Carl's son."

Dawson stood up, paced a few steps, then turned back to Headly. As though reading the myriad questions racing through Dawson's mind, he said, "Judging by your expression, I see that I don't need to spell out the significance of this to you."

Although Gary Headly had enjoyed a distinguished career, to his mind all his accomplishments had been overshadowed by what he perceived as his one failure—to bring Carl Wingert and Flora Stimel to justice. It had plagued his career, and now it was contaminating his retirement.

That was a cruelty that his godfather didn't deserve, and it made Dawson angry. "This Knutz, why'd he tip you to this?"

"He knows my interest. Worked with me when I investigated one of their jobs in Tennessee in the late eighties. He's aware of my impending retirement and notified me only as a courtesy to a colleague. He was careful not to divulge too much, but he did tell me that he's been digging into Jeremy Wesson's background looking for a link to Carl and Flora."

Dawson raised his brows in silent query.

"Nothing. Jeremy Wesson's birth certificate—a copy he used to enlist—is from Ohio. Says he was born to and reared by Mr. and Mrs. So-and-So Wesson. He graduated high school in the town where he grew up. Earned a degree at Texas Tech. Joined the Marines. His history looks commonplace until he wigged out and got mixed up with a redneck's wife."

"No leanings toward domestic terrorism?"

"None apparent."

"What's Knutz's take?"

"He advised me to leave it alone. The Bureau has bigger fish to fry these days. Nobody really gives a shit about Carl and Flora anymore. The consensus is that they're probably dead. That burglary at the armory in New Mexico was the last crime attributed to them. That was in '96."

"Seventeen years ago. A lot can happen in that amount of time."

"Doesn't mean they're dead."

"But with no indication that they're still alive, it's logical to assume otherwise."

"Logic and assumption be damned. I want to know, don't you?"

"At this late date, what possible difference does it make?"

"It makes a hell of a difference to me!"

Dawson sliced the air with his hands. "Okay. I get that. But this decorated Marine, who might have been their son—"

"He was. I know it."

"No you don't."

"The DNA says he was."

"It isn't foolproof."

"As good as."

"All right, even if he was their kid—"

"Aren't you curious to know what happened to him after Golden Branch, where he's been?"

"Not in the least."

"I don't believe that."

"Believe it. What good would digging into it—"

"I thought you'd want to."

"I don't."

"Then do it for me."

"Why? He's *dead*. End of story."

"It could be the biggest story of your career."

"It's certainly the biggest of yours!"

Simultaneously, they realized they'd been shouting. Headly glanced toward the door as though expecting to see his wife there, coming to check on the commotion. Dawson brought his voice down to a more reasonable level. "If you want to know the rest of the story, why don't *you* go to the trial in Savannah?"

"Because Eva would divorce me," he grumbled. "Besides, like I told you, I'm as good as out of the Bureau. If I went meddling down there, I'd look pathetic. Like a hanger-on who doesn't know when his time is up."

Dawson ran his fingers through his hair and released a sigh of agitation. He loved Headly. He knew how badly his godfather wanted closure on the defining incident of his career. But he was asking too much. Dawson was exhausted and disheartened by his experiences overseas. Even on his good days, his nerves felt raw and exposed. The last thing he needed was additional aggravation, like dredging up this unfinished saga. What possible good could come of it? Whether or not Jeremy Wesson was Carl and Flora's child, it didn't make one iota of difference.

Quietly he said, "I'm sorry. Even if there was no Harriet in my life sending me someplace else on another assignment, I wouldn't go to Savannah. Your pal Knutz is right. Some things should be left alone."

Headly gave him a searching look, then his shoulders slumped with acceptance of Dawson's mind being firmly made up. He tossed back the remainder of his drink and said no more about it. Shortly after that, Eva extended Dawson an invitation to stay for dinner. He declined, using as his excuse the need to pack for his trip to Idaho. Keeping eye contact with them to a minimum, he beat a hasty retreat.

He was leaking anxious sweat by the time he got into his car. At the first traffic light, he took another pill, washing it down with the lukewarm water left in the bottle. Rush-hour traffic out of DC into Virginia didn't improve his mood, making him really on edge by the time he let himself into his Alexandria apartment.

He was tugging off his boots when his cell phone chirped, alerting him to a text message. It was from Headly: *There's a clincher.*

He knew he was being baited, but curiosity won out over his better judgment. He texted back. *What's the clincher?*

The reply was quick in coming. *J Wesson only presumed dead. Body never found.*

Chapter 2

"Mr. Jackson, are you ready to call your next witness?"

The assistant DA stood. "I am, Your Honor. I call Amelia Nolan."

Like the other spectators, Dawson turned as a bailiff opened the double doors at the back of the courtroom and motioned in the former Mrs. Jeremy Wesson.

Today was the third day of the trial. The first witness this morning had been a veterinarian, a Dr. Somebody—Dawson had his name in his notes for referral if needed—who had droned on forever about the digestive processes of dogs, specifically pit bulls.

It took the better part of two hours for the prosecutor to wade through all the scientific rigmarole and get to the crucial point: bits and pieces of Darlene Strong had been found in the digestive tracts of three of Willard Strong's pack of illegal fighting dogs, which had been put down in order to search for evidence.

The second person to testify, the county medical examiner, had confirmed that those bits and pieces corresponded with the ones missing from what had been left of the victim's cadaver, which police had discovered locked inside the dogs' pen.

Darlene hadn't been killed by the dogs, but the state was asking for the death penalty, so Lemuel Jackson, a shrewd and meticulous prosecutor with a double-digit number of convictions, had wanted to impress upon the jury how heinous the crime had been. He'd wanted it on the record that her body had been fed to Willard's dogs, and since the animals were half-starved in order to make them fiercer competitors in the fighting rings . . .

The implication had made many of the jurors go a little green.

Blood samples taken from the ground inside the caged area, as well as a piece of scalp with hair attached found inside one dog's intestines, suggested that Jeremy Wesson had met the same fate.

By the time the defense attorney, Mike Gleason, had stumbled through an ineffectual cross-examination of the ME, it was almost twelve o'clock. The judge called for a lunch recess until one thirty, although Dawson thought it doubtful that anyone in the courtroom would have much of an appetite. Certainly not one that would require an hour and a half to appease.

But now they were back, and the third witness of the day had been summoned into the courtroom.

For background, Dawson had read news articles about the crime. He supposed he'd glanced at the photographs of the ex Mrs. Wesson that had accompanied some of those write-ups, but he really hadn't paid attention.

Suddenly he was.

The woman walking up the short center aisle wasn't at all what he'd expected. He'd seen Flora Stimel's Wanted posters and had imagined that Jeremy Wesson's ex-wife would be of a type similar to that of his mother. He'd expected her to be coarse, tough, and hard-looking.

But from her delicate bone structure to the pale right hand she raised to be sworn in, this woman was the polar opposite. She outclassed everyone in the courtroom, Dawson included. Dawson especially.

She was dressed in an ivory-colored form-fitting skirt, with a blouse of the same color but of softer material, topped by a sapphire-blue jacket. Her auburn hair was pulled into a low ponytail, but not so tightly as to prevent a few loose strands from framing her face. Her only visible jewelry were a pair of diamond stud earrings and a wristwatch. She struck the perfect note for a courtroom appearance, being neither too feminine and fussy nor too structured and severe.

As a journalist, he would have been interested in Jeremy Wesson's ex no matter what. There were a thousand questions he wanted to ask her, if not for his own elucidation, then certainly for Headly's.

But the woman about to testify awakened a different kind of curiosity in him, and he resented it, because he didn't need an additional complication, the worst possible one being the loss of his professional objectivity, on which he prided himself.

He cursed Headly again for dragging him into this. He hadn't wanted to come, but knew he had to. After receiving the taunting text from Headly, he'd packed his duffel bag. The following morning, rather than using the ticket to Idaho that had been foisted on him, he'd boarded a flight to Savannah.

While waiting in the rental-car line, he'd called Harriet.

"Are you already in Boise?"

"I took a detour."

He envisioned her seated behind her desk, smoke coming out her ears. "I assigned you a story, Dawson."

"I've got a better one."

"What is it?"

"For now, it's a secret."

"*Where* is it?"

"I'm hot on its trail."

"Dammit, Dawson!"

"I'll be in touch." And he clicked off before the people around him could hear the obscene invectives being shouted through his phone.

For the time being, he was covering his own expenses, so he'd booked a room in a midpriced downtown hotel. After taking a cold shower, he'd raided the minibar, turned on ESPN, and settled down on the bed with a room-service cheeseburger and his laptop.

He'd searched out websites that contained material pertaining to the crime for which Willard Strong was being tried. On every level, it was a disturbing case, and by the time Dawson had finished researching it, he'd developed a tightness in his chest that he wanted to attribute to the Tabasco with which he'd doused his cheeseburger. But he knew that wasn't the cause of the constriction.

He asked himself for the hundredth time why he'd let Headly rope him into becoming involved. But when he had stripped away all the plausible explanations for his capitulation, the truth stood alone, and it had nothing to do with Headly, but everything to do with himself.

Truth be known, he'd practically dared himself to come, as a kind of therapy.

Since his return from Afghanistan, he'd been unable to shake off the effects of spending almost a year in a war zone. They clung to him like a spiderweb, so fine as to be invisible, yet as tenacious as steel and, so far, impossible to escape.

Of course he was nowhere near as gone as Jeremy Wesson had been. No doubt the captain had suffered from the real thing, PTSD. It had cost him his family and ultimately his life, making him an ideal subject for a timely and relevant article, one certain to induce strong emotions in the reader.

But it was also the subject Dawson wished most to avoid. It cut too close to home.

And then there was the other element that made this story personally involving. Had Jeremy Wesson been Carl Wingert and Flora Stimel's son? Were they or were they not dead? Dawson didn't care. But Headly did, and he felt an obligation to his godfather to take the investigation at least one step further.

So, he'd come. And looking at it from a strictly journalistic standpoint, Jeremy Wesson's life was a treasure trove of material. How could he possibly pass up writing the provocative story of a man who'd entered the world as the offspring of fugitives from justice, had experienced a seemingly normal upbringing in the Midwest, had honorably served his country, had returned home from war emotionally and psychologically wrecked, and then had been violently murdered?

It was an American version of a Greek tragedy.

With that in mind on his first night in Savannah, he'd shut down his laptop, washed down a sleeping pill with a slug of Pepto-Bismol to neutralize the Tabasco, and gone to bed. Five minutes later, he got up and took another pill, swallowing it with a bottle of Jack Daniel's from the minibar.

He'd had the nightmare anyway. Twice.

Consequently he was groggy and ill-tempered for the first day of Willard Strong's trial. He'd arrived at the courthouse early—not to claim a front-row seat, but to secure one in the back row near the exit so he could make a speedy and unobtrusive getaway if he felt the need.

As soon as court had adjourned that first day, he'd headed straight for River Street, where he spent the remainder of the evening cruising the bars. Women were available, and sex would provide at least a temporary reprieve from the morbid thoughts that haunted him, but he hadn't acted on any of the invitations, subtle or overt, that he received.

He made friendships that lasted only for as long as a drink or two, limited conversations to impersonal topics, and stretched out the time until the bars closed and he had nothing else to do except return to the hotel room, and to the hard, unforgiving pillow where night sweats and bad dreams awaited.

Up to this moment, he'd been bored with the trial and was trying to devise a graceful way to disengage himself from everything relating to it.

The appearance of Wesson's ex-wife changed that.

Amelia's left palm felt damp against the Bible on which she swore to tell the whole truth. Then she stepped up into the witness box and took her seat.

Jackson approached her. "Ms. Nolan, thank you for appearing today. Will you please state your name for the court?"

"Amelia Nolan."

"That's your maiden name?"

"Yes. Following my divorce from Jeremy, I reverted to using it."

He smiled. "Nolan is an honorable name in this state."

"Thank you."

He glanced over his shoulder toward the defense table. "Ms. Nolan, do you recognize the defendant?"

For the first time since entering the courtroom, she looked toward Willard Strong. He sat with his shoulders hunched, his eyes peering at her from beneath the ledge of his prominent brow. His hair had been neatly combed. He was dressed in a suit that appeared to be two sizes too small. If she had to use a single word to describe him, it would be *brutish*.

She acknowledged recognition. "Jeremy introduced us."

"When did this initial meeting take place?"

"February twenty-second of 2011."

"You recall the exact date?"

"It was my older son, Hunter's, fourth birthday."

"Can you please tell the court the circumstances of this meeting?"

"Jeremy and I were separated. I had temporary custody of our two sons while our divorce was pending, but I had agreed to let Jeremy attend Hunter's party. When he arrived, Willard and Darlene Strong were with him."

"You hadn't met them before then?"

"No, but I knew their names. Jeremy had talked about them."

"How would you describe them that morning?"

"You mean—"

"The condition of the three when they arrived at your home."

"They were intoxicated."

The defense counsel stood. "Objection."

"I'll rephrase," Jackson said before the judge could rule. "Ms. Nolan, did you get the impression that the three of them had been drinking excessively?"

Gleason was about to object again, when the judge held up her hand. "Ms. Nolan may answer."

Jackson motioned for her to proceed.

"I'd seen Jeremy intoxicated before," she said. "Many times. He wasn't a pleasant and happy drunk. On the contrary. So I'd started watching for the signs. When he arrived for the party, I saw right away that his eyes were bloodshot. His smile was more like a sneer. His attitude was aggressive. The three of them laughed..." She paused, but could think of no other words that would adequately describe them. "They laughed drunkenly and inappropriately."

"What time of day was this?"

"The party was scheduled for noon. They got there shortly before that."

"Did you confront Mr. Wesson about these visible signs of intoxication?"

"Yes."

"Did he offer an explanation?"

"He said they'd come straight from a party of their own, that they'd been celebrating all night."

"'They?' He, Mr. Strong, and Mr. Strong's wife?"

"Objection. Leading the witness."

Jackson acknowledged the judge's ruling in favor of Gleason's objection, but he'd got his point across to the jury. The party referred to had been among the three of them exclusively.

Out the corner of her eye, Amelia saw Willard Strong mutter something to his lawyer. Gleason sternly shook his head as though admonishing him to keep quiet. It made her shudder to surmise what he might have said, but she seriously doubted that it could have been flattering to her.

Jackson continued. "I think the jury will agree that we've established that the defendant, his wife, and your estranged husband showed up drunk to your son's birthday party. Could you please tell the court what happened next?"

She put herself back into that scene, seeing again Jeremy's insolent grin. "I asked Jeremy to leave. Other guests had already arrived. They were in the courtyard at the side of the house. I was embarrassed for Jeremy, for myself."

"How did he respond to your request that he leave?"

"He became belligerent. He said that he had a right to see his son on his birthday, and that I wasn't going to stop him from doing so."

Gleason came to his feet. "Your Honor, I object. Why is this testimony relevant to this trial?"

"I'm getting to the relevance," Jackson calmly replied.

"Objection overruled," the judge said, but she asked Jackson to move it along.

He nodded and turned back to Amelia. "For the sake of time and defense counsel's limited patience, can you tell us how this confrontation was resolved?"

"I told Jeremy that he wasn't fit to be around children. Or anyone for that matter. I ordered him to leave. He refused. So I threatened to call the police. I also threatened to get a restraining order, preventing him from coming near our sons."

"What was his reaction to the threat?"

"He cursed at me. Called me names. He said that our sons were his flesh and blood and that nothing would or could keep him from being with them. He caused a terrible scene."

Friends of Hunter's from preschool, their parents, Hunter himself had heard Jeremy's profane shouting and had come inside to see what it was about. She would never forget the fear in her son's eyes as he watched his ranting father. Grant, her younger, was only a year and a half old at the time. He began to cry.

Amelia looked down at her cold, damp hands, which she'd subconsciously clasped tightly in her lap. She forced herself to relax them, reminding herself that her sons would never have to fear Jeremy again.

"Ms. Nolan?"

She raised her head and squared her shoulders.

"Ms. Nolan," Jackson repeated, "what were Willard and Darlene Strong doing while this scene was unfolding?"

She darted a look toward the defense table and felt the full brunt of Strong's animosity. "Mr. Strong was egging Jeremy on."

"Can you be more specific?"

"He was saying things like 'Darlene would never get away with talking to me like that.'"

"Did he indicate that she would suffer physically if she—"

"Your Honor, objection," Gleason whined. "Prosecution is leading the witness again."

"Sustained."

Jackson apologized, rather insincerely Amelia thought. Then he turned back to her. "Do you recall a specific threat made by Mr. Strong toward his wife?"

She closed her eyes for a moment, but when she opened them, she looked directly toward the jury box. "Jeremy had taken a grip on my arm. Here." She placed her hand around her biceps. "He was shaking me. Mr. Strong said, 'You're letting her off light. If Darlene threatened me like that, it would be the last thing she ever did.'"

The statement created a vacuum in the courtroom. It was several moments before the spectators began to breathe again. Feet shifted, clothing rustled as people readjusted themselves in their seats, someone coughed.

Dawson noticed the same was so with the jurors. They had seemed transfixed by Amelia Nolan, or at least by her story. Lem Jackson was no fool. He milked the tension by looking each of them in the eye before he walked back to the state's table and picked up a legal pad, flipping through several pages as though searching for a note. Dawson doubted he needed the reference. It was a plausible way to kill time while his witness's pertinent statement took root in the minds of the jurors.

Before he could pose another question, Amelia Nolan asked for a glass of water. While she was taking the short break, the judge invited everyone to stand up and stretch. Dawson used the time to send two texts. The first went to Headly.

Wesson's ex testifying. Very effective. Used the Viagra yet? I want salacious details.

The second text was sent to a researcher and fact checker who'd been at *NewsFront* since the magazine's first issue was published thirty years ago. She was scrawny, cranky, and always smelled of the cigarettes she claimed she no longer smoked, but Dawson trusted her speed, accuracy, and most of all her discretion. Every Christmas he corrupted her with a five-pound box of chocolate-covered cherries and a case of equally sweet wine.

Glenda, sweetheart: Amelia of the GA Nolans? Why "honorable"? Facts desired asap, please.

He used an app to tack on hearts and flowers at the end of the text.

No sooner had he pressed Send than the judge tapped her gavel and instructed everyone who'd stood to be seated. When everyone had resettled, she instructed Jackson to continue with his witness.

The prosecutor was ready. He set his legal tablet on the table and approached the witness box. When he addressed her, his tone was somber. "Ms. Nolan, how did this scene that you described eventually pan out?"

"One of the other parents called nine-one-one."

"The police responded?"

"Two officers arrived in a matter of minutes. But Jeremy and the Strongs had left before they got there."

"They left without further incident?"

"Grant was wailing. Hunter was cowering against one of the fathers there. I think their frightened reactions bothered Jeremy. And he was aware that everyone was witness to his grip on my arm, the shaking. I think he might have felt ashamed. I'm guessing. I don't know. In any case, he let go of me.

"When Mr. Strong told him he ought to do something about me and my 'smart mouth'—that's a quote—Jeremy told him to shut up and to mind his own business. With an expletive. Then he opened the front door and shoved Mr. Strong out onto the porch. Mr. Strong cursed him, and I believe he would have retaliated if—"

"Objection."

"Sustained."

Jackson asked quickly, "Did Mr. Strong retaliate to Mr. Wesson's shove?"

"No. He was too unsteady on his feet. He staggered off the steps and nearly fell down. Jeremy grabbed Mrs. Strong's hand and pulled her behind him through the door. The two men were angrily pushing and shoving each other as they made their way to Jeremy's car parked at the curb. I shut the door and didn't see anything more. When the police arrived, they were gone."

Jackson returned to the table to once again consult his notes, probably unnecessarily. He was letting his witness take a breather and giving the jury time to imagine the scene and the antagonism that obviously had existed between the two so-called friends.

Ms. Nolan took a sip from her glass of water. Even from the back of the room where Dawson sat, he could see that her hand was trembling.

As Jackson walked toward her, he frowned and slid his hands into his pants pockets, looking rueful, as though regretting the direction his questioning was about to take. "Ms. Nolan, you had a second encounter with Willard Strong, is that correct?"

"Yes."

"When was that?"

"The third of May last year."

"Again, you remember the exact date."

"Yes."

She lowered her head, causing a loose strand of hair to fall against her cheek. Absently she reached up and tucked it behind her ear. Dawson wondered if that was a nervous gesture, specific to these circumstances, or if it was an unconscious habit with her. He would bet the latter.

"Ms. Nolan, why do you remember that date with such clarity?"

When she raised her head to answer Jackson's question, Dawson realized that he, along with most everyone else in the courtroom, including the accused, was leaning forward in anticipation of her answer.

She cleared her throat delicately. "That was the day Mrs. Strong and Jeremy went missing."

Chapter 3

Jackson asked her to describe that day.

"It started out like any other weekday. I dropped the boys off at their preschool at Saint Thomas Episcopal Church and went to work."

"You work at the Collier War Museum?"

"I'm a curator. I specialize in the Civil War."

"It's a full-time job?"

"Yes, but the museum allows me a lot of flexibility, which, as a single parent, I require."

"On that day of May third, did anything out of the ordinary happen to alert you to what was coming?"

"Nothing. Not until I got a call from the school. It came shortly after one o'clock in the afternoon. The museum director, George Metcalf, and I were in his office."

"Because, George, it's crap."

"Humor him, Amelia. Humor me."

"It has no value. Either on the open market or to the museum."

"That may be."

"Not 'may be.' Is."

"Okay. It's little more than a trinket. The Confederate Army handed out hundreds—"

"Thousands."

"Thousands of them. But the medal is valuable to Patterson Knox. It came down through his family from his great-great-great-grand something or another, and he's named after that particular ancestor. I don't need to remind you—"

"But you're about to."

"—that Patterson Knox contributed over one hundred thousand dollars to us last year. Mrs. Knox is—"

"On our board of directors. I'm not stupid, George. I get it. It's just that you and I approach these issues from different directions. As a curator, it's my job to protect the integrity of the museum."

"That's my priority, too."

"Yes, but as director you must also pander to people who keep our doors open. It galls me to display junk in order to ensure that a large donor continues donating."

"I hear you. But—"

"Never mind. I recognize a dead end when I run into one. I don't concede defeat, but I acknowledge the futility of further argument, which I believe you had won even before it commenced. However, I had to give it my best shot."

"I would expect nothing less from you. Put Mr. Knox's medal in a corner somewhere."

"With a spotlighted brass plaque extolling his and Mrs. Knox's generosity?"

"It doesn't have to be a large one."

Continuing her testimony, she said, "We'd just concluded our meeting when my cell phone rang. I recognized the school's number and answered immediately. It was Mrs. Abernathy, the headmistress. She was extremely upset."

"Why?"

"A man had come to the school, barged his way into her office—"

"Objection. Hearsay."

Lem Jackson countered. The judge ruled in his favor and Amelia was asked to continue.

"The man demanded to know if Jeremy had been to the school that day. He hadn't, but Mrs. Abernathy had difficulty convincing him of that. Finally he left, but only after she threatened to call the police."

Jackson reminded the jury that Mrs. Abernathy earlier had testified to the same, and that she had identified Willard Strong as the irate man. He then asked Amelia if it had been her ex-husband's habit to visit Hunter and Grant at the school.

"No. To my knowledge he'd never gone there, not even on visitation days. Our divorce had become final. Given the incident at the birthday party, his visits with the boys were supervised. He resented that, bitterly, and hoped to have the restriction revoked. But in the meantime, he was adhering to it."

"Did this call from the school's headmistress alarm you, Ms. Nolan?"

"To put it mildly. When she described the man to me, I recognized him as Willard Strong. My knee-jerk reaction was to go immediately to the school. But Mrs. Abernathy assured me that Hunter and Grant were in her office, that they were safe, and that they knew nothing about the incident.

"Nevertheless, I wanted to see them myself and make certain that they were all right. Mrs. Abernathy offered to personally deliver them to me at home. I left the museum immediately to meet her there."

"Did you talk to anyone?"

"I tried to reach Jeremy. I wanted to know what was going

on. But my repeated calls to his cell phone went straight to voice mail. I also tried his workplace. I was told he had called in sick that morning. No one at the construction firm had seen or heard from him since the day before."

"You went home?"

"That's right."

In terms of mileage, the museum wasn't that far from her townhouse, but it seemed to take forever to cover the distance. The streets were familiar, so she could drive them without having to concentrate. But that only allowed her mind to spin wildly with chilling thoughts. Jeremy's relationship with Willard and Darlene Strong was obviously volatile, and the possibility of it endangering her sons to any extent and on any level was untenable.

Would she have to get a restraining order after all? Should she appeal to the family-court judge to deny Jeremy all visitation rights until he got himself sorted out? Perhaps a drastic move like that would wake him up to how self-destructive his behavior had become. Maybe withholding his sons would compel him to seek treatment, to get counseling, before he completely ruined his life.

Such were her thoughts as she pulled onto Jones Street, which looked absurdly placid. Enormous live-oak trees cast welcome shade onto the sidewalks buckled by their roots.

After moving out of the house where she and the boys had experienced so many unhappy times, she'd leased the townhouse. The walled courtyard provided a safe place for the boys to play. The neighbors watched out for one another. Until she decided where she wanted to settle, it was a comfortable and convenient stopgap.

To her disappointment, Mrs. Abernathy hadn't yet arrived. She turned in to the narrow, oyster-shell driveway and followed it along the side of the building to her parking space in back. She alighted quickly, climbed the steps, and unlocked the back door, which opened directly into the kitchen. Her alarm started beeping. It sounded unusually loud, and it took her a frustrat-

ing three tries before she punched in the correct sequence of numbers to turn it off.

When it stopped, her ears continued to ring—the only sound she heard above the portentous silence that pressed itself against her eardrums. All her sensory receptors seemed heightened to a thousand times greater than their normal capacity. Because there was no motion or sound, the absence of stimuli was deeply disturbing. It bespoke the void her life would be without her sons in it.

The rambunctiousness of two active preschoolers, which sometimes frazzled her, was now what she craved. She wanted to hear their laughter, inhale their little-boy smells, feel the pressure of their warm bodies against her chest and the damp smear of their kisses on her cheeks.

She went to the sink, turned on the faucet, and took a drinking glass from the open shelf. She filled the glass with water and drained it thirstily. Thinking that surely the headmistress had had time to get there by now, she glanced at the clock on the stove, then, thinking she heard a car on the street, turned.

When the glass slipped from her hand, it shattered on the floor, spraying her feet and legs with shards of glass.

Willard Strong was standing not three feet from her. He held a double-barrel shotgun crosswise against his chest, from shoulder to hip, one hand on the stock, the other on the barrels. "You scream and I'll kill you." Her back door was standing ajar. Calmly, he reached behind him and pushed it closed.

Amelia rolled her lips inward and took a deep breath through her nose, held it for several seconds, then released it slowly.

Jackson regarded her with concern. "Do you need a moment, Ms. Nolan?"

She shook her head, then murmured, "No, I'm fine." She wasn't, but hopefully no one in the courtroom would call her on the fib. She wanted no more delays in the proceedings. She wanted to get through this, past this, so she could get on with the rest of her life.

She barely remembered a time when she'd had complete control of her life and could make decisions without factoring Jeremy into them in one way or another. He'd been out of her life for more than a year, and still he was dominating her thoughts and dictating how her days were spent. But once she got through this—

"Mr. Strong used those exact words?" Jackson asked. "'You scream and I'll kill you?'"

Refocusing her thoughts, she answered yes.

"Did you feel that you were in imminent danger?"

"I did, yes. The threat seemed real. He was glaring at me, breathing hard. He was flexing and contracting his fingers around the barrels of the shotgun. He looked distraught. Furious. I was afraid for my life."

Jackson let that sink in as he walked over to the table where evidence, which had already been introduced, was exhibited. "Is this the shotgun he brought with him into your house?" He carried the weapon back to the witness box for her inspection.

"It looks like it. I remember the design carved into the stock."

He asked that the record note that she had identified Exhibit A, the shotgun with which Darlene Strong had been shot in the chest.

As he replaced the shotgun on the table, he asked, "Did the defendant say anything else to you?"

"He asked if my husband was there. I told him no and reminded him that Jeremy was no longer my husband. He said, 'But she's still my wife, and he's'"—she darted a glace toward the jury box, then finished—"'he's fucking her.' I told him that I knew nothing about it, that it wasn't my business to know, and that whatever was happening between them, Jeremy wouldn't come to my home."

"What did he say to that?"

"He laughed. With contempt. He called Jeremy a coward and said, 'He might, now he knows I'm on to them. Let's see.'" She paused to wipe her moist palms on the lap of her skirt. "He took me by the arm."

She went on to describe how he had roughly propelled her through the house, searching the rooms on both stories for Jeremy, all the while deaf to her denials that Jeremy would seek refuge in her house. "By the time we got back downstairs, he was even angrier and more frustrated than before. He was sweating profusely, swearing with every breath."

She paused, expecting an objection from Strong's lawyer, who was sitting perfectly still, staring at her as though contemplating his counterattack. Strong's stare was malevolent. Quickly she shifted her gaze back to Jackson.

He asked, "Was he still restraining you?"

"Yes. I thought this was the point where he would kill me. But then . . ." She swallowed, remembering the fear that had gripped her. "Then we heard the car pull up out front. Car doors slamming. My boys laughing and shouting excitedly, calling my name as they ran toward the townhouse. I heard Mrs. Abernathy cautioning them to be careful on the steps."

"What did Mr. Strong do when he heard them?"

"He started moving toward the front door."

"Was it locked?"

"Yes, but I was afraid that he would open it, and there my sons would be. Or I thought that he might fire the shotgun through the door."

"What did you do?"

"I dug in my heels and tried to bar his way."

"You placed yourself between him and the front door."

She nodded. "I didn't think about it, or plan it, I just reacted."

"You reacted to what you perceived to be mortal danger for your children."

Again, she swallowed drily. "Yes. I begged for their lives. By now I was on the verge of hysteria. Frantic. I asked him what he was going to do. He shoved me away from him with enough force to knock me to the floor. I was terrified that he would blast the front door." She looked over at the glowering defendant and said quietly, "But he didn't."

She hoped that in spite of Willard Strong's ferocity and the enmity with which he was glaring at her, he knew how grateful she was to him for sparing the lives of her children.

"What did he do, Ms. Nolan?"

She brought her gaze back to Jackson. "He stepped past me, went through the kitchen, and out the back door, the same way he'd come in."

"When you frantically asked him, 'What are you going to do?' did he offer a reply?"

She dampened her dry lips and looked toward the twelve people who would decide Willard Strong's guilt or innocence. "He said, 'I'm going to find them, and when I do, I'm going to kill them.'"

Lemuel Jackson was seasoned enough to know to quit when he was ahead. He told the judge that he had no further questions for Ms. Nolan.

The judge consulted both attorneys. Cross-examination was likely to take a while. Considering how late in the day it was, and the approach of the holiday weekend, they agreed that court should be adjourned until after Labor Day. The judge told Ms. Nolan that she could step down. A bailiff escorted her out through a side door.

The judge said, "Defense counsel will be ready to cross-examine Ms. Nolan when we reconvene at nine o'clock next Tuesday morning. Enjoy your holiday."

She banged the gavel. Dawson was the first one out of the courtroom.

A few minutes earlier, his phone had vibrated, signaling a text message. He claimed a relatively private place in the corridor and accessed the text. It was from Glenda, the researcher, asking him to call her. He wasted no time punching in her number, wanting to take advantage of her help while she was in a generous mood.

As soon as she answered, he said, "Have you finally decided to marry me? Please say you're calling to accept my many proposals."

Crossly she said, "Kiss my skinny ass, Dawson."

"You name the time and place."

She snorted, but he could sense that one of her rare smiles was behind it. "You ready?"

"Lay it on me."

"Amelia Wesson née Nolan is the daughter of the late US Congressman Beekman Davis Nolan—he went by Davis—who represented his district for thirty-two years."

"Huh."

"If you'd've been paying attention, you would've heard of him. He served on too many committees and advisory boards to list, presided over one congressional hearing in 1994 and another in '98. A public safety bill that was voted into law bears his name, because he wrote it and introduced it. He was well liked and admired on both sides of the aisle."

"Which side was he on?"

"He hailed from a state that usually goes red, but he didn't always toe the party line. He was a flag waver, for sure, but he was often outspoken against diehard conservatives, especially when it came to personal-liberty issues. Abortion. Gay marriage. Like that."

"Made enemies?"

"He had his critics. But his more liberal outlook also won him admirers on the other side. Basically, he was that rare bird that's almost extinct in politics—a man of integrity. Even the people who disagreed with him admired him. Couldn't be influenced by lobbyists, never backed down from what he believed in. His hero was Jefferson, and he quoted him a lot. By the way, do you want Harriet the Harridan in on any of this?"

"Not yet."

"I didn't think so. She's cussing you over something."

"Must have been that crack about her extra ten pounds."

Glenda cackled. "Watch yourself. I've heard rumors that she's into voodoo. Know what she did today? The portrait of her predecessor that hung in the lobby? She had it taken down. Said he was gone and that a new regime had taken over. Like we needed reminding. The bitch."

Dawson shared her sentiment, but the less said about Harriet the better for his frame of mind. He redirected the conversation back to Nolan. "What about the congressman's personal life?"

"Squeaky clean. Widowed in the midnineties. They'd been married since The Flood, and he never remarried. No scandals. Not one nekkid girl caught sneaking out of his office, no little boys in his shower. Social drinker, nonsmoker. On paper, he was a saint."

"Find anything on the daughter?"

"Amelia. Middle name Ware. These southern names just kill me," she mumbled as an aside. "Born May 1981, which makes her—"

"Thirty-two."

"I can subtract," she snapped. "Attended Vanderbilt. Active in various campus organizations. Took it upon herself to launch a food-and-clothing drive to help hurricane victims in Alabama and went herself to see that the goods got where they were supposed to go. Made national news. Yada yada.

"Graduated summa cum laude with a degree in history. Earned a master's while working at a museum in Boston. Then she spent two years working at another in Baltimore. But when her father retired from public office—"

"Do you know why he retired?"

"No specific reason given. He made an announcement that he wasn't going to seek reelection. Nothing noteworthy or suspicious. Just tired of it, I guess. He was nearing seventy."

"Okay."

"Anyhow... Where was I?"

"When her father retired..."

"Right. She moved back to Savannah and became his assistant. She served as his hostess, social secretary, Girl Friday. Together they sponsored fund-raisers for numerous charities."

"Was she married to Jeremy Wesson during this same time?"

"Let's see... yeah, there was an overlap of a few years. The congressman died in early 2010. Mrs. Wesson now works—"

"She goes by Nolan."

"—as a curator at the—"

"Collier War Museum. Specializes in—"

"Look, if you're so freakin' smart, why'd you have me look up all this crap? *Which*, if we're splitting hairs, you could've looked up yourself."

"But I'm clumsy at it and you're adroit."

"Adroit, my ass. You just don't want to take the time."

"I just don't want to take the time," he admitted.

"Your time's more valuable than mine?"

"No, you're priceless, and I couldn't do without you. You know that."

"Yeah, yeah," she muttered. "I've got photos of Ms. Nolan. She's at least an eight."

"Closer to a nine. And a half."

"I swear to God, Dawson, you had better not have me doing all this work just 'cause you've got the hots for the lady. I'm not running a dating service here."

"I swear, it's vital background information for a story."

"One you don't want Harriet to know about."

"Not yet." He glanced around and realized that the corridor had virtually cleared. He needed to hurry, but he had a few more questions for Glenda and was afraid that if he didn't ask them while she was being moderately agreeable, he'd be left wanting. "Do you have a current address for her?"

"Last one that surfaced was Jones Street in Savannah."

Considering what had happened, he doubted she was still living there. "Where did the congressman live?"

Glenda told him. "One website had photos. Oak trees with Spanish moss. White columns. Deep veranda. Your basic Tara."

"Is anyone living there now?"

"Don't know."

"See if you can find out. And work on getting a current address for her."

"We're looking at a holiday weekend, you know."

"But you love me. You know you do."

"In your dreams."

Grinning, he started toward the elevator bank. "Anything else you can dig up will be greatly appreciated. Text, call, or e-mail me. Any hour."

"I've got a life, too, you know. Never mind that it sucks."

"One more thing. How did Congressman Nolan die?"

"Well, finally! I've been itching for you to ask."

"Why's that?"

"Because I saved the best for last."

Diary of Flora Stimel—January 23, 1978

Today was awful, the reason being that Carl got furious at me.

I should have known better than to cross him. He's been out of sorts lately, and I know it's because of the guns that we were supposed to get, but didn't. Some Cuban drug dealers waved their money around (I guess they have a lot of it, because everybody in Miami seems to be stoned on something!), and the guy that was supposed to sell us the guns sold them to the Cubans instead. That pissed Carl off, and for the three days since then, he's been in a terrible mood.

He wanted to go after the Cubans, kill them, and take the guns, but Quirty (I still don't know his real name) talked him out of it. He said it was crazy to f—with the Cubans, who had just as soon cut your throat as look at you. Carl said if you shot them first, they wouldn't have a chance at cutting your throat. He was on a rampage.

But Quirty got some good smoke (probably bought off those

same Cubans) and that calmed Carl down some. At least me and Quirty were able to talk sense to him about getting revenge.

I didn't want to get into a war with those Cubans or anybody. I'm always afraid for Jeremy's safety. Anytime I say that to Carl, he laughs and says nobody would dare lay a hand on his kid. But I don't think the Cubans would be afraid of Carl, and maybe Carl knows that deep down because he didn't shoot anybody.

Which could also be why he's cross. He's bored, is all. Since that bank job in Louisiana when Jim got shot, we've been laying low. On the news they said the robber had died at the scene, killed by police. But Carl doesn't trust the news people to be telling the truth. He calls them puppets who only repeat what the cops and politicians want got across to the stupid public.

Carl says that if Jim lived even for a little while after he was shot, he could have talked, told them something about us. So we holed up in a trailer park in MS with a guy that Jim didn't know. That way, even if he had ratted us out, we were still safe from capture.

I was glad not to be on the move, because Jeremy and I both got sick with runny noses. His cough was worse than mine. What my grandma used to call croupy. Taking him to a doctor was out of the question. I didn't even ask Carl if we could, knowing what he'd say.

The man who put us up in his mobile home, Randy, thinks the world of Carl. Carl is his hero. He was nice to us even though Jeremy's coughing must've kept him up all night like it did Carl and me. It might have been that, instead of kindness, that caused Randy to buy a bottle of cough syrup for Jeremy without me even asking.

After a few days, Jeremy got better. He stopped being so puny and whiny and started eating. Which was good because Carl had decided that it was time to move on. We drove into

FL and kept going until we got here. Carl's sixth sense told him the heat was off and it was safe for us to stay put for a while.

Miami is okay, I guess, but I don't like this house. The mice seem to be making fun of me for even bothering to set traps. I hear them snapping shut all night long. I hate that sound! Come morning I'll have to empty the traps of those limp little bodies. Much as I hate their scurrying around in the dark, I hate to see them dead. But no matter how many I catch, there's ten more to take their place. The roaches are about as big as the mice.

I don't like Quirty's girlfriend, either. She's sneaky and sly. She reminds me of a cat we had when I was little. He'd had one of his eyes scratched out, which scared me already. But he'd come up on me before I knew it, and that gave me the willies. I was glad the day he crawled under the house and died.

Anyhow, this gal of Quirty's prances around and shows off, especially in front of Carl. The worst thing happened yesterday when Jeremy tipped over a bottle of red nail polish while she was painting her toenails. Barely a drop spilled on the floor and I got it right up. But she pinched Jeremy's arm, twisting the skin so it hurt him really bad. I lit into her, and before it was over, the men had to break us apart. I think I would have killed her if Carl hadn't stopped me.

The pinch left a dark bruise on Jeremy's arm, and that riled Carl, too. His mood went from bad to worse, so that today, when he saw me with the camera, he blew his stack.

It was an old Polaroid I found in a cabinet when I was setting a mousetrap. Quirty said I could use it to take some pictures of Jeremy. Carl's never allowed any pictures of us, but I wanted at least one baby picture of Jeremy.

I think it was the smell that gave me away. The chemicals inside the camera make the pictures stink when you peel them off and coat them with that stuff. Carl came storming in and caught me red-handed. He grabbed the camera and banged it against the edge of the kitchen table over and over again till it broke apart.

Jeremy got scared on account of all the racket and started crying. Carl ripped up the picture I'd taken and told me never ever to take any pictures.

After the blow-up, Quirty said maybe we'd worn out our welcome.

It's decided that we'll pull out tomorrow. I won't be sorry to leave this mousy house and that sneaky slut. But at least here in south FL the weather is warm. We spent all last winter in MN and I nearly froze. But I won't complain no matter where we go, so long as Carl keeps us together.

I haven't let myself wonder about what will happen when Jeremy is old enough to understand that we're outlaws and don't live like other people. I daydream about us having a normal life and being like other families. But it will never happen, so I had just as well stop daydreaming about it.

Carl's been saying things that scare me, things like our lifestyle being hard on kids, like Jeremy will be needing to go to school in a few more years. When Carl starts talking about the future—and I know how he is once he gets an idea into his head—I get petrified that he'll leave Jeremy behind somewhere.

I think back to Golden Branch. That horrible day. The worst day of my life so far. The labor was bad. I thought for sure I'd die of that. Then all that shooting! Lord, I was scared!

When Carl bent over me and told me that the others were dead and that he had to go *right that second*, I couldn't believe he meant it. I was bleeding. Hurting something awful. But he was serious as serious can be. He said if he stayed, he'd be killed or caught. Did I want that?

The whole rest of my life was decided in that moment. Because, truth be told, I didn't want to be killed or captured, either. Which I guess makes me the worst kind of coward, the worst kind of person.

It was cold and rainy. I remember running through those wet woods to where Carl had hid the car. I was holding Jeremy against me so tight, afraid I'd trip and fall with him, or that he'd cry and give us away. I was still sorta scared that Carl would go off and leave us if we didn't keep up. I should count my lucky stars that he took us at all.

Even after we got away, I couldn't stop crying over it. To this day, every time I think back on that morning, I cry buckets.

Chapter 4

Please, Mom?"

"You can get back in after you've had some lunch."

"Five more minutes?"

"After lunch."

"One more minute?"

Placing her hands on her hips, Amelia gave six-year-old Hunter *the look.*

She got a very downcast "Okay" as he waded out of the surf. "We were just starting to play."

She draped a beach towel over his shoulders and used a corner of it to dry the saltwater off his face. "Funny that I always seem to make you stop just when you're starting to play. Race you to the umbrella?"

She took off in the direction of their camp up the beach, where Grant was already rummaging in the picnic hamper. She slowed in order to let Hunter overtake her and smiled as she watched his strong young legs churning.

The sand was warm against the soles of her feet. There was just enough breeze to counteract the sun's heat. She deeply inhaled the salt air and smiled over the simple pleasure of being here, on the sea island, her favorite place on earth. The courtroom and the taxing testimony of yesterday seemed far removed. God bless the judge for granting her five whole days before having to return to court and face cross-examination. She'd determined not to think about the trial or the disturbing memories it evoked and, instead, to enjoy these last official days of summer with her sons.

Who, at the moment, were squabbling over a peanut-butter-and-jelly sandwich.

"I want this one." Grant, who'd just turned four, clutched the plastic-wrapped sandwich to his chest in an effort to keep his brother from snatching it.

Removing her wide-brimmed straw hat, she ducked beneath the beach umbrella and dropped down onto the quilt. "Hunter, leave Grant's sandwich alone and choose another. They're all alike."

"Exactly alike." Stephanie DeMarco joined them, setting a small cooler between the boys to help defuse their spat. "Who wants a Capri Sun?"

Amelia had hired the twenty-year-old to be the boys' nanny for the summer, and it had proved to be an ideal arrangement for everyone. Stef, as she preferred to be called, was a college student majoring in elementary education. Having grown up in landlocked Kansas, spending three months on an Atlantic beach was her idea of heaven. She'd come with impeccable references.

Having Stef living with them, and more or less on call twenty-four/seven, had enabled Amelia to live in her beach house on Saint Nelda's Island for the entire summer, rather than having to go back and forth between the island and the mainland only for weekend stays. Stef kept the boys occupied while Amelia worked in her upstairs office for a few hours each day. If her presence at the museum was required, she had child care while she made the round trip to Savannah by ferry.

Thanking Stef for the drinks, Amelia thought again what a godsend the young woman had been. The boys adored her, but, being no pushover, she was strict about baths, bedtime, and behavior. During the day, she kept them busy and entertained with educational projects and ample playtime.

An easy relationship had developed between the two women, more like a friendship than that of employee and employer. As she passed Amelia a bottled iced tea, Stef shook her head with derision. "Beats me why you come to the beach at all, covering up as you do. You look like Lawrence of Arabia."

Amelia didn't take offense, but laughed with self-deprecation as she plucked at the damp hem of her sheer caftan. "I used to tan when I was younger."

"I know it's bad for you. But I love to be bronzed."

Amelia assessed Stef's voluptuous shape, barely contained inside the two pieces of her bikini. "Bronze looks good on you," she said, to which Stef laughed.

After lunch and as soon as Amelia had slathered the boys with more sunscreen, they grabbed their pails and shovels and headed toward the shoreline. "Don't get in the water until I'm down there," she called after them.

"Want me to take a shift?" Stef asked.

"Thanks, but they haven't had much time with me the past few days. I'll stay with them if you'll go to the store."

"Sure. I saw your list on the kitchen counter. I added plastic wrap. Have you thought of anything else?"

"Lightbulbs. The one on the back porch is out. And don't rush back. I've been gone a lot this week. You deserve some 'you' time, and I need quality time with the boys."

"Thanks, boss." She saluted Amelia as she started toward the dunes that separated the house from the beach.

Amelia joined Hunter and Grant and together they waded into the surf. "I thought this beach ball had a leak," she remarked as she tossed it to Hunter. The last time she'd seen the colorfully striped ball, it had been lying deflated in a corner of the porch.

"It got fixed."

"Did you thank Stef for doing that?"

"She didn't do it. It just got fixed," he said. Then, "Watch, Mom!"

He executed a belly dive, which Grant imitated and came up choking. They played in the shallows until they were good and pruney, then trooped back onto shore, where Amelia oversaw the building of a sand castle, complete with turrets and a surrounding moat that she filled with seawater. "A moat was used to protect the castle from attacking enemies."

"And dragons," Grant said.

Hunter rolled his eyes. "There aren't any dragons, stupid."

"Are too!"

"Hunter, don't call your brother stupid," Amelia said. "Never. Understand?"

"Yes, ma'am. But tell him that dragons are make-believe."

"Well, make-believe or not," she said, "this moat is keeping them out."

Later, they lay on the quilt in the shade of the umbrella while she read to them from two storybooks. Before she finished the second one, Grant had fallen asleep, his head in her lap. Hunter rolled over onto his tummy and pillowed his head on his folded arms. In seconds, he, too, was asleep.

Amelia set the books aside and gazed at the two loves of her life. Hunter's hair was dark and grew in undisciplined swirls around his head, as her father's had. Grant's hair was straighter and lighter with the russet tint of hers.

Both had blue eyes, a genetic gift. She was glad she didn't have to look into their eyes and see Jeremy's. Although, she had once found his dark eyes extremely attractive. It seemed another lifetime ago that he had looked at her with love and adoration. It *was* another lifetime ago. The last time he'd fixed his eyes on her, they'd been filled with hatred and wrath.

Pushing the unwelcome thought away, she stretched out onto her back, and, with a hand on each son so she could feel their sweet breathing, she fell asleep.

They had spaghetti for dinner. While they were eating, Amelia mentioned the beach ball to Stef. "Weirdest thing," the young woman said, as she helped Grant twirl noodles onto his fork. "I'd thrown it away, but it showed up yesterday patched and inflated."

"How'd that happen? It didn't heal."

"Maybe Bernie," Stef said, shrugging, more interested in the mess Grant was making than in the beach ball mystery.

When they finished, Stef began clearing the table. "If you'll do the dishes, I'll bathe the boys," Amelia told her.

"Are you sure? Compared with bath time, doing the dishes is a snap."

Amelia smiled. "True. But I've missed the boys this week. Even when I was with them, I was distracted."

Stef turned from the sink and said hesitantly, "There's a write-up about the trial on the front page of the local newspaper. It mentions your testimony. I brought a copy in case you want to read it."

"No, thanks. I've kept the TV off during news time, too. I know all I need or want to know about it."

She shooed the boys upstairs. They put up token protests, but she soon had them stripped and in the tub. She knelt beside it to supervise the dispensing of liquid soap, which often got out of control.

Just before plunging her hands into the bathwater, she automatically reached to remove her watch.

It wasn't on her wrist.

Although it wasn't an expensive, diamond-studded model, it

was the last gift her father had given her before his death, and for that reason alone she cherished it. Staring at her bare wrist, she mentally backtracked, trying to remember when she'd taken it off. While preparing dinner? Before joining the boys in the ocean had she dropped it into her beach bag? She couldn't remember doing either.

Her thoughts were interrupted by an arc of bright-blue soap being squirted from the dispenser and landing on the front of her shirt. "Hey! Enough."

After their bath, she was almost as wet as they were. She oversaw their teeth brushing, got them into their pajamas, and listened to their prayers. By lights out, she was exhausted.

Stef was waiting for her in the kitchen with a glass of cold white wine. Amelia took it gratefully. "I've misplaced my wristwatch. Have you seen it?"

"No, but I'll keep an eye out for it."

"I'm sure it will turn up." Amelia sipped her wine, sighing with pleasure. "You must be angling for a raise."

Stef laughed. "The pay is adequate, but I would like to go out for a few hours tonight if that's okay."

"Sure. I'll even loan you my car."

"Thanks! I appreciate that. It's a little nerve-racking riding my bike in the dark."

"Where are you going?"

"Well, as you know, choices are limited."

The island's only village amounted to several establishments clustered near the ferry dock: a general store; a boat-rental place that also had two gas pumps and a live-bait tank; a real estate office that was open only on weekends, when the sea island drew visitors from the mainland; and a café and bar called Mickey's.

After the café's dinner hours, the bar stayed open and was the only nod toward a nightlife on the island.

"Mickey's?" Amelia asked. Stef nodded. "Meeting someone?"

Stef grinned and said with cheek, "Maybe."

"Same guy?"

"Maybe."

Amelia laughed. "Does he have a name?"

"Dirk."

"What does he do?"

"He works on boats. I don't know the specifics."

"Is he a permanent resident? Maybe I know his family."

Stef shook her head. "This is his first summer here."

"When do I get to meet him?"

"We'll see how things go." Changing the subject, she asked, "Will you be all right here alone?"

"Of course. I've been staying here alone since I was eighteen and finally talked my daddy into allowing it."

"Yeah, but you've had a rough week."

"I'm fine. I may treat myself to a long bath. This will definitely help relax me." She raised the glass of wine. "Thank you."

"I figured you could use it." Stef picked up her small purse and lifted Amelia's key ring off the hook as she passed through the back door.

Amelia followed to lock it behind her. Noticing the bright porch light overhead, she said, "Thanks for changing the bulb."

Stef paused on her way to the car. She looked at Amelia, then at the porch light, then back to Amelia. "I didn't. The bulb just must have been loose. I guess it came back on by itself."

After she drove away, Amelia remained standing on the threshold, one hand on the door jamb, the other on her chest where her heart had begun beating hard and fast. The lightbulb hadn't been loose. It hadn't come back on by itself. Because when Amelia noticed that it had burned out, she had removed it from the fixture.

As if the lightbulb and beach-ball puzzles weren't enough to fray her nerves, she was upset over her missing wristwatch. In the utility room, she upended her beach bag and went through the contents item by item. She checked the windowsill above the kitchen sink where she sometimes placed it before doing the dishes. She even put her hand down the garbage disposal.

Upstairs, she thoroughly searched her bathroom, bedroom, and dirty-clothes hamper. The hamper yielded a piece of Lego, but nothing else that didn't belong there.

Sitting on the side of her bed, she reconstructed her morning. She distinctly remembered pulling on her swimsuit, slipping the caftan over her head, then fastening her watch onto her wrist as she slid her feet into a pair of flip-flops.

It had to have come off somewhere on the beach.

She checked on the boys, who were sleeping soundly in their twin beds, then went back downstairs, got a flashlight, and switched it on as she descended the front steps.

The boardwalk that connected the house to the beach was only two feet wide. The planks were old and weathered. Fearing splinters, she didn't allow the boys to walk on it with bare feet, although the soles of her own feet had been toughened on these same planks every summer for as far back as she could remember. Back to when her mother was in the kitchen humming under her breath as she peeled fresh peaches for the cobbler she would bake. Back to when her father had warned her from his rocking chair on the verandah to be on the lookout for jellyfish.

The saw grass on the dunes rustled in the breeze. The moon was still rising, but even if it had been high in the sky, it wouldn't have shed much light. It was a narrow crescent, what her father used to call a "fingernail moon."

The tide of nostalgia and homesickness that assailed her was far stronger than the gentle surf. The lacy foam left on the sand when the soft waves receded sparkled in the beam of her flashlight. She walked along the packed sand, searching for a glint of gold, that precious, tangible connection to her father.

Using the house as a reference point, she made a U-turn and started back the other way, going a little farther up the beach where the sand was drier. She repeated that slow, zigzagging route, moving a little farther away from the shore on each lap. Eventually she acknowledged the futility of the search. If the watch had been lost on the beach, it had probably been washed out to sea with the ebbing tide.

Nevertheless, she searched more carefully around the area where they'd set up camp that day, even dropping to her knees at the spot where she'd staked the umbrella. She sifted handfuls of sand through her fingers.

Finally, she sat back on her heels and despondently rubbed her hand over her bare wrist. Of all the things to lose, why that? Her mother had always said that tears should never be wasted on inanimate objects. Still, the watch had held enormous sentimental value for her, and while she could buy another, that particular one was irreplaceable.

Sighing with regret, she looked out across the water, then up at the moon. She missed her mother, but that was a familiar ache because she'd been gone for a long time. The loss of her father, however, remained an open wound.

In that moment, she felt very lonely.

But not alone.

Gripped by a sudden and inexplicable fear, she turned quickly to look behind her. Seasonal residents and tourists usually cleared out by Labor Day, so all the other houses along the stretch of beach, her neighbor Bernie's included, were dark. No campfires flickered. There was one boat anchored offshore, but at a distance, and only its safety lights were on. The breeze didn't carry any sounds of merrymaking.

Yet, she sensed she wasn't alone. And it was that, not the balmy wind that raised goose bumps on her arms. Grateful for the flashlight, she got to her feet and started up the boardwalk, moving swiftly, so that by the time she reached the steps to the porch, she was practically running and out of breath. She shut the front door soundly behind her and shot the dead bolt. Then she went through each room of the lower story, checking it. But for what, she couldn't say.

Feeling a bit foolish for the unwarranted panic, she ordered herself to get a grip. Even so, she poured a second glass of wine and took it with her when she went upstairs. The boys were just as she'd left them. In her bedroom, she finished her wine while preparing for bed.

But she didn't fall asleep. It wasn't until much later, after she heard Stephanie come in and quietly shut the door to her bedroom, that she relaxed enough to close her eyes.

"Knock, knock?" Without waiting for an answer, the back door was pushed open and a shock of white hair appeared in the crack. "Anybody home?"

"Bernie!"

"Bernie!"

Both boys scrambled from their chairs at the breakfast table and rushed to greet their next-door neighbor. They were instantly intrigued by the large sack he'd carried in. With unabashed greed, Hunter asked, "Did you bring us something?"

"Mind your manners, young man," Amelia scolded.

Bernie laughed. "It's okay. I did, in fact, bring them something. But they have to finish breakfast before they can have it."

Amelia gave him a look of thanks as the boys returned to the table and attacked their cereal bowls.

"Coffee?"

"Thank you, but stay where you are. I'll get it."

He had one bad hip, and the other had already been replaced. As he went to the cabinet for a mug, Amelia noticed that his tottering gait was more pronounced than usual. After pouring his coffee, he joined her and the children at the table.

"My feelings were hurt," she told him.

He blew on his coffee. "Why's that?"

"I thought you might have left for home while I was in Savannah." He lived in Upper Michigan.

"Without saying good-bye? Never."

"Your house was dark last night."

"I was packing up and cleaning all day yesterday. Tuckered me out. I went to bed early."

"The rental company has people who thoroughly clean the house after you're gone. You didn't have to do it yourself."

"I know, but I'm fussy. Hate the thought of people seeing my dirt."

"You should have asked Stef and me for help."

"It looked to me like you were having a grand time on the beach. I wouldn't have interrupted your play."

"Grant, blot your mouth, please." She rolled her eyes when he used the sleeve of his T-shirt rather than his napkin. Bernie chuckled. She asked him when he planned to leave.

"In a day or so. Have to get back and settle in for the long winter."

"You could stay longer. Better yet, you could move here permanently."

"Home's up there," he said with a touch of sadness. "You know how it is."

He and his wife of decades, of whom he often spoke, had lived in the same house from the day they'd married. She had died years ago, but he continued to mourn her and refused to move away from the town where she was buried and where one day he would be interred beside her.

"Well, I'm glad you didn't go before we could say a proper good-bye." She reached across the table and patted his hand.

"Hey, Bernie," Stef chirped as she passed through the kitchen carrying a bundle of laundry bound for the utility room. "You look smokin' this morning! I like that shirt."

It was flamingo pink and matched a stripe in his equally loud Bermuda shorts.

"Thanks. It's new."

Amelia hid her smile in her coffee cup. Stef's flirting never failed to fluster the senior. After dumping her bundle in the laundry room, she reentered the kitchen and pointed to the large sack he'd left on the countertop. "What's that?"

"A going-away present for the boys."

"Can we have it now?" Hunter pushed his empty cereal bowl across the table for Amelia's inspection. "We ate our breakfast."

"Yeah, Mom, please," Grant chimed in.

"I suppose so."

Bernie seemed as eager as they to open the sack and reveal the surprise. With touching pride, he reached into the sack and produced a box. On it was a picture of a kite in the shape of a pirate ship. It was an elaborate thing, with multiple sails.

"Oh my gosh!" Amelia exclaimed. "Will it actually fly?"

"Can we do it now, Bernie?"

He looked at Amelia. "Can they?"

She laughed. "Of course. But get your sandals on," she called after the boys as they charged through the back door.

"I'll see that they do," Stef said, following them out.

Bernie paused and looked back at Amelia. "Maybe I should have checked with you first. But I saw it in a store on Tybee, and immediately thought of them. I hope you don't mind."

"It was sweet of you. Thank you. Oh, and thanks for repairing their beach ball."

He looked at her quizzically.

"You didn't patch it for them?"

"Nope. Must've been Stef."

Amelia smiled woodenly. "Don't let me keep you from the fun."

Grinning like a young boy himself, he hobbled out.

She tried without success to convince herself that there was a logical explanation for the ball, just as there was for the porch light. Forcibly shaking off her uneasiness, she cleared the table and put the dishes in the dishwasher. Then, taking a last cup of coffee with her, she went out onto the front porch and sat down in one of the rocking chairs.

The kite-flying was well under way. Stef was doing the running for Bernie, who was gesturing wildly and shouting instructions. The boys were running alongside Stef and were so excited watching the kite, their feet got tangled up with hers and all three of them stumbled and fell into the sand. The pirate ship crashed bow first into the surf.

But they all came up laughing. Bernie reeled the kite in and soon it was aloft again.

Amelia's throat became tight with mixed emotions: joy in watching her boys play with such unbridled happiness; and sorrow that they were doing so with a hired nanny and an elderly neighbor rather than with their dad.

One day, probably sooner than she hoped, they would question her about him. They knew he had died, but of course they were too young to know the circumstances. Eventually, they would want to know.

She kept a picture of Jeremy on the nightstand between their beds, but she doubted they actually *saw* it. It was part of the furnishings in their room, nothing more. They mentioned him less and less frequently, especially Grant who was barely old enough to remember him at all. Most of their memories would be of angry shouting, slamming doors, boozy breath.

In the picture in their room, he was wearing his Marine dress uniform and a stern but noble expression. The first time she saw the photo, she had teased Jeremy about it.

"You look grimly determined."

"I am," he'd said with exaggerated gravity. "Grimly determined to bed you and make you my woman."

"Well, if that's the case, I'll surrender without a fight."

They'd laughed and kissed and made love. Life had been good. The future had seemed bright.

She would emphasize to her sons that aspect of their father's personality, his ability to tease and laugh. She would tell them stories about the months leading up to their wedding, when he'd courted her sweetly and with an earnest desire to please.

He'd been intimidated by the plantation house in which she'd grown up, awed by the number of statesmen and dignitaries with whom she and her father were friends. His efforts to fit into their circle had won her heart.

Friends and colleagues were impressed by his distinguished-service record in Iraq. When it was called for, he exercised a courtly politeness that charmed even the most discriminating of their acquaintances. By the time they walked down the aisle, he'd been wholeheartedly accepted into their society.

When she talked to her sons about him, she would emphasize those good times. Of course, she inevitably would have to tell them about the bad ones as well. She would wait until they were old enough to understand, but not so long that they heard about his downfall from a crueler source.

The thought of that brought tears to her eyes.

As she blinked them away, something in her peripheral vision glinted. She turned her head to see what it was and for several moments stared with incomprehension. Then, gripping the armrests of the rocking chair, she slowly levered herself out of it and walked the length of the porch to the corner of the railing.

There lay her watch, the clasp open, the band stretched out along the wooden rail, as though it had been carefully placed.

She knew positively that she hadn't been the one who'd put it there.

She nearly jumped out of her skin when Stef bounded up onto the porch. "The boys are asking for a drink. They're having a blast, although I worry about Bernie's hip giving out. Are you coming down?" Then she paused and asked, "Something wrong?"

Amelia picked up the watch and turned to her. "I found my watch."

"Great! Where was it?"

That wasn't the response Amelia had hoped for. If Stef needed to ask where she'd found it, then she hadn't put it on the porch railing, either.

Dawson glanced down at the LED of his jangling cell phone. Headly. He answered dispiritedly. "Hey."

"What's up?"

"Why ask me? You're the one taking Viagra."

Headly snorted. "I don't need it."

"If you say so."

"Where are you?"

"In my room."

"What are you doing?"

"Just hanging out."

"Working on the story?"

"I don't have a story yet."

"You heard Amelia Nolan's testimony."

"And I'll hear her cross-examination on Tuesday. Between now and then, there's nothing much for me to do, is there?"

"Rough draft?"

"I talked myself out of that. I don't want to write something only to have to scrap it and begin again if the defense attorney destroys her testimony."

"Which is unlikely."

"Still."

"So you're just hanging out."

"Watching the grass grow."

"Any leads on her current address?"

"The last one Glenda could dig up was the townhouse on Jones Street. As I predicted, she no longer lives there."

"Maybe she moved into her dad's mansion."

"No. Glenda learned that she's donated it to the state. It's closed up, but will possibly open next spring as a museum. That's under consideration with the historical society. Something like that."

"Well, she's gotta live somewhere," Headly said with impatience.

"Wherever that somewhere is, it's under wraps. A bailiff hustled her from the courtroom. I assume the same bailiff will escort her in on Tuesday at nine o'clock. Over the long weekend, the lady is keeping a low profile, and who could blame her?"

"Damn! I'd hoped you could have talked to her by now."

"As if she would talk to me."

"How do you know she wouldn't?"

"Because she's not talking to any media."

"The news outlets down there are full of stories about the trial. I've been following online."

"Then you should have noticed that there aren't any quotes from her, except what she was quoted as saying on the witness stand. The state prosecutor—"

"Lemuel Jackson. I understand that he's highly regarded."

"He held a brief press conference outside the courthouse immediately after court was adjourned on Wednesday. I listened from a distance. He didn't say anything about Ms. Nolan except that her testimony had been compelling. Nothing's happened since then. Dullsville. So there you have it, an up-to-the-minute report. How about your end? Anything from Knutz?"

"About the Wessons of Ohio? Not yet. This damn holiday."

"Hmm. Let me know when he gets back to you. Right now I gotta go."

"If you're only watching the grass grow, what's your hurry?"

"I gotta pee."

Dawson hung up, dropped the cell phone onto the cluttered table, and walked into the bathroom. At least he hadn't lied to Headly about having to go.

When he was done, he lingered for a moment at the sink, staring at the disheveled guy in the mirror who had haunted-looking eyes surrounded by shadows. Arms braced stiffly on the rim of the sink, he silently asked himself what the hell he was doing here, why he was putting himself through this, why he should give a fuck about Jeremy Wesson.

Arriving at no satisfactory conclusion, he turned on the cold-water tap and splashed his face several times, then dried it, and was doing up his zipper as he walked back into the other room.

Where he uttered a startled sound and drew up short.

Amelia Nolan was standing not ten feet from him, a can of pepper spray aimed directly at his face.

"Tell me now who you are. Because after getting a face full of this, it'll be a while before you can talk."

Chapter 5

He raised his hands, palms out. "I swear I'm no threat."

"Like hell you're not."

With her free hand, she gestured to the table behind her where the incriminating evidence was on display.

Shit!

Scattered across the table were dozens of photos of her and her sons playing on the beach. He'd taken the shots with his cell phone, enlarged them on his laptop, and printed them out. Standing on the windowsill were the binoculars through which he'd been watching them.

The pictures he'd taken of her alone made him particularly culpable. In some she looked reflective and a bit sad. In others she was laughing over her sons' antics, her loose hair like a fiery halo in the sunlight as the three of them capered on the beach.

He'd also captured a private moment of her standing at the waterline in her swimsuit, one hand anchoring her floppy-brimmed straw hat to her head. With the sun behind her, the swimsuit was absorbed into the dark silhouette, and her shape, in profile, was clearly delineated.

She was more modestly clothed now in the familiar caftan, a two-piece swimsuit beneath it. Sand clung to her bare feet, so she must have come directly from the beach. Her hat had obviously been left behind when she decided to storm the house next door to hers, the one that he'd rented two days ago.

He felt like a voyeur and couldn't fault her for being angry. But that anger was mixed with fear. The hand clutching the canister of pepper spray wasn't all that steady.

"Who are you?"

"My name is Dawson Scott. Middle name Andrew. See for yourself. My wallet is right there." He motioned toward the table.

Keeping her eyes on him, she picked up the wallet and flipped it open. Inside it were his Virginia driver's license. And the damning press-corps ID card.

Her hand dropped to her side as though the wallet was as heavy as an anvil. "You're a lousy reporter."

He gave a weak grin. "Actually I'm pretty good."

She tossed the wallet back onto the table, then wiped her hand on the gauzy material of her caftan as if she'd touched something foul. The pepper spray was still aimed at him.

He tilted his head toward it. "Are you going to squirt me?"

"I haven't decided yet."

He probably thought she was being facetious. She wasn't. His being a journalist was only slightly better than his being a pervert who took snapshots of potential victims. They weren't mutually exclusive, either. "Whom do you work for? Or are you a freelance hacker who sells to the highest bidder?"

"I'm going to lower my hands, okay?" He did so. "I think it's apparent that I'm unarmed."

Unarmed and disconcerting, dressed only in a pair of cargo

shorts, the fly of which was still partially unzipped. They were riding dangerously low on his hips. He was the one half-dressed, which made her wonder why *she* felt exposed.

She took a tighter grip on the canister and thumbed the sprayer. "Answer my question."

"I forgot it."

"Whom do you work for?"

"I'm a staff writer for *NewsFront*."

She was relieved and grudgingly impressed. She'd imagined him affiliated with a publication much more lowbrow, a tabloid possibly, not a serious-minded, hard-news magazine. From his long blond hair to his bare feet, she gave him a once-over and arrived at an uncomplimentary opinion. "You don't look that respectable."

"Well, you don't look like a museum curator." He grinned. "Not that I'm complaining."

She was about to snap, *Don't be cute*, but she didn't want to play into the mild flirtation even to that extent. She was still as mad as hell, and also as creeped-out as she'd been when she found her wristwatch and realized that someone had to have been spying on her.

After discovering her watch, she'd gone down to the beach and helped fly the kite until Bernie cried uncle and returned to his house to rest, promising to join them for supper that night. Then she and the boys played in the water while Stef finished her chores indoors.

At lunchtime, Stef brought the picnic hamper down to the beach, as she had the day before. After they'd eaten and were stretched out on the quilt, relaxing, Amelia experienced again that sensation of being watched.

Shading her eyes against the glare, she'd scanned the eastern horizon. The same boat was still anchored offshore, but was too far away to pose any threat. She looked back toward her house, then at Bernie's, and then at the row of houses that stretched down the beach in the direction of the village. Nothing had alerted her to danger.

She'd then turned toward the house on the other side of hers, the last one in the row. It had been vacated by long-term renters the previous Sunday. But when she'd looked toward it…

Speaking as calmly as possible, she'd told Stef she had something to do inside, and had left her and the boys beneath the beach umbrella. She returned to the house only long enough to retrieve the pepper spray from the drawer of her nightstand. Going out the back way, she walked to the neighboring house and let herself in through an unlocked sliding glass door. She had hoped to catch the window peeper, for lack of a better word, in the act. If he hadn't been taking a bathroom break from his spying, she no doubt would have.

When he'd emerged from the bathroom, it was all she could do to keep from gasping. She wasn't sure what she'd expected, but not this. Not *him*. He didn't look like a man who would require perversion to satisfy his sexual urges. Nor did he fit her image of a writer, which was someone with an absent-minded demeanor, delicate hands, and a pallor. Someone much softer around the middle. Much softer everywhere.

She said, "The IDs could be fake."

"They're not."

"I'll Google you."

"Be my guest. You can use my laptop."

She'd noticed it and the printer on the table, certainly tools of his trade, but she ignored his gesture for her to help yourself. "How did you track me here?"

"Two things I never reveal. One, a source who asks to remain anonymous. And two, how I tracked—Okay, okay," he said quickly when she thrust the canister toward his face. "There's a researcher at the magazine. Her name is Glenda. I ply her with candy and wine at Christmas. She comes through for me."

"My house was bought over twenty years ago."

"June 1985."

"Under a corporate entity—"

"WareHouse, LLC. Want to know the purchase price?" Reading the dismay in her expression, he said, "Glenda could find a flea on a single hair on a woolly mammoth. During a sandstorm."

That last was tacked on with a crooked smile, which only annoyed her. "Did you rent this house?"

"As opposed to what? Breaking in and squatting?"

"Nothing would surprise me."

"Saint Nelda's Island Rentals. I spoke to a nice lady. The house was vacant. I have a credit card."

"How long have you been here?"

"Since court was adjourned for the holiday weekend."

"Only since Wednesday?"

"I arrived after dark."

"Hmm."

"What?"

"Nothing. I thought you'd been here longer."

"Why?"

"Doesn't matter," she said, gesturing vaguely. "However long it's been, you went to a lot of trouble and expense for nothing. I don't grant interviews. Ever."

"My trouble wasn't for nothing." He motioned toward her wrist. "You got your watch back."

She glanced down at it. "Do I have you to thank?"

"I was watching you through the binoculars yesterday while you were building the sand castle. After you and the kids went indoors, I saw something glittering in the sand. I went down later to check it out and found your watch."

"Why didn't you just knock on my door and return it like any normal person would do? Any person who wasn't a sneaking, spying magazine writer."

"Because I wasn't ready for you to know that I was here."

"When did you intend to make your presence known?"

"I'm not sure." He squinted at her thoughtfully. "But I'm glad you know."

"I'm sure you are. You can turn the lights on tonight instead of stumbling around in the dark." He acknowledged the barb, but didn't comment. "Did you see me searching the beach last night?" Before he could answer, she said, "Of course you did." Then another thought occurred to her. "The lightbulb?"

"I noticed that it was out. The back of your house was dark. I thought—"

"Thank you for your concern."

"You're welcome."

"And for my watch," she said, although it galled her to thank him for anything. "It means a lot to me."

"Why?"

She wasn't about to answer a question that personal.

Seeming to read her mind, he said, "Okay, if that one's too tough, how about this one? How did you recognize me?" Holding her gaze, he took a step toward her. "You did, didn't you?"

She took a corresponding step back. "How would I have recognized you?"

"I don't know, but you did. If you hadn't, I'd be writhing on the floor, temporarily blinded and choking. At the very least, you would have called the police and reported me as a stalker."

"You *are* a stalker."

"I know for certain that I'd never seen you until Wednesday afternoon when you took the witness stand. I was seated in the corner of the courtroom, back row. You never so much as glanced in that direction."

"I didn't see you there."

"But . . . ?"

"I saw you after court was adjourned," she admitted reluctantly. "To avoid the media storm, Mr. Jackson put me in an office on the third floor that overlooks the front of the courthouse. I was watching from the window while he addressed the reporters. You were standing at a distance, leaning against a signpost."

"You noticed me? From three stories up?"

He shot her that grin again, and it was even more aggravating this time. "I took you for a homeless person. Unshaven. Shaggy hair. That's why I recognized you when you stepped out of the bathroom. I almost wish I'd gone ahead and sprayed you. It would have served you right for tracking me here." She looked at the canister of spray, then lowered her hand. "As it is, I'll leave you with a warning. Do not approach me or my children. If you do, I'll call the police after all."

When she turned to go, he said, "As long as you're here, can I ask you a few questions?"

"Didn't you hear what I just said? No interviews. Ever."

"Strictly background stuff."

"No."

"The girl. Kin to you?" He hitched his chin toward the window, through which Stef and the boys could be seen playing a game with paddles and a ball.

Amelia hesitated, but didn't see a problem with answering him. "No relation. I hired her as a nanny for the summer."

"And the old man who was flying the kite?"

"Family friend. He rents the house next door every summer. And that's all you're going to get from me."

She turned to go, but again he stopped her with a question. "What would be the harm in us having a nice, neighborly chat?"

"During which you hope I'll forget myself, let down my guard, and pour out my deepest, darkest secrets?"

He arched one sun-bleached eyebrow. "You have deep, dark secrets?"

"Good-bye."

Moving quickly, he planted himself between her and the door, but he also raised his hands again. "Look, I understand why you might not trust me."

"Oh, well, thanks for your understanding. Not that I care whether you understand me or not." With disgust, she glanced at the photos. "Do you plan to publish those? Sell them to a tabloid?"

He looked offended. "Of course not."

"Then why did you take them?"

"So I could..."

When he couldn't come up with an explanation, she sidestepped him. Or tried. He moved to block her path. "Would you have talked to me if I'd walked up to you, looking like a homeless person, and introduced myself as a writer for *NewsFront*?" He gave her only half a second to answer. "Exactly. So, rather than scare you off—"

"You simply scared me."

"You were scared?"

"Of course I was scared," she exclaimed.

"Of what?"

"Of... I don't know. I sensed—"

"What?"

"Something. I thought—"

"What?"

"I was afraid that—"

"That what?"

"I don't know! Stop asking me questions."

"That's what I do."

They did another two-step dance, and again he blocked her path to the door.

"Get out of my way."

"One more question? Just one. Please?" Taking her silent glare for consent, he asked, "How did you discover that I was here?"

"I saw the sun reflecting off something in the window."

"Must've been the lenses of the binoculars."

"Remember to guard against that the next time you spy on someone."

"When did you sense someone watching you?"

"That's two questions."

"Have you sensed it only since I moved in, or before?"

She opened her mouth to speak, but paused. Looking beyond him toward the beach, she recalled the eerie feeling that had swept over her last night. Speaking to herself, she murmured, "The sensation was strong enough to raise goose bumps."

After a moment, her eyes moved back to his. They were light brown, flecked with gold. Tiger eyes. And the intensity of that amber gaze shocked her out of her momentary fog. "I've got to go. They'll wonder where I am."

He let her pass, but said to her back, "I apologize for frightening you. You've been put through hell. I don't want to contribute to your troubles."

"Then don't," she said without turning around. "Stay away from me and my children."

Eva Headly barely allowed her husband through the back door before demanding to know where he'd been.

"Nowhere." He brushed past her and continued down the hallway and into his den.

She followed. "You've been gone for hours, Gary. You didn't answer your cell phone."

"You're keeping track? I can't go out now without asking your permission?"

"Don't take that tone with me."

Headly knew better than anyone that Eva, who had the face and disposition of a saint most of the time, was no shrinking violet when riled.

"Are you seeing another woman?"

He gave her a look.

"Well, it happens, you know. Men your age—"

"My age? Now I'm a classification? What, sixty-five to death?"

"Don't change the subject."

She stared him down. He was the first to relent. "I didn't tell you where I was going because I didn't want an argument."

She sat down on the upholstered arm of the sofa and looked up at him expectantly, with a listening aspect. He muttered beneath his breath and turned toward the bar. "Want a drink?"

"No. And you're not having one until you tell me what's going on. Where did you go?"

He sat down heavily in his chair and rubbed his hand over his face. "I went to Dawson's place."

"He's not there."

"That's why I went." He waited for her to erupt and call him on invasion of privacy, but she surprised him.

"I'm sure you had a good reason for going, knowing full well that he's in Savannah."

"Is he?"

"Isn't he?"

He sighed. "I don't know. He's supposed to be, but he's lying to me, Eva. To us. To everybody, I think."

"About what?"

"I'm not sure. Something. Everything. I talked to him earlier this afternoon, and he sounded okay, but the conversation was off. When I thought back on it, I realized that his answers didn't quite fit the questions I asked."

"You felt he wasn't being straight with you?"

"I didn't *feel* it, I know it."

"Why would he lie?"

"It might have something to do with this." From his pants pocket, he withdrew the brown plastic bottle and passed it to her. "Antianxiety drug."

She uncapped the bottle and shook out a few of the tablets. "I knew something was wrong. First he avoids us for two weeks.

Then he shows up looking like a scarecrow. These pills explain it. He's being treated for anxiety and doesn't want us to know."

"I agree with everything you said except the last part. He admitted to me that he's not sleeping. But he's not seeing a doctor for the anxiety. Notice there's no label on the bottle. He's getting his 'medication' from some other source."

The implication distressed her as much as it had him. "Did you find anything else in his apartment that we should worry about?"

"No. And I felt guilty for being there and pawing through his stuff."

"Only because you care. Seeing the horrors he saw in Afghanistan affected him more than he wants to admit, even to himself. Should we confront him about it, insist that he see a therapist?"

"He'd just get defensive and deny that he needs one. You know how he is. Mr. Self-sufficient."

"Which, of course, is something you know nothing about."

He looked over at her and smiled sheepishly. "I've been a grump recently, haven't I?"

"No, you've been a regular son of a bitch. But I don't know what I'd do without you." She got up and moved to the arm of his chair, leaned over, and kissed the top of his head. "As for Dawson, he knows that we're always here for him, and how much we care, and that anything we do or say, it's for his own good."

"That's the hell of it, Eva. That's what's eating at me. Knowing that he's barely hanging on, instead of helping him through it, I sent him to look for Carl Wingert and Flora Stimel."

Chapter 6

There's a hot, hot, hot guy sitting at the bar who keeps staring at you."

Amelia turned her head in the direction Stef had indicated and met Dawson Scott's steady gaze. Quickly, she came back around, only to notice that everyone else at her table had also turned to look.

"Boys." She patted the tabletop, bringing their attention back to her. "Finish your dinner, please. It's getting late."

Stef fluffed her hair and said, "I'll be right back."

Before Amelia could stop her, the younger woman slid from her chair and struck off in the direction of the bar.

"Where's she going, Mom?"

"Can we go?"

"No! Eat. Grant, your bottom in the chair, please. Hunter, turn around and finish your hamburger."

Whatever was going on at the bar had grabbed Bernie's attention, too. To draw him back to her, she gently admonished him. "I saw you carrying boxes out to your car this afternoon. You really should let us help."

He launched into a diatribe against his bad hip and its probable replacement. "I've got an appointment with the orthopedic surgeon soon as I get home."

Amelia murmured sympathetically and tried to follow everything he was saying about the tribulations of aging, but she was curious to know what was taking place behind her.

She got a fair indication when Bernie stopped talking and became fixated on something behind her. Something tall. About six foot four, if she had gauged correctly.

"Everybody, this is our neighbor," Stef announced. "He's staying in the house next door. Alone."

Amelia didn't miss the emphasis Stef had placed on that last word, and it was mortifying to know that it probably hadn't escaped him, either. She had no choice except to turn and acknowledge the introduction. "Hello. Amelia Nolan." Her tone was polite but cool. Discouraging, she hoped.

"Dawson Scott."

He extended his hand. She looked at it for several seconds before reluctantly taking it in a quick handshake.

Stef continued the introductions. "This is Bernie Clarkson, Amelia's neighbor on the other side."

"Hi, Bernie." His arm grazed the top of Amelia's shoulder as he reached across the table to shake hands. "You were rocking that kite today."

The old man's face lit up. "You saw that?"

"Hard to miss."

"Hard contraption to fly, too."

"Lucky for you, you had these two buccaneers to help."

To Amelia's dismay, he rounded the table to address her sons, both of whom had disobediently gotten out of their chairs and were curiously regarding the tall stranger.

He hunkered down to their eye level. "Hi. I'm Dawson. What's your name?"

"Hunter."

Dawson gave him a high five. Hunter happily slapped his palm. "That's my brother, Grant. He's littler than me."

Grant, not to be outshone, shouldered his brother aside in order to move closer to Dawson. "What kind of car do you have?"

"Car? Well, while I'm here, I'm driving a rental car." He told Grant the model, which was apparently a crushing disappointment. His only response was an unenthusiastic *Oh.*

Dawson turned his head and looked across the table at Amelia, as though asking *What'd I say?* "He's into cars," she explained lamely. "He likes fast—"

"Sexy ones."

"Ah, I see," he said, looking amused at Stef's flirtatious quip. Turning back to the boys, he asked if they liked to play with Hot Wheels and Matchbox cars.

They nodded vigorously.

"Me too. I collected them when I was your age."

"We have to keep them picked up and in their box," Grant informed him. "Or else Mom takes them and puts them up high where we can't reach."

Dawson nodded solemnly. "My mom did that, too. But it's a good idea. You'd hate for somebody to trip over one of your cars and get hurt, right?"

Hunter asked, "Do you have a dog?"

"No, I don't."

"But you like them, right?"

"Oh yeah. Dogs are great. But I'm away from home a lot with my work. A dog would get lonesome."

Hunter shot Amelia an accusatory look. "We don't have one, either. Mom says maybe we can get one when things settle down. But I don't know when that is."

Amelia came to her feet so quickly, she painfully caught her hipbone on the edge of the table, rattling glasses and silverware. "Boys, it's past your bedtime. Say good-bye. Nice to meet you, Mr. Dawson."

"Scott."

"What?"

"Dawson Scott."

"Oh, sorry, well, enjoy your stay on the island."

While the boys were reluctantly telling him good-bye, she slipped the strap of her purse off the back of her chair, then shepherded her sons around tables and out of the café. Stef and Bernie followed.

Her little group had almost reached the parking lot at the rear of the building when she was hailed from behind. Dawson was jogging toward them. Amelia asked Stef to go on ahead. "Get the boys buckled in. I'll see what he wants."

For the first time of the summer, Stef looked a little put out by Amelia's request, but she did as asked and shooed the boys around the corner of the building. Bernie went along, too, but not before giving Amelia a knowing grin and an exaggerated wink.

To his credit, Dawson Scott cleaned up well. He still had the scruff, but it worked for him. As did the long hair. Somehow. He'd changed into a more presentable pair of khaki shorts and a black linen shirt with the sleeves rolled to his elbows. And he smelled good.

But none of that made her feel any more kindly toward him. "I told you to stay away from us."

"Your nanny invited me over to your table to meet you. If I had refused, it would have looked like obvious avoidance, wouldn't it? To say nothing of being rude."

She didn't address that logic, because he was right. "What do you want?"

"An interview."

"Have a nice life." She started to turn away.

"Wait, that was a joke. That's not why I came after you."

"Well?"

"Do you always carry the pepper spray?"

"No. I have two curious children who could come across it when they're looking for something else in my purse."

"So where do you keep it?"

"Where it would be handy if I had an intruder."

"It wasn't handy when Willard Strong surprised you in your kitchen that afternoon?"

"No. But even if it had been, he had a loaded shotgun and his finger was on the trigger."

"If you don't keep the pepper spray with you at all times, then what good is it?"

"It got your attention today, didn't it?"

He smiled with chagrin. "Ah, you got me with that one."

"We've exhausted the subject anyway. Good-bye."

"Where did Jeremy work?"

The abrupt switch of subject threw her off.

He said, "You testified that you'd called his workplace. Where was he working?"

"Your flea-on-a-single-hair lady came up empty?"

"Easier just to ask you."

Seeing no reason to withhold the information, she cited the name of the construction firm. "They specialize in commercial buildings. Large facilities. Schools, factories, medical complexes. Jeremy was one of their electrical engineers."

"Okay."

"He was very good at it," she said, hating herself for sounding defensive.

"How did he get to that from sniper training for the Marines?"

"So, you *have* done your research."

"Some. I'm still in the process."

"Jeremy held a degree in that field. After leaving the corps, he applied for a position with the firm, met the qualifications, and—"

"Congressman Nolan called in a favor."

She stiffened her spine.

"Okay, that was a cheap shot."

"You're damn right it was. Good-bye."

"Just one more thing."

"I don't think so."

"This isn't even a question."

"They're waiting for me in the car, Mr. Scott."

"Check under your front doormat."

"What?"

"I left something there for you."

"Under the doormat?"

"The photographs."

"Oh, the photographs. How cavalier." She gave him a drop-dead look. "You could replace them with a keystroke on your laptop. Or just take more."

"I won't. I promise. I know they made you uncomfortable."

"Pictures of me and my children, taken by a total stranger. You bet they made me uncomfortable. Especially since you failed to explain the reason for them."

"I didn't explain?"

"No. And I asked."

"Oh. I took them so I could study you."

"As part of your research?"

"No, so I could get to know you."

"I don't want you to know me."

It could have been a trick of the lights along the dock, reflecting off the water. Or his gaze really did move down to her mouth when he said in a low and stirring voice, "That's too bad."

Mistrusting herself to come up with an appropriate put-down that would have any oomph behind it, she turned away from him without speaking another word.

Stef was on her way downstairs as Amelia was making tired progress up.

"What was that about?"

"What?"

"Why'd you brush him off like that?"

"Who?"

Stef propped her fist on her hip. "Seriously?"

"I didn't brush him off." She wanted to add that she also didn't need to defend herself to anyone, but especially not to an employee. But that would have sounded as peevish as she felt, so she let it go. "I've lectured the boys about being cautious with strangers. I was setting an example."

"He's not a stranger. He's renting the house next door."

"Anybody could rent the house next door."

"Point taken. But if that guy had looked at me like that, I would have—"

"Like what?"

"Like he wanted to lick you all over."

"Stephanie!"

The younger woman only laughed. "What did he want when he called you back?"

"He asked about, uh . . . garbage collection."

Stef's eyes narrowed. "Okay, don't tell me."

Time to change the subject. "Are the boys down?"

"They were waiting for a story from you, but they went unconscious the second their heads hit the pillows."

"Thank you. I had to see to some things in my office. Reply to some e-mails." *Look under the front doormat.*

"Mind if I borrow your car again? I'll cover the gas."

"Seeing Dirk?"

"Um-huh."

"You're welcome to invite him to come here one night."

Stef wrinkled her nose. "I don't think so. He wouldn't exactly fit into the cozy family scene. He's not the type."

"Oh? What type is he?"

"Hip. Tattoos and a beard. He's older than me."

"By how much?"

She laughed. "I think my instinct is right. You'd take one look at him and disapprove. But that's cool. It's not like I'm that smitten. At the end of next week, I'll be going back to Kansas, and Dirk will be a blurry memory of my summer."

After Stef left, Amelia continued upstairs and went into the boys' bedroom. She kissed each of them, then sat on the edge of Hunter's bunk and watched them while they slept. Usually that brought her a sense of peace and well-being.

Tonight, it only served to remind her how vulnerable they were, how young and innocent, and totally dependent on her to protect them. Many times, she'd had to shelter them from Jeremy's dark moods, his heavy drinking, his rants about her working at the museum. After returning from his second tour in Afghanistan, her job had been one of the first things he'd picked quarrels over.

He'd wanted her waiting at home for him when he got off work every day and had resented any evening event or meeting that she was expected to attend. He became increasingly belligerent over having to stay at home with the boys until, finally, she began making excuses to George Metcalf as to why she had to miss work-related occasions.

But their evenings spent at home together were far from idyllic. She couldn't say anything that didn't spark a touchy reaction or full-throttle fight. The boys' constant activity and noise grated on him.

At first Jeremy had been a proud and boastful father to both boys. She had photographs of him cuddling them. In those, he looked happy and content. He'd been playful and had dazzled them with tricks, such as pulling pennies from their ears. He'd indulged them with treats and small gifts, which she allowed because he had missed much of their infancy. His desire to spoil them was understandable.

But after that second tour, his interaction with them became unpredictable. He'd become too short-tempered and impatient to be a hands-on dad. The overindulgent daddy became an angry man that her boys grew wary of, and their wariness irritated him, making the time he spent with them volatile. Ultimately she became afraid to leave them alone with him. Which was one of the main reasons she'd left. Protecting her children had become more important than saving the bad marriage.

Disturbed by those memories, she kissed the boys one more time, then went into her bedroom. Now that she knew eyes were watching, she made certain to pull down the shades before undressing.

It was a large and rambling house, and Dawson occupied very little of it. He didn't generate enough noise to fill it, either, so he heard every creak of wood, every faucet drip, and every thud of unknown origin.

He'd chosen to use one of the upstairs bedrooms, solely because the windows on the west side of it afforded an unrestricted view of Amelia's house.

From it, he watched Stef get into Amelia's car and head toward the village. Shortly after she left, he saw Amelia enter her bedroom, walk straight to the row of windows, and pull down each shade with a purposeful tug, as though she knew he was watching. She wanted him to know with certainty that she was closing off not only his view but also his access to her life. A few minutes later, the light in the room went out.

With one hand propped high on the jamb, he continued to watch her house through his open window. The breeze off the ocean was balmy and moisture-laden. Against the skin of his belly, it felt like a woman's breath. Like the softest of open-mouth kisses.

Groaning, he turned his face into his raised arm and rubbed his forehead against his biceps, cursing himself for being every kind of fool. He should have heeded his impulse to call Headly and tell him to screw this trial, screw Jeremy Wesson and whoever his parents had been, he was coming home.

But he'd taken one look at Amelia, and his ennui had turned into razor-sharp awareness. His disinterest became avid curiosity. He wanted to know all there was to know about her.

No, scratch that. Not *all.* He could do without knowing about her personal relationship with her ex. Because every time he thought about her in bed with Jeremy Wesson, about Wesson or any man moving on top of her, inside her, he wanted to hit something.

The hell of it was, Headly expected him to turn Wesson's life inside out. Pivotal years of his life had been spent with Amelia. If he did this thing for Headly, and did it right, there was no way he could omit the active role she had played.

He gave her house one last careful study, then walked to the bed and lay down, stretching out on his back. The pills he'd taken earlier were kicking in. He'd caught a pleasant buzz from the combo of them and Kentucky's elixir, and he was feeling drowsy. Maybe tonight would be the first night that he would sleep through without having the nightmare. *Please, God.*

Closing his eyes, he forced back the ghastly images that continually lurked on the borders of his mind. To replace them, he conjured up Amelia's face. Having finally gotten to see her eyes up close, he knew they were a deep, deep blue. Hooking her hair behind her ear was an absent-minded habit, as he'd suspected when he saw her do it in the courtroom. She also had a tendency to bite her plush lower lip.

Thinking of that caused a physical response of unequaled lust.

For weeks, he'd been sleepless during the nights, wound up tight during the days, his nerves flayed by recurring memories and nightmares of war. So, probably, this intense physical reaction was based on nothing more than a critical need for solace. Like any straight guy, one of the first places he would seek it was a woman's body. It couldn't cure the malady, but it could provide temporary relief from the symptoms.

But if it was only comfort he needed, wouldn't any breasts feel as soft? Couldn't forgetfulness be found between any pair of thighs? Wasn't one woman's hand as effective a magic wand as another's, one woman's mouth as mind-numbing as the next?

He had thought so. He'd lived his adult life believing so. Whether a sexual relationship lasted for a few months or a few hours, he'd got from it what he'd wanted and no more than he'd invested.

His customary nonchalance didn't apply here. Not to Amelia Nolan. No, this was something else. This wasn't a crotch throb that would be easily pacified. This was different. A first and only. This was hell.

He hoped Jeremy Wesson was frying in one of his own.

Chapter 7

Mom!"

"Mom! You gotta come see!"

Amelia was in her office composing an e-mail to George Metcalf when the boys rushed in, tracking in sand and practically stumbling over each other in their haste. Their faces were sweaty and flushed.

"What in the world?" It had been less than ten minutes since she'd heard them leaving the house on their way to the beach. "Did a spaceship land on the shore?"

"No, it's better. You gotta come see." Hunter took her hand and tried to pull her from the desk chair.

"Hold on. Where's Stef?"

"She's down there. Come on."

"Okay, I'll come down, I promise. Just let me finish this—"

"No! You gotta come *now*." Grant was bouncing on the balls of his feet. "Come see."

"If it's that stupendous, I guess my e-mail can wait."

Laughing, she let each one take a hand and drag her from the room, down the stairs, and out through the front door. Her laughter subsided when she looked beyond the dunes. Stef, looking sleek and bronze and young, was chatting with "hot, hot, hot" Dawson Scott. He had on swim trunks. A ball cap worn backward was keeping his hair out of his face. Something he said caused Stef to tip her head back and laugh.

"Hurry, Mom!"

Hunter tugged harder on her hand and together the three of them went down the steps. When they reached the boardwalk, the two boys left her and bolted ahead. She was too miffed to remember to warn them against splinters.

As she crested the dunes, she saw what all the excitement was about. A dragon had been sculpted into the sand. It had fangs and scales and claws, and a body that arched in and out of the sand for twelve feet. She didn't need to guess who the sculptor had been. Her sons were dancing around him like aboriginals worshiping a totem pole.

He'd placed her in an untenable situation. She couldn't spoil the boys' excitement, and, damn him, he knew it. Pasting on a smile, she approached the dragon. "My goodness!" She pressed her hands together and placed them under her chin, as though completely captivated. It worked to fool the boys.

Both were grinning up at her, their rapture apparent. "Isn't it awesome, Mom?"

"It certainly is! I hardly know what to say." This last, she addressed to Dawson, whose eyes were concealed by a pair of aviator sunglasses. She sensed him watching her closely and gauging her reaction from behind the dark lenses.

"Dawson made it!" Grant said.

"Did he?"

"Yeah, and he said he could make other stuff, too. We're gonna build a battleship."

"And a castle for the dragon," Grant added.

It was all she could do to keep from grinding her teeth. "Wow."

Stef, who'd been carefully observing Amelia as the scene unfolded, clapped her hands. "Before all these projects get under way, we'd better put on more sunscreen."

The boys chorused protests, but she placed a hand on each of their shoulders and turned them toward the house. "March. The sooner we do it, the sooner you can come back."

Hunter dug in his heels. "Dawson, will you still be here?"

He hesitated and looked at Amelia, but when she remained stonily silent, he smiled at the boys. "I'll be around."

"Don't leave!" Grant shouted over his shoulder as Stef propelled him up the boardwalk.

Neither she nor Dawson spoke until the trio had topped the dunes. Then he said quietly, "I meant only to surprise them. I thought I'd be finished before they came outside. They caught me putting on the final touches."

"I asked you, more nicely than warranted, to stay away from us."

"My house shares the beach with yours."

"But you picked *this spot* for your . . . your dragon. What made it so ideal? As if I didn't know."

"I'm not going to interview your children, Amelia."

Her tummy fluttered in reaction to his using her first name, and in such a low and infuriatingly reasonable tone. But she didn't address it, not wanting him to know that she had noticed.

He said, "I don't see the harm in my spending some time with the two of them."

She dragged back a strand of hair that had defied her hat and blown across her mouth. "Well, let me tell you what the harm is. Aside from the fact that I don't know anything about you."

"That's not true."

"Okay, you've got credentials. They don't speak to the kind of person you are."

"I—"

She held up her hand to stop him. "Secondly, Grant is too

young to remember much, but Hunter can recall when his grandfather died. Then—"

"They lost their father."

"That's right."

"So they could use a little man-time, don't you think?"

"Absolutely. But not with a man I know virtually nothing about. Not with a snake-oil salesman who will be here today and gone tomorrow. Not with a man who's ingratiating himself with them only in order to get to me so he can write a big, juicy story for his magazine."

"That's not why—"

"Save it. I already know you're a liar."

Angrily, he whipped off his sunglasses. "A liar? How's that?"

"Hey, Dawson!" The boys came charging over the dunes, toting pails and shovels. Hunter was the first to reach them. "Can we build the battleship now?"

Grant was bouncing again. "No, I want to build the castle first."

Dawson, his angry gaze still locked with Amelia's, arched an eyebrow by way of asking permission.

She said, "What choice do you leave me?"

He told the boys to start filling their buckets with wet sand. As they raced off, he replaced his sunglasses and said to her, "You and I aren't done with this discussion."

"You're damn right we're not."

She returned to her office and finished the e-mail even though there was no urgency to it because George wouldn't read it until after the holiday. Attached was a proposal for a new exhibit that she'd been thinking about for a while. She expected resistance to the idea. It would require a combination of diplomacy and arm twisting to convince him and the board of directors that it would be a viable and important addition to the museum. She'd wanted to draft the memo while her thoughts were still fresh.

But also she'd come back from the beach shaky and angry and very much in need of putting some distance between herself, Dawson, and his intrusion on her family.

After killing an hour, she determined that she was calm enough to return to the beach and watch him undermine her and dazzle her children. Dressed in a pair of loose white cotton pants and a red tank top, she decided against changing into a swimsuit. She grabbed her hat and joined the party on the beach.

And it was a party. The battleship was splendid. Stef was christening it with a bottle of apple juice. Hunter, the first to notice her, shouted, "Hey, Mom! We named it after you." Proudly he pointed to the name crookedly etched into the side of the ship.

She bent down to inspect the lettering that read, USS *Amelia*. "Did you print that all by yourself?"

Proudly, he bobbed his head.

She ran her fingers through his unruly mop of hair, now matted with saltwater and sand. "Thank you. I love it. That was very sweet of you."

"Dawson said to."

"Oh." She looked up. He was silhouetted against the bright sunlight, so she couldn't read his expression. "That was nice of him."

"Can we go in the ocean now?"

"I'm not dressed for it. Stef?"

"On it." Telling the boys she'd race them into the water, the three took off.

Grant plunged in, then called back, "Dawson, are you coming?"

"In a minute."

"If you need to go to the bathroom, it's okay if you tinkle in the ocean, just not in a swimming pool."

He chuckled. "Thanks. I'll keep that in mind."

Amelia retreated to the umbrella and sat down in one of the beach chairs. Dawson rescued his T-shirt from the maw of the dragon, shook sand from it, and pulled it on. It was a faded, threadbare thing with the neck and sleeves cut out, forming large armholes that extended halfway down his torso. As he walked slowly up the beach toward her, the thin cloth molded to his damp chest. So much for his nod toward propriety. His calves and feet were coated with sand.

When he reached the umbrella, he looked at the empty chair beside hers, then at the quilt, but decided against pushing his luck, or so she assumed, and sat down in the sand just outside the circle of shade.

She cut to the chase. "This morning before anyone else was up, I did a Google search on you."

"Yeah?"

"It took a while for me to read everything. Impressive."

"Thanks."

"You didn't tell me that you'd spent months in Afghanistan."

"You didn't ask."

Up to that point she'd been watching the boys and Stef playing in the ocean with an inflatable dolphin. Now she looked at him. "Right. You're the one who asks questions."

He pulled his knees up and looped his arms around his shins. "Ask me anything."

In spite of her ire, she was curious. "Some of your stories covered particular firefights. Were you actually there, in the thick of the fighting?"

"Not often. A few times. If the fighting was in a real hotbed, the military wouldn't allow me in. I'd interview the troops when they came back." He frowned thoughtfully. "The trouble with that war, most often you can't predict where the fight is going to be. It can be the lobby of a hotel, an open highway, a heavily guarded checkpoint. The enemy isn't always obvious, either."

"But when you could, you placed yourself in harm's way."

"That's where the stories were."

She felt it only fair to acknowledge how good they were. "Your writing is very moving. You made the men and women you wrote about seem real to the reader."

"I'm glad to hear that. They are real. Their stories deserved to be told."

She paused to study him. He'd taken off his sunglasses, so his eyes were squinted almost shut to block the glare. But his attention was fixed on her. "Did you meet Jeremy in Afghanistan?"

She could tell the question surprised him. "No. How could I have? I just got back two weeks ago. I'd never heard of him until Willard Strong's murder trial was brought to my attention."

"By whom?"

"I can't reveal a source."

"How convenient."

"Ask me something else."

She picked at the fringe on the beach towel lining her chair. "Why didn't you approach me through normal channels?"

"Could I have found you?"

"Through the museum. Through Lemuel Jackson. On the Internet, for that matter. Anybody can be found. How about Glenda? She would have found me."

He cracked a smile, but quickly pulled it back in. "Would you have agreed to an interview?"

"You know the answer to that. I'd like an answer to my question, please."

"What didn't I try a straightforward approach? Honestly, I wasn't sure I wanted to write a story about Jeremy. I was urged to come down here, sit in on the trial, check it out. By the third day, I was basically bored, ready to cash in, go home, and find another topic of more interest to me. But I changed my mind and decided to stay, at least for a while longer. Take it to the next step." He shrugged. "You know the rest."

"I caught you at taking it to the next step."

"It wasn't my proudest moment when I came out of the bathroom yesterday and realized I'd been caught spying, with my pants down, literally."

She resisted the appeal of his crooked smile. "You always have an answer ready, don't you?"

"Not always, no."

"That hasn't been my experience. All of your answers are self-deprecating, designed that way to be disarming, I'm sure."

He turned completely serious again. "I haven't 'designed' my answers, Amelia, and I think you're anything but disarmed right now. In fact, you seem locked and loaded. Are you that mad at me for playing with Hunter and Grant?"

"Why would a grown man want to waste his time that way?"

"I don't consider it a waste of time."

"Even worse. That's an admission that you have an ulterior motive. I hazard to guess what it is."

"You think I'm into little boys?"

She didn't say anything.

"I took just as many pictures of you."

Recalling one in particular sent a rush of heat through her. "That's supposed to reassure me?"

"It should reassure you that I'm not a deviant."

"Perhaps. But it doesn't rule out that you're a slick opportunist."

He tipped his chin down and stared at his sandy bare feet. Or maybe he was staring at hers, their bare toes being only inches apart. In any case, it was several moments before he raised his head.

"You don't know me, so I don't blame you in the slightest for being suspicious. In fact, I admire you for being ultraprotective and careful of who you let near your children. But I would never harm those boys, or you. Please trust me on that."

His words were stirring and persuasive, and she resented her strong inclination to believe them. "Why should I trust you when you so blatantly lied to me?"

"About what?"

"The photos. What kind of game are you playing?"

"Game?"

"I'd call it that. All those creepy things you did to work on me, play on my mind. Returning my lost watch, the porch light, the beach ball."

"Beach ball?"

"And then there's the photographs. Why come on so sincerely apologetic about them and tell me you'd returned them, when clearly you didn't?"

"I don't understand."

Thoroughly exasperated, she said, "There was nothing under the doormat when I got home last night. As you well know."

He became very still and stared at her for a count of ten. Then quietly he said, "I swear to you, I clipped all the photographs together and put them under your doormat."

Diary of Flora Stimel—June 5th, 1980

It's taken me weeks to open this diary and begin to write about this. Up till now, I haven't been able to put words on paper. Or do much of anything except cry. I've cried an ocean.

When I'm not crying, I sit and stare into space, unable to make myself move. I don't care what I look like, or if I'm clean or not, or hungry, or sleepy. I don't care if the world comes to an end. I've even wished for that. I know now what it means when people say somebody has "shut down."

I knew the day would come. I've had years to get ready for it, but that didn't help. I wasn't ready at all. As the date got closer, even Carl would turn quiet and thoughtful, like he was reconsidering. I knew he wouldn't change his mind, though, so I didn't even try to talk him into it.

But I couldn't leave Jeremy as easy as he did, and when I started carrying on, pleading with him to let him stay with us, he got mad. So I stopped begging. It was only making the separation harder on all of us.

Of course, I see the sense of it. It will be best for Jeremy. If I didn't think so, I would have fought Carl tooth and nail over it. Jeremy has to go to school. It will be good for him to make friends with other boys and do the things they do. Baseball and stuff. But, all the same, when I had to let go of him for the last time, I thought I would die. No mother should have to go through that.

Randy is a good choice to play his daddy. He helped us out that one time down in MS. I guess he formed an attachment to Jeremy then, because Jeremy was sick and had a terrible cough. Randy is kindhearted and still thinks the world of Carl. He shares the same ideas, but he doesn't have the "guts," he says, to do the things Carl is willing to do for our cause.

I thought he was going to faint when Carl asked him to raise our son. He said he was honored. He even cried a little and said he felt "anointed." I thought Carl would laugh at that, but he didn't. He told Randy he was playing his part, that he was as much a Ranger of Righteousness as anybody who carried a gun. He just wouldn't be fighting on the battlefront, so to speak.

Randy's gotten married since that time we stayed with him in MS. Patricia is also one of us, because she hates cops and everything government related. Here's her story: Her stepdaddy abused her and wound up killing her mother when she stood up to him. He went to the pen for it. Patricia was put into the foster care system. I gather it wasn't all that good for her. She doesn't talk about everything that happened to her, but her face turns hard and mean-looking whenever the subject is brought up. (Usually she's pretty.)

She's been on her own since she ran away at fifteen. She also doesn't talk about the things she did in order to survive, but I don't hold anything against her, because look at what all I've done. Anyhow, for being such a slight little thing, she knows how to take care of herself.

People Carl knows faked IDs for them. They've got new identities. They're going by the name of Wesson, which Carl picked out of the phone book. They've rented a house in a town in Ohio.

Patricia, who's also smart as a whip, is going to school to learn to be a court reporter. We laughed our heads off about that! What an inside joke. Here she'll be, sitting in courtrooms recording the words of lawyers, cops, and judges, while we're out breaking every law there is. Or just about.

But that job will be a good cover. Randy could sell ice cubes to Eskimos because of his easy, soft-spoken way. He got a job at a car dealership. His coworkers like him. They wouldn't believe it if somebody told them that mild-mannered Randy was raising the child of Carl Wingert and Flora Stimel, two of the FBI's Most Wanted!

Carl told them to go to church like the faithful. Randy was okay with it, but not Patricia. She said she wants no part of a God who'd put a kid through the shit she'd been put through. But she finally agreed to pretend to worship, because she knows it makes them look like ordinary folks, and Carl says that's the main thing.

They plan to join the PTA the day they enroll Jeremy in kindergarten in the fall. It breaks my heart that I won't be there to see him off on his first day of school. I hope he doesn't cry. Carl says he won't. He calls him his "good little soldier" because even when we were hugging him good-bye, his lower lip was trembling, but he didn't shed a tear.

He knows Carl has big plans for his future. He understands why we can't all live together. He also knows—because I've told him often enough—that even though he'll be living with Patricia and Randy and pretending to be their little boy, I'm his real mother and Carl is his real daddy. He'll call Patricia and Randy Mom and Dad, but he's our flesh and blood. Nothing will ever change that. We love him.

I hope he grows up understanding how things must be. I'm not sure I do.

Chapter 8

The boys had had such a full day, they practically fell asleep at the dinner table, and didn't object to an early bedtime. After getting them down, Amelia took a glass of wine out onto the porch and settled into one of the rocking chairs.

Stef joined her a few minutes later. "Kitchen's done. Unless you need me for anything else, I'm going up to bed."

"No Mickey's tonight?"

"I'm bushed."

"Same here. Sleep well."

Stef hesitated on the threshold. "Are you okay?"

"Why wouldn't I be?" Realizing how snappish that sounded, she softened her tone. "I'm fine."

"Are you mad at me for encouraging Dawson to hang out with us?"

"I can't be mad. The boys had a wonderful time. Being in male company was good for them."

"That was my thinking. But this particular male bugs you, doesn't he?"

She turned toward the younger woman, ready to take umbrage. Instead she ducked her head, admitting quietly, "A bit."

"His crooked tooth is awfully cute."

Amelia had noticed his slightly overlapping incisor. It actually made his smile more interesting.

"And I'd like to take a bite out of his biceps."

"You're incorrigible, Stef."

"Well, wouldn't you?"

If pressed, Amelia would have to admit that Dawson Scott was physically attractive. More times than she was comfortable with, her eyes had strayed from the novel that she was reading in the shade of the umbrella to the surf where he played with the boys. They had vied for his attention all day. He had seemed to be enjoying himself, too. But...

"There's something wrong with him." Amelia didn't even realize she'd spoken the thought out loud until Stef moaned.

"Oh, shit. He's *married*?"

Amelia laughed. "No. I mean, I don't know if he's married or not. I haven't—"

"Shh! Here he comes."

Amelia turned to see him approaching the porch. When he reached the bottom step, he said, "I saw you out here. Thought I'd bring a peace offering for monopolizing your sons all day." He had the neck of an uncorked wine bottle and two glasses clasped in one hand. Noticing the wineglass she held, he frowned. "But I see I'm too late."

"I'm going to bed. 'Night, you two." Stef went inside and closed the front door. Half a second later, the porch light went out.

Amelia and Dawson looked at each other through the sudden darkness, and when she saw a grin tugging at his lips, she had to laugh also. "She's got romantic notions."

"Would you rather I go?"

She considered it, then asked, "What color wine?"

"Red."

She extended her glass toward him. "As long as you bothered, you can top this off."

"I found the bottle in a cabinet. I can't vouch for the vintage."

"I can vouch for this one. Blending it with another will be an improvement."

He climbed the steps, refilled her glass, then poured one for himself. As he sat down in the rocker beside hers, he groaned. "I'm going to be sore tomorrow. Hunter and Grant gave me quite a workout."

She ran her finger around the lip of her wineglass. "All things considered, it's hard for me to say this, but thank you for spending time with them."

"You're welcome."

"They especially loved the roughhousing. I try, but..." She trailed off and shrugged.

He stretched his legs out in front of him. "Moms don't make good wrestlers. They're too afraid someone will get hurt."

She smiled. "You're right of course." She paused to sip her wine. "Do you have children of your own?"

"No."

"Married?"

"No."

"Stef wondered."

"Hmm." He sipped from his glass. "Am I allowed to make some observations?"

"About Stef?"

"About your children."

She made a motion for him to continue.

"I don't know much about kids, but, in my amateur opinion, you've done a good job with yours."

"Thank you."

"They don't pee in swimming pools."

She laughed.

"They say please and thank you. And even though I did suggest naming the battleship after you, they jumped on the idea."

"I wouldn't trade them for any others."

"Hunter is the more cautious of the two. He has his exuberant moments, but basically he's serious-minded. It's like he already realizes that being the oldest child comes with implied responsibilities that he accepts, even if it isn't fair.

"Grant," he said, pausing to grin, "wears his emotions on his sleeve. He's impulsive, capricious, approaches everything at full tilt. I'm betting that he'll get into more mischief than his older brother."

"You've given them a lot of thought."

"I'm naturally curious about people and what makes them tick. My job requires it. I observe closely and analyze my observations." When she merely nodded without comment, he added, "People reveal as much by their silences as they do by what they say."

"Do they? I'll have to remember that."

"Damn. By sharing a trade secret, did I just shoot myself in the foot? Will you be constantly on guard from here on?"

"We don't have a 'from here on.'"

He waited several beats. "Okay. But Tuesday morning, I'll be in the courtroom for your cross-examination."

"Be there or not. It's up to you. I've made it plain that I don't grant interviews."

"Right, you did. So I had better ask you now, while I have the chance."

She sharpened her focus on him. "Ask me what?"

"What was it like to be with a man who suffered from post-traumatic stress disorder?"

After posing the question, he kept his gaze averted. And, in that instant, she knew. "That's it, isn't it?"

"That's what?"

"You didn't fight in the war, but you brought it home with you."

He gave her a hard stare, then left the rocker and moved to the porch railing. Setting his wineglass on top of it, he gripped the wood so tightly it appeared he was trying to uproot it from the porch floor. He was in a struggle to contain his anger. God only knew what other emotions were tenuously bridled.

Her first instinct was to go inside and bar the door. Maybe she would have if he hadn't suddenly bowed his head low between his shoulders in a gesture of defeat. He let go of the railing with one hand to comb his fingers through his hair. He held it back for several seconds before releasing it and returning his hand to the railing.

She questioned the advisability of taking the conversation farther. But he'd had no compunction against intruding into her life. Why should she be hesitant to poke into his?

Beyond that, because of her personal experience with Jeremy, who suffered similarly, she was interested in the disorder. That had been the subject of the e-mail she'd composed to George Metcalf. She believed the museum should have an exhibit on this invisible casualty of war and give it the same importance as other consequences of armed conflict.

Quietly she said, "I sensed something about you, but I didn't know what it was until just now. You could have asked about Jeremy's affair with Darlene Strong, his quasi friendship with Willard, the murder scene, the probability that he was chewed to pieces by dogs. But instead of all that more titillating stuff, his PTSD was the one aspect of the whole mess that you wanted to know about."

She gave him time to respond. When he didn't, she continued. "Today on the beach, when we talked about the war, you didn't elaborate. I was complimenting you on the stories you'd written. Most men would have used that as an excuse to brag and try to impress me with their exploits."

"You've got that many men trying to impress you?"

His tone bordered on insulting, but she bit her tongue and let it pass. "Yesterday, I noticed the empty liquor bottles on your kitchen bar. Alongside pill bottles."

"Millions of people imbibe alcohol and take medication."

"True. That wasn't the giveaway. It's your eyes."

Slowly he came around to face her.

"They don't match a man who's physically fit and athletic," she said softly. "They belong to a man who is chemically dependent, or seriously ill and in pain, or who suffers insomnia. They look haunted by memories that won't go away."

He remained motionless and said nothing.

"Who are you seeing for help?"

Nothing.

"You *are* seeing a counselor or therapist?"

Finally, his voice gruff, he asked, "Did your husband?"

"No, which is why he became my *ex*-husband."

Moments of silence passed. Finally, he leaned back against the railing, folding his arms and crossing his ankles. "That subject is a whole lot more interesting than my empty whiskey bottles. How did you and Jeremy meet?" When she didn't answer, he said, "Anything we talk about tonight, I won't include in the piece. If I even write the piece, which is yet to be decided. In any case, nothing you tell me now will appear in print unless you authorize it."

"How can I trust you?"

"I promise."

Those shadowed eyes were more convincing than the vow. She cleared her throat, swallowed. "We met at a wedding. The bride and I had been sorority sisters. The groom was a Marine officer that Jeremy knew from Parris Island. He looked very handsome and dashing in his dress uniform. We danced, drank champagne together, had a good time. The following week he asked me out to dinner, and I accepted. We dated for six months, became engaged, and married ten months to the day from when we met."

"Hmm."

"What?"

He tilted his head to one side. "Was it the stud factor that attracted you?"

"Stud factor?"

"Here you are, a rich girl—"

"How offensive."

"But a fact. You grew up privileged, had your picture taken with presidents, received the best education money can buy. Here's Jeremy, who's been to war in Iraq, spiffy officer's uniform, stationed at Parris Island in charge of rifle training."

"Glenda?"

"Actually I looked that up myself. My point is, what attracted you to him? From the standpoint of someone on the outside looking in, you two wouldn't appear to be a match."

A lot of outsiders looking in had thought the same. "I suppose we were opposites who attracted."

"What kind of suitor was he?"

"Ardent."

"Really?"

"Yes. He could be terribly sweet and romantic."

"He carved your initials in a tree?"

"Yes."

He laughed. "I was kidding."

"I wasn't. He did that once. Why does it surprise you?"

"Because it doesn't mesh with the Jeremy who cheated on you by shagging his friend's wife." Before she could comment on that, he asked, "What about the congressman? What did he think of his new son-in-law?"

"Above all else, Daddy wanted my happiness."

"That's not what I asked."

Since she had his promise none of this would see publication, she decided to be brutally honest. "At first Daddy was concerned about the very differences in our backgrounds that you've cited. Jeremy wasn't like the men I'd dated before."

"I'm guessing preppie types."

"For the most part. Doctors, lawyers, men destined to take over a long-standing family business."

"I get the picture. Jeremy was a little rougher hewn."

"But earnest. Appropriately respectful. Daddy came to like him very much, and they got along well."

Dawson picked up his glass and, swirling the wine in it, asked, "What were Jeremy's parents like?"

"They were deceased when we met."

"Brothers, sisters?"

"He didn't have any family. It's a rather tragic history, actually. He rarely talked about it. Both his parents died in a house fire just weeks after his high school graduation."

"Jesus."

"Yes, it was very sad. Their home and everything in it was destroyed. His whole life history to that point was consumed. He didn't have any photographs or memorabilia of his babyhood or youth."

"Huh." He took a moment to assimilate that. "Was your marriage happy?"

"At first."

"No serious quarrels? Infidelity?"

"No. At least I was faithful. I believe he was until Darlene Strong."

"When was he deployed to Afghanistan?"

"Summer of 2007."

"Wasn't he a little old to be going?"

"He was highly specialized. He was needed."

"How'd he feel about going?"

"He couldn't wait. Even having experienced Iraq, he wanted to go. I admit that I didn't take it so well. I feared for his safety, and I hated that he'd miss so much of Hunter's infancy. He was only a few months old when Jeremy shipped out."

"That was shit luck."

She smiled wanly. "I think I said that myself a few times. But I tried to keep my correspondence with Jeremy upbeat. I didn't want to make him feel guilty over having to leave us. He didn't like the timing particularly, but he was excited to be going. More than that, he was willing to make the sacrifice because he considered serving a sacred duty."

"To his country."

"Yes."

"He loved America? He was a patriot?"

"Of course."

"He never questioned the war, or America's motives behind it, never said anything negative about the government?"

"He was a Marine. And, anyway, why would you even ask that?"

"I'm not implying anything. It's just that those are popular topics of debate these days." He looked into his wineglass, but didn't take a drink. As a lead-in for her, he said, "When he came home..."

She took a deep breath. "I immediately noticed changes in him. He seemed glad to be back, but he didn't laugh as much. I'd catch him staring into space, and when he realized I had noticed, he would force a joke. The baby's crying annoyed him, especially when we..." She cut her eyes up to him, then away. "When he wanted my undivided attention."

The sexual implication hovered there between them. Self-consciously she waited for another question. None came. For a long moment they only stared at each other. Then she remembered what he'd said about how revealing silences were.

"I feel terrible about saying this now." She spoke softly as though to underscore her reluctance. "But it was almost a relief when he left for his second tour. He took the tension in the house with him. Hunter became a happier, more contented baby. Which was good, since I discovered a few weeks after Jeremy left that I was pregnant again."

He shifted his stance against the porch railing and turned his head to one side, giving her his profile. She noted that he was chewing the inside of his cheek, but whether in consternation or simply deep thought, she didn't know.

Finally he looked back at her. "Did he ever tell you about conditions over there?"

"Only in the most basic of terms. 'It's hot.' 'It's turned cold.' 'Today I had my first shower in a month.' Like that."

"Nothing specific?"

She shook her head. "He commanded snipers. That's all I know. Most of the time, he couldn't even tell me where he was. He probably wouldn't have told me even if it hadn't been classified. He didn't want me to worry."

"You had a baby and another on the way."

"And with Grant I suffered terrible morning sickness."

He grinned, revealing that crooked tooth. "Yeah?"

"With Hunter, not a day of it. With Grant, I threw up several times a day for six months."

"Told you he'd cause mischief."

She laughed. "Very perceptive."

Gradually, their smiles receded and he brought them back to their conversation about Jeremy, which she was finding therapeutic. When had she actually talked to someone about this? Not to her father, whom she hadn't wanted to burden with her unhappiness. Not to a friend. Not to anyone.

Perhaps it was easier to unload on a stranger whom one would never see again. Or maybe it was easy to talk to Dawson because he could relate to Jeremy's condition. That was a reasonable assumption, but it was also a disturbing one. It bothered her to think that he could be as unstable as Jeremy had become.

She said, "I wish Jeremy had talked to me about what he was going through. If he had, things might have turned out differently."

"You mean when he returned from the second tour?"

"Things went quickly from bad to worse. At first I thought he missed the corps, the camaraderie, that he was having trouble adjusting to civilian life. He claimed to like his new job, but he didn't make friends with any coworkers. He became more withdrawn and antisocial.

"Tension at home mounted. There were two babies now. Jeremy was intolerant of Grant's crying, Hunter's chatter. He would pick fights with me over the slightest things." She hesitated before adding, "He drank excessively. Sometimes to the point of passing out."

Dawson gave her a wry look. "I've never passed out."

"You shouldn't let it get to that point."

"I have no intention to."

After a moment, she continued. "Jeremy would leave without telling me where he was going or how long he'd be gone, and he'd become enraged if I asked. He had trouble sleeping, and when he did, he had nightmares. He refused to talk about them.

"I begged him to get professional counseling. The suggestion always sparked an argument. His refusal to get help created more conflict. He got progressively short-tempered with me and the children. Hunter grew to be afraid of him, especially when Jeremy..."

He waited for a count of ten before he prodded her. "When Jeremy what?"

She looked down into her unfinished wine. "Became aggressive."

"You mean violent."

She raised her head and looked at him. "Please, Dawson," she said, using his name for the first time. "I wouldn't want anybody to know this. For my sons' sake."

He searched her eyes. "The motherfucker hit you. Didn't he?"

She lowered her gaze again. "Things had escalated to a crisis point. One night, he came home in the wee hours. When he got into bed, he smelled like perfume and sex. I told him to get away from me. He refused, so I left the bed. He came after me, grabbed me by the arm, and backhanded me across the face."

The handsome, dashing, romantic Marine who'd won her heart had morphed into a man she didn't know and couldn't relate to, even remotely. He was a mean stranger, whose temperament she mistrusted. All the new and terrible traits he'd acquired had manifested themselves that night. To this day, she could see the rage in his eyes, feel the hateful blow to her face, and taste her fear of him.

"Did you call the police?"

She shook her head. "I waited until he'd passed out, then got the boys up, left the house, and drove to Daddy's. When he saw my face, he became livid. I was afraid he'd do something rash, and it was all I could do to keep him from going after Jeremy and extracting his pound of flesh.

"Short of that, he wanted me to file a police report. But I just wanted to be away from Jeremy and out of the marriage as soon as possible. I moved into the Jones Street townhouse and filed for divorce that week.

"Jeremy contested it, but when he realized the futility of that, he fought me over child custody. He dragged his feet, intentionally created delays. I persisted. You heard in court how it all played out." She finished the last of her wine, then looked across at him. "Long answer to your question about my life with him."

He returned to the rocking chair, spread his knees wide, propped his forearms on his thighs, and clasped his hands between them. He turned his head toward her. "It's an ugly story, Amelia."

"Which you promised not to write."

"I did, and I won't." Then he looked past the railing toward the dunes and the beach beyond. The only sounds were the squeak of the rocking chairs and the whish of the surf. When he looked at her again, she knew what his next question was going to be before he asked it.

"Who took the photographs from under the doormat?"

"I don't know," she whispered, her voice cracking.

"Last night, I watched the four of you pile into your car. You stopped and picked up Bernie at his house. As soon as you were out of sight, I carried the photos over here and placed them there." He pointed to the jute doormat. "Then I got in my car and drove to the village. When I got to Mickey's, I couldn't have been more than five minutes behind you."

"You saw us leave Mickey's parking lot. I dropped Bernie at his back door. As we were getting out of the car, I asked Stef to take the boys upstairs and start the bedtime ritual. I came straight out here and looked beneath the mat."

"Somebody took them while we were all in the village."

"But who?" She wet her lips. "Maybe someone on the beach saw you leaving something and—"

He was shaking his head even before she finished. "The beach was deserted. I checked."

"But someone must have seen you."

"Exactly. Someone saw me because someone is watching."

"Other than you."

"Other than me. Tell me about the beach ball."

She remembered his bewilderment when she'd mentioned it earlier. "It was nothing."

"Then why not tell me?"

She did.

"It miraculously reappeared after being thrown away," he said. "Patched and inflated."

She shifted uneasily in her seat. "I'm sure there's an explanation."

"There is. Someone is making it his business to know everything that's going on in your life."

"I don't believe that."

"I think you do. Yesterday, when you were flaying me alive, you told me that you'd been feeling afraid, that you'd sensed—"

"Yesterday, I was upset and angry, talking out of my head, trying to make you feel bad for spying on me."

"You were just spouting nonsense?"

"Yes!"

"Amelia."

She shot from her chair and escaped to the railing as he had earlier. He followed, coming to stand close to her, close enough for her to feel his body heat.

"You're afraid he's still alive, aren't you?"

She turned to him. "No!"

"Denying it to me won't make you fear it any less. Nor will it make it untrue."

"He was killed by Willard Strong."

"His body was never found."

"But there was forensic evidence."

"Of what kind?"

"His blood on the ground inside the dog pen. A piece of scalp . . ." She buried her face in her hands. "God, what that man is accused of is too horrible to think about."

"I agree. But I question that Jeremy's fate was the same as Darlene's."

"All right. Maybe not. If not, Willard dumped Jeremy's body somewhere in the marsh. He sank it. Or it washed out to sea. There are alligators." Her voice carried a plea that he agree with at least one of those possibilities. But he just looked at her with a mix of skepticism and sympathy, which were equally vexing. She demanded, "Then where is he?"

"I'd like to know."

"Why would he disappear?"

"For the same reason anyone chooses to vanish. To escape trouble. Or the law. To start another life as someone else."

"Okay, say that's right. Why wouldn't he go far, far away from here? Why would he stay in this vicinity and risk being recognized? Faking your death is a crime, isn't it? Wouldn't he be afraid of getting caught? If he was going to disappear, why would he hang around and spy on me?"

"To make you anxious and afraid as punishment for leaving him."

She gave a hard shake of her head. "He didn't care that I left. By the time our divorce was final, he no longer loved me, only the boys. They were all he wanted." Realizing what she'd said, she sucked in a sharp breath and jerked her head up to look into Dawson's incisive gaze.

He gave a slow nod of his head.

"No," she said, her voice little more than a fearful whimper.

"This has occurred to you, Amelia. I know it has."

She wet her lips and rapidly formed an argument. "If Jeremy wanted the boys, he could have snatched them at any time. Before he ever met Willard and Darlene Strong."

"He could have. But in all probability he would have been caught and charged with kidnapping. If they were snatched now, no one would suspect a dead man of taking them."

She felt it was imperative that she argue fiercely against that logic. "You're only trying to frighten me."

"Why would I do that?"

"To get me to say things that'll make your story more intriguing, lend it an air of mystery."

"You know that's not true."

"Then why are you here? I told you that I wouldn't cooperate with *any* story you intend to write. Why don't you just go away and leave us alone? You weren't even all that interested in the story of Jeremy Wesson. You said you were about to reject it and move on to something else more interesting. Why didn't you?"

"Fair enough. You want to know why?"

He slid his hands under her hair behind her neck and drew her forward until her body was flush against his, his legs sandwiching hers, their faces not quite touching. "Why didn't I leave this goddamn story alone?" He brushed his thumbs across her lower lip. "Because you walked into that courtroom."

He held her there for several beats, his hot gaze moving over the features of her face as though he was trying to decide which to kiss first. Then he swore under his breath and abruptly released her.

Before she had time to fully recover her senses, he was gone, and she was alone.

Chapter 9

The next day, rainy weather kept everyone indoors. In their confinement, the boys became restless, bored, and whiney. None of the pastimes Stef suggested were greeted with enthusiasm. Worst of all, the cable went out, so watching television wasn't an option.

Lunchtime turned into a battle royal over who was responsible for Grant's spilled milk. Each blamed the other, arguing over who had bumped whom. To prevent a full-blown sibling feud, Stef offered to take them outside during a lull between showers.

"I would appreciate it," Amelia told her. "Just long enough for them to burn off some energy."

As they were putting on their tennis shoes, Hunter asked if they could invite Dawson to come out and play.

"No. Definitely not."

"How come?"

"I don't think he's at home."

"He is. His car is there."

"That piece-of-crap car."

"Grant! Where did you hear that?"

"Hunter said it."

"I did not!"

"Okay, okay. Whoever said it, it's inappropriate language. Don't say it again. And stay away from Mr. Scott's house."

"Why? He likes us."

"He's probably working."

"But, Mom—"

"Hunter, I said no." As she escorted them through the front door, she said to Stef in an undertone, "If he comes out, bring them inside."

"Okay," Stef grumbled. "I don't get it, but okay."

Amelia didn't have a single ally in her camp, but she was still the commander of this little band, so the rest of them could like it or not, they were having nothing more to do with their neighbor.

In the utility room, she attacked the piles of clean laundry waiting to be folded, realizing that in a week, she would be packing up their clothes to move back into Savannah. She didn't look forward to it. The boys disliked the apartment into which they'd moved after leaving the Jones Street townhouse, but her encounter with Willard Strong had made it impossible for her to continue living there.

Hunter and Grant wanted a house with a yard so they could have a dog, and, in fairness to them, they hadn't had a permanent home since she'd left Jeremy. She planned to begin house hunting immediately after the trial ended.

Thank God that tumultuous chapter of her life was about to close.

Unless Dawson Scott's theory was correct and Jeremy was still alive.

Despite her determination to dismiss his unsettling notion, she couldn't. Because the possibility that Jeremy had faked his death had crossed her mind with disturbing frequency. More so lately than before. Dawson had lent it credence. Now she couldn't shake her misgivings no matter how badly she wanted to.

After a restless night, she'd awakened at dawn, thinking about the boat that had been anchored offshore for the past several days. She had scrambled out of bed, gone to the window, and anxiously scanned the horizon. The inclement weather had made the water choppy, and the surf was stronger than usual. The boat she sought was no longer there, only a shrimp boat and an oil tanker, both commonplace sights.

She'd climbed back into bed, hoping to catch another forty winks, but she was too fidgety to go back to sleep, partially because of her general uneasiness, but also due to reexperiencing the sensations that Dawson's embrace had elicited.

Her mind refused to stay away from the memory. She felt the brush of his thumb against her lip, heard his roughly whispered *Because you walked into that courtroom*, and recalled the solid imprint of his body. The particular kind of agitation she was feeling was definitely inconvenient, because nothing could be done about it, and judging by the truculence in Dawson's eyes as he'd looked into hers, he was no happier than she about the chemistry between them.

She'd welcomed the appearance of her sons, who'd come from their beds to climb into hers. She'd gathered them against her, one under each arm, snuggled them, and kissed the tops of their tousled heads in fervent gratitude that they were hers. To keep. Forever. She would protect them with her life... and kill anyone who tried to take them from her.

Now, less than an hour after they'd gone outside, a sudden downpour called an end to the beach excursion. They barreled in through the utility-room door, all three of them sopping wet and shivering. Sand had blown into Hunter's eye. He was crying. Grant's lips were blue with cold.

"Stef, please get Grant into some dry clothes while I wash out Hunter's eye." At the prospect of that, he began to howl.

Amelia asked herself how this day could possibly get any worse.

Dawson watched Stef and the boys hurtling through the torrent toward the house. He'd watched their play from indoors, believing it best for everyone if, from now on, he made himself scarce.

As he turned away from the window, he checked his cell phone and saw that he had a signal, something that had been sporadic all morning. Knowing he should make the call while he could, he punched in the Headlys' house number. Eva answered. When she heard his voice, her relief was obvious.

"Are you all right? Gary's been trying to reach you."

"Cell service is dicey."

"In the city of Savannah?"

"Weather's moved in. Can't guarantee how long I'll have a signal. Is your old man around?"

"Yes, and he's as grumpy as you sound. I swear, the two of you..." She didn't finish, leaving him to infer that they tested her patience in equal measure.

Headly came on the line and began with an accusatory, "I've called you three times."

"Hello to you, too."

"Why haven't you answered your phone?"

"As I explained to Eva, cell service here comes and goes."

"Where exactly is *here*?"

Dawson ran his hand around the back of his neck where tension had collected. "I wasn't completely honest with you the last time we talked."

"Oh really?" Headly said, ladling on the sarcasm.

The ornery son of a bitch wasn't about to make this easy on him. "Everything I told you was the truth. I just omitted some things."

"Like where you are. What's that racket?"

"Rain. It's pelting. I'm on Saint Nelda's Island."

"Nelda was a saint?"

"Somebody thought so. It's a sea island off the coast of Georgia, slightly south of Savannah, reachable only by ferry, six miles long, two miles wide."

"Thanks for the geography lesson. I'm ready for *Jeopardy*. Why there?"

"I rented the house next door to one owned by the late Congressman Nolan."

A huff of surprise, followed by a short silence, then, "I don't even have to ask, do I?"

"She's here with her two sons and a nanny."

"Does she know you're there?"

"Yes."

"Does she know why?"

He skimmed the surface, omitting details, but got the facts across to Headly. "She knows about *NewsFront*, knows that I came down to cover the trial and see if there's a story worth writing, knows I followed her here to the island hoping for an interview. Nothing about you or the rest of it."

"How'd she react to the idea of a story?"

"She sure as hell didn't embrace it. She all but wears a sign around her neck warning off trespassers."

"Can't blame her. Most of her life has been lived in a fishbowl, first because of her father, now because of her husband."

"*Ex*-husband. *Late* ex-husband."

"Those qualifiers seem awfully important to you."

Dawson ignored the implication. "What I'm trying to tell you is that the lady is on red alert. She's particularly protective of her sons."

"Have you seen them?"

"Of course."

"Why 'of course'?"

"Because the houses share the beach. The little boys play out there. Build sand castles, splash in the ocean. I went out there yesterday and horsed around with them for a while." Dawson stopped and gnawed the inside of his cheek, refusing to say anything else until Headly supplied something more eloquent and intelligible than a grunted *Huh*.

After an extended silence, Headly asked, "Who do they look like?"

"Both have blue eyes like hers." The second the words were out, Dawson wanted to kick himself. Crossly, he added, "I don't know who they look like. They look like kids."

"Okay, no need to bite my head off."

"This is why I didn't tell you up front. I knew you'd pester me with questions."

"They could be Carl Wingert's grandkids. You don't expect me to be curious?"

Dawson didn't respond to that.

"What's she like?"

"She's—" A dozen adjectives crowded into his mind, but none he wanted to share with Headly. "Intelligent. Articulate. Assertive. Self-controlled. Guarded. Modest."

"You've just described my old-maid third-grade schoolteacher."

"All right, she's—" Desirable. Kissable. Fuckable.

"Fair of face," Headly said. "I've seen pictures."

"Then why ask me to describe her?"

"What's her mental state?"

"She's scared."

"Of you?"

"That he's alive."

"Jeremy."

"Yeah." Now he had no choice except to explain how he knew that. "I led her into casual conversation, learned a little about their life together." He gave Headly the gist of what had been said, and passed along what Amelia had told him about Jeremy's parents. "What has your pal Knutz uncovered about them?"

"Haven't heard back from him yet." He gave a snuffle of skepticism. "But, come on, a house fire that killed them both and destroyed all the family memorabilia?"

"I figured you'd find that a little too pat. I did. Knutz needs to check it out. A house fire with two fatalities must've made local news. Maybe there was a photo of Mr. and Mrs. Wesson in the newspaper obit. If they were in fact Carl and Flora, that means they've been dead for years, I'm on a wild-goose chase, your search is over, end of story."

"Not if their son faked his death and is still alive."

Dawson swore under his breath.

"Don't cuss at me," Headly said. "It's not a 'voilà' idea. His wife—*ex*-wife—advanced it herself."

"No, *I* advanced it. She denied the possibility."

"But you said—"

"She protested too much."

"Huh. Indicating to you that the possibility has occurred to her."

"Yeah," he said around a sigh. "Under all her self-possession, I think she's scared shitless."

"Where'd you leave it?"

"With her afraid to think the unthinkable. But she's thinking it anyway."

"What's the atmosphere like between the two of you?"

"I won't count on a birthday card."

After a moment of thought, Headly said, "I'll check out the victims of that house fire myself. But it's Sunday of a holiday weekend. I don't know how far I'll get until everybody goes back to work on Tuesday. What are you going to do in the meantime?"

"Wait until court reconvenes. I'll stay and see the trial through to the verdict, I guess. After that, I don't know. Harriet keeps calling, but I don't answer. I may already be fired."

"May not be a bad thing."

"May not."

"How are you doing otherwise?"

"I got a lot of sun yesterday."

"Sleeping better?"

"The sound of the ocean has a lulling effect. Look, I'm down to one bar. If my phone cuts out..."

Headly gave another grunt that said he knew Dawson was skirting the issue, but he wasn't going to waste limited cell phone service beating a dead horse.

"Don't get mad if you can't reach me," Dawson said. "On my way from the mainland, the ferry captain told me that cell service on the island is unreliable on good days. When a storm blows in, forget it."

Shortly after eight o'clock that evening a lightning bolt knocked out the power in Amelia's house, plunging it into darkness.

"Mommy?" Grant said tremulously.

"It's okay." Her reassurance was drowned out by the booming thunder.

Fortunately they were all gathered around the kitchen table playing Chutes and Ladders. Had she and Stef not been within reach, the boys would have been even more frightened than they were. Grant left his chair and climbed onto her lap. Stef reached across the corner of the table and took Hunter's hand.

Amelia had thought the afternoon would never end. She'd managed to rinse the sand from Hunter's eye, but he'd squalled through the process. To soothe him afterward, she'd made him and Grant cups of cocoa and marshmallows.

Paintboxes and pads of paper were brought out, and those had kept them entertained for a while. Hunter painted a seascape featuring her, himself, his brother, Stef, and a tall, shirtless figure with shoulder-length yellow hair sticking out from a baseball cap.

"That's Dawson," he told her proudly. "I'm gonna paint a battleship and give it to him, too."

Not wanting to incite another trauma, she didn't tell him it was unlikely he would ever see his hero again.

She and Stef stretched dinner out for as long as possible, killing time until they could put the boys to bed. They had agreed to play one more round of the board game before taking them upstairs.

And now the lights had gone out.

"Everything's fine," she said brightly. "There's a flashlight in that big bottom drawer." She tried to get up, but Grant clung to her. "No, Mommy, hold me." She carried him with her and got the flashlight from the drawer. She clicked it on. "See? This is an adventure. Grant, you can help me check the fuse box. Maybe the lightning just tripped the breaker switch."

But after she flipped every switch with no success, Grant said dolefully, "The 'lectricity isn't working."

"No it's not, but we have flashlights."

She went through the house collecting them. But they had to use them continually in order to keep the boys' fear of the storm at bay. Soon the flashlights began to weaken and then to go out one by one.

"I've just used our last two batteries," she confided to Stef. "We'll need more before morning."

"Maybe Bernie has some to spare."

Amelia went to the window above the sink and looked out. "His house is completely dark. He's probably sleeping."

Hesitantly, Stef said, "We have another neighbor."

Amelia looked toward Dawson's house. "His piece-of-crap car isn't there," she muttered. With unreasonable annoyance, she asked, "Where could he be on a night like tonight?"

Stef offered to start gathering up candles.

She had to take their only remaining working flashlight with her, leaving Amelia and the boys huddled around the kitchen table in the dark. She suggested they see how many rounds of "Row, Row, Row Your Boat" they could sing before Stef returned, but their voices faltered each time the kitchen was filled with a silvery flash of lightning and a cannon blast of thunder.

After several minutes, Stef returned to the kitchen with four tapers and three votives. Putting a match to a vanilla-scented candle, she said cheerfully, "It'll start to smell good in here."

With the candle lit, Amelia switched off the flashlight. Grant whimpered. "Turn it back on."

"We need to save the batteries, sweetheart."

He lay his cheek against her chest.

Hunter said, "He's such a baby."

"Hunter."

"I'm not a baby!"

Amelia ran her hand over his hair. "Well, it's bedtime anyway. After you close your eyes and go to sleep, you won't even realize it's dark. And when you wake up—"

"No!" he wailed. "I don't want to go to bed without a light on."

Amelia had hoped in vain for a miracle, but apparently she wasn't going to get one. "I have to go to the village for batteries."

But when she tried to get up, Grant began to cry and cling to her. "No, Mommy! Don't leave."

"It only makes sense that I go," Stef said.

"It makes no sense at all. I've been driving on this island in storms for years. It can be tricky if you don't know the road well. Sometimes it floods."

"I've driven it enough times to become familiar. Besides, I don't think our two boys here would let you out of their sight." Amelia acknowledged the rationality of Stef's going. Reluctantly she agreed.

Stef got her purse and Amelia's car keys.

"While you're there, get some nonperishable food items, too. We may not have a fridge and stove for a while. If lines are down, it takes a while to get repairmen out here. They restore service on the mainland first."

"If you think of anything else, call me." Then, checking her cell phone, Stef said. "If you can. Right now, I'm not getting a signal."

A half hour passed, during which Amelia told every silly "Knock-Knock" joke she knew, and which the boys had already heard dozens of times. She told them the story of "The Three Little Pigs" and then devised a contest to see who could huff and puff the best. Neither of the boys got into the game.

After another thirty minutes, she called Stef's phone. It went straight to voice mail.

The storm continued to rage without any sign of letting up. The boys grew increasingly anxious, in part because they sensed her own mounting nervousness. She was near her wit's end by the time she heard the utility-room door burst open, bringing a gust of wind in with it.

"Thank God," she breathed. "Stef?"

But it wasn't her nanny who stepped into the kitchen, dripping water, his hair plastered to his head.

"Dawson!"

Her boys, who'd been competing for space on her lap, abandoned her and ran to him, wrapping their arms around his legs and impeding his progress. He looked at Amelia through the wavering candlelight. "I was on my way home and noticed that your house is dark."

Hunter tugged on the hem of his shirt to get his attention. "The lights went out, and Grant was afraid, but I wasn't. I got sand in my eye, but it's out now. I painted you a battleship."

Grant, not to be outdone, informed him that candles make things look wavy. He added a hand gesture to demonstrate.

Hunter spoke over his brother. "Mom said if we'd go to bed and close our eyes, we wouldn't know it was dark, but I think we would."

"And she told us today that if we didn't stop whining, she was going to pull her hair out, but she didn't."

Dawson smiled. "Well, that's good. She's got such pretty hair." He brought his gaze back to Amelia, who had stood up to face him, rebuking herself for being relieved and glad to see him.

"Thank you for stopping. We're okay. Just waiting on Stef to get back from the village. She went for supplies."

"I just came from there. I doubt she'll get back anytime soon, if at all. The power is off everywhere. Only the store and Mickey's have generators. People are hunkering down in one or the other. I hope she does. The road is virtually impassable."

"I've tried calling her, but—"

"No cell service."

"You said the road was impassable?"

"That tidal pool halfway between here and—"

"It usually overflows during heavy rains."

"It has. All the way to the road."

"Then how'd you get here?"

He hesitated before saying, "Determination."

The gravelly tone behind the word made her tummy flutter. "I appreciate your checking on us. We're fine, but I could use some batteries if you have extras."

"Better than that, my house has a generator. It's listed as an amenity on the fact sheet I picked up at the rental office along with the key. If the power goes off, it comes on automatically, keeps the fridge, stove, and a few circuits working."

He glanced at the flickering candle on the table as well as at her scant reserves. "Those aren't going to last long. It's unlikely Stef will get back tonight, and it would be dangerous for her even to attempt it."

Amelia shifted from one foot to the other. "What are you saying?"

"I think you know."

She did know, and she shook her head. "I can't do that."

"Why not?"

"Because. Because I wouldn't think of putting you to the trouble."

"No trouble. It's a big house with lots of bedrooms, already made up for occupancy."

They looked at each other for several moments. Finally she said, "You know that's not the reason."

"Yeah. I know the reason. Last night. Just before I left."

She bobbed her head once.

"You don't have to worry about that."

"Of course I do."

"Okay, maybe you do. But you've got bigger worries than me, and I don't have to spell them out. Do you really want to be here alone in a dark house?"

"Mom, what are y'all talking about?"

She looked down at her eldest, who, she kept forgetting, was perceptive beyond his years. He sensed the tension between her and Dawson, but was unable to understand it. Seeing his young brow wrinkled with anxiety subverted Amelia's resolve.

When she looked again at Dawson, he extended his arms away from his sides, palms toward her. It was a subtle gesture, but meaningful, communicating that he didn't pose a threat.

"Dawson has asked us to spend the night at his house because he has lights."

Her last few words went unheard because of their whoops of glee. "Can we, Mom?"

"Can we go now?"

"Can I take some of my cars?"

"Let's save the cars for another time," Dawson told Grant. "I suggest you come right now, as you are, before the storm gets any worse."

"Can we, Mom?"

"I suppose that's—" Needing to hear no more, they left the kitchen at a run and pounded through the utility room. "Don't open the door till I get there!" She scribbled a note to Stef on a paper napkin, telling her where they were, and anchored it to the table with the salt shaker, then blew out the single candle, pitching the room into total darkness.

"Here, take my hand."

She was entrusting much more than her hand to the man who reached for her.

Chapter 10

Although the boys were clamoring to leave, Amelia took time to grab each of them a change of clothing from the stacks of folded laundry on the utility-room table. Dawson had parked as close as possible to the back door, but it would still be impossible to reach his car without getting soaked.

He didn't worry about himself. He couldn't possibly get any wetter than he already was. They made a mad dash for the car. The boys were shrieking with laughter and excitement by the time they clambered into the backseat.

"Suddenly, they're not as cranky and afraid as before," she remarked when Dawson slid behind the wheel.

"It's an adventure now."

"I told them earlier we were having an adventure. They didn't buy it."

"Sitting in the dark is a different kind of adventure from running through the rain."

"True. But the real difference is you."

The statement gave him pause, but now wasn't the time to think about it. He started the car; the tires spun before gaining traction. As they pulled away, she remarked on Bernie's dark house.

"Do you mind if we stop and check on him?"

"Not at all. In fact, he should come with us."

He drove the short distance, got out of the car, and ran up to Bernie's back door, finding a sliver of shelter beneath the eaves. He knocked three times before Bernie appeared wearing a baggy pair of undershorts and a white T-shirt, with slippers and black socks on his feet. He was rubbing his left eye. His white hair was sticking out at odd angles.

Since they'd only been introduced once, the older man seemed astonished to see him, but he remembered his name. "Mr. Scott?"

"Sorry if I got you out of bed."

"I was reading. Just like Boy Scout camp." He held up the flashlight in his hand. "What are you doing out in this?"

"Amelia's with me. She and the boys are staying at my house for the rest of the night." He gestured toward the car.

Bernie regarded him with surprise, then leaned around him and peered at the car. He waved at it, although the passengers were blurs behind the foggy, rain-streaked windows. "Stef, too?"

"She's stuck in town."

"Oh."

Before the old man drew the wrong conclusion, Dawson explained. "The boys were afraid. The house I'm renting has a generator. Lights."

"Ah, of course."

"We think you should spend the night there, too."

"No, no, I'm fine here."

"You'd be more comfortable."

"I'm snug as a bug, and I've got plenty of backup batteries."

A bolt of lightning cracked nearby. Dawson instinctively ducked. When he recovered, he noticed Bernie regarding him curiously. Embarrassed by his conditioned reaction to the boom, he said, "That one was close."

"You'd better get Amelia and the kids tucked inside."

"I can't talk you into joining the party? There are more than enough bedrooms, and it could be a long night."

"Thank you. I appreciate the invitation, but I'm fine."

"At least agree to come over for breakfast."

Bernie smiled. "If you insist."

Dawson bade him good night and plunged back into the torrent. He couldn't help but sling rain onto Amelia as he got into the car, but she seemed not to notice.

"Is he all right?"

"I think I woke him up. He seemed to be okay. He didn't want to relocate."

"You explained why we were doing this?"

He placed his hand over his heart. "I made a point of preserving your reputation."

"Thank you for checking on him."

"No problem." The road was a morass, but they made it to the back door of his house without mishap. "Hold on, boys, let me help you up the steps. They could be slick."

He got out and opened the back door on the driver's side. Taking a boy by each hand, he walked them quickly but cautiously up the three wooden steps, unlocked the back door, then ushered them inside. When he flipped the switch, the overhead light came on. He'd been keeping his fingers crossed that the generator did, in fact, take over during a power loss.

"Wow!" Hunter exclaimed. "Look at that ship model." It was displayed on the long table that divided the kitchen from the living area.

"First, take off your shoes and leave them here by the back door so you don't track up the floor. Then you can go look at the ship. But don't touch. It doesn't belong to me."

He went back out, intending to assist Amelia, but she'd already alighted. Protecting the armload of clothes she was carrying, she was picking her way around the deepest puddles. He went down the steps and took her elbow. "I was coming back for you. You should have waited."

"I'm okay."

As soon as she'd cleared the threshold of the back door, she pulled her arm free of his grasp. "I haven't been in this house since the owners renovated it. It's—"

He stepped directly in front of her, blocking her view. "Are you going to flinch every time I come near you?"

"I didn't flinch."

"Hell you didn't."

Her chin went up a fraction, but the trace of defiance was short-lived, and she dropped her gaze to somewhere in the vicinity of the second button of his shirt. "You're smart enough to understand how awkward this is for me."

"Because of the near kiss."

He didn't phrase it as a question, and she offered no reply, but only continued to stare straight ahead until the silence between them became strained. Finally she looked into his face again.

"Your virtue is safe with me," he said. "Okay?"

She nodded.

"Okay?" he repeated.

Even though she nodded a second time, he felt that she wasn't entirely convinced. He certainly wasn't.

Hunter and Grant missed the awkward exchange because, as with everything having to do with Dawson, they were fascinated by "his" house.

It was tastefully furnished and had amenities to recommend it, but it lacked the warmth and personality of hers, which had been purchased strictly for her family's use and was never rented out. Over the years it had accumulated personal keepsakes, family photographs, the marks and scars of living that made a house a home.

However, her sons didn't seem to miss the hominess. They were enthralled, particularly by the matching set of bunk beds in the upstairs bedroom to which Dawson led them. "Each of you can have a top bunk."

"Be careful on those ladders," Amelia cautioned as they started up the rungs.

Grant said, "I wish this was our room all the time."

Hunter declared that he wished they could live there forever.

Amelia smiled. "Well, before you get the bedcovers wet, come back down and change."

They climbed down and went to inspect the adjoining bathroom. "There's a room right across the hall for you," Dawson said.

"Thanks, but I'll sleep on one of the lower bunks."

He shot the beds a dubious glance. "You sure? The other room—"

"No sense in messing up two."

Although he looked like he wanted to argue further, he didn't. "Fine. I'm going to get dry. Make yourself comfortable."

A half hour later and now much more comfortable, she descended the open staircase which was dimly illuminated by night-lights that had been placed on every third tread. She'd towel-dried her hair and changed into the clothes she'd brought with her. In her haste, and in the dark of her utility room, she'd grabbed the first articles her hands had landed on, which turned out to be a pair of cotton pajama bottoms and a fleece hoodie. They were mismatched, but she didn't see what possible difference it made.

When she reached the bottom step, Dawson asked, "Everything all right?"

Her eyes searched the vast great room and spotted him in the semidarkness, sprawled in an easy chair. The lamp at his elbow cast only a faint glow.

"Sorry if I startled you," he said. "This is the only socket working in this room, and the overhead light is out."

The overhead light in the kitchen had been turned off. Had it been left on, it would have shed light into the living area. She chose not to remark on that. Nor did she comment on the disappearance of the liquor and pill bottles that had been conspicuously on the kitchen island when they arrived.

"There wasn't a glass in the bathroom," she said. "In case the boys wake up in the night and want a drink of water, I came down to get one."

"Come sit. Before hiding the incriminating evidence of my vices, I poured you a whiskey."

His right hand was dangling over the arm of the chair. In it, he loosely held a tumbler. Another one sat on the end table beneath the lamp. The amber contents reflected the light.

When she hesitated, he said, "Bourbon is all I have. Is that okay?"

"My father was a southern gentleman. What do you think?"

He smiled. "I think he probably spiked your baby bottle with it." He tilted his head toward the chair next to his. "Come on. You looked pretty wound up when I got to your house. This will relax you and help you sleep."

Said the spider to the fly, she thought.

But she joined him anyway. The chair was soft, cushy, and enveloping. Pulling her feet up, she tucked them against her hip.

Noticing her striped socks, he said, "Fetching."

"I'm afraid the whole outfit leaves much to be desired."

He looked her over and seemed to be on the verge of saying something, but changed his mind. Instead, he picked up the glass of whiskey on the table and extended it to her. "Drink up."

She took a sip and sighed as the liquor spread a pleasant

warmth through her middle. Letting her head fall back against the cushion, she sighed, "Lord, what a day."

"Mine didn't have many highlights, either."

"What happened?"

"Work-related hassle." He made an offhanded gesture and took a sip of his drink.

"You went to the village?"

"I didn't want to be caught in short supply."

"Of batteries?"

"Of booze." He raised his glass in a mock toast. "I was almost out."

"Thanks for sharing."

"You're welcome."

He smelled of soap. His hair was dry, brushed back away from his face, making the sun-lightened strands distinguishable from the darker ones beneath. He'd put on a pair of gym shorts and a T-shirt, which, like the one from the beach, was practically threadbare. But at least this one had sleeves that partially covered the bite-worthy biceps. The lamplight cast the features of his face into harsh relief, emphasizing the sharp angles, the spikiness of his eyelashes. It also glinted off the tawny hair on his legs.

Her teeth clinked against her glass when she took a hasty sip.

He said, "May I ask you a question? A harmless one."

"Chocolate or vanilla? It's a tie. My most favorite is peach."

He grinned. "Not quite that harmless."

She weighed the pros and cons of letting him pry further into her life, and specifically into her life with Jeremy, and finally consented to at least hear the question. "Then I'll decide if I want to answer it or not."

He waited a second or two, then asked if she had a picture of Jeremy's parents.

"His parents? No."

"If you did, would you show it to me?"

"The point is moot, I don't have one."

"Did you ever see one?"

"No, because, remember, everything was destroyed in the house fire."

"Did he ever take you to Ohio to tour his hometown, show you the site of the home that burned, visit the cemetery where his parents were buried?"

"They were cremated. He didn't keep their remains. He wasn't sentimental or nostalgic. He told me that, when he left Ohio, he left for good and never had a desire to return, not even to high-school class reunions."

"Did he say why?"

"The memories were too sad. He dealt with them by severing any and all ties."

"He didn't have one single shred of something that linked him to his parents? Nothing to indicate what they and his childhood had been like?"

"Why are you fixated on this?"

"I'm interested."

"But why? It's ancient history. And what does his childhood have to do with anything else?"

"Maybe nothing. Maybe everything. His parents could have impacted him in ways that even you're unaware of."

"I don't think so."

"Of course they did."

"How do you know?"

"Because parents do."

"Did yours?"

"Yes." He shot the rest of his whiskey and set the tumbler on the table. "Just like you'll influence Hunter and Grant, like your dad influenced you. From something as simple as what goes into a good meat loaf to the not-so-simple. Religion. Culture. How you should vote. Every damn thing you think or believe, your reactions, your behavior, were partially shaped by who and what your parents were."

"Genetics versus environment isn't a new controversy."

"I don't think it's one versus the other. I think it's a blend."

"Why are you so hung up on Jeremy's *blend*?"

"Because when I write about somebody, I want to know these things."

He had admitted to carefully observing individuals in an effort to learn what made them tick. Gauging by the stories she'd read online, he did more than that when he wrote about a person. He provided his readers a cross-section of their mind and soul. Which was disconcerting.

"Are you going to write about me?"

"I don't know yet."

"If you do, will you dissect me and hang me out there for all to see?"

"In order to do that, I would need to know things about you."

"You already do."

"Not enough. Not nearly."

"What else could you possibly wish to know?"

He stared into her eyes for a ponderous moment, and that should have warned her of what was coming. It didn't. She was totally unprepared.

"I want to know about your father's suicide."

Chapter 11

For several seconds she was too stunned to move, then she bolted from her chair and marched across the room. He caught her just as she stepped onto the bottom stair. Hooking her upper arm with his hand, he brought her around to face him.

"Let go of me!"

"Calm down."

"Go to hell!"

"Keep your voice down. You'll wake up the boys."

"You bet I'll wake up the boys." She jerked her arm free. "I'm taking my sons and getting far away from you, and I don't care if we have to wade to Savannah tonight!"

She shoved his chest and pushed herself out of his grip, then turned and started up the stairs. But on the third one, her socks caused her to slip. She fell forward, catching herself on the step above her, but knocking one knee hard against the edge of the tread. She clasped her knee and sat down on the step, rocking in pain.

"Dammit! Are you okay?"

He sat down on the step beneath her, bringing his face level with hers. His concern looked genuine, which only made her more furious. She placed her elbows on her knees and lowered her face to her hands. "Get away from me."

He didn't, of course. He just sat there, silent and unmoving, for as long as she did. Finally, when she had composed herself, she lowered her hands and wiped her tear-dampened palms on the legs of her pajamas. Looking anywhere except at him, she noticed the overturned tumbler in front of the chair where she'd been sitting.

"I dropped my glass. The bourbon spilled."

"Who gives a fuck?"

The vulgarity was unexpected, and she realized immediately that he'd used it intentionally to shock her out of her anger. It worked. She laughed, or choked out a laugh.

He motioned toward her knee. "I'll be happy to kiss it and make it well."

His genial smile completely defused her anger. She gave another involuntary laugh, then shook her head with chagrin. "Ah, Dawson."

"What?"

"I didn't want to like you."

"Then we're even. I didn't want to like you, either." The admission surprised her, and it must have shown. Leaning back, he rested his elbows on the step on which she sat and stretched his long legs out in front of him. "I resented this story being thrust on me."

"Was it thrust?"

"Yes. In the sense that I couldn't say no."

"Why?"

He closed one eye in a grimace. "That's complicated." He didn't divulge why.

Absently she rubbed her sore knee. "From a layman's standpoint, Jeremy's story has a lot of intriguing elements. Why weren't you interested?"

He stared at a spot in the distance for a long time, and when he answered, it was in a soft voice. "I saw guys blown to bits. Saw men risking their lives to save a wounded buddy whose odds of making it were nonexistent. Watched men and women putting themselves in harm's way to save a stranger. A hostile, even.

"Having witnessed incredible acts of bravery, I was disgusted by a decorated Marine who came home after surviving all that and then let his life—a damn good life, it seemed to me—go into the sewer. I didn't know Jeremy Wesson, but I didn't like him. Still don't." He looked at her then. "But I can relate to him. And that's what really disgusts me."

"The post-traumatic stress?"

He raised his shoulders in a small shrug.

Since that was the first time he had acknowledged that he suffered it to any degree, suspicion crept in, and she angled away from him. "Is this an I'll-show-you-mine-if-you-show-me-yours?"

"Your what and my what?"

"Vulnerability. You've revealed yours. Now you expect me to reveal mine?"

"Your vulnerability being your father." When she didn't answer, he asked, "Do you really think I'm that manipulative?"

"If not, why did you refer to his death as a suicide? The coroner ruled it an unintentional overdose of medication."

"I'm aware of that. But there were rumors and speculation."

"Which I squelched under threat of suing for libel if they were printed or broadcast. They were never made public, not even by the most jaundiced media. So how did you—" She stopped. "Oh. Glenda again."

"She has a ferret in her gene pool."

"So now I'm trapped into talking to you about it."

"No you're not."

"Sure I am. How can I dispel your misconceptions about my father's death without talking about it?"

"You can leave me with my misconceptions."

That wasn't a desirable option, and he knew it. "Do I at least have your word that anything I say is off the record?"

"Yes."

Perhaps she was swayed by the intimacy of the situation, or his masculine appeal, or the sincerity in his eyes. But, for whatever reason, in that moment she accepted him as trustworthy. "I'll never believe Daddy did it on purpose, especially knowing that I—the boys and I—would be the ones to find him."

"Christ."

"We were expected at his house at three o'clock, after I had picked them up from preschool. His time of death was placed at somewhere around two. He wouldn't have done that to me. I know it. The boys rushing in, seeing him slumped at his desk?" She shook her head adamantly.

"Never in a million years would he have deliberately left us with that memory. And that's assuming that he had a reason to take his life, when there was no evidence of any. He embraced life and lived it to the fullest."

"Incurable cancer? Financial troubles? Woman problems? A political scandal about to come to light?"

"Nothing. I swear to you, Dawson. I would know."

"Would you?"

"Yes."

"Fathers don't tell their daughters everything, especially ugly things."

"I would have known if something were terribly wrong."

"Okay."

"You say okay, but I feel your skepticism." She continued trying to convince him. "It was his housekeeper's afternoon off. Which explains how he could have overdosed. She'd been with us for years, even long before Mother died. She adored him, as everyone did.

"She nagged him about diet, exercise, and taking his various medications. She knew which were to be taken with or without food. She kept track of all that. So it's conceivable to me that he simply made a mistake, and she wasn't there to prevent it."

He frowned doubtfully. "It was a lot of pills to swallow by mistake."

"Says one who takes a lot."

"Exactly," he said with matching curtness. "And I know better than to eat a whole damn bottle full."

She put her hand to her forehead and rubbed it with her fingertips, noting that they were chilled. "He loved me and the boys to distraction. He was devoted to us. I'll go to my own grave believing that his death was a tragic accident, not a suicide. Jeremy..." She waved her hand. "Everything associated with him was terrible, including the way he died."

She glanced at him, thinking he might dispute that point. He didn't. "But I would gladly go through the whole Jeremy episode of my life again, I would endure anything, if I could have my father back. If only for long enough to ask him if he did it intentionally, and if he did, *why*? I'd ask him how he could have abandoned me so cruelly?"

Dawson's eyes seemed to be lit by an internal fire that burned through her. After a long moment, he relaxed his intensity, stood up, and extended his hand to help her up. "It's late, and you must be exhausted." He left her only long enough to get a drinking glass from the kitchen, then they climbed the stairs together.

"How's the knee?"

"I'll have a bruise tomorrow."

"You need some skid-proof socks."

"I'll put them on my Christmas list."

When they reached the bedroom where the boys slept, she opened the door and peeked inside. "I don't think they've moved."

"You're a good mother, Amelia."

His tone had the ring of unmitigated sincerity, and when she came back around to face him, she saw that his expression was just as serious.

"Thank you."

"You would never abandon them, would you?"

"Absolutely not."

"What about him? Would he?"

Jeremy. His murder would have orphaned Hunter and Grant. Faking his death would be abandonment of another sort entirely. As cruel as a suicide.

Gruffly, she said, "I appreciate your hospitality. Good night."

Dawson went into his bedroom, closed the door, and leaned back, gently knocking his head against it as though trying to beat some sense into it. If the door had had a lock, he would have locked himself in. Tonight he'd protected Amelia and her family from the storm, as well as from any unknown perils.

But who or what was going to protect her from him?

Her heartbreak over her father's death had almost broken his determination not to touch her again. He didn't trust himself to lay a hand on her, even in a comforting gesture.

He moved to the window. The wind still howled, the rainfall was torrential, and occasional lightning revealed the thick cloud cover. The storm hadn't yet blown itself out. He looked toward Amelia's house. No car. No Stef.

While Amelia had been preparing the boys for bed, he'd slipped back down to the kitchen and retrieved his pills and a bottle of bourbon. Now he sat down on the side of the bed and self-medicated with two tablets and two slugs of whiskey. He undressed and got into bed.

Lightning flickered across the ceiling. Thunder rumbled. It was a menacing night, but he didn't have to worry about

Amelia, Hunter, and Grant. Tonight they were safe. Which was probably why he was able to fall asleep faster than usual.

The nightmare left him in peace for the better part of the night. But it was merely stalking the perimeter of his subconscious, biding its time as it gathered momentum, because when it pounced, it did so with renewed ferocity.

"Dawson! Hey, man, up here!"

He turned toward the direction of the voice. The sun was blinding, silhouetting one of the soldiers against its glare on the crest of the ridge. Dawson raised his hand to shield his eyes and, making out Hawkins, waved.

"Dawson?"

"Dawson, get up here."

"Be right there."

"I ain't gonna wait forever. You want a story, haul your ass up here."

"Let me grab my laptop."

"Fucking now, man!"

"Dawson."

As he made his way up the unforgiving incline, time and again he lost his footing in the loose sand and rock. It seemed an endless climb. Hawkins became increasingly impatient, urging him to hurry. He was out of breath by the time he reached the ridge. Sweat was dripping into his eyes, stinging them. He tried to wipe it away, but the salty film remained, so it was through blurred vision that he saw Hawkins grinning at him.

Then—"No!"

"Dawson."

As always the noise ricocheting inside his skull woke him. He sat bolt upright, drenched in sweat, futilely trying to wipe it from his eyes with a hand that was bathed in the brine of his own terror, his mouth still open around the scream that invariably came too late.

This was like every other time he was jolted out of the nightmare, except now Amelia was here, her hand resting on his shoulder, and he realized that she'd been here for a while, her voice mingling with that of the smiling young soldier from rural North Dakota.

Dawson drew up his knees and placed his elbows on them, holding his head in his hands as he gasped for breath. The terror gradually receded, but not the humiliation, made even worse when Amelia sat down on the edge of the bed. He was as sharply aware of her pity as he was of her nearness.

"You were calling out."

"Sorry I woke you. Go back to bed."

She removed her hand from his shoulder, but stayed. Knowing what a frightful and pathetic sight he must be, he shook back his hair and used the hem of the sheet bunched around his waist to wipe the sweat off his face, neck, and chest.

She asked, "Is it always the same dream?"

"Yes."

"Do you want to—"

"No."

"It might help if you—"

"I'm not going to talk about it."

"Not with me or not with anyone?"

"Anyone."

"No one would think less of you if—"

"I would."

"You'll never get rid of it until—"

"I'll work it out, okay?"

"How?"

"Leave me alone."

"To do what? Take more pills?"

"Maybe."

"You have a problem, Dawson."

"Oh yeah?"

"Yes. And drugs and alcohol aren't the solution."

He whipped his head toward her and snapped, "What the fuck do you know about it?"

She recoiled as though he'd struck her.

Realizing what he'd said, he muttered an expletive and

reached for her, catching her hand as she shot off the bed. "I'm sorry. I'm sorry."

Applying only light pressure so as not to frighten her, he brought her around to face him. He looked directly into her eyes, silently appealing for forgiveness and, short of that, understanding. She remained unmoving.

"Please don't look at me like that." Then he closed his eyes and raised her hand to his mouth. He kissed the inside of her wrist, whispering repeatedly against her pulse, "I'm sorry." Bending his head low over her hand, he kissed the base of her thumb, and finally pressed his lips into her palm, hoarsely whispering, "Don't be afraid of me. Please." He touched his tongue to the hollow of her hand.

She made a small sound that brought his head up. Her expression had turned into one of confusion and indecision. She was breathing lightly and rapidly through her lips.

Caution and conscience kept him from dragging her down to him.

Caution and conscience be damned.

He pulled on her hand, gently but inexorably, until she was again sitting on the edge of the bed. Wide-eyed, she watched him as his fingertips explored the features of her face. Brows, cheekbones, nose, lips, jawline, and chin. He memorized them by touch.

Since she allowed that, he brushed her hair aside and nuzzled her neck until he felt the warmth of her skin against his lips. "I wouldn't...I *couldn't* ever hurt you. Believe that." He planted a tender kiss on the side of her neck. Then another.

Her head tipped back. Taking that as encouragement, his kisses on her neck became more fervent. By the time they reached her ear, there was intent behind them, and she responded. Tension escaped her on a sigh. Her body settled, ever so slightly shifting closer to him. Tentatively she placed her hands on his shoulders.

He eased his head back and looked into her eyes. "I'm not him, Amelia. I'm not like him. I swear to you, I'm not. I have it under control."

"I'm not afraid you'll lose control." Her voice was low and husky, and he wished it was something he could touch, stroke, taste. "I'm afraid I will."

With a rasped curse, he cupped her head between his hands and claimed a kiss that was unapologetically deep from the start. There was no buildup to the intimacy, because he'd been thinking about making love to her mouth from the moment he saw her in the courtroom.

She didn't shy away, but kissed him back in kind, with heat, her fingers alternately kneading his shoulders and tugging handfuls of his hair. Her unrestraint was as much a surprise as it was a delight.

He lowered her back onto the bed, where the kiss grew hungrier. As their mouths feasted on each other, he angled his body above hers. The sheet had become displaced, so there was nothing between the sensitized tip of his erection and her soft pajama bottoms. The contact caused a low groan to vibrate in his throat.

Amelia rubbed against him seductively, each movement sweetly feminine and small but breath stealing. He wasn't as subtle. His hands roved selfishly and impatiently, greedy for the feel of her skin. He pushed his hand into the loose waistband of her pajama bottoms and caressed the curve of her hip. In response, her thighs shifted, separated. He fit himself into the notch.

When the doorbell rang, he was in such a fog of lust that it didn't at first register with him what it was. When it rang a second time, they jerked apart and stared at each other, breathing loudly, sharing incredulity over someone's ill timing. Blistering the walls of the room with a scorching curse, he rolled off her.

She scrambled off the bed and yanked her clothing back into place. "It must be Stef."

"Or Bernie." He snatched his gym shorts from the chair beside the bed and pulled them on. "I invited him for breakfast, but, Christ, it's barely dawn."

He went to the window that overlooked the front of the house, expecting to see a familiar person below. He didn't. When he turned back to Amelia, she must have read the foreboding in his expression, because her hand moved to the base of her throat.

"What?"

"It's the police."

Chapter 12

Quickly, she checked on the boys, but they had slept through the ringing of the doorbell. By the time she got downstairs, Dawson was admitting a uniformed officer and a man in plainclothes into the house and saying to them, "She's here."

They introduced themselves as deputies from the Chatham County Sheriff's Office in Savannah. Saint Nelda's Island didn't have a police force of its own. To Amelia's knowledge, there had never been a need for one.

The uniformed man was young, so cleanly shaven that his cheeks were abraded. The tops of his ears turned red when he looked beyond Dawson's bare torso and took in her dishevelment.

It was clear to her that he was the junior official of the pair, probably serving as a chauffeur to the other man, who introduced himself as Deputy Tucker, a detective for the sheriff's office. He was potbellied, ruddy-faced, and all-business.

Amelia asked him why he was looking for her.

He took a small spiral notebook from the pocket of his rain jacket. "Do you own a car with Georgia license plate number..." He flipped open the notebook and read out the characters of her license plate.

She confirmed that that was her car.

"Are you acquainted with a young woman named Stephanie Elaine DeMarco?"

"She's my children's nanny. Is something...Has she been involved in an accident?"

"No, ma'am. I'm sorry to have to tell you that Miss DeMarco was found dead this morning."

Her knees gave way. Dawson and the uniformed deputy both reached for her, but Dawson got to her first. He supported her as he backed her into the nearest chair, where she sank down onto the seat. "Dead?" she wheezed. "Stef is dead?"

"My condolences, ma'am."

Madly, she wondered if she was dreaming. Or if someone was playing a vicious practical joke. Or if a dreadful mistake had been made, a mix-up of identities, perhaps. It happened, not often, but she'd read about such instances. Anything was possible except that vibrant, healthy, funny Stef was *dead*. Her mind refused to accept it. "There must be some mistake."

Tucker said, "A purse containing her identification was found on the passenger seat of your car. Her body was discovered just a few yards away."

"Discovered by whom?" Dawson asked. "Where?"

"In the parking lot behind the café. Kid who works the kitchen at Mickey's was taking out trash, noticed the car and wondered what it was doing there that time of morning. Then he saw the body behind the Dumpster. When my partner and I got to the island, we were told she worked for you. Your numbers were programmed into the cell phone found inside her purse. We've been trying to reach you."

"I haven't checked my phone this morning, but the last time I did, I didn't have service. I've been here since late last evening. I left Stef a note so she'd know where we were when she got home." Her voice cracked with emotion and she stifled a sob.

Dawson took over the explanation. "Practically the whole island lost power last night. This house has an emergency generator. I invited Ms. Nolan and her two young sons to ride out the storm here."

"You own this house?"

"I rented it for the Labor Day weekend."

"Are you Dawson Scott?"

"That's right."

"Mickey mentioned you. Where're you from, Mr. Scott?"

"Alexandria, Virginia."

He moved to the table where his laptop sat and took a business card from the pocket of a brown leather messenger bag. He handed it to the deputy, who studied it thoroughly before placing it in his pocket. "Did you know the girl?"

"I met her a few days ago, along with Ms. Nolan's family."

At the sound of her name, Amelia raised her head and realized that she'd been following their conversation with only half an ear. Her mind was still trying to process the inconceivable. "You said Stef was 'found dead' near the car. Was she struck by lightning?"

Tucker divided a glance between her and Dawson, but addressed his answer to her. "We're in the process of conducting a full investigation."

"But you know what killed her, so why don't you just tell us?"

It was clear that Dawson's impertinence was an affront to Tucker, but Dawson stared him down until he relented. "She suffered a head wound. She might have been struck from behind by debris carried by the strong winds, but foul played hasn't been ruled out."

Amelia couldn't speak at all, leaving Dawson to say the unthinkable out loud. "You mean she could have been murdered?"

"The ME will make a determination as to the manner of death."

For several moments following that, no one said anything. Then Amelia asked, "Where is she now?"

"Miss DeMarco's body is being transported to the morgue in Savannah."

"Have her parents been notified?"

"They're on their way from Kansas, but since they have to make a couple of connections, they aren't expected to arrive until midafternoon."

"How did they take the news? Never mind," she said before Tucker could answer. "I know how they must have taken it." She exhaled a long, sad sigh.

At the sound of footsteps on the porch, Dawson moved to the door and looked through a flanking window. "It's Bernie." He opened the door just as Bernie, arriving for breakfast, was raising his hand to knock. He was carrying a basket of citrus fruit. His face was creased with worry.

"What's a sheriff's car doing here?"

Dawson stood aside and motioned him in. He nodded to the young deputy, looked Tucker up and down, then his gaze moved to Amelia, and, seeing her tears, he asked, "What's happened?"

She took a deep breath. "It's Stef." She told him as much as she could before emotion made speech impossible. At that point, Dawson finished imparting the terrible news.

Bernie's mouth worked to form words, but he achieved none. Finally he was able to say, "She was a sweet young lady."

Amelia hugged herself. "I feel responsible."

"You're not," Dawson said brusquely.

"She was on an errand for me."

"Don't do that to yourself."

She nodded, as though agreeing, but for as long as she lived, she would regret letting Stef go out into the storm on a mission that should have been hers.

Bernie asked, "Where are the boys?"

"They're still sleeping." Shakily, she stood up. "I'd better go wake them."

"I'll go up with you," Dawson said. "Telling them won't be easy."

"I'm not going to tell them. Not right now. But I want to leave for Savannah as soon as we can. I want to be there with Stef at the . . ." Because of the images it conjured, she couldn't bring herself to say the word *morgue.* "I want to be there when her parents arrive."

"I'll take you." Dawson closed his hand around her elbow and together they turned toward the stairs.

"Uh, actually, Mr. Scott, I'd like you to ride with me back to the village." The three of them looked at Deputy Tucker, who squared his shoulders and took a step toward Dawson. "Besides coming out here to inform Ms. Nolan of her nanny's death, I was coming after you."

"What for?"

The deputy gave Dawson a sly smile. "You're leaving it to me to tell them?"

Dawson didn't answer, not even when Amelia turned to him and spoke his name softly, with inquiry. "Tell us what?"

His jaw remained tightly clenched.

Tucker said, "Seems he was the last person seen talking to Miss DeMarco."

Her mind in turmoil, Amelia switched onto autopilot. When she woke the boys, they were grumpy and out of sorts, especially when they learned that Dawson wasn't there.

Along with Bernie, they trooped back to her house. The electricity was still out, so she fed the children a breakfast of cold Pop-Tarts and the oranges that Bernie had contributed. She herself couldn't stomach the thought of food.

While her neighbor supervised the kids' meal, she went upstairs and gave herself a cold sponge bath in the sink of the semidark bathroom. Once she was dressed, she summoned the boys up to change their clothes.

Hunter complained about the shirt she chose for him. "Not that one, Mom."

"You can't wear one of your beach shirts. We're going to Savannah. You'll be visiting Mr. and Mrs. Metcalf today."

"Who's that?"

"You know, the director of the museum. You like him. Remember, he does duck calls?"

With cell service restored, she'd been able to contact George. After learning of her emergency, he and his wife had agreed to watch the children for as long as she needed them to.

"They have grandsons near your age," she added as she wrestled the disliked shirt over Hunter's head. "They'll be there to play with you."

"Why can't we stay here and play with Dawson?"

"Yeah? How come?" Grant whined.

"Because you'll be playing with new friends today." She injected false cheer into her tone. "The Metcalfs have a swimming pool, and there was mention of a cookout and s'mores."

"I'll bet they're dorks," Hunter mumbled.

Grant's only concern was whether or not the other boys liked cars. "I don't know," she replied in exasperation when he asked her for the third time. "Put your shoes on."

Then, in response to their crestfallen expressions, she gathered them into a group hug and held them tightly. "I'm sorry I'm so cross. I'm not mad at you, I promise. I just have a lot of grown-up things on my mind today. So, please, do as I ask without an argument, okay?"

Sullenly they promised to obey, but they persistently asked about Stef and Dawson's absence. She realized that her vague answers would pacify them for only so long, and then she would have to tell them why Stef had left without saying good-bye and explain why she wasn't coming back.

She would have to talk to them about death. Again. They weren't strangers to it. First their grandfather's. Then Jeremy's. Now their nanny's. It was a lot for their young minds to wrap themselves around. It was almost too much for hers.

Because her car was integral to the investigation, it had been impounded, so Bernie offered to drive them to the ferry dock. She settled the boys in the backseat with a portable DVD player between them and dual headsets.

Once under way, Bernie said, "What do you think happened?"

"I don't know, Bernie. I really don't want to talk about it."

Her mind was still reeling over everything that had transpired since being awakened by Dawson in the throes of a nightmare. His angry rebuke, followed by that tender appeal for forgiveness, then the kiss. His fervency and her oh-so-eager response. The doorbell.

His reaction to the deputy's bombshell had been stoicism that bordered on surliness. Before they left, Tucker had allowed him to go upstairs to change clothes, accompanied by the uniformed officer. While Dawson was out of earshot, the deputy asked Amelia about the sequence of events that had taken place the night before.

"What time did Mr. Scott arrive at your house?"

"Eight thirty. Nine possibly."

Bernie chimed in. "That's right. They stopped at my place. Woke me up, actually. I automatically checked the time. It was eight fifty-two."

Tucker took notes. He asked Amelia if Dawson had been in the house all night.

"Yes."

"Can you swear to that?"

"He and I went upstairs around eleven. We parted at the bedroom door where my sons and I were supposed to sleep. I didn't see him again until shortly before you arrived." She hoped that neither man detected the heat that rushed to her face. "If he left the house during the night, I was unaware of it." Realizing why the time line was important, she asked, "How long had Stef been . . ."

Inferring the question she was unable to ask, Tucker told them that the time of Stef's death hadn't been firmly established.

At that point, Dawson had appeared on the stairs, trailed by the young deputy. As he walked to the front door, Dawson had asked, rather sarcastically, if the deputy wanted to handcuff him.

"That won't be necessary, Mr. Scott. This isn't an arrest. We just want to talk to you."

"Right." He'd then turned to look at Amelia, but she had difficulty holding his gaze. She heard him mutter something she didn't catch, then he pulled open the front door and went out ahead of the two deputies.

Now as Bernie, his hands at ten and two on the steering wheel, dodged flooded areas of the road, she contradicted herself about not wanting to talk about it. "For the past week or so Stef had been seeing someone."

"Dirk."

"She told you about him?"

"Not much. He works on boats."

"I know little more than that. I urged her to invite him to the house, but she seemed reluctant to introduce us. I wish now that I'd pressed her for more information about him, but she was a grown woman. I didn't feel it was my place to interfere."

"I know exactly what you mean."

His tone suggested an unspoken footnote. So did the discomfiture in his expression. "Bernie, do you know something that you're not telling? Whatever it is, you should share it with the authorities."

He shifted in his seat, glanced into the rearview mirror to make certain the boys weren't listening, then gave her an uneasy glance. "I saw them together."

"Her and Dirk?"

Looking miserable, he shook his head.

Her heart began a dull, hard thudding. "Dawson?"

He nodded.

"When?"

He screwed up his face in thought. "Thursday?"

"You must have the day wrong." She'd caught Dawson spying on Friday, and Stef hadn't met him until that evening at Mickey's.

"No, I'm certain it was Thursday, because that was the day I was packing up and my hip started giving me fits."

Without interrupting him, she listened carefully as he described to her the encounter he'd seen.

When he finished, he paused, and added awkwardly, "It wasn't anything. Not really. But when I teased her about it later, warning her that he looked too old for her, she just laughed and asked me not to say anything to you about seeing them together."

"Why did she care if I knew?"

"*She* didn't. He did. He'd told her not to tell you that they'd met."

Amelia was too heartsick to respond.

Bernie pulled up to one of the village's few stop signs and looked across at her. "I hate now that I told you."

"I needed to know."

"It's not my place to butt in."

"You didn't butt in. I pried it out of you."

"Who you spend time with is your business."

"It was only circumstances that brought Dawson and me together."

"That may be," Bernie said, "but I think you like him."

She turned her head aside so he couldn't see her face. "We'd better hurry or we'll miss the ferry."

Chapter 13

Dawson left the interior of the sheriff's administrative offices through a doorway that opened into a small lobby. He was shocked to see Amelia there alone. She was sitting in one of a row of preformed plastic chairs lined up against the wall. She seemed just as surprised to see him. Her eyes widened fractionally, then she looked away.

He walked over and sat down in the chair next to hers. "Are you all right?"

She turned her head and gave him a droll look. "I can't remember a Labor Day I've enjoyed more."

For asking such a stupid question, he figured he deserved the putdown. "Hunter and Grant?"

"They're with George Metcalf and his wife. I talked to them on the phone a few minutes ago. They've had fun, but they're ready for me to come get them." She glanced toward the door through which he'd emerged. "I don't know when I'll be free to do that. And maybe it would be better if I left them there overnight. I have to be in court early tomorrow morning."

"I'm sure Lem Jackson would speak to the judge on your behalf."

"When he heard about Stef on the news, he called and offered to ask for a postponement, but I told him not to."

"Can you bear up to a cross-examination?"

"I'm tired of dreading it, and want to get it over with as soon as possible."

He understood her wanting to have the court appearance behind her, but he questioned the wisdom of her decision. She looked completely wrung out. "Have you told Hunter and Grant about Stef?"

"I don't know how to tell them when I can't believe it myself."

He waited for a moment. Then, "You know her death wasn't caused by flying debris."

She swallowed hard before murmuring *yes*.

While being "interviewed" by Deputy Tucker and his partner detective, the ME's initial finding had been reported to Dawson: Stef was killed by a blow to the back of her head. It had fractured her skull. The depression indicated that brute force had been applied.

"How did you find out?" he asked Amelia.

She folded her arms across her midriff and tucked her hands against her sides. "When I got to the morgue, I was asked to positively identify her. The autopsy won't be performed until her parents have seen her, but the medical examiner has examined the wound. He told me what killed her."

"Have her parents arrived?"

"A short while ago. They were brought straight to the morgue. I talked to them. They're devastated. I left them to grieve."

"That's where I would expect you to be," he said. "Somewhere grieving."

"Now that homicide has been confirmed, Deputy Tucker called and asked if I would come here and answer some questions. When I arrived, I was told to wait." She nodded toward a uniformed officer who was manning the reception desk from behind a window. "That was half an hour ago."

The crime scene on Saint Nelda's Island was still cordoned off, but it had been determined by someone in charge that, due to the serious nature of the crime, the investigation be conducted from the main sheriff's office rather than from the precinct that served Saint Nelda's.

The headquarters shared a campus with the county jail, a sprawling, industrial-looking complex wrapped in concertina wire. Maybe the decision to center the case here was an intimidation tactic.

Dawson had spent the entire day there, being questioned off and on by the pair of detectives. It was getting dark outside, and he had only now been released, with the stipulation that he keep himself available for further questioning.

To bring Amelia up to date, he told her all that. "Tucker and his partner, a guy named Wills—'Tucker and Wills' sounds like a magic act, doesn't it? Anyway, when they weren't questioning me, singly or together, they left me alone in the interrogation room. I guess I'm a person of interest. They did the whole bad-cop/good-cop routine, which might have been scary if it hadn't been so obvious. Bad cop, Tucker, told me that they got a search warrant for the beach house."

She looked at him with concern. "They're that serious about you?"

"They won't find a murder weapon. I just hate that the rental company had to notify the home owner that his house was about to be turned inside out. I doubt they'll provide good references if I ever want to rent again."

"How can you joke?"

He raked his fingers through his hair. "Because if I don't, I'll get really pissed off for even being considered a suspect. You've got to know that I had nothing to do with it."

She searched his eyes, finally saying, "The estimated time of her death coincides with when you were seen talking to her in the village."

"True. Which sucks. But I've explained to the detectives how that came about. Stef and I bumped into each other in the general store. She had bags. They were heavy because she'd bought extra bottled water. It was raining buckets. I offered to carry her purchases to the car for her. Which I did.

"I left her there and drove over to the dock to fill up my car with gas. Then I headed back to the beach. I expected her to be ahead of me and was surprised when I reached your house and saw that your car wasn't there. I figured she'd ducked into Mickey's, as she'd said she might, to see if he had any carry-out food. You know the rest."

"This encounter with Stef slipped your mind? Even though we talked at length about the unlikelihood of her returning soon, you forgot to tell me that you'd just seen her?" He was about to reply, when she stopped him. "Don't bother inventing an explanation. I know why you didn't tell me. You didn't want me to know that you and Stef were . . . friendly."

"'Friendly,' spoken in that tone, sounds like a euphemism."

"Bernie saw the two of you together."

Bloody hell. He could kick himself for not telling her before. The omission made him look as guilty as her glare indicated he was. "It was innocent."

His disclaimer made it sound anything but innocent and did nothing to assuage her suspicion.

He drew in a long breath. "Thursday, the day after my arrival, I had gone for a run and was on my way back to the house. Stef was on her bicycle, returning from the store. We crossed paths, exchanged names. She asked where I was staying, and when I told her, she remarked that we were neighbors and told me not to be a stranger. She said, 'Maybe we'll catch each other on the beach tomorrow.' We parted."

"You helped her with her bicycle basket."

"That's right. The clamp was loose. She was afraid the basket was going to shake free of the mounting and dump her purchases. So, yeah, I tightened the clamp for her. It took thirty seconds, max. That was it."

"If that was 'it,' why did the two of you pretend that you hadn't met? When I caught you spying Friday afternoon, you asked me who she was, when you already knew. Friday night at Mickey's, when she brought you over from the bar to our table, she didn't say, 'This is our neighbor, who was kind enough to help me with my bicycle basket yesterday.'"

"I asked you who she was because when we met, she hadn't specifically explained her position in your household. I didn't know that she wasn't a relative. At Mickey's, I suppose she was sensitive to the tidal waves of hostility you were radiating. I can only guess, but I *guess* she didn't want to rile you."

"You took your cue from her and went along with the pretense of never having met."

"Something like that." She continued to look at him, making him wonder if she also knew about that other time. Whether or not she did, it would be better to come clean about it now. "I was alone with her one other time."

"When?"

"Also on Thursday."

"The same day you met?"

"Late that night. I went over to leave your wristwatch on the porch railing. As I was skirting around the back of your house, Stef drove up in your car and caught me in the headlights. I had no choice except to brazen it out. I told her that I'd heard something and had come to check for an intruder. Which wasn't such a stretch of the truth. I'd been keeping an eye on your house, particularly late at night, for reasons you know."

"You were sneaking around my house in the middle of the night, and she didn't think that was the least bit suspicious? She didn't raise a hue and cry and ask what the hell you were doing?"

"She was in no condition to do anything. She'd been drinking. Quite a lot. I had to help her from the car to the back door. She begged me not to tell you. Since I didn't want you to know that I was staying in the house next door—"

"Spying."

"—I promised that you would never hear it from me, in exchange for her promise never to drive again in that condition."

"You two formed a pact."

He wished he could deny it, but that was more or less the truth of it. "It was a nonissue."

"Was it? The authorities might disagree. Do they know about these secret meetings between you two?"

"Yes. I told them."

That calmed her a little, but she was still looking at him with anger and suspicion. "Did you see her as an excellent source of insider information on me? Or as something else entirely?"

"No to the first question. I don't dare guess what 'something else entirely' implies."

"Come on, Dawson, don't play dumb. She was a friendly, flirty girl, who also happened to be a head turner, especially in a bikini."

"She was. All that. She was also half my age. Near enough, at least."

"That didn't matter to her. She said the guy she was seeing was older."

He reacted with a start. "Dirk is older?"

"You know about him?"

"The night she came in drunk, she mentioned him by name. 'Dirk and I killed a bottle of Captain Morgan.' The detectives want to question him, but they haven't been able to track him down."

"That's one reason I was asked to come in," she said. "They want to know what I know about him."

"What *do* you know about him?"

"Not even his last name."

Dawson listened with mounting apprehension as she told him what little she knew about the elusive Dirk. "Did Stef tell you why she wasn't keen on you two meeting?"

"I gathered he wasn't keen on it, either. He wouldn't fit into 'the family scene.'"

"Did she describe him physically?"

"Older than she, but she didn't say by how much. Tattoos. A beard."

"Huh."

"Your brow is furrowed. What are you thinking?"

"Dirk comes across as excessively secretive."

He got up and walked over to a bulletin board that was papered with Wanted posters, forming a collage of sinister faces. One poster stood out, however, because the wanted individual had the benign countenance of an angel framed by curly blond hair. Not yet thirty years old, she was wanted for armed robbery and murder. A twenty-five-thousand-dollar reward had been offered for information leading to her arrest. She was considered to be armed and dangerous.

The criminal bent of one's personality wasn't always obvious.

He turned back to Amelia. "I didn't use Stef as a source of information on you. But maybe someone else did. Someone who wanted to keep track of you and your sons, who wanted to know where you were and who you were with. Someone having a great deal of personal interest in your activities, your daily routine, your comings and goings."

She took a deep, stuttering breath, indicating to Dawson that even though she didn't respond, she understood all too well what he was leading up to.

In a quiet voice, he said, "There's the age factor."

"We don't know how old this Dirk is."

"For the sake of argument, let's say his age fits."

"Let's not," she said, coming to her feet. "The man Stef described to me sounds nothing like Jeremy."

"Tattoos are easily acquired. The beard might take a week or two. He's been missing for fifteen months."

"You don't think I'd recognize the man I was married to, even with a beard?"

"You would, but the casual observer wouldn't. Furthermore, nobody's looking for Jeremy Wesson. The general consensus is that Willard Strong fed him to a pack of starving pit bulls."

She took a reflexive step away from him, but when the back of her knees touched the seat of the chair, she sat back down abruptly. He returned to his seat beside her. He wanted to caress her cheek, at the very least, take her hand. He refrained, largely because he feared a rebuff.

"Something else has been nagging at me."

She shook her head as though to stave off whatever it was he was about to say, but he didn't let it deter him. "I haven't shared this with the detectives because I wanted to run it past you, first." And Headly. Above anyone else, he would trust Gary Headly's instincts on this.

"When I ran into Stef in the general store, she was wearing a rain slicker. I teased her about the loud pattern. Red with bright-yellow-and-white daisies. She told me she'd taken it from the trunk of your car."

"It's mine. Jeremy and I went to Charleston for a getaway weekend. The weather turned bad, and I needed a raincoat in a hurry. That was the first one I found. It's not something I would typically choose, so I kept it at the beach house and never wore it except there on the island."

"Last I saw her, Stef was standing beside your car, wearing your slicker, with—"

"No."

"—the hood up."

"Stop!"

"Amelia—"

"Don't say anymore."

Just then the door adjacent to the reception window swung outward and Tucker and Wills walked through. "Well, Mr. Scott," Tucker drawled. "Glad to see you're still here. You saved us a trip."

"I ran into Ms. Nolan."

Tucker introduced his partner to her.

"Thank you for coming in, Ms. Nolan," Wills said. As tall and thin as Tucker was short and stout, he had the bearing and stooped posture of a tenured professor. He was also the more sensitive of the two, and noticed how shaken Amelia appeared. "Ma'am, are you all right?"

"Yes, fine. It's been a terrible day."

"Of course. We realize what an imposition it is to ask you to come down here this time of night."

"Not at all. If I can help, I want to."

"We'll be with you directly," he told her.

"Right now, it's Mr. Scott we want to talk to." Tucker hiked up his belt, or tried, and grinned at Dawson. "We were on our way to come find you."

"Here I am." Despite his wisecrack, Dawson got a bad feeling about the detective's smirk.

"Do you know a guy named Ray Dale Huffman?"

"Never heard of him."

"Are you sure?" Wills asked in a kinder tone.

"Positive. Who is he?"

"Repeat offender," Tucker said. "We've got him in lockup. He heard through the jailhouse grapevine—it's the damnedest thing how that works, truly. Anyhow, he got wind of us questioning you in connection to Miss DeMarco's murder, and he offered to make a deal."

"What kind of deal?"

Wills said, "We drop the charge against him in exchange for information about you."

"Sorry. You've been had. I don't even know the guy."

Tucker's grin turned even more smug. "Not what he said."

"I don't give a shit what he said."

"Well, you should." Tucker moved in close and leered up at him. "Because Ray Dale claims that one night last week, down on River Street, he sold you a whole bag full of drugs."

They allowed him one phone call. He called Headly.

"I can't talk now. We've got friends over. The cabernet is breathing, steaks are on the grill, and Eva's tossing the salad."

"Amelia Nolan's nanny was murdered last night."

Dawson could practically hear the gears grinding inside Headly's head. "Hold on."

While he went to notify Eva and their guests that dinner would be delayed, Dawson glanced over his shoulder. The two detectives were out of earshot but observing him closely. Tucker was stroking his jutting belly, which he used as other policemen did a billy club, to try and intimidate.

Dawson didn't know how long they would give him, so when Headly came back on the line, he said, "I'm in a time crunch, so listen and don't interrupt."

According to the oversized wall clock, he talked for one hundred and twenty-eight seconds, summing up as concisely as possible the events of the past few days, filling in pertinent facts he'd deliberately left out of previous conversations.

When he stopped, the first thing out of Headly's mouth was, "Jesus."

"Yeah. The wristwatch thing freaked Amelia out because she'd sensed somebody had been watching her."

"You."

"Not me. I told you, she got the feeling before I ever arrived on the scene. Then there were the photographs." He'd told Headly about them, too, ignoring grunts of disapproval for his having taken them in the first place. "We still don't know what happened to them. The beach ball also remains unexplained."

"You said the girl, Stef, was driving Amelia's car and wearing her rain slicker."

"A distinctive slicker. She had the hood up. It was dark. Cats-and-dogs rain. From the back, she could easily have been mistaken for Amelia."

"And Dirk's gone underground."

Dawson expelled his breath. "That's where we are. What do you make of it?"

"You know before asking."

Yes, he did. "Amelia won't admit it, but she's afraid my hunch is right."

"We could be wrong," Headly said, musing aloud. "Maybe the nanny got crosswise with somebody, and he or she whacked her."

"That's a possibility, of course. But if Stef had an enemy, she didn't show it. We know of none. And we know definitely that Amelia has one."

"Okay, if Jeremy's alive, what would he gain by killing his ex-wife?"

"His children."

"Shit," Headly said. "I walked right into that one."

"He once told Amelia that nothing would keep him from his sons."

"By the way, I called the local newspaper in Wesson's hometown, played the FBI ace, and asked that his parents' obit be e-mailed to me. I laid it on thick. A matter of national security, and so on. Anyhow, I got it this afternoon. It included a picture of two pleasant-looking individuals on their twenty-fifth wedding anniversary. She was wearing a corsage of roses."

"Not Carl and Flora."

"Not even close."

"So even if Jeremy was their son by birth, he wasn't reared by them."

"Looks like."

Before they could take that topic further, Tucker nudged Dawson's shoulder and mouthed, "Sixty seconds."

"I gotta go," he said into the phone.

"No need to rush now. Eva's already steamed. But she'll get over it. She always does." After a pause, he said, "Dirk needs to be found."

"Yeah, about that... I thought maybe you could come down."

"To Savannah?"

"If Dirk *is* Jeremy, you'll want to be in on the hunt and the capture. Right?"

"Definitely. I'll call Knutz first thing tomorrow morning. Have him start putting together a task force."

"Any chance you can get here tonight?"

"Tonight?"

"For a couple of urgent reasons. First and foremost, Amelia needs someone watching her back."

"I thought that was your detail. What's the other urgency?"

"I need you to bail me out."

Even before thanking Headly for picking him up, as they walked from the jail, Dawson asked him if Amelia was safe.

"Soon as our call ended last night, I talked to Knutz. He's got people he occasionally uses for surveillance, sorta freelancers. He put somebody on Amelia. A gal actually, but she's one of the best, he says.

"Anyway, she followed Amelia when she left the sheriff's office. She went straight to her apartment, spent the night there without incident. She left it this morning at eight o'clock." He checked his wristwatch. "About ten minutes ago."

"So she's okay?"

"Didn't I indicate that?"

"What about the boys?"

"They weren't with her."

"She must have left them with the museum guy and his wife. She said she might. It was probably for the best. But somebody should be guarding that house, too. They—" He caught Headly looking at him curiously. "What?"

"For a jailbird, you're awfully concerned about the welfare of a widow and her two kids."

"If something happens to them, it'll be on your head for not telling the locals about the possibility of Jeremy's resurrection."

Querulously, Headly said, "Another one of Knutz's free-lancers is watching the museum guy's house. Okay?"

"Why didn't you just say so?"

"Well, I've been a little busy lately getting your ass out of jail."

"Thanks, by the way."

Headly merely snorted.

Dawson said, "I wasn't worried about being formally charged." He'd spent an uncomfortable night in jail—fortunately not in the same cell with Ray Dale Huffman, whom, had he gotten close to, he might have strangled. "It was only a matter of time before they had to let me go."

Headly motioned him toward the rental car he'd picked up at the Savannah airport.

"How do you figure?"

"They didn't have any evidence."

Headly used the remote key to unlock the car doors. They got in on opposite sides, and Headly started the engine immediately. "Of illegal drug possession or homicide?"

"Certainly no evidence tying me to Stef's murder."

Headly just sat there with his hand on the gearshift, looking at him, silently asking about the other possible criminal charge.

"All right, I'd bought some pills from Ray Dale. Yesterday, a rookie deputy was sent upstairs with me while I changed clothes. He was green, easily distracted with jabber. I snatched the bottle of them off my nightstand, and when he allowed me to go to the john, I flushed them."

"Clever you." Headly backed out of the parking slot, muttering angrily under his breath.

"Will you relax?" Dawson said. "They were—"

"I know what they were. I found your stash in your apartment."

"Excuse me? You broke into my apartment?"

"Don't go all righteously indignant on me. I'm not the drug addict."

"I'm hardly an addict."

"No? Then why are your hands shaking?"

He'd hoped no one would notice. "Look, I only needed something to take the edge off."

"Off what?"

Dawson clammed up, then said, "I wasn't taking anything you can't get from a doctor."

"Then why aren't you getting them from one, instead of buying them off guys on the street with names like Ray Dale? God only knows what they're laced with."

Dawson was about to argue that, but truth be told, he couldn't vouch for the pharmaceutical integrity of the pills he'd been taking. His only criterion for quality control had been that they worked. Their numbing effect was swift and short-term, but even a moment away from the nightmare was worth the risk of taking compounds of dubious origin.

"I was careful," he mumbled.

"Buying only from reliable, upstanding illegal drug dealers."

Dawson didn't address his godfather's sarcasm, knowing it was justified. His recklessness was indefensible, so he didn't even attempt to excuse it. "Take the next right, then the hotel is up one block on the left."

When he'd relocated to Saint Nelda's, he'd taken only what he thought he would need at the beach and hadn't checked out of the hotel, a decision he was glad of now. He left Headly in the lobby while he went upstairs to shower and change clothes. He was back down in five minutes. In less than ten more, they were entering the courthouse.

Chapter 14

Court convened shortly after nine o'clock. The judge said she hoped everyone had enjoyed the holiday weekend, then asked Willard Strong's defense attorney if he was ready to cross-examine the witness.

Mike Gleason stood. "Ready, Your Honor."

Amelia was escorted in. As she took her seat in the witness box, she was reminded that she was still under oath.

Sitting beside Dawson in the gallery, Headly harrumphed. "What did you notice first, her intelligence, her modesty, or her self-control?"

Dawson didn't answer. Mike Gleason had already fired the first volley by asking Amelia if she had formed an opinion of Willard Strong even before meeting him.

"I don't understand what you mean."

"What I mean is this, Ms. Nolan. Your husband returns from war. He's obviously suffering from PTSD. What do you do? Encourage him? Nurture him? Exercise patient, loving kindness? No. You leave him and rob him of his sons."

Jackson was on his feet immediately. "Objection."

"In fact, Ms. Nolan, isn't it true that your first reaction to anything that diverted your husband's attention away from you, including and especially his friendship with Mr. Strong, was—"

"Your Honor—"

"Spiteful jealousy?"

The judge banged her gavel several times and sustained Jackson's objection.

Many more were to come. Despite them, Gleason tried his hardest to chisel away at Amelia's loyalty and integrity. *Merciless* and *selfish* were words he used to describe her efforts to get out of the marriage.

He grilled her about the two times she'd been with the defendant, at Hunter's birthday party, and then the day he had come to the townhouse looking for Jeremy. He tried to discredit her accounts of these incidents, to put a spin on them that would make her out to be a woman prone to either hysterics or malice.

It was an ill-chosen strategy. Amelia remained calm. She didn't get flustered, even as she stressed the immediate threat that Willard Strong had posed to her and her children.

Eventually the lawyer must have sensed that her composure was more persuasive than his theatrics and that all he was accomplishing was to irritate the jurors and make them more, not less, sympathetic toward her. After an hour of getting nowhere, he wrapped up rather quickly and told the judge that he had no further questions for her.

She stepped down, and the bailiff led her out through the same side exit as before. Dawson whispered, "Let's go," and together he and Headly left through the door at the back of the courtroom.

They intercepted Amelia in the corridor. Cell phone in hand, she was punching in a number when she noticed them walking toward her. Her hands dropped to her sides. "They let you out of jail?"

"You sound disappointed."

Headly stepped forward and extended his right hand. "Ms. Nolan. Gary Headly."

She shook his hand, but with a notable lack of warmth. "Are you his lawyer?"

"Second-generation family friend. Also his godfather. But please don't hold that against me." His friendly smile wasn't returned.

Dawson tilted his head toward the courtroom. "You did great in there."

"It wasn't a talent show."

"I know that," he shot back, matching her ire. "All I meant was that your reason was effective against his ranting."

"I'm just grateful to have it over and done with. Now, if you'll excuse me." She made to go around them, but Dawson sidestepped and blocked her path.

"Where are you going?"

"To pick up my children."

"Are they all right?"

"No. They're not all right." She pushed back her hair, hooking a strand behind her ear, which was a sure signal that the composure she'd exhibited in the courtroom was about to desert her. "They keep asking where I am and when I'm coming to get them. They sense that something is wrong, but they don't know what, and not knowing is frightening to them, especially to Hunter, who is remarkably perceptive for his age. At some point I must tell them that their adored nanny is dead." Her voice cracked, which she tried to cover by clearing her throat. "I have to go."

This time Dawson didn't physically try to stop her, but he spoke her name with appeal.

She turned back, but her body language remained hostile. "If you're still after a good story, why don't you write one about yourself?"

"I'm not interesting."

She gave a caustic laugh. "Oh, but you are. You're secretive, mercurial, a study in contradictions. Beyond that, you're…"

"What?"

"Just so I'm clear, those pills you were taking weren't doctor prescribed, were they?"

He wouldn't admit it out loud, not inside the courthouse. But he gave one shake of his head.

Softly, but bitterly, she said, "Right." As she turned to go, her cell phone, still in her hand, vibrated. She looked at the LED and answered immediately. "Deputy Tucker?" She listened for a moment, her face going pale. "Where did you find him?"

Dawson was beside her in an instant, whispering, "Dirk?"

She looked up at him and nodded. "I see," she said into the phone. "Well, please keep me—"

"Excuse me, Ms. Nolan." Headly took the phone from her hand and raised it to his ear. As he started walking purposefully toward the elevator bank, Dawson heard him say, "Deputy? My name is Gary Headly. I'm a friend of Ms. Nolan's. Also an agent with the FBI. We're on our way. Please be there to meet us."

Amelia felt disoriented from the shock waves that just kept coming.

She had spent a virtually sleepless night, alternately pacing the floor and tossing in bed, sometimes sobbing over what had happened to Stef, then trembling in fear that she had been the intended victim. Off and on she prayed fervently for the safety of her children, bargaining with God to preserve them.

And at any given time, she was despising Dawson Scott for his multiple deceptions and half truths and omissions, even as her body betrayed her with stirring recollections of his nakedness, his blatant arousal, the sheer carnality of his kisses, and her responses to them.

At dawn, she'd had to shelve all the emotional turmoil and pull herself together for her court appearance. Actually, it hadn't been as terrible as she had anticipated. Mike Gleason had raked her over the coals, but she, like everyone in the courtroom, realized that it was desperation, not conviction, that had fueled his fiery attack on her character. She almost felt sorry for Willard Strong, who'd had to sit by and watch his case being damaged rather than strengthened.

But it was over, and she didn't have to think about it anymore. She wanted to collect her children and return to the beach house, splash in the surf, feel the sea breeze in her hair, and taste the salt air. She wanted to laugh and romp in the sand with her sons. But even as she visualized such playful abandon, her heart felt anything but carefree.

The specter of Stef's murder clouded her happiness over having the trial behind her. She must figure out how to explain the nanny's sudden absence to her sons, how to tell them in a way that was honest but that wouldn't leave them with an acute fear of death.

She hoped that by now they would have forgotten about Dawson altogether so she wouldn't be required to talk about him.

But he had a way of turning up when she least expected him, as he had in the courthouse corridor. His night in lockup had left him looking hollow-eyed and underfed. But still incredibly good. At the sight of him, her body had quickened in spite of her determination to remain aloof.

The situation had turned truly bizarre when the older man, who'd introduced himself only moments earlier as Dawson's friend and godfather, seized her cell phone and started throwing his weight around.

Now, without being given sufficient time to process this staggering series of events, she was flanked by Dawson and Headly as they entered the building that was becoming uncomfortably familiar.

As instructed, Deputy Tucker was waiting for them in the lobby where she and Dawson had talked last night. His first words were for Dawson. "You should feel right at home."

Dawson ignored the dig and didn't respond.

Tucker acknowledged her with a polite nod, then turned to the older man. "You must be Agent Headly."

Headly shook hands with him and proffered his ID.

As the deputy handed it back, he said, "The sheriff's office is working the DeMarco case in conjunction with Savannah Metro PD. If we need additional help, we'll go to GBI. Why's the federal bureau horning in?"

"Not the Bureau. Me. And I'm here only as a friend of Ms. Nolan's."

"Huh." The deputy regarded Headly skeptically, then addressed her. "Reason I called you, I thought you'd want to know that Dirk's last name is Arneson. We've got him back there now talking to Wills."

"Where did you find him?" Dawson asked.

"Here in Savannah. One of those temporary apartments that rents by the week, but a nice one."

Amelia said, "Stef told me that he works on boats."

"Electronics systems," Tucker said. "Fancy, high-tech gizmos. We're running down his current employer to check that out."

Sizzling through her mind was the word *electronics*, which was closely related to Jeremy's field of expertise. She saw that Dawson had picked up on that, too. He had planted in her mind the possibly that Jeremy was alive and posing as Dirk. If that was true, just knowing that he was under the same roof was making it hard for her to breathe.

Headly asked, "Did he have identification?"

"Florida driver's license, an insurance card for a 2009 Ford pickup, one credit card, one gas card. All legit and nothing overdue."

"Has he been cooperative?" Dawson asked.

"More or less. Arresting deputies said he gave them some attitude. Probably because there's an outstanding warrant for him in Florida."

"For what?"

"Parking tickets."

"Parking tickets?"

The detective gave Dawson a look. "What? You were expecting something else?"

"Weren't you?"

Tucker merely shrugged. "When the deputies told him that parking violations weren't the issue, he claimed not to know why we wanted to talk to him."

"He denied knowing Stef?" Dawson asked.

"No. He admits to hooking up with her a couple of times, but swears that until the deputies told him, he didn't even know that she was dead."

"It's been on the news," Dawson said.

"We pointed that out to him. Still claims he hadn't heard anything about it. He also provided an alibi for the night she was killed. Says he and a couple other guys have been working on a yacht that's tied up over there on Saint Nelda's south dock. But the day Miss DeMarco was killed, they hadn't gone to the island, on account of the storm. They were afraid they wouldn't be able to get back, and they had nowhere to stay out there. He says that at the estimated time of her death he was playing poker with his friends in his apartment. He gave us their names. We're trying to track them down, but he tells us they went to New Orleans yesterday for another job."

"A poker night with suddenly absent friends?"

For once the deputy agreed with Dawson. "I hear ya. We talked to the captain of the ferry that goes out to Saint Nelda's. From the description we gave him, he knew right off who we were talking about. Says he's carried him back and forth many times.

"But he can't remember if Dirk was a passenger on the ferry on Sunday. Because of the weather, he had his hands full piloting the thing before they shut down ferry service altogether. He can't swear one way or another whether he hauled Dirk that day or not.

"And, too, the owners of that yacht are in North Carolina. Dirk had access to it, and he knows how to pilot it, even in bad weather, because he installed all the safety geegaws."

"You're saying he might not have needed the ferry to get himself to the island and back."

"Righto. We're looking at him hard," Tucker said. "He admits to being sort of a drifter, moving from job to job along the East Coast. His 'permanent address' is a post office box in Florida."

Amelia, Dawson, and Headly exchanged a look. Dawson came back to Tucker. "Does he have any kind of scar on his head?"

"Scar?"

"A patch of hair missing. Like he suffered a serious wound."

"The hell you talking about?"

Before Dawson was forced to explain the reason for his question, Headly intervened. "Ms. Nolan doesn't know Dirk by name, but she may recognize him by sight. If so, it could have some bearing on your investigation. Can she take a look?"

Tucker motioned them toward the door. "Any help we can get."

She said, "I don't want him to see me."

"He won't. He's in an interrogation room. There's a one-way window."

The four went through the door that opened into a large squad room furnished with work stations partitioned off from one another. A few personnel were about, doing various things. They all stopped what they were doing and watched them traverse the room. Tucker led them out of that room and into a sterile corridor. They made a left turn into another seemingly endless corridor identical to the first.

Tucker, in step with Amelia, asked, "Did Miss DeMarco seem to welcome his attentions?"

"From what I gather, yes," Amelia replied. "She always looked forward to meeting him."

"Did she ever tell you where their dates took place?"

"Mickey's is the only night spot on Saint Nelda's."

"For that reason, we started there. Neither Mickey nor any of his employees ever remember seeing her there with a guy fitting his description."

Amelia shook her head in puzzlement. "I don't know where else they would have spent time."

"Our guess: the yacht. It's snazzy. He probably wanted to impress her. But when we asked him if he'd ever entertained her on the boat, he denied it. I figure because he doesn't want to lose his job. If his alibi doesn't pan out, we'll get a search warrant." Absorbed in thought, he stroked his cheek. "Her purse was left behind with cash and credit cards. She wasn't sexually assaulted."

"You're wondering about Dirk's motive," Dawson said.

"His or whoever's. To have delivered a blow that vicious, the perp wanted her dead, no question. But we haven't determined why." He motioned them through another turn. "Almost there."

He went ahead of them and stopped in front of a door with a square window in the top half of it. In order to reach it, Amelia had to take what seemed the longest walk of her life. Then, for several moments after coming even with the door, she couldn't bring herself to look.

Finally, Tucker prompted her. "Ms. Nolan? Do you recognize him?"

She took a deep breath and turned her head toward the window.

He was sitting at a table, talking to Deputy Wills. Just as Stef had described him, he had a beard. Elaborate tattoos extended from his wrists up into the short sleeves of his shirt. His hair was buzzed so short, it showed up as more of a shadow over his scalp.

She fell back against the wall and expelled a gust of breath. “It’s not him.”

Dawson and Headly moved up to the window to take a look.

Tucker was completely flummoxed. “Not who? Who’d you expect?”

Feeling profoundly foolish, she stammered, “I thought… thought if I saw him, I might recognize him, but I’m sorry, I don’t. I’ve never seen this man before. I apologize for wasting your time, Deputy Tucker. But, please, keep me informed on the progress of your investigation. I want you to catch the person who killed Stef.”

“We’ll catch him.” He hitched his thumb toward the one-way window. “Maybe we already have. We combed Miss DeMarco’s clothing and your car for trace evidence. Collected some. Everything’s been sent to the lab.”

“A lot of people have ridden in my car. I have two little boys who track things in.”

“I’m aware of that. Would you be opposed to supplying us with hair, saliva swabs from the three of you?”

“Of course not.”

He looked at Dawson. “You, too.”

Dawson held up his hands in surrender. “Anytime.”

“May not be necessary,” Tucker said, somewhat grudgingly. “I’ll let you know.” Coming back to Amelia, he said, “I hate that you’re being put through this. Especially after, well, I know what you went through when… Your husband, and all. You testified at Strong’s trial this morning, right?”

“Yes. It’s over now.” She paused a beat. “I don’t think I can find my way out.”

He took the hint, and they retraced their path through the intersecting corridors. Tucker went as far as the lobby door with them. Holding it for her, he thanked her again for coming. With escape in mind, she walked toward the exit. Dawson stayed even with her. Headly followed.

Dawson's theory had been debunked. The possibility of Jeremy's still being alive was just so much hooey. Dirk Arneson wasn't a reincarnation of Jeremy. Jeremy hadn't seduced and then murdered Stef. He hadn't lifted photos from beneath her doormat or repaired a beach ball. He wasn't monitoring her every move. He wasn't a threat. *He was dead.* It was preposterous to think otherwise.

So why didn't she feel vastly relieved?

Because even though the matter should have been settled the instant she laid eyes on Dirk Arneson, it didn't *feel* settled. Instinctively she knew there was something she was missing. Something vital. She felt it simmering between the two men, who were talking to each other in a furtive manner that made her pause just as she was about to push open the exit door.

She caught Headly asking Dawson, "Disappointed or glad?"

"You tell me. They're your obsession."

Abruptly she turned to face them. They drew up short and ceased talking. She gave each of them a hard look, growing angrier with each loud tick of Dawson's saucer-sized wristwatch. Looking him square in the eye, she said, "It's time you explained to me just what the hell is going on."

Chapter 15

Dawson and Headly followed her in Headly's rental car to a restaurant that was preparing for its lunch trade. A line had already formed for people who desired tables, but they secured a small round one in the bar, which was separate from the restaurant. It was quieter and dimly lighted. The darkness provided a sense of privacy and fit their somber mood.

Amelia and Headly ordered iced tea. "Bourbon on the rocks," Dawson told the waitress, and when she moved away to fill the order, he read the censure in two pairs of eyes. "I went cold turkey on the pills. Cut me some slack."

No one said anything until after they'd been served. Headly stirred two packets of artificial sweetener into his tea. Dawson rattled the ice in his drink, then took a sip. He noticed that Amelia didn't touch her glass, but kept her hands clasped together in her lap as though holding on for dear life. In that small, quiet way, she was bracing herself. Dawson doubted the measure would be sufficient for what was coming.

Headly folded his forearms on the edge of the table and

leaned slightly toward her. "Have you ever heard of Golden Branch, Oregon?"

"No."

"The shootout there in '76?"

"Shootout?"

"Between several law enforcement agencies and members of a radical group called Rangers of Righteousness."

"I think I've heard of them. Domestic terrorists?"

"Precisely. We went to Golden Branch to serve several arrest warrants. It resulted in disaster. Seven people died. Two lawmen, five members of the group. The first one to die was a deputy US marshal. He was standing no more than a yard away from me when he took a bullet in the throat."

He gave her his account, which, for nearly forty years, he'd related officially and unofficially at different times to various people. Throughout the telling, Dawson watched Amelia's face, looking for hints as to what she was thinking.

When Headly paused to take a drink of tea, she looked at Dawson as though to ask, *Why is he telling me about this?* But when Headly continued, she returned her attention to him and didn't interrupt.

When he finished, she didn't say anything for several seconds. Finally, she cleared her throat. "The two . . . the couple who escaped . . . ?"

"Carl Wingert and Floral Stimel. The leaders. The worst of them. They were never apprehended."

"Even after all this time?"

"To my great disappointment and embarrassment," Headly said. "They're officially still wanted by the FBI, but . . ." He gave a rueful chuckle, "I'm not."

"What do you think happened to them?"

"God only knows. No crimes have been attributed to them for seventeen years, so they're presumed dead."

"What about the baby?"

Headly glanced at Dawson, who suddenly realized that his heart was beating as though he had never heard the story before and couldn't wait to learn the fate of the characters involved.

Headly reached over and placed his hand over Amelia's, which had begun to nervously fold and unfold the corners of the cocktail napkin beneath her sweating glass of tea. "During the investigation of your ex-husband's murder, his DNA was retrieved."

Her chest rose and fell with a shallow breath. Apprehension filled her eyes. She pulled her hand from beneath Headly's and clasped her two hands together. "I'm aware of that."

"What you don't know is that Jeremy's DNA sample was matched to one already in our data system," Headly said quietly. "It came from that house in Golden Branch."

She stared at him for several seconds and, after making a few unsuccessful attempts to speak, asked, "How is that possible?"

"We're still trying to piece together the 'how' of it. What we know is that the Wessons weren't his birth parents. We retrieved Flora Stimel's DNA in Golden Branch. She was Jeremy's mother."

"You can't be positive."

"DNA doesn't lie."

"Jeremy's samples were taken almost forty years apart, from different areas of the country."

Dawson knew the futility of arguing that the biology was in error. Amelia realized it, too.

Not quite as emphatically as before, she said, "Even if the outlaw couple were his parents, which I'm not accepting, Jeremy couldn't have known."

"I think the probability is high that he did," Headly said. "Did you ever see his birth certificate?"

"The original was destroyed in the house fire."

"That's right. He used a copied birth certificate to enlist in the Marines. Easily fudged. Did he ever mention to you that he'd been adopted?"

"No."

"Or give you any indication that he questioned his parentage?"

"Never. The subject of his parents—"

When she broke off, Headly asked gently, "What?"

She struggled with her answer and finally said, "Was closed to discussion."

"Doesn't that tell you something?"

It was plain to Dawson that she was warring against the logic of Headly's question. She fought back with the only argument left to her. "What difference does it make now who his parents were? It would be a different matter if he were still alive. But he isn't."

Headly didn't say anything either to back that assertion or to dispute it. Nor did Dawson. But their weighty silence spoke volumes.

Finally Headly said, "I'm going to try to find the connection—if there was one—between the Wessons and Carl and Flora. But it's been decades. The trail has long since gone cold. According to the reports I've read about that fire, the Wessons' whole life history, fictional or true, went up in flames. And I'm running out of time. In a couple of weeks, I'll be officially retired."

"Then why not just let it go?"

He glanced at Dawson. "You're not the first person to ask me." He took several moments to carefully consider his answer. "I was resigned to living with my failure to capture Carl and Flora. Then I learned about their son, Jeremy. It's a new development in a cold case. As a law enforcement officer, I can't ignore that."

"Even though he's dead."

"A murder without a body?" He frowned. "That's a gaping hole, Amelia. A giant uncertainty that I can't turn my back on. This story began for me that day in Oregon. I can't leave it with an open ending like that."

"The story." She turned to Dawson. "That explains your interest. You must've been dying to know what I knew about Jeremy's history, which makes the tale even more intriguing, doesn't it? Now I understand why you asked all those questions about his upbringing, his parents."

"I was hoping your answers would confirm a blood relationship with the Wessons."

"Or were you trying to establish that he was Carl and Flora's love child?"

"I don't want it to be true, either."

"Of course you do! It adds such drama to your story."

"That's not—"

"All that playtime spent with Hunter and Grant. Were you looking closely for signs of a criminal bent?"

"For God's sake!"

"And me. No wonder you've been so . . . attentive."

"Amelia—"

Before he could say anything else, she held up both hands, palms out. "I've had it. I won't listen to any more." She stood up. "The *story* ended for me this morning after my court appearance. That gothic myth about Dirk . . ." She gestured with impatience. "I feel like a fool for giving it one iota of credence. Jeremy's heritage, whatever it was, is irrelevant. He's dead. Leave me out of your ghost chasing and get the hell out of my life." She strode away and through the exit door.

Headly turned to Dawson. "Are you just going to sit there? Why aren't you going after her?"

"Because I'm getting the hell out of her life."

"But—"

"And I'm not going to discuss my reasons with you." He figured Headly already knew them anyway. "You heard the lady. She wants to be left out of it, and, frankly, so do I." He pushed his chair back. Before walking away, he said, "I'll call a taxi. Thanks for the drink."

Since her car was still impounded—and, under the circumstances, she never wanted it back—Amelia was driving her second car, an older model that had become hers upon her father's death. Ordinarily, she derived a sense of comfort from being behind the steering wheel that had known his touch. But as she pulled out of the restaurant parking lot, her anger didn't allow for any additional emotions.

After the upheavals of the morning, she felt like she'd been put through a shredder and knew that she wasn't up to being "mommy." She placed a brief call to Molly Metcalf, George's kindhearted wife, and asked if the boys could stay a while longer. "I need to go to Saint Nelda's and close up the house. I'll get it done a lot faster if they're not underfoot. And I'm really not up to answering questions about Stef yet. I should be back around nightfall."

Having been reassured that they were happily playing with the Metcalfs' grandsons, she took the ferry over to the island. As she passed Mickey's, she noticed that the yellow crime-scene tape was still stretched around the parking lot behind the building. The sight made her choke back a sob.

Bernie was puttering around the back of his house and, seeing her approach, waved. She pulled over and lowered the driver's-side window. He closed the lid of his car trunk and hobbled over. "You're just in time to see me off."

"For good?"

"I'm driving as far as Charleston this afternoon. Eat a dinner of shrimp and grits. Then I'll get an early start tomorrow. I see the boys aren't with you. I hate to leave without saying goodbye."

"I hate that, too. I had planned to bring them back for the remainder of the week, but I've changed my mind. I haven't told them about Stef. Until I do, I thought I should keep them away from the beach, where they're sure to wonder about her sudden absence."

"Probably for the best. I saw two deputies tromping into your house earlier."

"Deputy Tucker called and asked if they could look through Stef's room, see if anything would point them to the person who killed her." She told him about Dirk Arneson. "He owns up to knowing Stef, but claims to have an alibi."

"Dawson Scott?"

"He spent last night in jail, but was released this morning. Tucker hasn't ruled him out. Just to be obtuse, I think. They don't like each other."

"I don't think he ever laid a hand on Stef."

"Neither do I," she said, meaning it.

He hesitated, then asked, "What about the two of you?"

"There's no such thing, Bernie."

Leaving that subject, she told him that she'd offered to relieve Stef's parents of one unpleasant task. "I told them I would pack up her things, then I'll close up the house. That job always makes me sad, especially when I don't know when I'll be back. Today will be particularly unhappy."

"Want me to stay and keep you company? I could wait till morning to leave."

She glanced toward her house. It looked terribly empty, and for half a second she was tempted to accept his offer. "No, thanks. You don't want to miss your shrimp and grits." She reached across the car's interior and patted his age-speckled hand resting in the open window. "Be careful on the road."

"Did I give you my e-mail address?"

"Stef—" She said the name automatically, and it was a cruel reminder. "She jotted it down for me."

"Stay in touch. Tell Hunter and Grant I'll see them next summer."

"The kite will be here."

After saying a final good-bye, she drove the remainder of the distance to her house and went in through the back door. The power had been restored, but that didn't dispel the sadness she felt as she moved through the silent rooms. Not since her first visit to the house after her father's death had she felt this forlorn.

Sandy footprints had been left on the stairs by the deputies who had searched Stef's room. Her bedroom was no longer as neat as before. Articles had been left out, rearranged.

For five minutes, Amelia sat on the bed and cried for her young friend. Then, forcing herself to get to the unwelcome chore, she neatly folded all Stef's clothing into her two suitcases. She packed all her personal belongings, too, leaving it to her parents to determine what they wanted to keep. When everything had been zipped into the suitcases, she carried them down to her car and stowed them in the trunk.

Bernie's car was no longer there. She was completely alone, and she felt it.

The loneliness became a pressure inside her chest as she began shutting down the house for the season. A service would come later to do the deep cleaning, but she emptied the refrigerator and pantry of all perishables, stripped the beds, and gathered the laundry from the various hampers into one big bundle and took it down to the utility room.

It was a familiar routine, which she'd performed dozens of times. Today, the project left her severely depressed. Tears threatened as she went from room to room one last time, checking for lights left on, for ceiling fans still circulating, for dripping faucets, and unlocked windows.

Conversations with Stef, the boys' laughter, echoed in her memory.

She went into her bedroom for a final inspection to see if she was leaving anything behind. As she went to pull down the window shades, unable to stop herself, she looked across the expanse of beach toward the neighboring house.

She knew which of the upstairs windows were in Dawson's bedroom. He'd watched her through those windows. Disturbingly, her mind lingered less on the invasion of privacy than it did on the kiss he and she had shared inside that bedroom, on the bed, among twisted sheets redolent with his scent.

As much to block out that erotic memory as to block the view, she quickly pulled down the shades.

She made it to the bottom of the stairs before realizing that she'd left her laptop on the desk in the room that she used as an office. Leaving her handbag, she quickly retraced her way back up to the second floor.

The sun was setting, shadows were deep, as she entered the room and went over to the desk. There she hesitated, and, before she could talk herself out of it, pulled out the chair, sat down, and booted up the computer. All the while trying to talk herself out of it, she accessed the Internet and ran a search for Carl Wingert.

In a matter of keystrokes, she was on a website for the FBI's Most Wanted, looking into the face of the man who had been a fugitive from justice for decades, searching his glowering features for any resemblance to the man she had loved and married, then had grown to fear.

There wasn't one. Between the photograph on the monitor and Jeremy, she didn't detect a single similarity. But maybe she wasn't seeing it because she didn't want to. Was desperation making her blind to it?

She rejected the thought that Jeremy, the father of her children, was the son of criminals. Murderers. It simply couldn't be.

Yet FBI Agent Headly, certainly no fool, was convinced, and had DNA evidence backing him up.

Jeremy had manifested a violent streak.

Burying her face in her heads, she expelled a long breath, carrying on it a fearful prayer, "Dear God, please no."

Harriet was beside herself with excitement. "He fed them to *dogs*?"

"Willard claims his wife was dead when he found her." Dawson, seated on the foot of the bed in his hotel room, pinched the bridge of his nose till it made his eyes water. Only by inflicting physical pain could he make the agony of this conversation tolerable by comparison. "She died of a close-range shotgun blast to the chest."

"Willard's shotgun. You said his fingerprints were the only ones on it."

"Yeah, but he swore under oath that he didn't shoot her."

"What's his version?"

"On the witness stand, he admitted that he'd been drinking all day while he searched in and around Savannah for the cheating lovers. Eventually he gave up and drove out to this place in the woods where he cages and trains his fighting pit bulls. He claims he was so drunk he couldn't even get out of his pickup before passing out.

"When he came to, it was hours later, after midnight. He noticed immediately that his shotgun was missing from the cab of his truck. He climbed out, stumbled around in the dark, trying to figure out which end was up.

"He made it into the shack—his crash pad out there—and found a flashlight. He said the dogs were going nuts, and that's a quote. So he staggered over to the pens, shined his light around, and inside one of cages was Darlene. What was left of her. His shotgun was propped up against the outside of the cage."

"He expects the jury to believe that?"

"I don't know what he expects. That's what he testified. In doing so, he admitted to committing several felonies by participating in dogfights."

"What did he have to say about Jeremy Wesson?"

"Doesn't have a clue what happened to him. Evidence that he

met the same fate as Darlene is inconclusive. A patch of hairy scalp in the stomach of one dog. Blood in the pen."

"That's not conclusive?"

"When the ME testified, that's the word he used. The defense attorney picked up on it and made it his mantra."

"Okay. Go on."

"Willard saw Darlene's remains, panicked, bolted. It took police a couple of days to track him down, and only then after they got an anonymous tip about his possible whereabouts. In that amount of time, the digestive process—"

"Jeremy was doggie poop by then."

Dawson was thinking why, if the dogs had made a meal of Jeremy, they would have been ravenous for Darlene. But he didn't address that incongruity. Vampira was lapping up the grisly elements of the story.

He continued. "Willard swears he never saw Jeremy. His attorney tried to plant in the minds of the jurors that it was Jeremy who took the shotgun from Willard's pickup while Willard was unconscious, killed Darlene, pushed her body into the dog pen, then hightailed it into the marsh, never to be seen again. Possibly it was he who called in the tip."

"His wife's lover framed poor Willard for her murder."

"The lawyer didn't use those words, but that's essentially the seed of reasonable doubt he tried to sow."

"Does he have a snowball's chance in hell of being acquitted?"

"Juries sometimes pull surprises."

Dawson was past ready to wrap up this obligatory call. The less interaction he had with Harriet, the happier he was. Beyond that, he was whipped. Straight from that disastrous meeting with Headly and Amelia, he'd gone to the courthouse. Having invested days in Willard Strong's trial, he needed to come away with something to show for his time and expenses or there would be hell to pay with Harriet when he got back to DC.

When court was adjourned, he'd been tempted to cruise River Street until he found someone of Ray Dale's ilk, who could replace the stash of pills he'd flushed away. He resisted the temptation. Deputies Tucker and Wills would love nothing better than to get another crack at him, and he hadn't been completely cleared of suspicion of murder.

Besides, taking prescription drugs bought on the street was stupid, self-destructive behavior. He hadn't needed Headly or Amelia pointing that out to him.

So he'd returned to the hotel room and, with no more fortification than a shot of whiskey, finally responded to the dozens of voice mails Harriet had left for him. The first sixty seconds of their conversation had been a blistering diatribe about his unreliability. Was it true that he'd been questioned by police about a young woman's murder? Someone in the magazine office had seen it on the Internet. She wouldn't have believed it had she not linked to the story and read it for herself.

Finally cutting in, he threatened to hang up if she didn't shut up. "Keep talking to me like that, and I walk, Harriet, and I mean it."

"Like I fucking care."

"Fine. You can explain to your new boss why your best staff writer sold his sensational story to another magazine."

He'd hooked her with that, and she had calmed down enough to listen to his glossed-over, abbreviated explanation about his night in lockup and how it had come about. "I was questioned along with everybody else who was seen with the victim that day." Which wasn't quite true, but it wasn't wholly false. "Worse thing about it, I didn't get to brush my teeth till this morning."

He'd then outlined the story he wanted to write.

She said now, "I have to hand it to you, I thought you were blowing smoke. This is a great story, especially since Jeremy Wesson was a decorated war veteran."

"That's the angle. War hero meets a bad end back home."

"Good, good. Go with that. What's Willard Strong like?"

"Mean-looking. Hulking."

She picked up on his qualifying tone of voice. "But what?"

"I don't know," he said thoughtfully. "He also seems thick-skulled. This was a complex crime."

"You don't think he's capable of committing it?"

"Capable of shooting the cheating pair with a shotgun, yes. But then I think his instinct would be to run like hell and keep running until he was caught. To hang around and try to destroy the evidence, especially in such a bizarre fashion... That strikes a sour note with me. The overkill seems out of character, too well planned. I think—"

"That's your problem, Dawson. You think too much. Analyze too much. Not every story has to be about the subject's goddamn psyche, originating when the cell divided. Just write the story as though it's a crime piece. For once, don't trowel on the psychological bull crap. Make it titillating, make it gory, make it sentimental from the war-hero angle. Readers will eat it up. No pun intended."

"Ha-ha. I get it."

"Can you finagle an interview with him?"

"With Willard? Not until after the trial, if then."

"What about Amelia Nolan?"

A shaft of desire and pain went straight through him. "I gave it a shot. She slammed the door."

"Figuratively or literally?"

"Doesn't matter. She's not talking. Especially now that she's dealing with another tragedy."

"The nanny's murder. Hmm. The dual tragedies could be a new angle. Try again. Use your charm."

"Don't hold your breath. Right now, I'm beat. I'm gonna grab a shower, a burger, and a ball game on TV. If you want more of the gruesome details, you'll have to read them in my story, like everybody else."

Dawson clicked off, put his phone on vibrate, then fell back onto the bed and laid a forearm across his eyes. He hadn't lied about being exhausted. He needed sleep, but he'd sworn off antianxiety pills and sleeping meds. Whiskey had lost its dulling power, providing only a temporary buzz followed by a cottony head and queasy stomach.

Which left him to his own devices to find tranquility. By God, he'd get there by sheer force of will.

But when he closed his eyes and tried to focus only on clouds drifting across snowy mountain peaks and brooks rippling through primeval forests, his mind stayed stubbornly fixed on the woman who had walked out of his life earlier today.

The woman he wanted like hell, but couldn't have.

Headly had asked him why he didn't go after her. Wasn't the answer clear enough? She hadn't wanted him to. She'd "had it." He was an opportunist, a con artist, working the inside track, even baiting her children, to get the goods. That was her opinion of Dawson Scott.

But even if he'd been straightforward with her from the start, had come clean and told her everything, won her confidence and possibly even her affection, he still would have let her walk away today. He was no martyr, but he wasn't a completely selfish bastard, either. The last thing Amelia Nolan needed was another man in her life who woke up every night screaming.

He was struggling with that humiliating memory when he felt his phone vibrate. He picked it up and, seeing Headly's name, swore. He started not to answer, but that would only delay the inevitable. He clicked on. "I'm about to get in the shower. Can I get back to you?"

"No. This is urgent."

"You sound out of breath."

"I am."

"What have you been doing?"

"Yapping at their heels."

"Whose heels?"

"Sheriff's office, Savannah Metro, finally got Knutz involved. Good thing I kept yapping."

"If your blood pressure goes up, Eva will—"

"They lifted a fingerprint off the rain slicker."

Dawson bit back the rest of what he was about to say.

"It matched so well I got a hard-on. Guess whose print."

"Jeremy Wesson's."

"Skip the shower and get over here."

Chapter 16

Against her will or reason, Amelia was captivated by Carl Wingert's Wanted poster.

In 1970 he had launched himself from the rank of petty crook and troublemaker to notorious outlaw by boldly robbing a federal bank in Kansas City. He did it in broad daylight on a busy Friday afternoon. He didn't wear a mask or disguise of any kind, as though he'd wanted to be recognized and given credit for the crime, which included the execution-style shootings of the bank president, the teller who'd emptied her drawer for him, then ill-advisedly set off an alarm, a guard who made a valiant attempt to thwart him, and a city policeman, who, by sheer happenstance, had been waiting in line to deposit his paycheck.

Security cameras had captured numerous photographs of Carl that day because he'd made no attempt to avoid them. The time-lapse photos had been enlarged, enhanced, and were the only images of the criminal that existed except for class pictures, which chronicled a public-school boy's transformation from a scowling child into a thug who looked progressively angrier with each advancing grade. He dropped out after his sophomore year.

The best of these exclusive pictures of Carl as an adult had been selected for his Wanted poster, and as Amelia studied them, she asked herself repeatedly if this man was, as Gary Headly claimed, her sons' grandfather?

That possibility alone was upsetting. But it was especially disturbing to think that Jeremy might have known. If he had, had he kept it a secret because he was ashamed of his heritage and wanted to protect her and his children from disgrace? Or had the reason for his secrecy been more sinister? It was a chilling possibility.

Suddenly she became aware that the room had grown dark except for the laptop's screen. She hadn't meant to stay this late. But as she made to push back the desk chair, her motion was arrested by a noise coming from downstairs.

She knew every nook and cranny of the house, each stair tread that groaned beneath someone's weight, every hinge that squeaked unless oiled regularly, which drawers stuck when the humidity was especially high.

Only someone that intimately familiar with the house would recognize the scraping sound the kitchen door made against the floor when it was pushed open.

That's what she'd heard. And then silence.

That, even more than the sound of the door being opened, caused her heart to lurch. Quickly she closed her laptop, pitching the room, indeed the whole house, into total darkness.

"Remember, just act normal."

"Got it."

"You're just coming back to get your stuff from the beach house before you leave for home. If he's out there somewhere watching her, that's what he needs to think."

"Got it."

"We don't want him—"

"Goddammit!" Dawson snapped. "I said I've got it."

Headly had been giving him instructions since they'd left the ferry dock. Dawson was driving Headly's rental car at an unsafe speed. Headly was hunkered down out of sight in the backseat.

Behind them were two sheriff's units and an unmarked car carrying four FBI agents from the Savannah office, including Cecil Knutz. All were driving without headlights, keeping back so that it appeared that Dawson's car was the only one on the road.

"Until Amelia is safe, the last thing we want—"

"Is to tip him that the cavalry is out of sight behind the hill," Dawson said, quoting Headly, who'd used the analogy earlier when he was talking through the plan with the swiftly assembled team as they crossed the sound to Saint Nelda's.

"If he realizes we're on to him, he'll have nothing to lose by killing her, if only so he can go out in a blaze of glory."

"If he hurts her, I'll personally see to it that he does. I'll blow his fucking head off."

"See, that's what I'm talking about. You're a writer, not a law officer."

"A wordsmith."

"What?"

"That's what that asshole Tucker called me." *You're gonna let this pill-popping wordsmith do police work?* Dawson's impulse had been to launch himself at the deputy and demonstrate just how dangerous a wordsmith could be when provoked, but he'd let the insult slide. The personal satisfaction he would have derived from a one-on-one with the guy wasn't worth the precious time it would have cost.

Already an hour had elapsed since Headly had called him and told him about the fingerprint. During that agonizing sixty minutes, no one had been able to reach Amelia. She hadn't answered either her cell phone or the landline at her Savannah apartment.

It had been Dawson's idea to contact George Metcalf, who confirmed that the children were still with him and his wife. Amelia had told them she would be spending the afternoon at her beach house, and that her chores there might extend into the evening. There wasn't a landline in the house on Saint Nelda's.

The deputy who'd been guarding the crime scene in Mickey's parking lot had been pulled off the detail and returned to the mainland when his shift was over, and *someone* had deemed it unnecessary for a replacement to be sent. No one claimed responsibility for that regrettable decision, which had left no one available to drive out to Amelia's house, check on her safety, warn her of the possible danger, and remain with her until reinforcements could arrive.

"Tucker's a blowhard," Headly said now from the backseat. "Forget him. But remember that he and the others are trained law enforcement officers. You're not. The only reason you're in on this is because you can reconnoiter for us without setting off Jeremy's alarm bells. If he's even in the vicinity. He could be in Canada by now."

"Do you think he's in Canada?"

Headly didn't respond. If he thought that, they wouldn't be racing to alert Amelia of the latest development.

"Bernie's house looks deserted," Dawson told him as he blasted past it. "Jesus, she's been out here all by herself. There's a car at her house, but not a single light on. And she hasn't answered her phone."

"Drive on past."

"Fuck that."

He braked and got out of the car, practically in one motion. Leaving Headly cussing a blue streak, he ran toward the back door of Amelia's house. It was unlocked. He eased it open and paused to listen.

The silence was profound and portentous. If everything was okay, the lights would be on and there would be sounds of activity.

He glanced around to see that Headly was coming up behind him, talking softly into his cell phone, describing the situation to the personnel in the vehicles behind them.

Dawson, realizing that their covertness was about to be compromised anyway, banged into Amelia's kitchen, hit the light switch, and shouted her name. From the kitchen he charged into the formal dining room, from which he could see the living area, the front door, and the porch beyond. Nothing. Moving swiftly, he rushed toward the stairs and tripped over her handbag on the bottom step.

His gaze tracked up. She was standing at the top of the staircase, poised and tense, gripping the banister. Then, upon recognizing him, she sank down onto the top step.

He took the stairs two at a time. "Are you all right?"

She whispered yes, but clearly she wasn't. She was trembling and looking beyond his shoulder with dismay, watching as her house filled up with armed men.

Her eyes were wide with shock and bewilderment when they reconnected with Dawson's. He placed his hands on her shoulders. "Jeremy's fingerprint was found on the rain slicker."

She nodded her head slowly, as though resigned to acknowledging what she had so persistently denied. Then she gripped his arms. "The boys?"

"Safe. Guards have been posted around the Metcalfs' house."

"They'll be frightened."

"They won't know. The Metcalfs have been informed, but Headly gave the order for the officers to remain invisible. No marked cars, or light bars, nothing like that."

"This is all so..." It seemed she couldn't find a word that adequately described the circumstances. With her misery apparent, she said, "I didn't want to believe it. Any of it. But it's all true, isn't it?" Tears spilled over her lower eyelids.

Dawson placed his hand on the back of her head and tucked it between his neck and shoulder. Sliding his fingers up through her hair, he whispered into it, "If I could make it untrue, I would."

Deputies were dispatched to patrol the beach and surrounding area on foot.

Tucker and Wills, the FBI agents, Amelia, Headly, and Dawson gathered in Amelia's living room. To bring everyone up to speed, Headly summarized Carl and Flora's criminal career and disclosed Jeremy's relationship to them. He shared the theory that Jeremy had killed Stef, mistaking her for Amelia.

He explained to Tucker why they'd been interested in seeing Dirk Arneson. "We thought perhaps Jeremy had assumed another identity and was using the girl to get information on Amelia and his sons."

"Instead of doing that song and dance, why didn't you just tell me?"

Headly threw him a bone. "In hindsight, I probably should have." Tucker looked mollified.

Cecil Knutz was as agreeable a guy as Headly had described him. He was a few years younger than Headly, but wore the aging process more visibly. He was paunchy and balding, but savvy and senior enough to be the RANC.

Dawson admired his gentle and respectful attitude toward Amelia as he questioned her. She gave him an overview of her marriage and divorce, but, unfortunately, had nothing new or enlightening to tell him.

"To me, Jeremy died more than a year ago. If he's alive, I have no idea where he's been or where he is. Although, lately, I've felt a *presence*, like someone was watching me. I blamed my uneasiness on Willard Strong's trial and having to talk openly about things I'd rather forget."

She told the group about the beach ball mystery and about a set of photographs of her and the children that had disappeared without explanation. "A friend delivered them when no one was at home, but they weren't where they'd been left." Dawson appreciated that she didn't cite him as the "friend."

She also told them about a boat she'd noticed. "It remained anchored offshore for several days. Other than that, nothing's been out of the ordinary." But as she said that, she'd glanced at Dawson.

The team debated whether she and her sons should be moved into a safe house until Jeremy was captured. Headly nixed the idea. "At this point, he thinks he's in the clear. If she's placed in protective custody, we'd just as well go on loudspeakers throughout the Deep South and tell Jeremy that we're on to him."

Tucker said, "All this is assuming he is alive. That hasn't been firmly established."

"What do you need to firmly establish it?" Dawson demanded.

"Something more than a latent fingerprint lifted from a wet raincoat. It could have been there for years."

"Unlikely," one of the FBI agents said. "On a nonporous surface like that? Most likely it would have been wiped off or badly smudged by now."

"It hasn't been digitally enhanced yet," Tucker argued. "I'm not going to accept with one-hundred-percent certainty that Wesson is alive until—"

"He whacks Amelia like he did her nanny?" Dawson said.

"Why are you so eager for me to buy into this? So I won't arrest *you*?"

Deputy Wills stepped in. "Considering all the unexplained things that have happened to Ms. Nolan lately, plus the fingerprint, which I grant needs further analysis," he said to his partner, "plus the fact that we never located Jeremy Wesson's body, I think we should proceed as though he is alive.

"If we err on the side of caution, the worst that can happen is that we'll look like a bunch of bozos for supposing even for a moment that a dead man killed Miss DeMarco. But the alternative, which is to ignore the possibility, comes with considerably more risks to Ms. Nolan and her children."

Even Tucker agreed that taking safety precautions was warranted.

Headly submitted a plan. "Actually this house is as easy to guard as any. This is the tip of the island. On an open stretch of beach there aren't that many good hiding places. Jeremy can't get here by water—either the sound or the ocean—that we won't see. He can't drive on without coming over on the ferry."

"And he can't walk on water, even though he can rise from the dead." Wills's joke eased lingering tension, but his statement was a further indication that he believed their quarry was Jeremy Wesson, alive and well.

Before they dispersed, Tucker got in one last potshot. He said to Dawson, "If I need you, do I look for you here first?"

The question and its embarrassing implication toward Amelia caused everyone else to go still and silent. Dawson saw red and wanted to knock the deputy on his fat ass. But Headly, sensing his fury, clamped a hand on his forearm and said blandly, "If you need to locate Dawson, you can always go through me."

Everyone left except for the deputies who were to guard the house. Personnel from the sheriff's office in Savannah were dispatched to pick up Hunter and Grant and bring them to the island. Amelia requested that the Metcalfs be allowed to accompany them. "They'll be afraid of strangers."

They were delivered about an hour later by two deputies, one a young woman. The Metcalfs were mild-mannered people, who seemed a bit overawed to find themselves in such a situation.

The boys knew no such restraint. After the two-day separation from their mother, they were excited to see her, talking over each other to gain her attention. Dawson stood back and watched as she hugged them tightly, kissing their faces when they let her, running her hands over them as though to reassure herself that they were well and safe.

The kids' joy over finding Dawson there was almost as exuberant. Amelia introduced him to the Metcalfs by name only. They probably took him for a plainclothes policeman assigned to guard the family. In any case, they hadn't questioned his staying behind when they and the two deputies left.

The boys then conducted him on a tour of the house that included everything from their Playstation to the empty bowl where their goldfish had met his demise at the beginning of the summer.

The tour concluded in their bedroom, where Amelia announced that it was time for bed. They put up an argument. A compromise was reached only after Dawson agreed to read them their bedtime story.

That had been nearly an hour ago. It had taken him that long to get them settled. Now as he entered the kitchen, he said to Amelia, "Ah, alone at last."

Her smile was grim. "Except for all the guards outside."

"A necessary evil."

"The boys finally went to sleep?"

"Took two stories."

"Thanks for doing that."

"My pleasure."

"Did they ask why Stef isn't here?"

"Grant mentioned her in passing, but nothing more was said."

"I'm surprised they're not more curious."

"They're kids." He shrugged philosophically. "To them, two days is a long time. They've been distracted."

"By you being here."

"I filled a gap."

"And then some."

As she plugged in an electric kettle, she gave him a sidelong glance, possibly noting how ill at ease he felt in the homey kitchen. There was a bear-shaped cookie jar on the counter. The boys' artwork was stuck to the refrigerator door with Disney-character magnets. The cookbooks lined up on the open shelf looked well used, not for show.

By comparison, his apartment's galley was sterile.

She motioned him toward the dining table. "Have a seat. I cleared out the pantry today, but I found tea bags and cocoa mix in a canister. That's all I have to offer."

"No apology necessary. My cupboard in Alexandria stays as bare as Old Mother Hubbard's."

"You know nursery rhymes?"

"My mom recited them all the time. I remember that one."

"Do your parents live in Virginia?"

He told her about the fatal accident. "You know parents, always telling you to be careful anytime you get the behind the wheel. More than anything, mine worried about me being in a car wreck. Which turned out to be ironic, since that's what killed them. They were driving home from a movie, on a weeknight, on a street they'd driven a million times. The driver of an oncoming car swerved to miss a squirrel crossing the street, lost control, hit them head-on."

"I'm sorry," she said softly.

"The driver of the other car walked away from it. Devastated, of course. The Headlys took the loss of my parents almost as hard as I did. Headly and my dad had been friends since grade school."

"So it wasn't just a figure of speech. He really is your godfather?"

"He is. He held me at my baptism, which he often says didn't take."

She gave a soft laugh. "You're obviously very close."

"He's a pain in the ass."

"My dad could be one, too, but his admonitions usually proved to be wise."

Seeing the recurring sadness creep over her, he said, "Hey," and reached behind him for the jacket he'd hung on the back of the stool earlier. He pulled a Hershey's bar from the pocket and produced it with a flourish. "I got this out of the minibar in my hotel room earlier today. Forgot about it till now. Want to flip for it?"

"No thanks. I'm not hungry."

"When did you last eat?" When she had to stop and think about it, he said, "That's what I thought. This is good energy. I'll split it with you."

The kettle began to whistle. He chose cocoa over tea. When she set it down in front of him, she said, "I'm sorry I don't have anything stronger. Not even a bottle of wine."

"Doesn't matter. You jinxed it for me."

"Drinking?"

He tilted his head up and met her eyes. "You told me the booze and pills wouldn't help my problem. After that, they stopped working for me."

"I don't think it was anything I said. You came to your senses."

"Maybe. Or maybe the night spent in jail turned me around. But don't expect me to send Tucker a thank-you bouquet."

"What is it between you two?"

"He hated me on sight. Don't know why."

"You're a head and a half taller."

"Ohhh. Is that it?" Seriously, he added, "I wanted to deck him for embarrassing you."

"Doesn't matter. Around the sheriff's office I'm sure it's well known by now that we were together in your house at dawn when they notified me about Stef."

She went back to the counter for her tea, then sat down across from him. He unwrapped the candy bar, broke it in two, and passed a half to her.

She nibbled at it as she thoughtfully regarded him. "Dawson, what are you doing here?"

"Having some cocoa."

She gave him a look.

Unsure how to answer, he rolled his shoulders uncomfortably. Finally, in a quiet voice, he asked, "Do you want me to go?"

She dunked her tea bag in the hot water several times, but left it steeping. "We've known each other for less than a week. I'm in a crisis situation. I don't get why you're hanging around, or why..." She looked at him wryly. "Or why I'm comfortable with it."

"Beats the hell out of me, too." He could tell that his response surprised her. "Believe me, I didn't plan on this."

"This...?"

"You, Hunter and Grant, bedtime stories." He glanced toward the smiling-bear face on the cookie jar. "It's a far cry from a war zone, but damn near as nerve-racking for a man like me."

"Then why are you here?"

Because it was too late now for him to pull back without feeling that he was abandoning them. He should have kept them at arm's length. He hadn't. He was sunk in deep, good and involved, and there was no backing out without looking like a heel. Besides, he didn't want to leave them. He couldn't explain it to her, because he had no explanation for it himself. Except that he wanted her.

There was that. But to become romantically involved would bugger up both their lives. Hers was already in upheaval, and his was a mess. It was neither wise nor honorable even to fantasize about making love to her.

But he did. Constantly.

He cleared his throat. "You need a friend right now. It's as simple as that." He was lying, because it wasn't simple at all.

She studied him for several seconds, then lowered her gaze. "I need a friend, and you need a story."

"That's not why I'm here."

"Isn't it?"

"No. Hell, no." When she raised her head, he saw the misgiving still in her eyes. "Amelia, my objectivity took a nosedive the instant I met you. You know it."

After a moment of shared staring, she busied herself with removing the tea bag from the mug and taking a sip. Then she observed him polishing off his portion of the candy bar and washing it down with a sip of cocoa. "That's a lot of chocolate. Won't the caffeine keep you awake?"

"If I'm lucky. You know what happens when I sleep."

The reminder of his nightmare brought back memories of what had come after: the kiss. It wavered there between them, as real as the steam rising from their beverage mugs. The atmosphere in the kitchen seemed to pressurize, but they didn't look away from each other.

He said, "I never properly thanked you for being there when I came out of the nightmare."

She made a dismissive movement that was so slight, anyone not eating her up with his eyes would have missed it.

He wanted to tell her how many times since then he had thought about that kiss and how badly he wanted to repeat it, how much he wanted to touch her again, *now*. To hold her, stroke her soft skin, feel her breath against his face, have her naked and warm and shifting beneath him, to be inside her.

If she knew the prurient drift of his thoughts and how difficult it was for him not to act on them, she wouldn't be nearly so comfortable sharing tea and cocoa. She'd doubt that he was here only as a friend. But he couldn't help thinking about it and wishing it were otherwise. He felt it only fair that she know that.

"If I could have you after every nightmare, I'd have ten a night."

They were still staring into each other's eyes when his cell phone jangled, which was probably just as well, since his resolve not to touch her again had all but evaporated.

Dawson answered his phone on speaker. "I'm coming in," Headly said. "Don't shoot." Without replying, Dawson clicked off. "That reminds me," he said to her, "maybe you should rethink carrying the pepper spray at all times. And, for God's sake, your phone."

"Not having my phone was a terrible oversight. I didn't hear your calls. It and the pepper spray were in my handbag at the bottom of the stairs. But if I'd had the spray, you might have got it in the face. Why didn't you identify yourself immediately?"

"In case Jeremy was in here with you, Headly didn't want to tip him off to our presence."

She sighed. "I almost wish it had played out that way."

"No," he said emphatically. "You don't."

"At least it would be over now."

"True. But you would probably be dead."

Diary of Flora Stimel—April 16, 1984

We killed three people yesterday. Last night we celebrated to the point that everybody except me is still unconscious.

It was a great day for us, not only because the robbery was successful (over $60,000), but it also took place on income tax day. Which was symbolic. That was Carl's way of thumbing his nose at the federal government.

I don't feel so bad about the two guys guarding the armored truck. They were careless and—when you think about it—let down the people they work for. As Carl said, if they'd been doing their job the way they should have been, they'd be alive, the money would still be there, and we'd be the ones dead. None of us got hurt, except that I broke a fingernail when I pushed our hostage into the back of the van.

I don't know her name yet. The news people said it won't be released until her next of kin is notified.

She was Latino. Her hair had a bit of gray in it. In her

younger years she might have been pretty. She was wearing little gold cross earrings. She was scared half to death and as we sped away from the scene, she started crying and blubbering in Spanish. I don't know the language, but I guess she was pleading for her life. Carl was frantic to escape and kept yelling at Mel to drive faster.

Carl was nervous because taking a hostage hadn't been part of the plan, and he likes to stick to the plan. But the armored-truck driver must have sent a silent alarm before Carl shot him, because a cop car roared up out of nowhere, taking us all by surprise.

The Mexican lady was an innocent bystander—that's what the newsman called her. Carl grabbed her and pushed her toward me and told me to get her into the van while he held off the cop. The cop, seeing that we had a hostage, didn't shoot back. Carl shot him, though. He's in the hospital in critical condition. On TV they showed all the cops who'd come to the hospital to show their support. Carl laughed and said it was too bad we couldn't attack the hospital and take them all out at once, save ourselves the trouble later.

Anyway, back to the Mexican lady, she didn't do as Carl ordered. She kept crying and chattering until she became hysterical and started wailing something terrible. But I've never heard anything as loud as the gun blast inside that van. After Carl shot her, it was awfully quiet except for the ringing in my ears. I guess it was that way with Carl and Mel, too, because nobody said anything for the longest time.

We left her body in that van when we switched to another. I think because I touched her, they may get evidence off her clothes that will nail us. Since we started this, more than ten years ago now, the feds have gotten real smart about forensic stuff like that.

Sometimes I wish we could just quit, collect Jeremy, and go someplace quiet and pretty and be a regular family. Jeremy is in third grade now. He's making straight A's and he's on a Little League team. I doubt I'll ever get to see him play, but I got to talk to him on the phone last week for ten whole minutes.

Carl says maybe we can meet next month. I hope so, but, after today, he might not want to risk it. So far, nobody's caught on to Randy and Patricia. To look at them, you'd think they were Beaver Cleaver's mom and dad. But Carl says when you stop being careful is when you get caught. And if we got caught, that would be the end of us seeing Jeremy at all. They'd lock us away for a long, long time, if they didn't just skip that part and execute us.

I got off the subject again. (Jeremy is always on my mind!) We left that Mexican lady's body in the ditched van. By the time we got to this hideout, we had all calmed down and started breathing easier. Carl declared the day a victory, especially after we counted the money.

That's when the party started. Everybody got wasted. I smoked and drank more than usual, because it bothered me some, the way Carl had shot that woman just because she was making a fuss. We had nothing against her. She wasn't guarding that truck. Just happened to be in the wrong place at the wrong time. She looked to be in her midforties, making it almost certain that she had a husband, kids, grandkids maybe. I couldn't help but feel sorry for them. They weren't partying last night.

This is the first job Mel has done with us. He came recommended as a driver with nerves of steel. He lived up to his reputation and got us out of there, so I guess Carl felt that he deserved a reward. Me.

I hate it when he lets another man you-know-what me. Because after, when Carl sobers up, he's mad at *me*, like it had been my idea. When actually, I never like it. It makes me feel dirty. Like I'm trash. And I get to thinking that if I'm no more valuable to him than that, he might leave me behind if we ever got trapped.

But I really don't think he would. He didn't leave me behind at Golden Branch, when I thought for sure he was going to.

He'd have my skin, though, if he ever caught me with this diary. I don't want to think about how mad he'd be. He might give me to somebody like Mel and never take me back.

Chapter 17

Jeremy Wesson idly scratched his full beard as he listened to a ten p.m. local radio news update, which obliged him with a shorthand summation of Willard Strong's courtroom testimony earlier that day.

Willard's time line had been off by a few hours, but otherwise his recollections and suppositions were damn near on the money as to how things had gone down the day Jeremy had killed the man's wife with his shotgun while he was sleeping it off in the cab of his pickup truck.

Whether or not a jury bought Willard's explanation was a wait-and-see, but it wasn't looking good for the accused. Jeremy didn't hold a personal grudge against Willard, who had been handpicked to play an essential role, and he'd served his purpose well. He looked the part. He'd acted the part. And had Jeremy not been directing those events, Willard was of such a violent nature, he eventually might have killed both Jeremy and Darlene for their cheating.

However, there was never a chance of that happening. Jeremy had propelled the plot from the beginning to the end. Willard's conviction would seal the deal, so to speak. In everyone's mind, beyond a *reasonable* doubt, Jeremy Wesson would be dead along with poor Darlene.

The mission—to set up Jeremy Wesson's ruination as a testament to America's turpitude—had been painstakingly planned and meticulously carried out. He had set himself up as someone who'd seemingly had everything a man could want: beautiful wife, esteemed father-in-law, two perfect sons, a bright future. Ruination of that American dream had occurred when he returned from war—damaged, self-destructive, and on a slippery slope to a disastrous end.

It had taken years to pull off, and some of the guises he'd had to assume were more easily adaptable and maintainable than others.

He'd made a good Marine. Applying his marksmanship skills had come naturally, but so had instructing others. He'd enjoyed the camaraderie, particularly during his tours to the Middle East. He'd even cultivated a few friendships that, later, he regretted having to sever. Of course he hadn't bought into the God-and-country dogma of the corps. He'd had to fake that, but he'd done so convincingly.

Becoming Amelia Nolan's suitor had been much more challenging. His callowness hadn't all been pretense. He felt much more at home in a military barracks than in a ballroom. Randy and Patricia had taught him the basic rules of comportment, and he'd attended enough officers' functions to know how to conduct himself on formal occasions.

But the Nolans lived in a rarified society that had intimidated him as an enemy target never had. The guidelines of southern gentility hadn't been written down in any book, yet everyone in the Nolans' circle seemed to know and understand them. Often, he'd reconsidered the choice of whom he should court with a goal toward marrying. He'd thought perhaps the bar should be lowered a notch or two.

However, to his amazement, his gauche bumbles had made him more lovable to Amelia, not less. He was different from the beaux she was accustomed to, and that was his allure. His etiquette missteps appealed to her rather than appalled. Once he realized that, he'd played into the role and became a puppy, whose efforts were ardent if clumsy and who was eager to win favor.

The ruse backfired somewhat, because her unqualified acceptance had made him fall in love with her. A little. Much more than he'd bargained on. He'd expected never to feel anything except contempt for her and everything she represented—the wealthy, rapacious, greedy, soul-stripping aristocracy of the US of A.

Often he'd wished she didn't love him so much. If she'd been judgmental and critical, if she'd patronized him, if she'd been intolerant of his postwar condition rather than extremely concerned, it would have made the mission easier. His goal had been to break her, not to break her heart.

He'd also wanted to despise with a passion his father-in-law and his patriotic, flag-waving idiocy. He'd scorned the statesman's politics and the government he represented, but he'd discovered that it was hard to work up that level of antipathy for the man himself. Nolan was a fair-thinking, generous gentleman.

But the hardest act of all was the evolution of a loving daddy into a drunken, abusive brute that his sons feared. They'd gone from running toward him, arms raised, all smiles because he was home, to cowering whenever he walked into a room and cringing at his raised voice. He had a lot to make up to them.

Soon he would.

After all these years, the goal was days away from being achieved. Willard Strong would be convicted of killing Darlene, and, by extension, Jeremy Wesson. After that, he could wage his private war with impunity. He could wreak havoc in all fifty states, and nobody would be looking for a dead man.

There *was* one hitch that needed to be ironed out.

He'd been shocked to learn that the woman found dead behind Mickey's wasn't Amelia. Jesus, he still couldn't believe he'd mistaken another woman for her.

The day of the storm, the ocean had become so choppy, he'd decided against going all the way back to Savannah, and instead had docked the boat on Saint Nelda's. He hadn't been to the island that much, so he wasn't concerned about being recognized.

If he happened to cross paths with someone who'd known Jeremy Wesson, it was still unlikely they'd see through the thick beard that covered the lower third of his face, or beyond the cap he wore to cover the patch of missing scalp he'd sliced off himself and tossed into that dog pen. In the fifteen months he'd been in hiding, he'd also put on thirty pounds.

So when he tied up at Saint Nelda's pier during the downpour, he hadn't felt in danger of being discovered. He'd been standing inside the wheelhouse of the boat, drinking a cup of coffee and staring out at the water-logged village, when he spotted her.

The rain had been like a curtain, and it was well past dark. She might have gone unnoticed if not for the raincoat. That loud, ugly rain slicker Amelia had bought in Charleston was hard to miss, even in the feeble glow of light coming through the windows of the general store.

For the four hundred and eighty-something days since he'd left those damn dogs fighting over Darlene's remains, he'd been biding his time until he could remove Amelia and reclaim his sons. It would have been lunacy to attempt anything as bold as kidnapping Hunter and Grant while Amelia remained a key factor in Willard's trial and was frequently the subject of news stories. Besides, he knew that her testimony would help convict Willard, and he hadn't wanted to hamper that.

But over those boring days and lonely nights, he'd contemplated several scenarios, thinking hard about how he would bring about her removal when the time was right. He searched for an option other than death, because . . . Well, just because.

There was such a thing as overplanning, however. Sometimes one could miss an opportunity while strategizing. When a plum was dropped into your lap, it was practically obligatory to accept the gift from Fate, wasn't it?

Reclaiming his sons would be more easily accomplished with their mother permanently out of the picture. The unfairness of that could be contemplated later. But at that moment in time, he had to act.

He'd set his coffee aside, secured a ball-peen hammer from the toolbox, and tucked it inside his own slicker. A man making a mad dash through pelting rain wouldn't arouse suspicion. But it didn't matter, because he made it to the parking lot behind Mickey's without anyone seeing him.

He'd hunkered behind the Dumpster to wait.

But—*damn it all*—when she emerged from the store, the guy was with her, the one who'd been playing on the beach with his kids, the tall, rangy stranger with whom Amelia had sat on her porch the night before, in side-by-side rocking chairs, drinking wine.

Heads down, they ran to her car. He could hear them laughing as they dodged puddles. The guy opened the car's rear door and stowed her purchases in the footwell. She opened the passenger door and tossed her purse onto the seat. They exchanged a brief good-bye, then he jogged away, back toward the store.

As she was making her way around the rear of the car, she dropped her keys. She bent down to pick them up. He seized the moment. He didn't think of her face, her eyes, the body he'd made love to. He didn't think of her kind nature, her musical laugh, or her cute frown of concentration. He thought nothing of her humanity. She was a target, like the dozens he'd taken out in Iraq and Afghanistan from hundreds of yards away. She had to go. That's all there was to it.

He heard the sound, felt the give, when the hammer breached her skull, only fractionally impeded by the hood of the slicker.

Never knowing what hit her, she fell face-first into the mud. He took her by the ankle and dragged her behind the Dumpster. He straightened the hood over her head. Then he ran back to the boat. It had been remarkably easy and quick. His coffee hadn't even gone cold.

Dawson Scott was the name of the guy who'd almost spoiled it. He was a hotshot writer for a magazine. Jeremy had heard all about him this morning while he was eating a tall stack with a side of sausage at a truck stop off I-95. He was sitting at the counter, so he could see the TV mounted up on the wall above it.

The sheriff's-office spokesman was coy, but, when pressed by reporters, told them that Dawson Scott had been held in jail overnight and was still a person of interest in the girl's murder. It had been all Jeremy could do to keep from laughing out loud.

Investigators were also questioning some other guy. Jeremy couldn't remember his name, but it was inconsequential. What mattered was that one person they were *not* looking for was the late Jeremy Wesson.

He'd feel damn good about things if not for that one hitch: he'd have to figure out something else for Amelia.

He was looking forward to the day when he could leave this cabin, with its moldy walls, saggy bed, clanking generator, and cookstove that smelled of propane even when not in use. Every critter in South Carolina seemed to find its way inside. He couldn't even identify most of the scat he had to sweep up every time he returned to the cabin.

Its one redeeming feature was that nobody knew it was here.

Which was why, as soon as he turned off the radio and heard the light thump, indicating that somebody had stepped onto the porch, he acted reflexively. A yank on the dirty string killed the single ceiling light. Moving soundlessly and efficiently across the buckled hardwood floor, he slid the pistol from his waistband and flattened himself against the wall on the backside of the door.

By habit, he kept a bullet chambered. The pistol was ready to fire. He raised it to chin height, held his breath, and waited.

Jeremy heard the doorknob move fractionally. After that, nothing. But even without that telltale, almost inaudible metallic squeak, he would have known someone was on the other side of the door. He sensed a presence that signaled danger, and hell if he was going to wait and let some yokel deputy arrest him. Or try.

He grabbed the doorknob, jerked the door open, and thrust his gun hand forward. The bore of his pistol came to within an inch of the other man's forehead.

Jeremy's breath whooshed out and his arm dropped to his side. "Hell, Daddy, I almost shot you."

Looking harried, Headly blustered into the kitchen through the utility-room door. Taking in the scene, he noticed the empty candy wrapper on the table. "Got any more Hershey's?"

Dawson said, "Fresh out."

Amelia offered to make him a cup of hot chocolate.

"That would be great, thanks."

He pulled a chair from beneath the table and sat down. "How are you?"

He'd addressed the question to Dawson, who raised his shoulders in a laconic shrug. "Fine. Why do you keep asking?"

Headly opened his mouth as though to answer, then seemed to think better of it. He turned to Amelia instead and asked about Hunter and Grant.

"When they got here, they were keyed up. It took two storybooks to get them to sleep."

"I'm sure they were glad to have you tuck them in."

"Actually, Dawson read them to sleep."

Headly's gaze swung back to Dawson and held until Dawson said querulously, "You barged in here like your hair was on fire. What's up?"

"The boat you noticed?" he said to her, nodding his thanks as she delivered his cocoa. "Coast Guard's routine patrols made note of it because it stayed anchored just offshore for several days. But it was only a guy fishing, they said. Nothing suspicious. No interaction with other craft."

"Did they get the name of it?" Dawson asked.

"*CandyCane*." Headly paused as though waiting for an *Ah-ha* from one of them. "Nothing?" he asked, looking at her.

"To my knowledge, Jeremy never did any boating and very little fishing."

"Where's it registered?" Dawson asked.

"Rhode Island. But to an owner who doesn't exist."

Amelia exchanged a glance with Dawson and when she looked back at Headly, he continued.

"We don't know that Jeremy and the *CandyCane* are connected, and we won't until we find it. But it fits. It was offshore and in sight of your house for days, during which time creepy stuff happened and you sensed yourself being watched. And..." He paused and sipped from his mug of chocolate. "It docked at Saint Nelda's pier on Sunday evening."

"Walking distance from where Stef was murdered," Dawson said.

"The guy who tends the gas pumps ran out to tell the boater that he was out of luck if he needed fueling. The power was out, so the pumps were shut down."

"I must have been his last customer," Dawson remarked.

"You were. He confirmed that to Tucker. Anyhow, the boater—only person onboard as far as the gas guy could tell—said he was just waiting out the storm."

"Did the gas guy note what time the boat pulled out?"

"No. He closed down and retreated to his one-room apartment behind the bait shop. He says he curled up with a book and a Coleman lantern, read for a while, then went to bed. The *CandyCane* was gone the next morning. That's all he knows. But I doubt Jeremy hung around for long after killing the girl."

Every time Amelia heard words to that effect, they jarred her. She was functioning as she must, speaking her lines correctly, but whenever Jeremy was cited as Stef's murderer, she underwent a cruel reality check. She was still finding it impossible to accept.

It had been a crime of such deliberate but detached violence, she tried to imagine it of the sweetly smiling man with whom she'd exchanged wedding vows, who'd held Hunter for the first time with endearing awkwardness, who'd swung Grant in his arms until he'd squealed with delight.

In her mind these images of Jeremy the husband and father, and Jeremy the killer, were irreconcilable. It was even hard to imagine that level of depravity from the man she had fled the night he struck her.

How many faces had Jeremy worn? Which was the real Jeremy? Would she ever know? Did she want to?

Her mind came back to the present and to Dawson, who was asking Headly why Tucker hadn't bothered to ask before now about boats that had docked at Saint Nelda's on Sunday.

"He did. People who live or work around the dock were canvassed. The gas guy mentioned the *CandyCane*, but Tucker didn't follow up because he didn't think he needed to. You and Arneson were better prospects."

Amelia asked, "What did this boater look like?"

"Stocky, full beard."

"Stocky doesn't sound like Jeremy."

"Weight gain is as easy as growing a beard," Dawson said. "It just takes longer, and he's had time."

Headly finished his hot chocolate and pushed the mug aside

so he could lean forward on the table. "Amelia, I need you to tell me every single thing you can possibly remember about him."

"I have."

"Not even close. You gotta dig. Friends, enemies, likes, dislikes, fears, phobias, people, places, and things, anything he ever mentioned to you, any name he ever dropped. A receipt you found on his dresser. Matchbook. Post-it note. Movie ticket. Itinerary."

"You're talking about years," she exclaimed.

"I realize that. But he's proven himself to be incredibly resourceful. He's successfully faked his death for more than a year. He might have been shadowing you for all this time, and you never knew he was there. He wants his children and—"

"You don't know that."

"Then why isn't he long gone from this area? Why did he kill a girl he didn't even know unless he mistook her for you?"

She looked at Dawson, who said, "You know what I think."

Yes. He had already argued these same points with her.

"He wants his kids, Amelia," Headly said gently. "And you're an obstruction he must eliminate."

She hugged herself tightly. "You're scaring me."

"You should be scared," Dawson said. "You *need* to be. Because this guy is not screwing around, and if you ever doubt that, you only have to remember how viciously he killed Darlene and then Stef. Defenseless women. In cold blood. Think about that. Remember who his father was."

Thinking back to the photograph of Carl Wingert, which had held an inexplicable fascination for her, she recalled the ruthlessness that had defined his features. She pictured Jeremy as he'd looked during one of his rants, and while their facial features bore no resemblance, the intensity of their malevolence was identical.

She exhaled and said with resignation, "Of course I'll do whatever I can to protect my children."

Headly appeared satisfied. "With any luck, he'll make a mistake and trip himself up. He did with the fingerprint. Same as Carl." He chuckled. "The slippery bastard had never been fingerprinted, which was a major frustration to those of us trying to catch him.

"That is, not until the late eighties when he used a homemade bomb to blow up a mail truck. First and last time he ever used explosives, because apparently he wasn't very good with them. The thing went off as soon as Carl set it into place. It's a wonder it didn't kill him, but all he lost was his thumb and index finger. He also left the print of his middle finger on one of the bomb fragments. We didn't—"

He must have realized that both she and Dawson were gaping at him. Dawson hissed, "Son of a bitch." Then he came out of his chair so suddenly it toppled backward. *"Son of a bitch!"*

"What?" Headly demanded.

She wheezed, "Which hand? Which hand is missing fingers?"

"The left."

She covered her gasp with her hand. Dawson spoke for her. "He's Bernie."

Chapter 18

Jesus, I can't tell you how glad I am to be ditching this old geezer."

Carl pulled the loud pink shirt over his head, balled it up, and tossed it into the trash can. He popped a pair of contacts out of his eyes and sighed with relief. "Hate those damn things." The contacts went the way of the shirt. They wouldn't be needed again. Bernie wouldn't be needed again.

Jeremy took two beers from the rusty refrigerator, twisted off the caps, and passed one to his father. "I didn't expect you until tomorrow."

"I didn't expect to leave the island until tomorrow, but things were getting too hot over there." As he exchanged plaid Bermuda shorts for a pair of khaki pants, he told Jeremy about the deputies who'd been at Amelia's house earlier that day.

"Why so nervous? They weren't looking for you."

His son's amusement annoyed him. "I haven't escaped capture this long by being careless. Cops get close, I get as far away as possible as soon as possible."

"You went to the writer's house on Monday morning while the cops were there."

"Ordinarily I wouldn't have gone anywhere near the place. But then you had gone and killed the wrong woman. Here you had crowed in my ear—by the way, you weren't supposed to call me."

"I've explained about burner phones, Daddy. They can't be traced."

"I don't trust them. None of that technology shit. Don't use the phone again. Anyway, you boasted that you'd killed Amelia. Next thing I know, Dawson Scott is at my back door and Amelia is cozied up in the passenger seat of his car! The following morning, I had to go over there to see what was what. For all I knew, they were telling her that her supposedly late ex-husband had killed her nanny."

"A dead man can't be suspected of murder."

"You could have been identified by the guy who runs the filling station."

"Not a chance. We shouted at each other through a downpour for ten, fifteen seconds tops, then he ran back into his shop. He was at least twenty yards away from me. I couldn't tell you what he looked like. I'll be a blur to him, too."

"You'd better hope."

"I don't exactly look like a spit-and-polish Marine anymore," he said, patting his expanded belly.

"What about the boat?"

"Taken care of."

"You sure?"

"Positive."

"Weapon?"

"At the bottom of the sound."

"Because we've come too far with this to start making mistakes."

"Nobody is after me. Okay?" Hitching his thumb over his shoulder, he said, "I picked up groceries, if you're hungry."

"In a while. I need to think."

They sat in mismatched chairs and drank their beers. Jeremy was the first to speak. "How are my boys?"

"Good, last I saw them, which was Monday morning when I drove Amelia and them to the ferry. When I talked to her this afternoon, they were still at the curator's house."

Jeremy thoughtfully picked at a loose corner on the label of his beer bottle. "Do they ever talk about me?"

"Not that I've heard." Noticing Jeremy's pained expression, he said, "You haven't been around for a long time. They'll have to get to know you again."

"When can we get them?"

"We've got to take care of Amelia first."

Jeremy shifted in his seat. "About that, why don't we just snatch the boys and disappear? Why does she have to die?"

"Because she would never give up looking for them, that's why. You were married to her, you should know. Even after the law dusted their hands of ever finding them, she wouldn't. She's got the means to hire people to track us down. I don't want to be worrying about that for the rest of my days. Better to simply—" He made a chopping motion.

"I guess," Jeremy mumbled and took a swallow of beer.

"Needs to be soon, too."

"You're right. If we're going to do it, let's get it over with. I want my boys. The longer we wait, the dimmer their memory of me becomes."

Carl murmured in agreement, but he was only half listening. Thinking out loud, he said, "Something's not right."

"Not right with what?"

"This situation." He finished his beer, then got up and began to pace. "I feel like I'm missing something, and when you miss something, you get caught."

"Amelia doesn't suspect that I'm still alive, does she?"

"She's given no indication of it. Even when I saw her today, she was definitely upset over the nanny, but she acted like herself and said her sweet good-bye to dear old Bernie. 'Until next summer…' Like that. She was sad to be closing up the house and leaving the beach. She loves that place. The kids, too. They play—" That sparked a thought. "Where are the pictures?"

"Bottom drawer of the bureau."

"None of me, right?"

"No. First thing I looked for. I know how you feel about pictures of us. Mom told me that the maddest you ever got at her was when you caught her taking pictures of me as a toddler."

That wasn't the maddest he'd ever got at Flora, but Jeremy didn't need to know that.

He found the pictures—apparently taken by Dawson Scott—in the drawer, paper-clipped together. He took them over to the dining table so he could spread them out for better viewing.

"Damn fool thing you did to get these," he said to Jeremy as he joined him at the table.

"Curiosity got the better of me. I saw y'all leave, saw him jog over to her house and put something under the doormat. He was dressed up, so I figured he was going to dinner, too, and wouldn't be back for a while. I got back to the *CandyCane* with time to spare."

Carl still thought his son had been reckless to row a dingy to shore and then back to the boat. The margin for error had been huge. And for what? The photos seemed harmless enough, hardly worth the risk Jeremy had taken to obtain them.

Jeremy picked up a picture of his sons playing in the surf. "As long as he was at it, I wish he'd taken more shots of them and fewer of Amelia."

"Why'd he take them at all?" Carl asked. "You checked him out on your computer?"

"Didn't even have to dig. He's exactly what he claims to be. He's won prizes. He covered Afghanistan for his magazine. Just back from there, actually."

"So what's he doing down here?"

"Besides lusting for Amelia, you mean," Jeremy said as he held up a photo of her.

"Feeling's mutual, I think," Carl said.

"Really?"

"Something's there. She looked kinda sick when I told her I'd seen him with Stef."

"Is she sleeping with him?"

"Do you care?"

"Not really. I'd be surprised, is all. Pregnancy killed her libido."

Carl wasn't convinced of Jeremy's indifference when it came to Dawson Scott and Amelia, but his concerns about the man were much more serious. "What gets me," he said, "is that this writer showed up out of nowhere, moved into the house next door to your ex-wife's, and edged in on her and the boys."

"You said yourself that he was running down the story of me, Darlene, and Willard."

"That's what I said, but..."

"What else could it be?"

"I don't know," Carl muttered. "That's what worries me."

"It makes perfect sense that he'd want to interview Amelia to get background stuff about our life together."

"True. But it seems to me that he went to an awful lot of trouble to cover a murder trial in out-of-the-way Savannah."

Jeremy blurted a laugh. "The man went to freakin' Afghanistan for stories."

Carl turned to Jeremy and must have telegraphed his rising anger, because his son's amused grin collapsed. "Are you humoring your old man?"

"No, Daddy."

"You think I'm getting soft in the head?"

"Of course not."

"You think you're smarter than me?"

"No! Jesus!"

"Others have thought they were. They didn't listen to what I told them, and you know what? They're either dead or fighting off queers in a goddamn prison."

"Daddy, I—"

"The day you think you're smarter than me—"

"I don't think that."

"Is the day somebody will take you down." His left hand had been maimed, but his right hand worked just fine, and he emphasized those last words by poking Jeremy in the chest with his index finger. Carl held him in a hard stare for several moments more, giving the message time to sink in, then removed his hand and turned away. "I've worked up an appetite."

They fixed thick sandwiches of deli meats and cheeses. The freezer wasn't that great, so the ice cream was soft, but it tasted good. Over cups of coffee they continued their discussion.

Carl said, "Look, son, I get cranky sometimes. I know you're eager to get your boys back. Hell, I can't wait until we're all together, either."

"They're gonna love British Columbia. I remember those days we spent there as the best time of my life."

During one summer vacation, Carl had agreed to meet the Wessons—after so many years, even he had come to think of Randy and Patricia by that name—near Vancouver. They'd rented a cabin on a lake and had spent their days fishing, lazing about, and having cookouts on the shore.

They were scheduled to stay for two weeks. He and Flora left after six days. She'd cried when he'd made her leave, but he'd become anxious and paranoid. Even the patrolling park rangers made him nervous. It was never a good idea to stay in one place for too long.

As an afterthought, Jeremy added now, "That was the summer before my senior year. It's the last time I remember feeling like a kid."

"You had to grow up soon after that."

Jeremy sipped his coffee and lapsed into a brooding silence that reminded Carl of Flora. He left the table and began to pace again.

Watching him, Jeremy asked, "Does your hip hurt?"

"No."

"Then what's with the face?"

"I still think that something is off."

"Off?"

"Like I don't have the full picture. I'm missing a critical piece and it's nagging me."

"What could it be?"

Carl scowled. "Hell if I know. I'm thinking."

Chapter 19

It certainly wasn't the worst sight that had ever greeted her first thing in the morning. Dawson, his back to her, was bent low over the countertop, watching freshly brewed coffee as it dripped into the carafe.

"Can't brew fast enough?"

He straightened and turned around to face her as she entered the kitchen. "Not nearly fast enough, and this is the second pot."

"How long have you been up?"

"A few hours."

"*Hours?* Did you get any sleep?"

"A few minutes."

"The sofa is too short for you. You should have taken the bed when I offered." She had also offered him Stef's room, which he'd declined.

"I wouldn't run you out of your bed. Besides, it wasn't the sofa keeping me awake."

"Nightmares?"

His gaze moved over her, causing fillips of sensation everywhere it lingered. "General restlessness."

"Me too."

He arched his eyebrow with interest.

Quickly, she went to the cabinet and opened it to get a coffee mug for herself, but her movements were arrested when he crowded in behind her, trapping her between him and the counter.

Pushing her hair aside, he nuzzled her neck behind her ear. "What did I ever do to deserve this?"

Her head tipped toward her shoulder as his mouth applied damp pressure to the side of her neck. "Deserve what?"

"Two mornings of you showing up, fresh out of bed, looking all rosy and warm, like you've either been well fucked or are about to be, and making me crazy wanting to be the man who's given you that look."

She offered up no resistance when he turned her and drew her to him. Being held flush against his torso made her weak with longing to be skin-to-skin. One of them, maybe she, made a throaty sound of both hunger and appeasement when their mouths came together in a blatantly carnal kiss. Several times they changed the angle of their heads, but they didn't break contact until he withdrew so his lips could nibble at hers.

Those sweet pecks tingled and delighted and excited, especially when paired with the prickle of his scruff. His hands moved over her back, their possessiveness tempered by the syllables of longing whispered against her lips.

Bending his head lower, he pushed aside the strap of her tank top to give him access to her collarbone. But even as she sighed with pleasure, she plaintively murmured his name.

"Hmm?"

"We can't."

"I know." But he didn't stop at her collarbone. He continued down, placing soft kisses on her chest.

"Really," she said weakly.

"I know."

Through the thin cotton tank top, his hand cupped her breast and pushed it up to swell above the neckline. He rubbed his rough cheek against it, then turned his face into the plumpness and kissed it open-mouthed. Hard with arousal, he fit himself into the V between her thighs. The sensation was so intense, she gasped.

"Dawson, we can't. I mean it. We can't."

He went perfectly still, then raised his head and looked down at her. His eyes were glazed with passion, but he gave a slow nod, released her, and moved back a step. They stood there, breathing unevenly, staring at each other.

Finally he said, "Afraid the people guarding you will see us?" He gestured toward the window above the sink.

"That, yes, but..." She swallowed. "I wouldn't even if they weren't out there. I wouldn't with the boys in the house. I know it's old-fashioned, laughably old-fashioned, but I made myself a rule never to... It wouldn't have happened the other morning, either. I'd have come to my senses before it got that far. I'm sorry."

"It's okay."

"It's *not* okay. I know it's not. But I have to think about how impressionable the boys are. Even—"

He stopped her by reaching out to slide her strap back into place, then put both hands on her shoulders. "I understand."

"That's very decent of you."

He gave a lopsided grin. "Yeah, I'm a rock."

She smiled. "You agreed that we had to stop."

His grin faded as he removed his hands from her shoulders. "But not because of the boys."

"No?"

He shook his head.

"Then why?"

He looked away from her for several seconds. When his darkly ringed eyes came back to hers, he said, "Because I won't subject you to me."

Dawson collected his socks and boots from the living room where he'd left them on the floor near the cursed sofa and took them upstairs to the bathroom designated as the boys'. By the time he had showered and dressed, their beds were empty. Following the sound of their voices, he went downstairs to the kitchen to find the family and Headly gathered around the dining table.

"Look, Dawson, doughnuts," Grant chirped. In the center of the table was a large white box from which Grant picked out a doughnut frosted with pink icing and covered with sprinkles. He passed it up to him.

Amelia said, "Grant, you should have let Dawson choose which one he wanted."

Because of Grant's handling, the icing had smeared and some of the sprinkles had shaken loose, but not for the world would Dawson have refused it. "Just the one I wanted. Thanks, buddy." He ruffled the boy's hair as he took a big bite.

"He brought them," Hunter said, pointing to Headly. "His name's Mr. Headly."

As observant as a hawk, Headly was leaning back in his chair and sipping from a cup of coffee with a casualness that Dawson knew was phony. He missed nothing, possibly not even the faint whisker burn on Amelia's throat.

"Mom doesn't let us have doughnuts for breakfast except sometimes on Saturdays. But she said it was okay today since Mr. Headly already brought them."

"Then this is a treat." Dawson licked the icing and sprinkles off his fingers.

Up to that point, he and Amelia had avoided looking directly at each other, an avoidance also noticed by Headly. Now, still not quite meeting his eyes, she offered Dawson coffee and started to leave her place at the table.

"I'll help myself."

He filled a mug with coffee and leaned against the counter to drink it while the boys finished their doughnuts. When they were done, Amelia sent them to wash their hands and faces. "Just what they needed," she said, looking askance at Headly as she wiped the table with a damp sponge. "A sugar high."

He chuckled. "We'll figure out a way to let them run it off later."

"Thank you. I would appreciate that."

"In the meantime, the three of us need to talk."

Amelia said, "Then I'd better figure out something to entertain the boys."

Everything that she'd packed into her car the day before had been unpacked and put back in its proper place. While she was settling the boys down with a DVD on the TV in the living area, Dawson joined Headly at the table and assessed the doughnut inventory. "Any with Bavarian-cream filling?"

"Sorry, no."

"Then this will have to do." He selected a plain glazed.

"How'd it go last night?"

The question immediately put Dawson on the defensive. "How'd what go?"

"Did you get the shakes?"

"I told you. I'm not a damn addict."

"Any nightmares?"

He rolled his shoulders in a gesture that could have meant anything or nothing.

"Only because you didn't sleep at all."

Dawson silently endured Headly's appraisal of his haggard face and the dark circles under his eyes.

"If she ever sees you looking normal, she might not be attracted. It may be the zombie effect she finds appealing."

Dawson finished the rest of the doughnut, asking around the last bite, "Haven't you got more important things to do than to try and piss me off?"

"What's giving you nightmares?"

"I don't recall telling you I had nightmares."

"You didn't deny it, either."

Dawson folded his arms over his chest, letting his body language speak for itself.

But Headly wasn't through with him. "When are you going to tell me what happened to you over there? Why are you afraid to fall asleep?"

Dawson mentally counted to ten, then repositioned himself in his chair to signal a change in topic. "Have you talked to Eva?"

"This morning."

"How is she?"

"Worried."

"She knows you don't eat right when she's not around."

"Not about me, about you."

"Then she's worrying for nothing. How many times do I have to tell the two of you that I'm all right?"

Headly took a deep breath, blew it out. "I shouldn't have sent you down here."

Dawson snorted a laugh. "Too effing late."

"I know." Headly looked at him meaningfully, then glanced over his shoulder toward the living room where the boys could be heard arguing over which movie they would watch. "How is she?"

"She slept alone, if that's what you're asking."

"It isn't."

Dawson knew the more defensive he was, the more Headly would browbeat him, so he addressed his question about Amelia without reading a subtext into it. "She's brave. Tougher at the core, I think, than she appears on the surface. Steelier."

"I'm afraid that before this is over, she'll need to be."

Before Dawson could ask what that remark portended, Amelia rejoined them, expelling a breath as she sat down. "Be concise, Mr. Headly. Buzz Lightyear will pacify them for only so long. I promised them playtime after the movie."

"Can't blame them for wanting to play outside."

"They want to play with Dawson."

Headly turned and looked at him expectantly, obviously waiting for a comment. All he said was, "You'd better get started. You're wasting valuable time."

Headly snuffled as though to say that Dawson was dodging an issue, but that for the moment it had to wait. "Okay, here's where we are. Bernie was conveyed to the mainland on the ferry late yesterday evening."

"He said he was driving to Charleston."

"Well, he didn't. Not in that car, anyway. They found it parked in a public lot just a few blocks from the ferry pier. No sign of him. We'll keep an eye on the car, but my guess is that he abandoned it."

"Why do you think that?" Amelia asked. "He doesn't know his true identity has been discovered."

"The car's license plate was bogus. It's been a few years since Michigan used that design, but few people down here would notice. Carl did such a good job of altering the year of expiration that it was undetectable from a distance. Plus, the VIN number has been scratched out so that it's unreadable. No prints inside the car. None on the door handles. He wiped it clean."

"Is the parking lot attended?" Dawson asked.

"No. Only monitored by meter maids. You park, feed bills into a metal box or use a credit card. The box spits out a receipt you leave on the inside of your windshield. His was good for twenty-four hours, and, from the time stamp, we know he was back on the mainland for forty-seven minutes before our band of brothers launched our raid on this house last night. He got a good head start."

"Security cameras?"

"Several on the pier. We have him driving off the ferry. That's it. The bags and boxes you saw him loading into the trunk?" he said to Amelia. "All empty. They were for show."

"The bad hips, too, in all likelihood," Dawson remarked sourly. "Nice touch, though." He hitched his chin in the direction of the house Bernie had occupied. "What about that?"

"Techies are still gathering evidence, but so far it hasn't yielded anything substantive. Full of fingerprints, of course, but I doubt any of them will be Carl's."

"He didn't walk around wearing rubber gloves."

"I'd bet my left nut—excuse me, Amelia—that we don't find a print that matches. Don't forget, all we have is a print for the middle finger, left hand."

"Hair in the shower drain?"

"Gathered. Skin cells off the linens. But we don't have Carl's DNA. Believe me, if he was easy to catch, I'd have caught him."

"What about his house in Michigan?" Amelia asked.

"No such house number or street."

She was amazed. "But I sent Christmas cards. They never came back."

Headly raised a shoulder. "All I know is, the house address doesn't exist and neither does the e-mail address he left with Miss DeMarco to give to you."

Dawson said, "There must be a record of his leases for the house next door."

"One would think. We got the manager of the rental office out of bed late last night to serve the search warrant. He was obstinate at first, didn't want to divulge personal information on a repeat client. But after some arm twisting to the tune of 'obstruction of justice,' he told us that Bernie Clarkson always paid him with a money order."

"Like you buy at Seven-Eleven?"

"Exactly like that. I asked the guy if that hadn't seemed odd to him. His answer, 'He was from Michigan.' As if that explained why he didn't pay with a credit card or check. Anyhow, the little old man from the Upper Peninsula didn't leave a paper trail."

He focused on Amelia. "Did he always come alone?"

"Yes. The first summer he spent here—"

"2009."

"That's right. Jeremy was overseas. Grant was just a baby. I stayed the whole summer out here. Dad came off and on, but I spent a lot of time with Bernie because we were both lonely. He was grieving the recent death of his wife."

"That's what he told you. Doesn't mean that Flora's dead. Did he ever show you a photograph of her?"

"No. Which, now that I think about it, was odd. He talked about her with affection."

"Did Jeremy ever meet so-called Bernie?"

"No. Even after he mustered out, he rarely came here. He couldn't take time away from work. On one rare occasion when he did spend a few days, I invited Bernie to join us for dinner, but he excused himself, saying he didn't want to intrude on our family time."

"He declined because they were afraid you'd notice a resemblance."

"I doubt I would have," she said. "I see nothing of Jeremy in the Wanted-poster photograph of Carl."

"I wasn't struck by a similarity, either," Dawson said. "I was totally taken in by Bernie."

"Don't beat yourself up," Headly said. "That's a lousy picture on the Wanted poster and it's over forty years old. Carl was just launching his criminal career then. He must look a lot different now."

"Like a septuagenarian," Dawson said. "Wrinkled, age spots. His hair has thinned considerably and it's completely white. The limp could be faked. But maybe not." He thought of something else. "The night of the storm, when he answered my knock, his eyes were red and he was rubbing them. I thought I'd woken him up. Now I think he must wear contacts to change his eye color. I'd caught him without them."

Addressing Amelia, Headly said, "Bernie and Jeremy never let you see them side by side because you might've detected something. If not alike in looks, in mannerisms."

"You're still of the opinion that Jeremy knew who his father was, and that they were—"

"In cahoots? Absolutely. Bernie entered your life around the time your marriage started deteriorating. That wasn't coincidental. He came here to keep an eye on you while Jeremy was in Afghanistan."

"I was alone year-round. Bernie lived next door only during the summer months."

"But when you're in Savannah, your schedule is more structured," Dawson said, picking up on Headly's thread. "You stick to a routine built around your work, the boys' schooling. You see the same people, go to the same places, do the same things. Basically, your life is under constant scrutiny."

"That's right," Headly said. "You aren't as free in town as you are at the beach."

"Free?" She asked with a light laugh. "To do what?"

"To spend the night in another man's house."

Headly's words fell like bricks. Amelia lowered her gaze to the tabletop. Dawson sat there seething for a moment, then said, "Tucker must've gotten a real kick out of telling you."

"I'm surprised you didn't."

"Nothing to tell. Amelia stayed that night only because of the power outage."

"Yeah, Tucker said you hammered that home. About two dozen times." He divided a look between them. "Look, you're grown-ups. I don't care. I'm only saying what it looked like to—"

"That asshole Tucker."

"No, to Jeremy and Carl. But let's leave that for a moment. We'll come back to it."

While Headly paused to take several sips of coffee, Dawson

looked over at Amelia with apology. For all their protests to the contrary, they hadn't fooled anybody into believing that their night together had been entirely chaste.

Headly resumed. "They found the *CandyCane* tied up at a public, out-of-the-way dock on a channel on Tybee Island. I haven't been there, but I hear it's perfect for Jeremy's purposes. Boaters come and go. Nobody pays much attention. Easy for him to get over here to spy on Amelia or watch his kids play on the beach. Last time somebody noticed the boat being there was early Monday."

"He may not have been the man on that boat," Amelia said.

"Knutz has a couple of people working it. Here's a giveaway. The craft has been scrubbed down with bleach inside and out. So either it was piloted by a stocky, bearded, law-abiding germophobe who's made himself scarce, or Jeremy made certain that if the authorities somehow linked the boat to the murder on Saint Nelda's, it couldn't be linked to him."

"It wasn't that hard to find," Dawson said. "Which tells me that he didn't see much risk of it being connected to the crime."

"Or maybe," Headly said, "he knows he won't need it anymore and abandoned it like Carl did his car."

"Either way, Jeremy doesn't realize that he's been had."

"For the time being," Headly said. "And that's good. The longer we can keep him and Carl in the dark, the better."

Dawson didn't like the way Headly was eyeing him as he tacked on that last part. "What?"

"It would be nice if we had a decoy. Somebody to feed to the media sharks like chum. A pseudosuspect to throw Carl and Jeremy off."

Dawson pointed to his own chest. "Me? I?"

"I'm just saying."

"Forget it. What about Dirk Arneson?"

"He's off the hook for everything except using his employer's yacht as a bachelor pad. His poker pals were located in New Orleans and questioned. They backed up his alibi. He was released with an apology."

"Poor Tucker. Foiled again."

"He doesn't like you, either. And he'd write me off as a crackpot for accusing a dead man of killing that girl if not for that fingerprint. But there *is* the print. And there *is* Jeremy's kinship with Carl Wingert, a notorious criminal at large. Tucker's wading through Carl's history now to familiarize himself, but in a way that's working against us."

"How so?" Amelia asked.

"He can't quite reconcile that Carl the terrible could pass himself off for years as Bernie the tenderhearted. So far, we haven't got anything forensic to prove that Bernie is Carl's alter ego, and until some turns up, Tucker's waffling."

"You've gotta be kidding me!" Dawson exclaimed.

"He says a lot of older people have missing fingers, because reattachment wasn't always the option it is now, and he's right. He also backed me into a corner until I admitted that I've never seen Bernie, so I can't ID him as Carl, whom I've also never seen in the flesh."

Amelia asked, "How do they explain his car being abandoned, all that?"

"They can't, except to say that maybe he's having senior moments and forgot where he left it."

"The phony addresses, the absence of public records?" Dawson said.

"All suspicious, but not a smoking gun." Headly turned to Amelia. "I don't suppose you have a picture of Bernie."

"No."

"Figured that. Carl wouldn't have let himself be photographed. The SO is going to have one of those computer programs age the picture from Carl's Wanted poster, see if it resembles your seventy-something neighbor, but for right now, they're soft on him. Additionally—"

"Jesus. There's an additionally?" Dawson left his chair and made an aimless circuit of the kitchen.

"*Additionally,* Tucker's wrestling with Jeremy's motive for killing Miss DeMarco. And if you believe that he wielded the murder weapon thinking he was killing her, then I allow that there's a problem with it."

"But he didn't think he was killing Stef. He thought it was Amelia."

"Tucker's not sold on that, and he's got some strong arguments."

"Like what?" Dawson asked.

"Like how Jeremy could have planned it. How would he have known that Amelia would be in the village that night?"

"He couldn't have known," she said.

"Right. That's the hangup. Even Knutz, who's on my side, winces when I assert that it was a crime of opportunity. My take? Jeremy tied up at Saint Nelda's dock to ride out the storm. He saw Miss DeMarco, mistook her for you, and seized the opportunity."

Wryly Dawson said, "It was a dark and stormy night."

"To them my theory sounds just that clichéd. Homicide detectives deal in facts and hard evidence. We're short on those."

"Except for the fingerprint," Amelia said.

"*If* it's a recent print—which is being argued—it places Jeremy there."

"Then what's the problem?" Dawson asked.

"I say again, motive. Murder is quite a leap from spooking Amelia with a busted beach ball. If Jeremy is only trying to mess with her mind, when he spotted her running through the rain, why didn't he just jump out of the bushes and shout *boo*?"

"Tucker didn't actually say that, did he?"

"It was almost that inane. But here's their refrain," Headly said, going back to Amelia. "Why would Jeremy want to kill you? Now, to me, his motive is obvious."

"The children," she replied.

"Ultimately. Hear me out," he said, holding up both hands before she could say more. "What I think, Jeremy and Carl were too cautious to act before Willard Strong's trial ended. They'd been impatiently biding their time until Willard was residing on death row and the dust had settled. They were almost there, days away from completion, the end was in sight when...a strapping, good-looking lad appears on the scene."

He tilted his head toward Dawson, who realized they'd come back to the disconcerting topic of him and Amelia.

"He shows up out of nowhere," Headly said, "and you start spending time with him. The children also seem gaga, which wouldn't have set well with their father. To Jeremy, the new man in your life was a catalytic event."

She looked at Dawson uneasily. "He's hardly in my life."

"And they wouldn't want him to be."

"But we'd just met."

"Sometimes that's all it takes." After a short but awkward silence, he continued. "A romance between you two at least *appeared* to be blossoming. Jeremy had to stop it."

"This means that Stef died because of me." Shooting a glance at Dawson, she added, "Because of us."

"No." Headly propped his elbow on the table and shook his index finger at her. "Listen to me. Your perceived attraction to Dawson was only an excuse for Jeremy to act sooner rather than later. Eventually, no matter what, whether or not you'd ever met Dawson, he would have killed you. If not Jeremy, then his father would have. Because—and make no mistake about this, Amelia—the man is evil.

"Sweet, lovable Bernie is a sham. In truth, he never existed. It was Carl Wingert all along, and he duped you well. Because, behind the limp and age spots, he's a terrorist who believes that you deserve to die. I'm as certain of that as I am that it's gravity holding me onto the planet."

"Why would he want me dead?"

"Punishment for leaving Jeremy."

"Jeremy was the one who destroyed our marriage. I wasn't the one having an affair."

"This isn't about morality. Do you think Carl cares who slept with whom? No. It's about loyalty. He has strong feelings about it. But—and here's the kicker—it's one-sided. It's loyalty to *him* that he's a fanatic about.

"Conversely, he doesn't blink over leaving someone behind. He saves his own skin first. He's done it time and again. At Golden Branch, he sacrificed one of his men so he could escape, and, frankly, I'm amazed that he took Jeremy and Flora, straight out of childbed, with him when he ran.

"Once, during a standoff, one of his gang members tried to surrender. He walked out of a motel room with his hands raised. He was killed on the spot, but not by police. Carl, from inside the motel room, shot him in the back of the head and then escaped during the confusion that ensued."

Headly was laying it on thick, perhaps for shock value, but Dawson was glad he wasn't sparing Amelia the cold reality of the kind of man her father-in-law was. Jeremy had the same bloodline.

Headly continued. "Carl Wingert is unconscionable. He believes his actions, no matter how detestable, are justified. He'll vanquish anyone he considers disloyal, and you, Amelia, were disloyal.

"I'm sure Jeremy's mind has been poisoned against you. But even if he still worships the ground you walk on, even if he is madly in love with you and entertaining a fantasy about reuniting with you and his sons, Carl will never allow it. He'll kill you."

"Then why didn't he yesterday when I was alone at the beach house?"

"Because he's too smart to have followed up Jeremy's mistake with another. He couldn't kill you and then disappear. That would have been too obvious. It probably galled him, but he had to continue playing Bernie until he was safely off the island. Now he has time to plan something else."

"What am I supposed to do in the meantime? While he's *planning*. The boys and I can't remain under lock and key indefinitely."

"It won't be indefinite."

Dawson stopped prowling around the room and looked sharply at Headly, whose expression was as grim as he'd ever seen it. "What does that mean?"

"Everything I've told you up till now?"

"Yeah?"

"That's the good news."

Chapter 20

Is this Harriet Plummer?"

"Isn't that who you asked for? Who's this?"

"My name is Bernie Clarkson. I'm calling you from Saint Nelda's Island."

"Where?"

"Offshore from Savannah. I hate to bother you, Ms. Plummer, but he wrote your name on the back of his business card."

"Who did? Dawson?"

"Uh... let's see, I had it right here... Yes, Dawson Scott. Tall, long hair?"

"Why did he give you my name?"

"So you do know him? He does write for the magazine?"

"Yes."

"Good. That makes me feel better."

"About what?"

"About what he's up to."

"Look, if you're a reporter—"

"Reporter?"

"The magazine has no comment other than to say that

Dawson was questioned by the police, but it was pro forma, nothing came of it, and he was released. That's it. Okay?"

"I know all that. I'm not a reporter. Just an ordinary person who wants to know if Mr. Scott is, well, safe to talk to."

"Safe? Maybe you'd better back up and start at the beginning, Mr. Clarkson."

"Well, I was walking on the beach, which I do twice a day. The exercise helps my hips."

"Uh-huh."

"Mr. Scott approached me and struck up a conversation. Seemed to be a nice enough fellow. We chatted about this and that, then he asked if he could interview me."

"Why would he want to interview you?"

"That's why I'm calling you, to ask why he would want to interview me."

"He didn't tell you?"

"He said he was working on a story for the magazine."

"He's covering the Willard Strong trial. Are you familiar with it?"

"It's big news down here."

"Well, Dawson is writing a story about the double murder of Strong's wife and her lover."

"Jeremy Wesson."

"You knew him?"

"I never met him, but I know his ex-wife very well. Amelia and her children spend summers next door to me on the island."

"Well, there you go. That's the connection. The last time I spoke to Dawson, he was hoping to get an interview with her."

"Why?"

"Because typically an ex-wife is a great source of information on a subject. If you're well acquainted with the former Mrs. Wesson, it makes sense that Dawson would want to talk to you, possibly as an inroad to her. Okay? Now if there's nothing—"

"I don't know that I'd want to be quoted."

"If you ask Dawson not to quote you, he won't. Or he'll refer to you as 'an unnamed source.'"

"I wouldn't want to hurt Amelia's feelings by talking behind her back."

"That's very noble of you, but I can vouch for Dawson's journalistic integrity. He treats his subjects with sensitivity. Sometimes to an irritating degree, if I'm being honest."

"What made him want to write about this particular crime?"

"I don't know."

"Maybe an inside source tipped him to it?"

"I don't know."

"You don't know, or you won't tell?"

"I don't know. But if I did, I wouldn't tell."

"Then I guess I'll have to ask him myself."

"Good luck with that."

The bitch hung up on him. After patronizing him, she'd rudely hung up. About what you'd expect from a woman put in charge.

Carl had learned what he'd wanted to know, however. Dawson Scott had come to Georgia to cover the Willard Strong murder case and write a story about it.

What Carl still didn't know was *why*? Why would a writer based in Washington, DC, recently back from overseas, become intrigued by this particular crime? When compared with writing about war, a double murder in Georgia seemed tame. Why would it have captured Dawson Scott's interest?

There were several logical explanations, of course. But Carl mistrusted logic. Too often it didn't apply to a situation. He had never staked his life on what was logical, and he wasn't about to change that practice now.

"I'm coming in!"

The shout came from outside. He went to the door and opened it for Jeremy, who was tramping through the undergrowth toward the cabin, carrying several grocery sacks.

A road to the dwelling would have certainly made access more convenient, but one had never been included in the plan. Roads led people to places, and Carl hadn't wanted anyone to accidentally happen upon this hideout after taking a wrong turn or following a road simply to see where it went.

He had bought the property under a name that meant nothing and continued to pay annual taxes to keep nosy bureaucrats from coming to check it out. He liked it okay, and having it had come in handy, but at any given time, he was willing to walk away from it and not look back. He never became attached to a piece of real estate. For that matter, he didn't form biding attachments to anything. Sentimentality could get you killed.

After murdering Darlene and setting up Willard to take the fall, Jeremy had left the scene on foot, following Carl's instructions to cover his tracks well. Carl had picked him up on the main road, provided some antiseptic cream and a gauze patch for the self-inflicted wound on his head, and drove him as close as he could get to the cabin. Jeremy had gone the rest of the way through the marsh on foot.

Sandwiched between that brackish marsh on one side and a dense forest on the other, the cabin was so far off the beaten path that Jeremy had been able to hide in it for fifteen months.

During that time, he'd changed his appearance. He'd let his hair grow out long enough to cover the bald spot, which had healed, but was unsightly. He'd also cultivated a beard and gained weight.

Carl had brought him supplies once a week. Occasionally Jeremy had complained about the isolation, the leaky roof, and the lousy TV reception, which could only be obtained with a camouflaged antenna on the side of the roof. But he'd endured these inconveniences, knowing that the sacrifices would eventually be rewarded by getting his sons back.

He and Jeremy had built the cabin themselves while he was stationed at Parris Island. Although it lacked amenities, Flora had loved it because it had allowed them to see Jeremy periodically. She had campaigned for it to become their permanent home. Carl had refused to live permanently anywhere, so she'd had to be content with short visits to the place.

Those times spent here with Jeremy had made her happy. In truth, she was easily made happy by the smallest of things and the most insignificant of gestures. But she also became sad easily and anguished over things that couldn't be helped and should have been long forgotten. That was a character trait he'd found maddening.

Jeremy clumped inside. "Well?" Carl asked. "What did you learn?"

"The car was still in the lot where 'Bernie' left it. I didn't get too close, but it looked to me like there was a parking ticket under the windshield wiper. Other than that, there was no sign that it had been noticed."

Carl gnawed on that. "Strikes me as odd that they haven't impounded it. How long do they usually wait to haul in cars with parking violations?"

Jeremy shrugged as he took a carton of orange juice from one of the shopping bags and gulped directly from it.

"You didn't spot any cops staked out to watch it?"

"No, but there are industrial buildings surrounding that parking lot, each of them several stories tall. They could be surveilling it from any one of a thousand windows, but I don't think so, Daddy. Who would be lying in wait for Bernie to return? Bernie is a nobody, a nonfactor in any of this."

Carl eyed his son shrewdly. "Then why don't you look happier?"

"They're all over the boat."

Carl muttered a stream of obscenities.

Defensively, Jeremy said, "They were bound to follow up on any boats that had put into Saint Nelda's dock on Sunday. I guess the gas pump attendant remembered the name of it."

"Stupid name. No wonder he remembered it."

Flora had suggested the boat be named *CandyCane* because they had acquired it on a Christmas Eve. They'd used it to escape following the burglary of a church after its midnight mass when the coffers were full.

The owner of the boat, an embittered veteran of the Vietnam War, and a devotee of Carl's, was also an atheist. He'd been so delighted over the theft of a church, he had graciously offered his boat to convey them far away from Maryland. He'd taken them all the way down to the Florida Keys.

When the need arose for a boat, the embittered vet, now suffering several forms of cancer, had been willing to oblige his hero again. He taught Jeremy basic boating and navigational skills, enough so that he could get himself to Saint Nelda's from other islands and marinas along the coasts of the Carolinas, Georgia, and Florida. Marina slips were rented under assumed names.

"That guy on Saint Nelda's might be able to describe me," he said now, "but he can't identify me as Jeremy Wesson. Besides, I told you, the boat has been wiped clean. They won't find any trace of me onboard."

"One hair is all it would take."

"That's a worry, but a minor one. They're still looking at Dawson Scott."

"He was released."

"Yeah, but the investigators are 'reconstructing the time line,' making me think he hasn't been altogether cleared." He gestured to the plastic bags he'd dropped on the table. "I bought a newspaper. The murder has been demoted to page five."

Carl found the newspaper in one of the bags, opened it to that page, and scanned the text. Jeremy turned on his tablet PC. "If you'd ever learn to navigate the Internet, you wouldn't need a newspaper anymore."

"I don't like computers."

"By the time you read a newspaper, it's old news. You get continual updates on the Internet."

They'd had this conversation many times before. With the exception of firearms, Carl loathed gadgetry. He was leery of anything he saw or read on the Net.

According to the newspaper story, the sheriff's office was being tight-lipped about the progress of its investigation. Deputy Tucker was quoted. He used the same hackneyed phrases that every law enforcement officer in the country uses whenever what he is saying, basically, is that they don't have jack shit.

Dawson Scott had cooperated with the investigation. They hadn't made an arrest, but were analyzing evidence. They were following a new lead. Blah, blah. Carl knew that whenever a lead petered out and cops were stuck, they always lied and said they had a new one to follow.

Jeremy had been reading aloud off the newspaper's website, and the write-up on it more or less matched what Carl had just read. "So much for constant updates," he said snidely.

"But here we get a color photo, too. The newspaper didn't even have a black-and-white."

Carl glanced at the tablet from over Jeremy's shoulder. "Tucker is a tub o' guts," he remarked, pointing to the potbellied deputy pictured standing in the foreground of a group of uniformed officers.

Then, in the motion of turning away, he said, "Wait! Give me that." Roughly he snatched the tablet out of Jeremy's hands. "How do I enlarge the picture?"

"Tap…"

The photograph filled the screen. Carl looked hard at a man standing in the background. Although a deputy in a cowboy hat was blocking one half of his face from the camera, instant recognition suffused Carl with feverish heat. He clenched his teeth and sailed the tablet across the room like a Frisbee.

"Hey! What's the matter?"

"I knew it! I sensed it! Didn't I tell you something was out of joint?"

"What? What do you see?"

With unmitigated hatred, Carl said, "FBI Special Agent Gary Headly."

Diary of Flora Stimel—Christmas Day, 1993

I'm so blue, I can barely stand it. We stole from a church last night, which I'm pretty sure means I'll go to hell. Of course I already knew I would, because I've killed people. Well, helped kill people. I've been there when Carl killed, and I think that's the same as doing it myself.

Carl had me go into the church before the midnight service started. I watched people as they came in. Mommies and daddies and grandfolks. Some of the children were sleepy, being as the service started at 11:15, way past their bedtime. Others were excited and couldn't sit still. I guess they were anxious to get home and into bed so Santa Claus could come.

It just made my heart ache, because I never got to spend a Christmas Eve with Jeremy and play Santa for him, and now he's too old. He's a senior in high school! I wish that just once I could have watched his face on Christmas morning when he found his presents under the tree.

It's been a long time since he believed in Santa Claus, of course. What he believes in now, mostly, is his daddy. He thinks Carl hung the moon. Randy and Patricia have seen to it that he knows Carl's ideas about things. They tell him about how men like Carl are smart enough to see everything that's wrong in this country, and that's why the government and the law hate and fear them and want to shut them up. Jeremy has caught on. Grabbed on, really. I'm glad of it. But it worries me.

I got off the track, which I do a lot whenever I write in this diary. I start thinking back and then... See? There I go again.

After the congregation sang "Silent Night" at midnight to candlelight (I had a candle, too. Everybody did. The people on either side of me had no idea that they were sitting next to a noted outlaw! Bet they would have croaked!)... Anyhow, everyone started filing out of the church. Except me. I went into the ladies' room, which I'd made sure to locate before I took my seat in the sanctuary.

Only one other woman came in. She did her business quick and left. Her family was probably waiting on her. I stood on the toilet seat in case a janitor or somebody came in to check the stalls and see if everybody was gone, but the lights went out with me still balancing up there.

I waited another ten minutes like Carl had told me to, then turned on my flashlight and left the restroom. What had looked so pretty in the candlelight looked kinda spooky in the dark. The statues and all. But I tried not to look at anything except the circle of light I directed to the floor.

I let Carl and Henry in through a side door. No alarm sounded, but Carl said it was probably a silent one. Henry joked and said, "Only God can hear it, I guess." I didn't think it was funny. Carl sorta laughed, but he was focused on picking the lock on the church office door.

We grabbed the bags the ushers had emptied the offering plates into and got the heck out of there. But there must have been a silent alarm, because when we ran out of the church, there was a policeman just stepping out of his patrol car. He pulled his pistol and hollered for us to halt. Carl shot him in the chest. Henry got him in the head, I think.

As we were running to the car, Henry fired at the figures in the Nativity on the church lawn. He claims he doesn't believe in God or Jesus or Allah or anything, but he sure bears them a grudge.

We made a safe getaway and came away with good cash. But I felt awful about it and didn't get high like the men did after we boarded the boat and started south. I hope the sailor, or whatever it is you call the guy who drives the boat, can drive it when he's stoned. They all got stoned good. Carl included, which is why I felt it was okay to get out my diary and write.

I hope Jeremy likes his presents. I haven't seen him since we went to Vancouver this past summer. I can't get over how grown he is! A man, really. I was shocked when we hugged and I felt whiskers on his chin! I don't know when I'll get to see him again. I've started mentioning his high school graduation which will be in the spring. I say over and over again how much I wish I could be there. Carl acts like he doesn't hear me. But maybe he'll take the hint.

The sun's coming up and I'm seasick from writing, so I'd better put this way. But not before saying, Merry Christmas, Jeremy. I love you.

Dec. 25th, later. We get TV even out here on the ocean, and on the news they were talking about the burglary at the church. The policeman died. He was only twenty-seven. He had a two-month-old baby girl. Hearing that kinda made me sick to my stomach, so I used that as an excuse to come below and get away from Carl, who's in a mean mood.

I think because the news people quoted that FBI agent Gary Headly, who's been after us for years. Carl hates him with a passion. I think on account of he's a little afraid that one of these days Agent Headly is going to capture us like he's pledged to do.

Also Carl hates him because he was at Golden Branch, and he never fails to mention that whenever he's interviewed about us. Carl hates being reminded of that day. So do I. Even if Carl doesn't admit it, I think deep down he was awfully scared that day, too. Scared of being killed or of getting caught. I also think he feels guilty over doing what he did and leaving like that when everybody else was dead or dying.

Anyhow, he blames everything that happened that day on the feds and, in his mind, Headly sorta represents all of them. Carl won't be happy till Agent Headly is dead.

Chapter 21

Headly's bad news had to wait.

Just as he was about to impart it, Hunter and Grant came into the kitchen asking for a snack. Since breakfast had amounted to an overdose of sugar, Amelia offered them milk or nothing. They took the milk, but dawdled over it as though aware of the adults' impatience for them to finish. When they were finally done, she wrangled them back into the living area to continue their movie.

The moment she reentered the kitchen, Headly picked up where he'd left off. "For all the reasons we've discussed, Tucker isn't convinced that Stephanie DeMarco's murder is related to Amelia beyond the fact that Amelia was her employer."

"Stubborn jerk," Dawson said. "Wills?"

"Leaning toward Knutz and me. But, you know, we're the big, bad, buttinsky FBI, and he's loyal. Sheriff is backing his man, too. Tucker shared the Jeremy-is-alive theory with him. No fool, he recognizes that it will be hard to live down if we're wrong. He's asked for further analysis on the fingerprint. Now, about Bernie. The sheriff was quick to point out that he hasn't been charged with a crime."

"Not as Bernie, no."

"Well, he thinks the Carl-Bernie connection is thin and is demanding more concrete evidence of that before launching a full-scale manhunt for a fugitive that nobody's heard from in seventeen years."

"The Bureau doesn't need his authorization."

"No . . ." Headly said with marked hesitancy.

"But what? What's the upshot?"

"Keeping guards on Amelia and the children isn't warranted. They plan to withdraw them."

"They can't."

"I asked for forty-eight hours."

"That's not enough time to—"

"They gave me twenty-four." Headly glanced at the wall clock. "Now twenty-three and thirteen minutes."

Dawson swore under his breath.

Headly said, "The Bureau will pursue Bernie Clarkson, if only to rule out that he's Carl."

"Fine. Good. But that still leaves Amelia and the boys vulnerable."

"Knutz made a suggestion." Headly looked at Amelia. "But I doubt you're going to like it."

Speaking for the first time in several minutes, she asked, "What is it?"

"You could call a press conference and announce that you have good reason to believe that your ex-husband wasn't murdered, that he's still alive and stalking you, that possibly he killed your nanny mistakenly, and that he represents a threat to you and your children."

No one said anything for a moment, then Dawson asked, "What purpose would that serve?"

"Public opinion would likely favor her. Press would be all over it. That could jostle the local authorities into taking some action."

"I won't do it," she said, brooking no argument. She looked

toward the living area where Hunter and Grant could be heard laughing. "Can you imagine the effect it's going to have on our lives when it's disclosed that Jeremy is alive?"

"That's an inevitability," Headly gently reminded her. "Whenever and however it comes about, it's going to have a dramatic impact."

"Of course I know that. But I don't want to be the ringmaster of the media circus when it happens. Eventually my sons will be identified as the children of a murderer, grandchildren of domestic terrorists. I can't protect them from the truth, or prevent it from becoming public knowledge. But I also can't conceive of how we'll cope with the backlash. How will they live with that stigma?"

She looked to both men for an answer, but, of course, none was forthcoming, because there wasn't one. Dawson held her tortured gaze for several seconds, then turned away. Headly was the first to break the strained silence.

"Okay, we'll sit on the disclosure for as long as we can. In the meantime let's try to find the sons of bitches. Did you come up with anything overnight, something you've remembered that could be useful? Where Jeremy might be hiding, who could be sheltering him?"

"I made a list of his friends, ones whose names I could remember. But by the time he disappeared, Jeremy had alienated most of them."

"Where's the list?"

"Upstairs on my desk."

"Would you get it, please? Let's take a look. I know it's a long shot, but our time is running out. I still believe that as long as Carl and Jeremy don't know—" Headly broke off when Dawson's cell phone rang.

He checked the LED. "Harriet."

Amelia looked to Headly for clarification. "*NewsFront*'s managing editor. A harpy."

Dawson answered, but his editor cut him off in midsentence. He listened, then asked tersely, "Did the call come through the switchboard? What time?" He looked at his wristwatch. "What exactly did he want to know?"

She and Headly could tell by the tension in his posture that Harriet was passing on unwelcome news. After a full minute of listening, Dawson said, "Okay, thanks for letting me know. Yeah, yeah, I'm still trying to woo her." He glanced at Amelia. "Right. She'd be a plum interview for sure. Which is why I gotta run now. Bye." He clicked off and, after a beat, said, "A man identifying himself as Bernie Clarkson called her to get the skinny on me."

Headly hissed through his teeth. "Carl knows."

"At the very least he smells a rat."

Amelia sat down heavily in the nearest chair. "What did he say specifically?"

Dawson recounted the conversation that his editor had repeated to him. "She said he sounded like a dotty old man. Cautious and suspicious. The last thing he asked was what or who had brought the Jeremy Wesson story to my attention. She told him she didn't know, and she doesn't. She believes that my interest was sparked by the Willard, Darlene, Jeremy love triangle and its deadly consequences, partially the result of his PTSD."

Headly said, "But 'Bernie' thought there might be more to your interest, and acted on that hunch."

"Apparently. He lied about the business card. I didn't give him one. Which means that he went to the trouble to find out whom to call to check me out."

"Well, at least she didn't tell him anything that would arouse more suspicion," Amelia said. "The opposite, in fact. She only confirmed that you're a journalist on the trail of a good story."

"I am that." He stared thoughtfully into space for several moments, then rapidly punched in a number on his cell phone.

"Glenda, love of my life, will you marry me? Okay, how 'bout we just have a hot affair? One-night stand, then. All right, all right, listen. Two things.

"First, Harriet took a call at her desk around nine fifty this morning. I can't remember the number of her extension, but... Is it any wonder that I love you? Can you get me the number of the caller? God, no, don't go through her. Go through the main switchboard, and make it casual.

"Second thing," he paused and took a deep breath. "I need to go to jail without passing go. Can you help me?"

A female deputy assumed the role of nanny. The boys took to her immediately, especially when she set up a lengthy race track for their many cars. It wound from room to room and even up the staircase. They were enthralled with the makeshift ramps.

Another sheriff's deputy arrived with groceries to replenish Amelia's refrigerator and pantry. Having provided for her sons made her feel better about leaving them while she returned to the city with Headly and Dawson.

Headly was interested in seeing what remained of Jeremy's effects that were still in her possession. "They're in a strongbox in my apartment," she told him. "Don't expect too much. I've kept only some things the boys may want when they get older. His marksmanship medals. Things like that."

Deputies in unmarked cars were in front of and behind her car when they drove off the ferry and made their way through Savannah. To Amelia, the caravan looked obvious, but she supposed the law officers knew what they were doing. Headly was wearing a shoulder holster beneath his jacket, which was both comforting and disconcerting.

The plan was for them to drop Dawson off at the jail visitation center and come back for him after their errand to her apartment.

"I could grease the skids for you," Headly offered. "Make it more official."

"Thanks," Dawson said, "but I want to avoid being 'official.' A private citizen is more confidence inspiring."

"You hope."

"I hope." As he got out of the car, he gave Amelia a meaningful look. "Later."

"Good luck."

After pausing to make certain that the unmarked cars were still serving as unobtrusive escorts as she drove away, Dawson entered the building where Willard Strong's lawyer, Mike Gleason, was waiting for him in the lobby, as arranged by Glenda, who had passed herself off as a top-ranking executive at *NewsFront.* The attorney had fallen for her schmooze, which was as good as any when she set her mind to it.

"I appealed to his vanity, and he fell for it," she'd told Dawson when she called him back to confirm the appointment.

He'd forgiven her for being unable to obtain more information about Carl Wingert's telephone call to Harriet. As Dawson had expected, it had come in on a number that was blocked. "Sorry, I couldn't help you there," the researcher had said.

"You're still a sweetheart. You got me this meeting, and that's a coup."

Now, puffed up with self-importance, the lawyer approached him. "Mr. Scott?"

They shook hands. "Thank you for agreeing to talk to me."

"With no guarantee of granting you an interview with my client."

"I hope to convince you that it would be in his best interest."

"Then you've got your work cut out for you."

Gleason accompanied the snarky comment with a gesture toward a sitting area where they could chat.

He was about the same age as Dawson, nice-looking, and well dressed. But he wasn't an effective trial lawyer. His cross-examination of Amelia had been disastrous, and he hadn't recovered much ground by putting his client on the witness stand.

He talked tough, but Dawson guessed that the chest thumping was to compensate for basic insecurity. He was in over his head and he knew it, but he would go down kicking.

"I thought *NewsFront* had folded."

It was a mild but intentional gibe. Dawson responded with a bland smile. "We're hanging in there. One of the few."

"I was told that you're covering the trial for the magazine."

"I'm covering the trial for myself. It's a compelling story, start to finish." He didn't have time to pussyfoot around or spare Gleason's inflated ego. He laid it out there. "The way things stand now, the story will end with Willard Strong going to death row."

Gleason took exception, which Dawson had anticipated. He talked over the attorney's sputtered protests. "Which will be a tragic miscarriage of justice, because your client is innocent."

That stopped the spate of objections. Dawson raised his eyebrows as though asking permission to continue. Curtly, Gleason bobbed his head.

"Willard was framed for his wife's murder."

"What makes you think so, Mr. Scott?"

"I'm not prepared to divulge that."

Gleason looked disappointed, then put out. "You're trying to pull a fast one, aren't you?"

"No."

"Did you try to get an interview with Lem Jackson, too? Did you tell him you think we wasted the state's money on a trial, that Willard is as guilty as sin and should have gone straight to prison?"

"No."

"But you'll admit that an interview with my client would embellish the story you intend to write."

"Damn straight it will. But by letting me talk to him, you'd be doing him a favor as well as me."

He crossed his arms over his chest. "Tell me how it could benefit him."

"You mean in addition to setting him free instead of condemning him to death?" Dawson didn't expect a reply, and Gleason didn't bother to make one. "Your client has a major PR problem. Even if he isn't a killer, he looks like one. He carried a massive chip on his shoulder into the courtroom each day. Then you put him in the witness box and suddenly he's earnest, woebegone, pathetic. A man trying to save his life would be expected to have a change of heart and become more humble, but I don't think the jury bought Willard's sincerity."

"You can't influence the jurors' perception of him. They won't have access to anything you write."

"True."

"Then—"

"I can possibly change the course of the trial. But first you must let me talk to him. Only then can I help Willard help himself."

"Helping him is my job."

"With all due respect, you're failing."

Again, the ego reared. "The jury's not in yet, Mr. Scott."

"The odds for an acquittal are slim to none. Admit it."

He admitted nothing, but he said, "Give me another reason why this is a good idea."

"Unless there's a major upset, something like a mistrial, he'll be convicted."

"I'm not conceding the point. But if he is convicted, I'll immediately file for an appeal."

"Your appeal *could* coincide with a national magazine story slanted in Willard's favor."

"You'd do that? You'd write it that way?"

"Yes."

"Why?"

"Because I'd stake my career on his innocence."

"Are you yanking my chain?"

"No."

That seemed to impress him, but he still wasn't ready to concede. "I looked you up on the Internet. You've written your share of smear stories."

"About people who deserved to be smeared."

"So, how do I know that isn't what you plan for my client?"

"You don't."

"How do I know you aren't bullshitting me when you say you think he's innocent?"

"You don't." After a second, he added, "I know you're taking a leap of faith here, but it will pay off."

The lawyer chewed on that, literally. The inside of his cheek was being brutalized by his molars. At last, he said, "Let me sleep on it."

"Nope. This is a onetime offer."

"But I need time to—"

"No time. Tell me now. Yes or no?"

"You're working under a deadline?"

He'd posed the question tongue-in-cheek, but Dawson answered solemnly. "You have no idea."

Dawson could tell that the attorney's pride struggled with the concept of surrender and that it got the better of him. "Sorry, Mr. Scott. No soap. At least not until I've considered it, consulted my client, and weighed our options."

Dawson wanted to grab him by his well-tailored lapels and shake him. He didn't, but he leaned forward and spoke rapidly, aggressively. "What options? *What options?* You have two. Twelve people are ready, even eager, to have a needle shoved into Willard's vein. He dies an innocent man and you chalk up a big ugly black mark in your loss column. That's one option."

He leaned even closer. "And then there's me, the town crier

on Willard's behalf. He goes free, you're hailed a hero, you go on TV to talk about it, and every felon in the South is begging you to be his defender."

Dawson could tell he liked the sound of that, but still he was wrestling with it. "That all sounds good, but—"

"What?"

"It might not work out that way."

"It for damn sure won't if you turn me down."

"I'm not turning you down flat. But caution is called for here."

"No time for caution. You've got to decide."

"But—"

"You gotta say yes and say it now."

"You—"

"I'm the only hope for your client."

"He—"

"Hasn't got a prayer and you know it."

"I—"

"*Grant me the goddamn interview.*"

Dawson's imperious shout took him aback, but it also worked. He unfolded his arms. He licked his lips. "It'll be like a webcam."

"Fine."

"I'll be right there the whole time."

"Fine."

"I'll record the entire interview and have it transcripted afterward."

"Fine."

"If you slander him, I'll sue you and your magazine."

Dawson stood up. "Deal."

The short-notice meeting with the prisoner took time to arrange. It seemed interminably long to Dawson, who paced while Gleason dealt with staff who seemed to have nothing but time on their hands. Eventually, they were situated in a room that allowed them a video interview with Willard Strong.

In another part of the jail, Strong was led into a room, manacled and shackled. Radiating hostility, he slumped down into the chair in front of the monitor through which he could communicate. He regarded his lawyer with patent contempt. Then his belligerent gaze shifted to Dawson. "Who the fuck are you?"

Dawson gave him a lazy smile. "Be nice, Willard. I'm the guy who's here to save your sorry self."

Amelia and Headly were headed back toward the jail. She was driving. Headly was in the passenger seat, talking on his cell phone to Knutz. A minor collision on the expressway had slowed traffic to a crawl. The sheriff's unmarked cars were having as much difficulty switching lanes as she.

Headly ended his conversation. "Knutz is trying to buy us more time, using that phone call to Dawson's boss as leverage. Why would little ol' Bernie phone her in the first place? Why would he lie?"

"Unless he was Carl."

"Knutz is acting on that. Meanwhile the boat hasn't given up any clues."

Nor had the strongbox. Nothing useful was discovered: no map, property deed, lease, or paperwork of any kind.

That having proved fruitless, they'd divided the list of Jeremy's former friends that she'd compiled, and working on their separate cell phones, the two of them had placed dozens of calls. In preparation for the inevitable question *Why are you asking me about Jeremy now?* Headly had made up an explanation involving a fictitious tax return with a questionable deduction that was affecting the trust funds set up for Hunter and Grant. He'd advised Amelia on the buzzwords to use.

"Do you think they'll understand that gibberish?" she asked.

"No. And to avoid any further involvement, no one will ask for clarity. That's the point."

Many of the numbers they called were no longer in service. Some had been answered by voice mail, on which they'd left messages asking the individual to call them back on a matter of grave importance.

Of the few people with whom they'd spoken, all were reluctant to talk about Jeremy and were actually ill at ease for having been singled out as a former acquaintance. Most reactions were wary, some downright hostile.

Repeatedly both Headly and Amelia were told that the questions they were putting to them now had already been asked by police more than a year earlier, when Jeremy went missing and was presumed dead. They'd told everything they knew then.

She braked for a pickup truck trying to wedge its way in and looked over at Headly. "Where do we go from here?"

"Maybe Dawson got something out of Willard." He shifted in his seat and turned slightly toward her. "What do you think of him?"

"He gives me the creeps."

He laughed. "I meant Dawson. Or does *he* give you the creeps?"

"Oh. Dawson."

Headly waited her out, and she was the first to look away. Taking her foot off the brake pedal, she rolled forward only a few yards before having to stop again. "Dawson and I didn't get off to a great start. Did he tell you about our initial meeting?"

"He began playing with the boys on the beach. Things went from there."

"More or less," she murmured.

"Huh. More, I think."

When she said nothing, he chuckled. "Okay. Keep that story to yourselves. Back to my original question."

"What do I think of him? In what way?"

"In any way."

"He's good with the boys."

"Surprisingly."

"Why?"

"He has no former experience with kids. He was raised an only child. He was around our daughter, Sarah, a lot, but she's a few years older, so they squabbled as much as they played." He told her that Sarah was married and living in London.

"Children?"

"Not yet. My wife drops hints about as subtle as crashing meteorites."

Amelia laughed. "In the meantime Dawson receives parental doting from you and Mrs. Headly."

"Which he resists, of course."

Temporarily stopped in the logjam, she looked at him. "Why 'of course'?"

"The detachment that makes him a good journalist carries over into his personal life. He sets himself apart, sees himself only as an observer, a loner. That's why he's never married. Why he hasn't even come close."

She gave him an arch look. "Mind you, I didn't ask."

"No, but I figured you wanted to know." He grinned at her and winked. "Oh, there have been a few women who stayed on longer than others. A couple of them were lovely ladies, who met Eva's rigid standards. But even with them, once things got too warm and fuzzy, he called it quits."

"Commitment issues are common. Especially for a man who's a loner."

"I didn't say he was a loner."

She looked at him with puzzlement. "You just did."

"I said he *sees* himself as a loner."

"What's the difference?"

"His true nature. Would a natural-born loner have gravitated to your children the way he has?"

"Wait." She held up her hand, wanting to understand. "You're saying Dawson fights his natural tendencies?"

"With a vengeance."

"Why?"

"It's a defense mechanism."

"Against what?"

"You'll have to ask him." He held her gaze for several beats, then called her attention to the traffic. "You have an opening." Once past the fender bender, he continued. "When you've exhausted that subject, ask him what happened in Afghanistan."

"I have. He refused to talk about it. You?"

"The same."

"I witnessed him in the throes of a nightmare. We weren't sleeping together," she added hastily.

"Mind you, I didn't ask," he said, throwing her words back at her.

She gave him a smile of chagrin, then turned serious again. "I heard him crying out and went to check. He was in quite a state. Visibly tormented. He woke up screaming. Like Jeremy used to do. Except…"

"What?"

"Dawson was drenched with sweat and trembling. Even after he was fully awake and aware of his surroundings, it took him several minutes to recover. He experienced the horror of the nightmare physically and emotionally. After seeing him that way, I believe Jeremy was faking."

"The nightmares?"

"All of it. I think he was only pretending to suffer from post-traumatic stress. If so, that's yet another betrayal, isn't it? They're adding up."

"Amelia." Headly spoke her name quietly. When she turned her head toward him, he said, "Dawson isn't like Jeremy. Not in any respect."

That reassurance, coming from someone who knew him well,

was what she'd needed and wanted. They drove the rest of the way to the jail without further comment. But as they approached the visitation center, she said, "He's not out front."

"That's a good sign. The longer he's able to talk to Willard, the better his chances of obtaining information. Park and let's wait inside, where it's cooler."

It was a full half hour before Dawson reunited with them in the lobby of the center. Headly reached him first. "Well?"

"Gleason was four square against it, but he finally caved."

"You saw Willard?" Amelia asked.

"Ten minutes on webcam, but I might have got something. He was all attitude at first, but when I told him I thought Jeremy was still alive, and that it was he, not Willard, who had killed Darlene, he grew considerably more cooperative." He smiled grimly as he crossed his index and middle fingers. "We're like this now."

"Congratulations," Headly said. "Skip to the good part."

"I don't know how good or reliable it is. It's not like Willard has won my unqualified trust. But when I asked him if he knew about a place that Jeremy might run to, he didn't even have to search his memory. Which lends credibility to what he told me. Once, when he and Jeremy were out at the dog pens, Jeremy made an unflattering comment about the shack. He said something to the effect that it made his look like a Hilton."

"His *shack*?"

Dawson shrugged. "Willard couldn't be more specific, because when he asked Jeremy for details, he blew it off. What he had *meant* to say was that *if* he had a place like that, it would be better than the shit hole Willard had.

"However, Willard is convinced that it was a slip of the tongue, something Jeremy hadn't intended to mention, but when he did, he tried to talk his way out of it. Do you know of any such place?" he asked Amelia.

She shook her head dejectedly. "If Jeremy owned anything like that, I'm unaware of it."

"Fishing cabin, deer blind, hut, boathouse, cowshed?"

"I don't know of anything."

Headly made a sound of disgust. "The whole thing sounds far-fetched. I think Willard is pretending to remember something that was never said. Or telling you tales to amuse himself."

"Or something he knows I want to hear," Dawson said. "I asked him why he didn't tell the cops about this conversation when they were searching kingdom come for Jeremy or his remains. He said he did tell them, but, to his knowledge, nobody acted on the information. They were searching the marsh for a decomposing body, not a shack with a living Jeremy inside."

Headly dragged his hand down his face, stretching the skin. "A shack that may or may not exist, and if it does, it could be anywhere in the forty-eight contiguous states."

"South Carolina."

Dawson and Headly looked at Amelia, who'd spoken as though thinking out loud. Realizing that she had their attention, she said, "I found a speeding ticket on our closet floor. It must have fallen out of a pocket when he hung up his clothes. I noticed it had been issued in South Carolina, so I asked him about it."

"When was this?"

"Shortly before we separated. He'd already made Willard's acquaintance, and even then I wasn't keen on this new friendship. I hoped he'd gone to Beaufort to visit some of his old friends from Parris Island and the naval air station.

"When I showed him the ticket, he became irrationally furious. That's why I remember it. He took it from me, tore it into pieces, and threw them away. He cursed me for meddling and told me to mind my own business. Obviously I'd hit on something he didn't want me to know about. I suspected it was another woman. But perhaps…" She trailed off to let them draw their own conclusion.

Dawson looked at Headly and shrugged. "It's something."

Energized, they started toward the exit. Headly said, "With Jeremy's Social Security number, the DMV over there should be able to look up the ticket. Once we know where it was issued, we'll have a starting point to begin a search. I'll get Knutz on that."

He punched a number into his phone. Dawson held the door and allowed Amelia and Headly to precede him. They emerged into the bright sunlight and headed toward the parking lot.

Headly, phone to his ear, turned his head to say something to Dawson from over his shoulder when suddenly a strange expression came over his face. Then his eyes went completely blank.

Dawson's brain processed instantly what that vacant look signified, even as Headly's knees folded beneath him and he toppled forward. Dawson gave a shout of horror and outrage as he pushed Amelia to the sidewalk and followed her down.

The second bullet missed her by a hairbreadth.

The one intended for Headly had found its mark.

Chapter 22

Carl Wingert was one of the few criminals in American history who had the gall to bring the fight to the authorities.

He and Jeremy had spent hours on the roof of a seven-story office building that, due to the recession, had run out of renters. The management company had gone bankrupt, and after being foreclosed upon, the building had stood empty and neglected.

Situated in an industrial park where other businesses had similarly succumbed to the bad economy, it was a quarter mile away from the jail complex. In between was a four-lane thoroughfare divided by a wide median planted with crepe myrtle trees.

Trees presented a problem in general, but from that roof, one of the tallest in the whole area, Jeremy could have taken several clear shots. Partially obscured by a ventilation shaft, they'd waited for an opportunity to strike FBI agent Gary Headly where and when he would least expect it.

The playing field had changed for Carl the instant he saw Headly in the photograph. The only reason the veteran agent would be here in Savannah working in conjunction with the sheriff's office to solve the Stephanie DeMarco murder case was because Jeremy had been linked to the homicide and, even more damning, to Carl Wingert.

The authorities hadn't publicly declared that Jeremy was indeed alive and the suspected culprit, or that he had a direct bloodline to a notorious fugitive from justice, but Carl knew that those dots of information had been connected. That was the only explanation for Headly's involvement.

Whether or not Headly had linked him to Bernie Clarkson, he didn't know. But even if he hadn't, he would still be hot on Jeremy's trail if only because he was Carl's son. Either way, Carl resolved not to wait on the agent to find him. No, by God. The guy wanted him, the guy was going to get him. Just not in the way he planned on it.

Carl had reasoned that sooner or later Headly would show up at the sheriff's office to confer with the blubber-gutted deputy and that when he did, Jeremy could pick him off, even from that distance.

The assassination of an FBI agent on the campus of the sheriff's office and jail complex would create chaos. Panic and confusion would ensue. Before anyone figured out from which direction the fatal bullet had come, he and Jeremy would be long gone.

The plan had the stamp of Carl Wingert all over it. It was just audacious enough to work. Certainly there was an element of risk, but it was low enough that Carl was willing to take it in order to rid himself of his nemesis. By doing so, he would also let the rotten American society know that Carl wasn't done with it quite yet. He may be old, but he was still a fear-worthy entity, a force to be reckoned with.

He regretted not having taken a bold action such as this decades ago, and blamed Flora and her whining for his years of inactivity. So his resentment toward Headly had had decades in which to ferment, and it now made his revenge even sweeter.

The hours they'd spent waiting on the roof for Headly to

appear had given Jeremy time to assess the conditions, do his calculations, and practice his aim on uniformed personnel and visitors to the sheriff's office and jail who entered and exited the various buildings on their various errands, little knowing that they were in his crosshairs.

Jeremy needed no coaching, but Carl kept up a stream of instruction. "You'll have one chance to take him out, possibly two, but no more before they hear the report. Within seconds, we need to be on the fire stairs."

When the time came, Jeremy was mentally primed. All he had to do was make the shot. Carl, who'd been watching the complex through binoculars, recognized Amelia's car when it wheeled up to the entrance of the visitation center. He reported this to Jeremy. "See her?"

"On the car," Jeremy said, his voice tense with concentration. "This could be it."

But it wasn't. Dawson Scott alighted and went into the building alone, and while Jeremy would have loved nothing better than to blow him away, he hadn't had a clear shot, and besides, Dawson Scott wasn't today's target.

Amelia drove away. They waited, ate energy bars, drank from water bottles. Going on two hours later, Amelia returned and parked. This time she and "Guess-fucking-who," Carl chuckled, parked and went inside. "Got to come out sometime. Set up, son."

This time the wait was short. Amelia was the first one out. Headly right behind her, his phone to his ear.

"Got him?" Carl asked Jeremy.

"Roger Dodger."

But just as Jeremy squeezed the trigger, the agent turned to speak over his shoulder. Carl, who was expecting to see the agent's head explode, cursed when he collapsed and fell, cranium intact. "Not a head shot, but he's down. Let's go!"

The binoculars hung from his neck by a cord, so his hands

were free to grab the tripod as choreographed. Jeremy retrieved two shell casings. The shots had come in such rapid succession, Carl hadn't realized Jeremy had fired a second time. "Amelia?"

"Missed her."

Carl didn't waste time on disappointment. There would be another occasion for Amelia. As for Headly, if he wasn't dead, he was ruined.

The two of them jogged across the gravel roof and squeezed through the heavy metal door that had given them access to it. Their footsteps echoed loudly in the enclosed stairwell, but there was no one to hear them as they descended through the deserted building. Jeremy was carrying the rifle, but he could still move with more speed and alacrity than Carl, whose hips pained him with every tread.

Jeremy asked if he needed to take a sec to rest. Carl shoved him aside and went past him. "You'll have trouble keeping up with me, sonny."

As though to underscore their need for haste, the wail of sirens reached them through the exterior walls.

"Christ, that was fast," Jeremy said.

"Don't think about them. Just keep moving."

By the time they reached the ground floor, both were laboring to catch their breath. They left the building through the back door by which they'd entered after destroying the lock. Jeremy opened the rear door of his car and was carefully placing the rifle in the floorboard behind the driver's seat when a patrol car, running hot, lights flashing, turned into the alley between the abandoned building and its vacant neighbor. It screeched to a halt about ten yards away from them.

"Stay calm," Carl said, instantly adapting the persona of Bernie Clarkson.

The officer behind the wheel was middle-aged, which told Carl a lot about him, namely that he wasn't the sharpest of cops or he wouldn't still be on routine patrol. He clambered out while unsnapping the holster on his right hip.

"Put your hands where I can see them!" He worked the pistol out of the holster and aimed it at them in turn.

"What's going on, officer?" Carl asked in Bernie's age-rusty voice.

He shouted, "Come out from behind that door! Hands up!"

Jeremy eased away from the open door of the backseat and, along with Carl, raised his hands shoulder high. "What are all the sirens—"

"Who are you? What are you doing here?"

"As of this morning, we've leased this building for our medical supply company," Jeremy said. "Came to check it out, see if the utilities had been turned on yet. We were just about to leave when those sirens started screaming."

Carl asked, "Was there a robbery in the area?"

The officer's eyes sawed between them. "Stay where you are." He reached for the transmitter clipped to his shoulder.

"Daddy?" Jeremy said.

"Got him." Carl yanked a pistol from his waistband at the small of his back and pulled the trigger only once. The cop went down. "They never learn."

Shooting a cop hadn't been part of their plan. Jeremy said, "We need to get out of here *now*." He turned to close the car's rear door.

Carl hobbled around the front of the car to the passenger side and was halfway in when he heard the crack. It was still several seconds before he realized that the policeman, lying crumpled on the pavement with a pool of blood forming beneath him, had managed to get off a shot.

That infuriated Carl. He walked over to him, bent down, and jammed the barrel of his pistol against the officer's temple. Looking into his fear-stricken eyes, he smiled. "Impress the devil. Tell him you got killed by Carl Wingert."

He left the body and the car where they were, but made note of the name on the tag pinned to the officer's uniform and yanked the squawking police radio from off his belt.

Jeremy was behind the steering wheel with the motor running by the time Carl slid into the passenger seat. "Drive toward the bridge. Easy like."

He jacked up the volume of the radio and had listened for several minutes before anyone tried to contact the officer he'd killed. Muffling his voice, he said, "Nothing moving over here." The dispatcher gave the officer new instructions, which Carl acknowledged, then switched off. "We should be miles away before they start looking for him." When Jeremy didn't respond, he looked over at him. He was sweaty and grim-faced, focused on his driving.

Then Carl noticed that his hand was flattened against his right side. Blood was leaking between his fingers. "Jesus! He hit you with that shot?"

Jeremy peeled his lips back to form a parody of a grin. "Just a scratch, Daddy."

"We, uh, found an SPD officer and his unit behind an abandoned building. He'd been shot twice. Once in the abdomen, once…" Tucker glanced at Amelia, who was sitting beside Dawson on a short sofa in the trauma center waiting room. The deputy amended whatever he had been about to say. "He was dead."

Dawson felt Amelia flinch. He was too shocked by what had happened to Headly to react.

Deputy Wills cleared his throat, his prominent Adam's apple sliding up and down his long, wrinkled neck. Dawson thought he looked like a turtle with his small head poking out of his shirt collar, which was too large.

Entertaining such nonsensical thoughts was the only thing keeping him sane. If he started thinking about the reality he found himself in, about Headly inexorably dying while he stood futilely by, he'd go crazy, destroy something, kill somebody.

He was only barely holding on to his reason, and he was able to do that only because Headly hadn't been pronounced dead at the scene. Perhaps he had died in transit to the hospital, or on the operating table, but no one had had the courage to tell Dawson yet. That was a distinct possibility, because the deputies were regarding him as though mistrustful of his outward stoicism and in fear of an eruption of violent fury at any moment. They were justifiably afraid.

Wills cleared his throat again. "You were right about the direction the shots came from."

"I didn't spend nine months in a war zone for nothing."

"Well, anyway, on account of you, we knew where to start looking for the shooter. They were on the roof."

Dawson fixed him with a stare. "They?"

"We found two sets of shoe prints in the gravel. And Jeremy Wesson's fingerprints on the doorknobs."

"Carl was with him."

"We don't know that," Tucker said.

"I do." Dawson closed his hand into a tight fist. "Carl would want to take credit for killing Headly."

After a taut silence, Wills said, "We don't know who pulled the trigger, but—"

"Jeremy was a sniper, for chrissake."

Wills nodded. "From that vantage point, with a fancy scope, a skilled shooter..." He didn't take that thought any further. "The fingerprints—"

"Weren't an oversight," Dawson said. "They don't care who knows it was them."

"Look," Tucker said, "you're making assumptions that—"

Wills nudged Tucker hard enough to shut him up. He, the

good cop, realized that every contrary word out of his partner's mouth was riling Dawson. Like jerking a sleeping tiger's tail.

After a moment, he continued. "The downed officer had been on patrol over in that industrial park where some vandalism had recently been reported." He shrugged his bony shoulders. "Must've intercepted them as they were fleeing. His radio was missing. Which explains how they eluded us. They could follow our communications and keep track of our movements."

Tucker said, "Plus, we don't know what they're driving. The car Bernie—Carl—left in that parking lot is still there."

Dawson shot him a baleful look. "You've finally come around to accepting that Bernie is Carl Wingert?"

Tucker had the grace to look abashed.

Amelia slid her hand beneath Dawson's arm and rested it on his thigh, which served to keep him from lunging at the deputy who'd questioned Headly's superior knowledge. His muttered epithets toward Tucker were heard by her alone.

He'd tried to persuade her to return to the beach house and take advantage of the protection she'd be afforded there, but she had refused to budge from his side, and secretly he was glad. Over the course of the last few tumultuous hours, her invisible steeliness had manifested itself in quiet but emphatic ways.

She'd spent ten minutes talking on her cell phone to the deputy who'd been watching Hunter and Grant all day. She later told Dawson that they'd been thoroughly entertained until, after a pizza dinner, they'd been tucked safely into bed and were now fast asleep.

She'd also been assured that they were unaware of the personnel, which had been doubled in number, to guard them. Satisfied that her children were being well attended, she'd declared that she would stay with Dawson, at least until they knew the extent of Headly's injury and the status of his condition.

Several times she had tried to thank him for saving her life, but was unable to complete the sentence without becoming too emotional to speak. He'd told her that thanks were unnecessary, that he understood the depth of what she was feeling. She seemed to understand how he felt as well.

When fear of the worst had caused him to lapse into brooding silences, she hadn't filled them with mindless promises that all would be well, when the possibility of catastrophe loomed. When he felt like talking, she had listened as though absorbing each word into her skin. She was a soft but stalwart presence he was grateful to have.

Because of the tension between Tucker and Dawson, Wills continued as spokesperson. "All gloves have come off. A manhunt is under way for Carl Wingert and Jeremy Wesson. Every law enforcement agency in five states is on high alert.

"Knutz would be here himself, except he's gone into overdrive, coordinating the effort. Coast Guard's put up choppers to patrol the beaches. First thing tomorrow morning, police boats will start searching the inland waterways. Canine units will be called up if they're needed. US Marshals Service. State police. You name it, he's got them working it.

"But the problem is," he continued, tugging at his long earlobe, "we're talking about a huge area and we don't have a starting point. Apparently Wesson was using a bogus license when he got that traffic ticket, because none was issued in South Carolina to his SSN. We don't know of any kinfolk they have in the area except Ms. Nolan here. Jeremy's Marine buddies are being canvassed, but—"

"They're the last people he would contact," Amelia said.

"That's what we think, too. But we gotta check. As Tucker noted, we don't have a make and model of the vehicle they were driving."

"Tire tracks?" Dawson asked.

"We tried, but there's nothing but hard pavement around that vacant building. Surrounding buildings are also vacant, so there was no one to question about vehicles seen in the area."

"Security cameras?"

"None operable, because the businesses are kaput."

"What about traffic cameras?" Amelia asked.

"Being checked all over the city, but most only capture the license plate, not the driver."

"Cameras on the bridges?"

"Are being checked. But lots of cars, lots of drivers. It'll take time."

Tucker broke a thoughtful silence by asking Amelia if she had duplicates of Jeremy's credit cards.

"Not for years. I've had my own accounts since we separated."

"We were hoping maybe he'd use an ATM or make a purchase."

"You don't think Carl would avoid leaving such an obvious trail?"

"Hey," Tucker said, taking offense at Dawson's snide tone. "We're doing our best here."

"That's what worries me," Dawson fired back. "If you had listened to Headly sooner—"

"Well, excuse me for not placing much confidence in a lawman who's been chasing the same guy for forty years."

Dawson was off the sofa in a blink, intent on ripping out Tucker's flabby throat. He might have, had it not been for Amelia grabbing a handful of his shirttail to hold him back.

Which coincided with Eva's sudden appearance in the open doorway.

Dawson worked himself free of Amelia's grip and shouldered past the deputies in order to reach her. His arms went around her, and he bent down low to murmur into her hair, "Eva, Eva, we can't lose him. We just can't."

He held her tightly while she cried into his shirtfront. But she was made of stern stuff and eventually set him away from her and wiped the tears off her face. "I was told by the policeman who met me at the airport that he's still in surgery."

"They took him back"—Dawson glanced at the wall clock—"over three hours ago. No word since then."

"Did you see him before he went in?"

He shook his head. "By the time Amelia and I were allowed to leave the scene, he was being prepped in the OR. They wouldn't let us go back." He reached behind him for Amelia's hand, pulled her forward, and made the introductions.

Amelia bit her lower lip to keep it from quivering. "Mrs. Headly, I'm so sorry."

Eva took her other hand. "It's not your fault."

"He was trying to catch the men intent on hurting me."

"He was trying to catch Carl Wingert long before you were born."

Amelia gave her a watery smile and motioned her toward the sofa. Eva went to it and sat down. Amelia asked if she could get her anything. Eva declined, but patted the seat next to her. "Please." Amelia joined her and they began talking together in low tones.

Dawson turned back to Wills, who said, "We'll keep you apprised."

"I'll appreciate that."

"We're sorry about Agent Headly."

"Thanks." He said it brusquely, but the remorse in their expressions was genuine, even in Tucker's. He thanked them again with more sincerity.

The two left. Dawson, seeing that the women were involved in their conversation, stepped into the hallway. Disobeying the signs prohibiting the use of cell phones, he accessed his and punched in a familiar number. "Hey, Glenda. No, no word yet. He's still in surgery. Got anything?"

Five minutes later, as he was disconnecting, a wiry, compact man in green surgical scrubs came through a pair of double doors. "Mr. Headly's family?"

Dawson's throat seized up, but he managed to nod toward

the waiting area. He followed the surgeon into the room and stepped around him so that he was at Eva's side with a supporting arm around her shoulders when the surgeon introduced himself.

"I'm sorry it took so long, but the surgery to remove the bullet was painstaking because we didn't want to further damage surrounding tissue or nearby nerves. He's in recovery. Not completely out of the woods, but for someone who took a hollowpoint between his scapula and spine, he's doing remarkably well."

The surgeon provided them a much more detailed description of the wound and the repair it had required, but they absorbed little of what he said. What they heard was that, after the swelling went down, the paralysis Headly was currently experiencing in his shoulders and arms would be reversed and he should enjoy a full recovery.

Amelia knew that her relief couldn't match that of Eva and Dawson, but it was profound nevertheless. Although Eva had absolved her of any and all responsibility, had Headly died, she would have borne that regret for the remainder of her days.

For Dawson's sake, she was especially happy that Headly had survived.

In celebration of the good news, the three had hugged, laughing and crying in equal measure. Dawson was the first to pull himself together. He resorted to the masculine mechanism of dealing with a traumatic event by pretending he hadn't been sorely affected by it. He cracked jokes. "He's too stubborn to die. He wouldn't go without giving me one final lecture."

Eva saw through his ruse as clearly as Amelia did, but she didn't call him on it, knowing that he was coping with his emotions in a manner that was comfortable for him. Eva placed a call to their daughter, who'd been standing by in London to learn her father's fate. Soon after that they were told they could see Headly in recovery. Eva insisted that Dawson be allowed to go with her. He, in turn, refused to go without Amelia.

The three of them were shown into the curtained cubicle where Headly lay tethered to machines and roped in tubes. Surprisingly his eyes were open. As Eva approached the bed, he asked groggily, "Where'd you come from?"

She clasped his inert hand, and there were tears in her eyes when she bent down and kissed his lips gently. But she answered in a breezy tone. "They called to tell me that you'd been shot. I checked my calendar and it was clear. Having nothing else to do, I flew down."

His eyes were suspiciously moist as he gazed up at her. "Just as well flush the Viagra. I can't move my hands. Foreplay's out."

She laughed softly. "The paralysis is temporary."

His unfocused eyes roved over to Dawson. "She lying?"

"No. You'll live to screw another day."

"Really, you two!" Eva said in mock outrage. "What will Amelia think of us?"

Headly turned his head toward her. She expressed how sorry she was for what he was suffering.

"I'm glad it wasn't you he hit."

"He tried," Dawson said.

Headly closed his eyes. "Jesus."

"Dawson saved my life."

Headly whispered, "Are they in custody?"

"Don't think about any of that right now, Gary."

Despite Eva's admonishment, he forced his eyes open and looked to Dawson, who said, "Still at large."

"Shit."

Eva said, "Gary, if you continue to torture yourself, I'm going to leave. I swear I will."

No one believed her, especially not her husband, who smiled

at her drowsily. "I'm damn glad your calendar was clear. Wish I could hug you."

Dawson glanced over his shoulder at the flimsy curtain that enclosed them but provided only a modicum of privacy. "Listen, Amelia and I should split, let you two have a minute alone before they run us all out."

"What's your rush?" Headly asked.

"I just said."

Headly grunted. "What's going on?"

"Okay, if you must know, I'm hungry. On account of you, I haven't had anything to eat today except for those crummy doughnuts at breakfast."

"I apologize for the inconvenience."

Even though Headly garbled some of the syllables of the last word, Dawson smiled across at Eva. "Pissy is a good sign. He's gonna be fine." But when he looked down at Headly, his expression turned serious. "You had me scared." Being careful of the IV shunt taped to the back of Headly's hand, Dawson gripped it. Huskily, he said, "Rest. Cooperate with the nurses. Take care of yourself, hear?"

The long look the two men shared was rife with unspoken meaning.

"See you in the morning." Dawson returned Headly's hand to his side and, after winking at Eva, turned, held the curtain aside, and motioned Amelia through.

They didn't speak until they were out of the recovery area and walking swiftly down the corridor. "In here." He pushed open the door leading to the stairwell. Once the door had closed behind them, he said, "He's too smart for his own good."

"He knew you were lying when you told him you were hungry."

"I guess my technique needs work."

"So what is going on?"

"I'm due to meet Tucker and Wills downstairs in a few minutes."

"What for?"

"Glenda's been doing some research today. She unearthed something hinky they should know about."

"Hinky how?"

He shook his head. "Not that I'm brimming with admiration for the two, especially Tucker, but I really should share this with them first."

"Does it relate to the shack that Willard mentioned?"

He just looked at her, said nothing.

"You won't tell me even that much?" His silence, and the lack of trust it signified, came as a crushing disappointment. She lowered her head so she'd no longer have to look into his shuttered eyes.

After a lengthy silence, he said, "I don't expect you to understand."

"Well, I don't. I thought you... we..."

Placing his index finger beneath her chin, he tipped her head back until she had no choice but to look into his face. And in his expression she saw all she needed to know and more than she needed to understand.

"You thought right," he whispered. "I, we, *did*."

His hand slid around the back of her neck and pulled her up into a kiss so evocative and intimate that it aroused every cell in her body. Craving closeness, she clutched handfuls of his shirt and stood on tiptoe. His hand settled on her butt and secured her against him.

The kiss was bone-melting, intensely passionate, but short-lived. When he ended it, he cupped her face between his hands and stared into her eyes, then released her so abruptly she fell back against the tile wall. By the time she realized it was over, he was halfway down to the next landing, where he turned a corner and disappeared. He didn't look back.

She stayed there for several minutes, holding her fingers against her throbbing lips, tasting him still, and trying to make sense of the last few minutes. When she replayed the scene in her mind, she realized that dialogue was missing. What had been left unsaid?

Eventually she left the stairwell. Eva was in the corridor talking with a nurse. She ended the conversation and walked toward Amelia. "I recommended they increase the dosage of Gary's sedative. He's fighting it."

"He's in pain?"

"Mental anguish. Did Dawson leave to get something to eat?"

"No, he's meeting with the deputies downstairs. His researcher..." Noticing the strange look that had come over the other woman's face, she asked, "What?"

"The two deputies who were in the waiting room earlier? Tucker and—"

"Wills. Yes."

"I just left them talking to the surgeon. They wanted to know about the bullet's trajectory. Something technical."

For several seconds, Amelia could only stare at her with misapprehension. Then she jogged toward the direction Eva had indicated. When she rounded a corner, there stood the two deputies engaged in conversion with the surgeon.

Wills noticed her. "Ms. Nolan?"

"Where's Dawson?"

"Isn't he with you?"

"You weren't meeting him? About some information his researcher..." She could tell by their blank expressions that they had no idea what she was talking about. She turned quickly toward Eva. "He lied to me."

"He lied to all of us. And Gary knew it."

Diary of Flora Stimel—February 22, 2007

I'm so excited! Jeremy is a daddy! His son Hunter Davis Wesson (I think of it as Wingert) was born at four something this morning. Carl didn't remember the exact time. Men never remember the details! But he did remember that the baby weighed seven pounds, three ounces. I didn't get to weigh Jeremy when he was born, but I think he had to have weighed at least that much!

Jeremy called Carl, which he's not supposed to do unless it's an emergency, like somebody's discovered the cabin or something. (He's paranoid about Amelia's daddy. Calls him a shrewd old buzzard.) Carl would only talk for a minute, but Jeremy was able to tell him that the baby was born Cesarean. Both mommy and baby are fine.

Carl said maybe—just MAYBE—he'd take me to the hospital. We could pretend we were there for someone else and look at the baby through the nursery window. I'm holding my breath!

But I should know better than to get my hopes up. He wouldn't allow me to go to Jeremy's graduation from either high school or college. I've only seen him in his dress Marine uniform from a distance when he was serving as an honor guard at a football game. Carl said a drunk and rowdy crowd that big was safe for us to venture into.

I didn't even ask if we could go to Jeremy's wedding. I knew Carl would never hear of it. But I did ask if we could park across the street from the church and see them when they came out and got into the limo. Carl asked me if I had shit for brains. He said the wedding of a congressman's daughter would be crawling with cops. I hadn't thought of that. I guess maybe I do have shit for brains. Ha-ha!

My mama and daddy always said so. I thought about them today when I got the news about the baby. They're great-grandparents. Or they are if they're still alive, which I doubt. They'd be old now.

Over the years I've wondered if they followed my career. I've thought, wouldn't it be funny if sometime they saw my picture on a Wanted poster in the post office? Would they be proud that I'd made something of myself even if it was as an outlaw? Or would Daddy just shake his head and mutter, "Shit for brains," like he always did whenever I did something he thought was silly or a waste of time.

I might not have run away so young if they'd been just a little bit nicer to me and not always putting me down. I liked Carl right off because he boosted my self-esteem. He made me feel smarter and prettier than Mama and Daddy ever had.

Of course, that was years ago. He knows now I'm not all that smart. Living the way we have, I haven't been able to take good care of myself. Pretty I ain't!

Good Lord, where did all that come from? I was writing about Jeremy's wedding. I read the newspaper story about it over and over again. The reception must have been something to see. Like in a fairy tale. An orchestra played. Amelia is beautiful. (Her picture was in the newspaper.)

I must say, even though she was handpicked as part of Carl's plan, I don't think Jeremy looks on being married to a pretty thing like her as a hardship. He says she treats him good, too.

Carl got a little put out with him the last time he visited us here in the cabin. It was Amelia this and Amelia that until Carl told him to shut up, that he sounded like a moonstruck fool. "This is no love match, and don't forget it." I think Jeremy does forget, though. Because he talks about her like he loves her.

Like last time he came here to see us, he told about this picnic they'd had. She'd surprised him with it. She fried the chicken herself and packed it in a big basket. (I've seen picnic baskets like that in the movies.) Anyhow, he said that right in the middle of the picnic, it started to rain. But instead of it ruining things, they grabbed the chicken and ran back to the car, laughing their heads off.

I thought it was a funny story, the way Jeremy told it. But Carl didn't. He reminded Jeremy that his wife is only part of the grand scheme. Jeremy stopped laughing and got this sad look on his face. I think he likes his wife more than he lets on to his daddy. But Carl has this . . . what's the word? Influence. Carl has this influence over Jeremy that's so strong, I believe he'll do anything for him, even if his heart isn't in it.

I wonder how he feels about the baby? Not what he tells Carl, or even me, but what he feels deep down in his heart. I don't know what to wish for. Should I wish that he loves his baby boy? Or that he doesn't?

If he does love him, it'll be hard for him to see the plan through and leave his son with Amelia. Being separated from your baby is like having a piece of your heart torn out. I know, because I've had years of it. Maybe it's different for men. I hope so. I wouldn't wish that pain on anybody.

Now I have a new worry—Afganastan (sp?). Jeremy will be shipping out soon, and he's excited to be going back to war. He survived Iraq without a scratch. I was so thankful. Now I'll worry myself sick every day he's over there. Carl poo-poos my concern. He says Jeremy is a chip off the old block, a natural-born killer, who won't be afraid of any ragheads.

I pretended not to hear that, because I hate to think of my baby boy as a man who could kill as easily as Carl has. (But to be fair, he hasn't killed anybody in the past several years.)

What will become of little Hunter, I wonder. Will he ever know my name? I wish I could hold him just once. Is that too much to ask? I guess so, because I know it will never happen.

Chapter 23

Like everybody, when it was expedient, Dawson told white lies. Those small equivocations were harmless, usually told to protect the one being lied to as much as to shield himself from some unpleasantness. They rarely pricked his conscience.

But it chafed to be devious with three people who mattered to him. Eva had been too relieved over Headly's condition to notice his shiftiness. Headly had known something was up, but his sharp mind had been dulled by anesthesia. Amelia, however, had known he was lying. By omission, but that counted. He'd lied to her. Except for the kiss. That hadn't been a lie. And however this turned out, he hoped that she would come to realize that in that kiss, he'd been completely honest.

Since he'd left Savannah, there had been three calls from her to his cell phone, which indicated to him that she must have discovered he wasn't on his way out to meet Tucker and Wills.

He hadn't answered those calls, he hadn't listened to the voice mails she'd left, fearing that if he did, he would be persuaded to return. Short of making a U-turn, he might be tempted to tell her what he planned to do, in which case she would try everything within her power to stop him.

He couldn't allow that. He might fail, but he couldn't live out the rest of his life with even a semblance of peace if he didn't at least make this attempt to have a face-to-face with Jeremy and Carl.

Actually what Amelia had said this morning about their perception of him—that of a reporter on the trail of a good story—had reminded him of his one talent. The single thing at which he excelled was getting people to talk to him about themselves.

That had sparked an idea. After the attempt on Headly's life, the idea had crystallized and expanded into a resolve.

Acting on the tip Willard had given him, he had called Glenda even before reuniting with Headly and Amelia in the lobby of the jail visitation center. God bless her, she'd undertaken the task he'd requested, persisted throughout the day, and when he called her from the hospital corridor, she'd given him something to go on.

He should share what he'd learned with the authorities, but although he'd told Amelia that he was about to, he had no intention of doing so. If he was later brought up on charges of obstruction of justice, his defense would be that he hadn't wanted to get everyone excited if Glenda's information turned out to be useless.

But the real reason he'd kept the information to himself was because he wanted a crack at Jeremy and Carl. He wanted that badly. If they were arrested or killed, he would never get an opportunity to speak with them without being monitored. He had a sliver of a chance to have a candid, no-holds-barred, one-on-one conversation with them, and he was taking it.

Carl and Jeremy knew him only as an ambitious journalist who had ingratiated himself with Amelia and her children in order to write a story that would be fat with intimate details. They didn't know about his relationship with Headly. That was a major advantage.

Another was Carl's personality. *He has a colossal ego.* If Headly had told Dawson that once, he'd told him that a thousand times. Most sociopaths had elevated opinions of themselves, which was why they were capable of such derring-do. Dawson reasoned that Carl fit that profile and that he would welcome being given a soapbox from which to vent his spleen. Dawson could provide him a huge audience.

That is, *if* Carl or Jeremy didn't kill him before he could state his purpose.

He was taking a bold, possibly even foolhardy chance, but Carl should relate to that kind of chutzpah. He'd based a criminal career on it. Dawson's sheer audacity might make Carl curious enough not to pull the trigger before Dawson could make his pitch, and he'd have to make it fast.

"I want to commit your story to print."

That should get the megalomaniac's attention.

An interview with him wasn't unprecedented. Carl had granted one once before. Dawson had heard about it through Headly. "In the mideighties, a reporter for the *Washington Post* wrote and published an article about Carl. A lot of the background information on him and his crimes came from me. The writer wanted to be fair, give Carl a chance to rebut what I'd said, set straight any misconceptions about him. In the article, he made it clear that he wished for an interview with him.

"Carl took him at his word. A few weeks after the article appeared, the reporter was kidnapped. Several days after his disappearance, he mailed in a handwritten transcript of a lengthy interview. The newspaper published it in its entirety, and the reporter was awarded a Pulitzer for it."

Carl now had thirty more years to tell about than he had during that first interview. Dawson planned to ask him about the past seventeen specifically. Had he committed crimes that weren't attributed to him, or had he semiretired as he appeared to have done? Had he urged Jeremy to follow in his footsteps, or had that been Jeremy's decision alone? What about Flora?

There was much Dawson wanted to ask him.

But first, he had to find him.

The car he'd rented when he arrived in Savannah less than a week ago was still at the beach house, so he'd taken a taxi from the hospital to the airport, where he arrived at one of the car rental companies just as it was about to close for the night.

Avoiding I-95, he crossed into South Carolina on a dark, two-lane highway. It meandered through thick forests that had thus far escaped developers who sacrificed nature preserves to golf-based communities for retirees.

For miles, the only lights he'd seen were the twin beams of his headlights and a slender moon that was occasionally obscured by thin clouds. The air was soft and thick with humidity. Dotting the flat land were marshes and swamps of murky water.

You wouldn't want to lose your way out here. But if you were looking to hide, the conditions were excellent.

He'd had Glenda searching out parcels of land in the region that had switched hands during the time Jeremy was stationed at Parris Island. It was a long shot, but Glenda came through with a solid possibility. She reported her finding when he called her from the hospital.

"Twenty acres, located between Beaufort and Charleston about a half mile inland. It changed ownership in 2006."

"What snagged your attention about this particular transaction?"

"It was purchased by a corporation."

"Not that unusual."

"No, but the plot is in the middle of freakin' nowhere, no channel connecting it to the ocean, not even a county road's access. A third of it is marshland. What would a corporation want with it?" Before Dawson could form a reply, she said, "I checked to see what kind of business it did and—Hello!—the corporation isn't registered in any of the fifty states. Looks phony."

Dawson tried and failed to pat down his mounting optimism. "Corporations are dissolved. They change names."

"They do. But property taxes were paid as recently as two months ago, automatic draw on an account."

"Bearing the corporation's name?"

"You got it."

Holding a wrinkled piece of paper flat against the wall, he'd scribbled down the coordinates of the lot that had been mysteriously purchased the year that Jeremy Wesson met Amelia Nolan. "Glenda, you're an angel."

"You're an asshole, but you saved that lady's life today, so I guess that makes you okay."

"Who said?"

"That you're an asshole?"

"That I saved the lady's life."

"CNN."

That was disturbing. He didn't want to be alluded to as a hero. That would be the biggest lie of all. He wasn't a hero.

The road he'd been on had become progressively narrower with each mile. Then the hardtop had given way to gravel until, now, he was bumping along a dirt track. It tapered to a dead end about ten yards away from a seemingly impenetrable field of cordgrass.

He killed the car's engine and turned off the headlights. The darkness was unrelieved. Fumbling for his cell phone, he clicked it on and checked the GPS app that had brought him to this intersection of the property lines that formed the southeast corner of the twenty-acre plot. This spot also was nearest to the Atlantic and had the lowest elevation of the property.

Switching on his flashlight app, he got out of the car, walked toward the high grass, and sank to his ankles in viscous water.

Twenty acres of dry ground wouldn't be that difficult to navigate in daylight. But it would be crazy to strike out through a salt marsh in total darkness, not knowing where he was going or even what he was looking for. Until sunrise, he was stuck.

He got back into the car and turned off his phone. Then, as a safety precaution, he removed the battery, having heard that one could transmit a signal even if the phone was turned off.

He didn't want to be found until after he had found Carl and Jeremy.

Amelia and Eva had passed the night in the hospital waiting room. Eva hadn't even considered a nurse's suggestion that she go to a hotel and get a good night's rest. She wouldn't leave and miss even one of the periodic visits with Headly that she was allowed.

In the event that his condition changed for the worse, Amelia didn't want her to be alone, so she had declined Tucker's offer for a deputy to escort her back to Saint Nelda's. Further, she didn't want to leave the place where she'd last seen Dawson. She was entertaining a silly notion that if she stayed, he would soon return with a full explanation for his sudden departure.

Now as dawn approached, her eyes felt gritty and dry. She longed for a shower. She had stinging scrapes on her right palm and elbow, which had borne the brunt of her fall when Dawson had pushed her to the concrete. But these physical discomforts were negligible compared with her emotional upset. She was desperate with worry over him.

As Eva returned from a visit with Headly, Amelia lowered her cell phone from her ear and disconnected. "I'm not even getting Dawson's voice mail anymore. How's the patient?"

"*Im*patient. Cranky. Fretful. His blood pressure has gone up. The nurses are blaming it on pain, but I know better. Lying still, unable to move his arms is driving him crazy. He thinks we're not telling him the truth about the paralysis being temporary. And every time I go in there, he asks me about Dawson."

Amelia looked at her wristwatch, running her finger around the crystal, remembering that it might never have been recovered if not for Dawson. "He's been gone for hours. Why hasn't he called me back?"

"I'm sure there's a good reason."

"I'm sure of that, too. But I'm unsure I want to know what it is." The more she thought back onto their last conversation, the more convinced she became that Dawson had withheld something from her, not because he didn't trust her but because he predicted a negative reaction. "Should I share my concerns with Agent Knutz? The detectives?"

"What would you tell them?"

"That he lied about where he was going."

"Men frequently lie to women about where they're going."

"They would probably think he went out to buy drugs." Quickly she added, "He only needed antianxiety pills to help him sleep, you know."

"I know."

"He hasn't even had a drink in days."

"You've been a good influence."

"Me? No. I haven't had anything to do with it."

Eva smiled knowingly. "In a very short period of time, you two have become remarkably close."

"One step forward, two back."

"Oh?"

She hesitated. "Woman to woman?"

"Anything you tell me will go no farther, Amelia. I promise you."

"Truth is, he makes my head spin."

The older woman laughed softly. "So there *is* an attraction."

"Definitely."

"That's good, isn't it?"

"It would be, if he was consistent. One minute it's like he can't get enough of me. Then the next, he's pushing me away, literally keeping me at arm's length."

"Has he told you why?"

"Is there a why?"

"Obviously Dawson thinks so."

"Your husband says he regards himself a loner."

"We've tried to turn that thinking around."

"Headly told me that, too. But there's more to this resistance than general self-denial. I think he's resisting me for a specific reason."

"What makes you think so?"

"I feel it. I believe it must have something to do with Jeremy."

Eva said nothing, just waited for her to elaborate.

"Possibly with Jeremy's PTSD, with him being who and what he is."

"Dawson would never lay your ex-husband's sins at your feet. I know him well enough to assure you of that."

"No, I don't believe he would either. I think . . . I think . . . Actually, I don't know what to think." She bent her head low and massaged her temples. "Where did he go? What could Glenda have uncovered that sent him flying out of here?"

Earlier they had discussed the possibility of calling the researcher and asking her what she had revealed. But neither knew how to reach her or even what her last name was. They had decided to wait until morning and call her at the magazine office. Eva had cautioned Amelia against becoming too optimistic. "He's relied on her for years. She's like a secret weapon. I doubt his Glenda will betray his trust."

If the researcher was as protective of her sources as Dawson was, Amelia doubted they'd learn much from her, either. But she didn't know where else to turn for answers.

"For him to have left Headly tonight, it must have been something vitally important."

"He knew Gary was out of immediate danger."

"Yes. But still. He'd been agonizing over him for hours. What could possibly have prompted him to leave and not even to call to check on him?"

"I'll admit, that doesn't seem like Dawson. Tell me again everything he said."

Amelia reiterated the conversation in the stairwell. "Could it relate to what Willard Strong told him?"

"About a shack that Jeremy owned?"

"You don't suppose . . . Oh, Lord. You don't suppose that Glenda located it. Surely Dawson wouldn't go there alone."

"We've got to tell Gary." Eva stood up and headed for the door.

"Eva, no." Amelia followed her from the waiting room and down the corridor. "You can't tell him. His blood pressure."

"That can be controlled with medication. But if he learns later that I didn't tell him about this immediately, I can forget our Alaska cruise. He'd probably divorce me."

They entered the ward without any of the medical staff seeing them and slipped behind the privacy curtain. Headly's eyes popped open. He took one look at them and knew instantly that they weren't there to fluff his pillow. "What?"

"Tell him." Eva scooted aside so Amelia could move closer to the bed.

In a rapid whisper she filled him in, concluding with, "If Glenda gave him an idea of where this shack is, do you think he'd be foolish enough to go there alone and confront them?"

His gaze moved back and forth between them, ending with his wife, whose distress was as apparent as her resignation. Headly closed his eyes and gave a long sigh. "Fuck."

More than a profanity, the word was weighty with despair. Coming from a man of purpose and action, it heightened Amelia's fear. "They'll kill him, won't they?"

He roused himself and opened his eyes. "Not if I can help it.

But goddammit, I'm trapped here. Eva, call Knutz. His number's in my phone." Eva moved to the closet where his personal effects had been stored.

"I don't know what to tell him."

"Let Amelia do the talking." Looking at her, he said, "Tell him what you just told me. He'll have Glenda tracked down. He'll mobilize the local authorities and maybe, just maybe, they'll intercept Dawson in time."

"And if they don't?" Amelia asked.

"Carl will probably give him the interview of his career. He's done it before."

Eva stopped dealing with the cell phone and looked at him with alarm. "Gary, no."

Amelia, noting her reaction, said, "What? What about an interview?"

Ignoring his wife's distress, Headly told her about the coup a *Washington Post* reporter had achieved. "The day after the interview ran, Carl released him along a rural road in West Virginia. With a bullet through his brain. He was awarded the Pulitzer posthumously."

He was in the midst of his nightmare, laboriously clawing his way up the incline toward Hawkins, who was shouting at him from the crest, when he was startled awake by a heron that took flight out of the marsh with a noisy flapping of wings.

He'd been spared the horrible ending of his nightmare, but he was still shaky and leaking a cold sweat. He dried his face with his shirttail and took a sip from a bottle of water.

He was surprised he'd been able even to doze, and equally surprised that he was still alive. Had Carl or Jeremy come upon him, he could have been murdered in his sleep. Although he'd had about a two-hour nap, he didn't feel rested. However, despite his fatigue, and the sun not being completely up, he was impatient to get under way.

He replaced the battery in his cell phone. That amounted to beaming his location to the authorities if they were looking for him, but he had to take that risk. He needed the phone to help him navigate.

He took only it and the water bottle with him when he left the car. A weapon would have been superfluous. Jeremy had missed Amelia because of Dawson's quick action. The bullet he'd fired at Headly hadn't been a head shot, and it had lost velocity due to the distance, preventing it from inflicting the damage it could have. But regardless of his bad luck yesterday, his marksmanship skills were renowned. A man foundering in a marsh would be easy pickins.

Dawson had decided to take a zigzagging route from this point, working his way up the trapezoidal-shaped parcel, which was much narrower at the base than at the top, which was farther inland. If he reached the northwest corner without finding anything and this turned out to be a wild-goose chase, he'd follow a diagonal line back to his starting point.

The water he'd stepped into last night never got any higher than his knees, but it soaked the legs of his jeans and filled his boots. He fought his way through areas of thick cordgrass and clumps of palmetto palms, with their leaves that were shaped like knife blades and which were just as sharp. The insects were aggressive and merciless. He didn't want to think about the species of reptiles he might encounter.

He had estimated he could walk twenty acres in half an hour or less. But slogging through water and thrashing through the uncharitable plant life increased the effort and time required.

Fortunately, as the elevation rose, the soil became firmer and less brackish, and the marsh grasses gradually gave over to forest. Soon he was walking under tree branches that formed a tangled, dense canopy overhead, which kept the forest floor shady. Undergrowth flourished. Vines twisted up tree trunks. Lacy ferns formed patches of vibrant green. From every vantage point, the landscape looked like a diorama of shifting shadows, a wilderness of undisturbed camouflage.

Which is why he almost missed it.

Had it not been for a pair of redbirds that caught his attention as they streaked through the woods calling to each other and then lighting on the tilting television antenna attached to the edge of the roof, he might have gone right past without seeing it.

He stopped dead in his tracks and then quickly crouched behind a thicket of palmetto. He figured that if Carl or Jeremy had spied him or heard him, he would already be dead.

The structure was larger than what he would term a shack. More like a cabin. It squatted in a small clearing surrounded by trees. Tall grass and wild shrubbery grew right up to the exterior walls, which were constructed of raw lumber that had weathered to blend in with the dun tint of tree bark.

The low roof was completely covered with lichen and fallen tree branches, where vegetation had taken root in the naturally made compost. From the air, it would have blended in with the landscape. Not even from a helicopter, flying low, could it have been spotted.

He had come onto it from the front. There was a porch of sorts about a yard square, a door flanked by small windows, placed high. The window glass had been smeared with something to prevent it from reflecting light. No telephone or electrical lines were in evidence, but a generator, painted in camouflage, was tucked against one exterior wall and covered in vines.

Dawson thought wryly: this is the reward for a lifetime of crime? But then, one of Carl Wingert's grievances had been the obsessive materialism of the American people. In this, at least, he practiced what he preached.

Dawson waited ten minutes by his watch before daring to move, then began a slow and silent approach. When he could go no farther without stepping out from the cover of the trees, he stopped to take several deep breaths.

Two people came to mind: Corporal Hawkins, the young soldier from North Dakota who was featured in his nightmare. And Amelia, the last woman he would kiss. The first woman he would love. If he didn't live through this, he hoped that by some cosmic miracle they would both know that in his final moments he had acknowledged his unpaid debts to them.

He stepped from the relative safety of the trees and walked toward the cabin. No one called out a warning. No telltale shadows appeared at the foggy windows. He heard no rustling sounds, nothing to indicate that the dwelling was inhabited.

But as he was about to step onto the porch, he recalled something Headly had told him: *We should have known it was booby-trapped.* A snitch had told the FBI that Carl and Flora were hiding inside a house in southern Florida. A covert raid was planned and perfectly executed until a Special Ops agent stepped onto the wooden porch. He and the structure had been blown to smithereens. Three fellow agents had been critically wounded despite their protective gear.

Dawson equated booby traps to IEDs. He'd seen their handiwork up close. Thoughts of the ravages they were capable of went through his mind as he eased himself up onto the small platform.

Nothing detonated. He expected gunshots at the very least, but all he heard was the domestic spat between the redbirds. He reached for the doorknob and turned it. Surprisingly it wasn't locked. The door swung inward. The first thing that greeted him was the smell. Old garbage, sour sweat, blood.

"I could shoot you through the door, so you'd just as well come in."

Not a voice he recognized as Bernie's.

Heart thundering, hands raised, he stepped across the threshold, using his foot to push the door open wide until it came up against the wall. No one was behind the door. He swept the room in one glance.

Reeking metal trash can. Cast-off furniture. Dirty dishes piled high in a stained sink that didn't have a faucet. A wooden pallet in the corner stacked with packs of bottled water. A Frigidaire that was decades old.

And on a sofa was a bearded man, semireclined. He was holding a pistol, but listlessly. Upon identifying Dawson, he registered his surprise. *"You?"*

"Me."

All the things Headly had told Dawson about Carl Wingert came flashing back to him in an instant. *You can't be well enough prepared for Carl.* Dawson spun around to check behind him, but only the monotonous landscape lay beyond the open door.

One time, in New Mexico, he jumped from the rafters of an old horse barn. Shot the agent who'd chased him in there point blank in the chest. Dawson looked up at the low ceiling. No rafters. No attic.

The man on the sofa seemed amused by his jumpiness. "Relax. He's not here."

"Where'd he go?"

"Didn't say."

Satisfied that they were the only two in the place, Dawson said, "I'm not armed. I'm going to lower my hands."

Jeremy Wesson, a man about whom he'd been rabidly curious, a man he'd resented with every fiber of his being, a man he wanted to see severely punished for killing Stef and almost killing Headly, didn't look that evil or menacing.

He was regarding Dawson with equal curiosity, taking in the full measure of him. "You look even taller up close."

"You look like shit." Against his beard, Jeremy's complexion looked clammy and waxen.

"Rough twenty-four hours."

"They haven't exactly been a picnic for Headly, either."

"Is he alive?"

"He's going to be okay."

"In the split second it took the bullet to get there, he turned."

"You missed Amelia, too."

"I wasn't trying that hard."

Dawson wouldn't credit him with total sincerity, but Jeremy did dip his head for several seconds in what could have been remorse. When he came back to Dawson, he noticed that his boots and jeans were wet. "Tough to get here, huh? How'd you find it?"

"I never reveal a source."

Jeremy stifled a laugh, which caused him to cough. To cover it, he turned his face into his shoulder. When the coughing subsided, he asked, "Are the cops behind you?"

"I don't think so."

"You came alone?"

"Yes."

"Why?"

"I wanted to meet you face-to-face."

"What for?"

Dawson didn't respond.

"You fucking my wife?"

"She's not your wife. But, no."

Whether or not he believed that, Dawson couldn't tell.

"Did you come here to kill me?"

"No."

"Because if you did—"

"I didn't."

"—you're too late." He pulled his hand away from a bloody, festering mess on the side of his lower abdomen. "I'm already a dead man."

Chapter 24

Dawson was kneeling beside the ratty sofa before he even realized he'd moved. He pushed Jeremy's hand aside and raised the hem of his dirty shirt. Under it was a putrefying wound. The tissue was puckered, pussy, and red around the dark bullet hole, which was clotted with dried blood. "Jesus. This looks bad, but it's stopped bleeding."

Jeremy gave an ironic grin. "I've run dry."

Dawson feared he was right. Most of the bleeding must have been internal and considerable. Beneath his bushy mustache, his lips were gray. He let go of the pistol. It landed on the floor inches from Dawson's knee.

"I lied about shooting you through the door. It's not loaded."

Dawson yanked his cell phone from his belt.

"Don't bother."

Ignoring Jeremy's weak protest, he punched in 911. When the operator answered, he said, "Listen carefully." He told her his general location, then the geographical coordinates of the tract. "I need medical care for a seriously wounded man."

"What's the nature—"

"He's been shot in the gut."

"Is he—"

"We're in a cabin, but there's no road to it. Send a search-and-rescue chopper. They won't be able to set down. Tell them to come prepared for that and to look for smoke."

"Smoke?"

"That'll help them find us. And my phone will be on."

"What's your name?"

"Dawson Scott."

"The Dawson Scott everyone's looking for?"

"They're looking for me?"

"All over the place."

"Well, they can find me here. I'm with Jeremy Wesson. Got it? Jeremy Wesson. Tell them not to come in shooting. It's just the two of us, we're unarmed, and he's in a bad way."

"Okay, stay on the line, Mr.—"

"You do your job. I'm gonna do mine."

He disconnected and didn't answer when his cell phone rang almost immediately. Moving quickly, he dragged the overflowing trash can outside and upended it to dump the nauseating contents. He gathered up sticks and dead brush and crammed them into the can, then went back into the cabin. "Matches?"

Jeremy motioned feebly. "Shelf above the sink."

The rickety dining table was piled with newspapers. Dawson took them and the box of matches out to the trash can, stuffed the newspapers down among the kindling, struck matches to them, and left them to burn.

Jeremy was looking worse by the moment. Dawson steeled himself against the compassion welling inside him. Slipping on his professional objectivity, he started the video recorder on his cell phone. He didn't care about the quality of the picture, but anything Jeremy said could be very important later. "Who shot you?"

"The cop."

"The one you killed?"

"Daddy did."

"Carl Wingert. He's your father?"

"That's right. How did you find out?"

"Never mind that now. Where is Carl?"

"I told you. He left."

"How long ago?"

"Last night sometime."

"You've been here all night alone? Why didn't you call for help?"

Jeremy gave another dry laugh, which caused a fit of coughing. Gasping, he said, "I'd rather bleed out here than die in prison."

"Carl left you here to bleed out? Why didn't he take you to an ER?"

Jeremy looked down at the wound and when he raised his gaze back to Dawson, there were tears in his eyes. "He knows a lost cause when he sees one."

Dawson ran his fingers though his hair. "Christ. Doesn't the man have a heart?"

"You know about him? Beyond Bernie, I mean. You know about his past?"

"Yeah, I know. Much more than I want to."

"He's had to leave people behind before."

"He *chose* to leave them behind."

"Heroes are forced to make hard decisions."

"Hero?" Dawson sneered. "He's a chickenshit."

Jeremy said nothing, but he took a swipe at his eyes to brush the tears away. "He left me with one bullet. I knew what he expected me to do with it, so after he'd been gone for sixty seconds or so, I fired it." Dawson followed his gaze to the ceiling where the wood was splintered around a bullet hole.

Jeremy said, "Daddy hasn't made many mistakes, but he made one last night. He didn't come back to see that I'd really done it." He leaned back against the soiled sofa cushion and closed his eyes. A tear leaked from beneath his eyelid, rolled down his cheek, and was absorbed by his beard. "I didn't want to blow my own brains out, but I hoped to die before anybody got here."

"No such luck, Jeremy. I need you to clear up a couple of things."

Eyes still closed, he asked, "Are you going to write about me?"

"I haven't decided yet."

"Well, if it's deathbed confessions you're after, you'd better be quick."

"Willard Strong's version of Darlene's murder. True?"

"Close enough. Main thing, he didn't do it. I did."

Dawson looked down at his phone to make sure he'd got that. "The Wessons."

Jeremy opened his eyes as they filled with more tears. He struggled not to cry. "Randy and Patricia."

"Was their last name really Wesson?"

"No, but I don't know what their real names were. I lived with them for thirteen years and they took good care of me. They believed in Daddy and his crusade, as they called it."

"What about the fire?"

"Daddy said it was necessary. He called it martyring them for the cause." Jeremy wiped his eyes again.

It was a struggle for Dawson to maintain his objectivity as he asked the next question. "Amelia's father. Suicide, or not?"

He stared hard into Jeremy's eyes, demanding the truth. Slowly Jeremy gave a small shake of his head, then let it sink deeper into the cushion. "From the time we met, especially after we married, he would ask questions about the Wessons and other things I'd told him that didn't add up. Daddy was afraid he'd really start snooping after the divorce. I wasn't the congressman's favorite person."

"You'd hit Amelia."

He winced, but he didn't defend the abuse. "Daddy was afraid the old man would be out to get me. He said we needed to nip it in the bud."

"So you nipped it."

"I knew his schedule, knew when he would be in the house alone."

"How'd you coerce him into taking the pills?"

"Daddy gave him a choice. Take the lethal dosage, or stand by and watch Amelia die slowly and in agony. He was going to die, no matter what, but if he wanted her to live, he would fake his suicide. The old man tried to reason, then to bargain. He wound up pleading, but in the end he swallowed the pills. We waited there until we were sure his heart had stopped."

"And left him for Amelia to find." Dawson wanted to strike him, to beat him senseless for the grief he had caused her, not just over her father's death but over everything he'd done for a stupid, fanatical, baseless "cause."

"'Cause,' my ass," he muttered. Carl Wingert's treachery was propelled only by his ego, his sick, sociopathic delusions of grandeur. Dawson was suddenly consumed by rage. He grabbed Jeremy's hand as though he would arm wrestle him right there atop Jeremy's chest. "You also need to answer for killing Stef."

"Stupid move. I acted without thinking."

"That's not going to hack it as a defense."

As though he hadn't heard Dawson's remark, he continued. "I'd been cooped up here for so long, to get out of here and actually do something felt good."

"It felt good to kill a young woman?"

"I thought she was Amelia."

"You wanted to kill the mother of your children."

He turned away from Dawson's accusatory glare, and his chest deflated as he expelled a long sigh. "If I had to think about it, I couldn't have done it. So when I saw her—the woman I thought was her—it was like Providence. A sign. Something. If

I acted on impulse and did it right then, I'd be done with it and not have to think about it anymore. That's what went through my mind."

"Fucking twisted mind, Jeremy."

"Tell her that I'm sorry."

"I doubt she'll believe that."

"Probably not. Not after everything I've put her through." His gaze turned introspective. "My boys will be ashamed of who their daddy was, won't they?"

The answer was so obvious that Dawson didn't need to state it.

"I was jealous of you for playing with them on the beach," Jeremy continued. "I watched from the boat. Where'd you get the football?"

"Found a bag of beach toys in the rental house."

"Grant's got a good right arm for a kid his age."

"For a kid of any age."

"Hunter's better at soccer."

"He's got some moves."

"They're good boys, right?"

"They're great boys."

"Do they ever talk about me?"

This man didn't deserve his pity, his compassion, not even one of those magnanimous white lies. But to tell the harsh truth to a dying man... "All the time," he heard himself say. "They're proud of your service to your country."

Jeremy knew he was being lied to, and looked at Dawson in a way that silently thanked him for the mercy. Then he closed his eyes and Dawson feared that he'd lost consciousness or soon would. He shook his shoulder. "Don't pass out yet. Tell me where Carl went."

"I don't know."

"I don't believe you."

"He left me here to die. You think I give a shit about where he went?" Again tears filled his eyes.

Dawson did in fact believe him when he said he didn't know his father's whereabouts. A man who would abandon his dying son wouldn't bother to tell him where he was going. He battled another onslaught of pity. "Jeremy, where's Flora?"

His eyes jerked into focus on Dawson's face, then he made a raw, sobbing sound. "Don't ask me—"

"Where is she, Jeremy? Is your mother still alive?"

Another harsh sound erupted from him. "Leave me alone. I'm dying."

Dawson gripped his hand more tightly. "Tell me, damn you."

"I—"

"Tell me!"

Just then they heard the clatter of a helicopter approaching. Dawson ran to the door and looked out. The trash can was emitting a thin ribbon of smoke, and it had worked as a signal. The helicopter appeared, hovering barely above the treetops. He stepped out of the cabin and waved his arms over his head, then went back inside and knelt beside the sofa.

Jeremy's head had lolled to one side. "No!" Dawson worked his arm beneath Jeremy's head and, supporting his limp nape in the crook of his elbow, lifted it off the cushion. "Don't die on me. Come on, wake up!" He jostled his head.

Jeremy groaned. His eyes fluttered open.

"Help's here, man. Hang on."

"I don't want help."

"What happened to Flora?"

Jeremy's lips moved, but Dawson couldn't hear him for the racket outside. Forest debris caught in the downwash of the helicopter blades was striking the exterior walls like stones. Men were shouting. A heavy footfall landed on the porch, and someone shouted his name.

He bent his head low. "Tell me where to find Flora. Jeremy. Tell me."

Jeremy clutched the collar of Dawson's shirt and pulled him

down until his ear was directly above Jeremy's lips. He whispered his last words, then he looked into Dawson's eyes, and for a millisecond they connected. Then Jeremy's became unseeing.

Dawson stared into the vacant gaze for several moments, then eased Jeremy's head back onto the cushion and pulled his arm out from under him. When he tried to stand, he had to tug his collar free from the dead man's grip.

Amelia was in Headly's hospital room with the restive patient and Eva when she received the call that Tucker had promised her. "Deputy Tucker? I'm putting you on speaker."

She clicked over in time to hear him say, "We found him."

"Is he all right?"

"He's fine."

Eva folded her hands beneath her chin in an attitude of prayer. Headly muttered inaudibly, which was probably just as well. Amelia felt light-headed with relief.

The deputy continued. "But I'm sorry to report that your . . . that Jeremy is dead."

She lowered herself into a chair. "I see."

She wouldn't have expected the burst of grief she experienced. He'd been dead to her for more than a year. She had already mourned his passing once; she wouldn't have thought there was any bereavement left for him. Knowing the things he'd done, she was amazed that she could feel anything at all. Yet she did. Regret over his bad choices, sorrow over his wasted life, and, even more sadly, relief. She and her sons were free of him.

Tucker said, "The Savannah PD officer we found dead had got off one shot from his service revolver. Jeremy took it low in the abdomen. He bled out slow."

She nodded, then, realizing that Tucker was waiting on a verbal response, repeated the only words she seemed capable of uttering. "I see."

"The details will have to keep for now. Scott got a video recording on his phone, but we still have a lot to ask him about what transpired when he got here."

"That's why they're not letting you talk to him," Headly said, not caring if Tucker overheard him. More loudly, he said, "Tucker, what about Carl?"

"No sign of him."

Headly's lips tightened to a thin line. "The bastard left Jeremy there to die alone."

"Looks like."

Amelia felt another stab of heartache. "When can we expect Dawson back in Savannah?"

"Can't say. This place is reachable only by foot. A helicopter can't set down. May take a while to get him out. Right now, he's being questioned by Knutz's people. I'm needed. Got to go."

"Thank you for calling." She wasn't sure he heard all of that before disconnecting.

It was several moments before she raised her head. "At least we know that he's safe." Headly and Eva were watching her closely. She supposed they were gauging her reaction to the news about Jeremy. She stood up. "I'm going home to my sons."

"We'll have to keep your phone for a while," Tucker said.

Dawson nodded.

"A local deputy will walk you out of here. We've set up a quasi camp on a road about half a mile that way." He hitched a thumb over his shoulder.

"My car's in the opposite direction."

"This is the shorter route out. It's not far, but it's not an easy walk through the woods. The road swings around to the south and connects to the one that dead-ends in the marsh where your car's at. Couple of deputies are watching it till you get there. Someone will drive you to it."

"I'll appreciate it. Thanks."

A uniformed man approached at a jog. "Deputy Tucker? Can I have a sec?"

Dawson turned away to let them confer and looked toward the cabin, which had become a beehive of activity. Over the course of the past few hours, crime-scene personnel had arrived. Some were uniformed. Others wore civilian clothes. One was in a suit and lace-up shoes, others wore blue jeans and T-shirts with the various agency names stenciled on them. The options depended on rank, Dawson supposed. They came and went as their duties required.

He was happy to remain as detached as possible.

He had, however, been questioned at length by Tucker and Wills, who'd arrived shortly after the first responders, thrashing their way through the forest to reach the spot. They'd soon been joined by sheriff's deputies from the South Carolina county and by several FBI agents from Knutz's office. Apparently he was coordinating things from Savannah.

Each agency wanted to question him independently, so he was called on several times to describe Jeremy's condition when he arrived. The video off his cell phone, as he'd guessed, was poor, but Jeremy's confessions could be clearly heard, the most shocking of which was that of staging Congressman Davis Nolan's suicide.

The day had turned hot and sticky, the overcast sky creating a greenhouse effect that by noon had shirts sticking to backs. It was long past midday now. Dawson was bone tired and emotionally drained, but he had answered their multitude of questions patiently, realizing that the sooner he did so, the sooner he would be allowed to leave.

It seemed that that time had finally come. After his brief

conference with the uniformed officer, Tucker walked back toward him, accompanied by Wills who was mopping sweat off his hangdog face with a folded handkerchief.

Tucker said, "False alarm. They were holding a white-haired man who roughly fit Carl Wingert's description at a Dairy Queen. The old guy had stopped to get a Blizzard. Wasn't Carl."

"He won't be that easy to take," Dawson said.

"The son of a bitch," Wills said under his breath. "I'm no fan of Jeremy Wesson, but . . . Jesus. What kind of man could run away and leave his kid like that, knowing he was dying?"

Only one answer came to Dawson's mind: Carl Wingert.

A suspension of activity drew their attention to the cabin. The three watched solemnly as the stretcher bearing Jeremy's body was maneuvered through the narrow doorway, carried by members of a rescue team. They placed it on the ground in the clearing to wait for the helicopter that would lift it out.

"Where will he be taken?" Dawson asked.

"Back to us, eventually," Tucker said. "He died in their county, but he was our fugitive. They're cooperating with us." Turning back to Dawson, he said, "They're more than a little curious about you."

"Why?"

"They want to know if you should be arrested."

"For what crime?"

"Stupidity, mainly. Care to share what the hell you were thinking to come out here on your own, track them down, approach without caution?"

"I was after an interview."

"Well, you got one. More than you bargained for."

"A lot more," he said quietly.

"Much as it pains me to say it, we're glad you found him. The video will exonerate Willard Strong. It'll also close the book on the DeMarco girl's slaying."

"And reverse the ruling on Congressman Nolan's suicide," Dawson said.

"How do you think Ms. Nolan will react to that?" Wills asked.

"With mixed emotions."

They must have read from his expression that he wasn't going to discuss it further with them. Tucker said, "You'll be around?"

"Until Carl is captured."

Tucker didn't like the sound of that. "Look, don't pull any more fool stunts, okay? You're not a cop."

"So you've said."

"I don't want to have to cart you away in a body bag."

"I'll keep that in mind."

"Say, listen." Tucker backed down, glanced toward the cabin, flicked a bead of sweat off the tip of his nose. Coming back to Dawson, he said, "I'm man enough to admit when I'm wrong. I was wrong. Bygones?" He extended his right hand. Dawson shook it.

Tucker nodded, but as he was about to walk away in step with Wills, Dawson said, "You're not done here." His solemn tone grabbed their attention. They looked at him expectantly. "The porch was an add-on," he said. "Jeremy built it to protect the grave."

"Grave?" Wills said. "Whose?"

"His mother's."

Diary of Flora Stimel—2010

I'm not sure of the date, whether it's still January or if Feb. is here. It's cold, I know that much. The cabin stays damp, and that hasn't helped my chest cold. It's hung on for weeks. I try not to cough too much, because it irritates Carl.

He's short-tempered because we stay cooped up in here for days at a time. He doesn't like to venture out when it's rainy because tracks can be left in wet ground.

What I think—who's looking for us after all this time? I bet most cops these days have never even heard of us. But Carl is as paranoid as ever. That FBI agent Headly makes him nervous. We haven't pulled a job in years, but Carl says that doesn't matter. We're still wanted. Headly's still out there and he'll never give up till we're caught or dead.

Makes me tired just to think about it. And I miss Jeremy. He hasn't been out to see us since before Christmas. He's going to Af. again soon. Carl says that he's too busy to come see us. He's "setting things up," whatever that means, but I think it means that their big plan is about to be launched.

Breaks my heart that Jeremy's gotta leave his family again. Last time he was here, he brought me pictures of the boys and told me stories about them. He had a picture of Hunter holding his new baby brother. Their faces are so sweet! I wanted to keep the pictures, but after I'd looked at them for a while, Carl took them away and burned them. In case this place is discovered, he didn't want anything around that would connect us to Jeremy. But when I saw the fire eating up the pictures of our grandbabies, I cried. It took me a long time to stop.

I don't know for sure how many days have gone by since I wrote that last part. The days sorta blend together. I don't know why, because it's not like I sleep through them. I'm so tired, but I can't sleep at all. I think I have fever.

Earlier today, I was lying here on the bed with my eyes closed. When I opened them, I caught Carl just sitting there at the table, staring at me. I asked him what was wrong. He said, "Nothing," and got up to fix himself a can of soup. I think he just hates me being sick.

I told him that cough syrup and maybe aspirin for the body aches would make me feel better and get me well faster. He said he'd go buy some when the weather clears.

He's asleep now, which is why I'm able to write in this diary. I don't like what I'm thinking, which is this: Much as I'd like to have some medicine, I hope Carl doesn't leave me here alone to go after it. I'm scared that if he left, he might not come back.

Like last summer, when he was away for weeks at a time, and I had to be here by myself while he was at the beach. He got to see the grandchildren every single day! Lord, how I wanted to be there, too, but he said he couldn't risk me making a fool of myself over them and ruining everything. He's probably right. I don't think I could have been around them and not loved them to pieces!

He came every few weeks to bring me food, just like he said he would. But each time he left, I got afraid that I'd never see him again. I don't mind the cabin, but I don't like being in this wilderness alone. Who besides Jeremy and Carl know I'm here? It's a scary thought.

Oh, happy day! Jeremy came. I didn't let on how sick I was, but I could tell he knew, and it worried him. His eyes were wet when he kissed me good-bye. He's a sweet boy. I hung on to him for as long as I could. I can still feel how his palm felt sliding against mine and the very last brush of his fingertips as he finally let go of my hand.

I need to get some things off my conscience. I guess God already knows my sins and doesn't need for me to write them down in this tacky little book. But anyway, I can't today. I'm not up to it. The coughing fits wear me out. Maybe tomorrow.

Carl left a while ago. He went after groceries and promised he'd bring back some medicine and a PayDay candy bar, my favorite.

Carl knows that my biggest fear has always been that he'd run off and leave me. When I asked if that's what he had in mind, he told me the fever was making me loony. I guess it is. Because if he didn't leave me in Golden Branch.

I wish I hadn't thought of Golden Branch. Now it's all I'm thinking about.

Stop crying, Flora! My crying always makes Daddy so mad. I mean Carl. *He's like Daddy that way.*

He's been gone for hours. I should use this time while he's gone to write as much in this diary as I can, and then hide it before he gets back. But it's dark and

---

it's day again, I think. Carl isn't back yet, but he will be soon, I know. Maybe I'll sleep for a while and when I wake up

Chapter 25

Amelia was in the beach-house kitchen when Dawson knocked once on the utility-room door, then walked in. She wanted to melt at the sight of him, but somehow maintained her dignity. Both of them seemed a bit shell-shocked, unsure of what to do or how to behave. Was there a rule of etiquette for this situation?

They stared at each other until it became awkward. Finally she spoke. “Hi.”

“Hi.”

He was wearing a white cotton shirt, tail out, sleeves rolled to his elbows, over a pair of jeans, all of which looked great. But he seemed immeasurably fatigued. “Are you all right?”

He raised one shoulder in a slight shrug, nodded once. “All things considered.”

“They called from the ferry dock to tell me you were on your way.”

“Had to run quite a gauntlet to get through. Island is crawling with cops of various sorts. But that’s good.”

"I feel safe. As long as I don't look toward Bernie's house. I can't look at it without shuddering. I hope I'll get over that in time."

He gave a nod. "Is the woman deputy still staying here in the house?"

"She is. She's on break at the moment. Several of the officers are staying in the house you rented. They take shifts sleeping, eating. Since you were coming, she figured it would be okay if she went next door for a while."

"Hmm." After that noncomment, his gaze moved aimlessly around the kitchen—more to avoid looking directly at her than to look at something else, she thought.

"Are you all right?"

He sharp-focused on her again. "You asked me that already."

"Oh, right, I did. I'm sorry."

"I'm fine. Are you?"

"Yes. Except, about Jeremy…" She took a deep breath, let it out through her lips. "I'm not sure what I should be feeling."

"Understandable."

"I don't grieve for him. But I do feel sad."

"I can relate. Believe me."

Dozens of questions about Jeremy's final minutes were on the tip of her tongue, but she couldn't bring herself to ask them. Not yet. She wasn't ready to hear the details, and Dawson seemed equally disinclined to provide them.

They were acting like strangers, not like two people who had shared a passionate farewell kiss the night before. Although she wanted to feel his arms around her, to be surrounded by him, warmed by him, she hadn't made an initiating move. Neither had he. It wasn't for lack of desire. That hadn't changed. His eyes burned with it.

But Jeremy's death had made a difference. Had he died remotely, distantly, it might not have had this divisive effect. But Dawson had been there when he drew his last breath, and that had created an indefinable chasm between them. They were trying to find a way to bridge it.

Unable to bear the teeming silence any longer, she said, "Eva called to tell me that you'd stopped by at the hospital."

"Briefly. Soon as I'd gone to the hotel and cleaned up. I knew Headly would want to hear everything firsthand. He was—"

"Oh, I know how he was," she said, laughing softly. "I wouldn't be surprised if the nursing staff has a picture of him they're using as a dartboard. He's not an ideal patient."

"His mood will improve soon as he starts getting feeling back." A few seconds elapsed, then, "Eva said you stayed with her all night. She appreciated it and so do I."

"I wouldn't have left her alone. Despite the surgeon's positive prognosis, she was terribly worried about him. And about you."

He shifted his weight from one foot to another, looking uncomfortable. "Tucker said he called you."

"I'd made him promise to the moment they located you."

"I would have called you myself, but they wouldn't let me speak to anyone until I'd been questioned."

"Headly told me that."

"Then when I was free to call, I didn't have my phone. They took it as evidence because Jeremy was recorded on it. Besides—"

"You didn't feel like talking."

He gave her a weak smile. "Right. After going over it repeatedly with the authorities, no, for a while there, I didn't feel like talking anymore."

"I needed some down time to let my mind settle around it, too. I wanted only to be with my children."

"Do they know?"

"What would be the point of telling them?"

"None."

"I didn't think so, either."

"How are they?"

"Want to see them?"

He grinned. "I could do with some innocence."

They climbed the stairs and moved down the hallway, past the closed door to the guest room that Stef had used. "I spoke with Mrs. DeMarco a short while ago. They'd been notified of Jeremy's confession. Stef's body will be released to them tomorrow."

"Good," he said. "And terrible."

"Yes."

When they entered the boys' bedroom, they heard them quarreling in the connecting bathroom. "Hey, what's going on?"

At the sound of her voice, their silence was abrupt. Amelia shot a suspicious look over her shoulder at Dawson as she pushed open the bathroom door. When the boys saw him, they shoved their way past her and launched themselves at him.

He hooked his hands under Grant's arms and used him as a weight to do a biceps curl, clenching his teeth and groaning with the effort, which caused Grant to giggle. When he set him down, he socked Hunter's shoulder. They fired questions at him, but, talking over them, he asked what all the noise had been about.

Hunter quickly gave the classic reply. "Nothing."

"Hunter said we shouldn't tell Mom, but I think we should."

"Shut up, Grant!"

"Hunter, I've asked you not to tell your brother to—"

"It's about our—"

"Grant, shut up!"

"—penises."

Hunter looked like he wanted the floor to open up and swallow him. Bright spots of color appeared in his cheeks.

Amelia cleared her throat and, with as much composure as she could muster, asked, "What about them?"

"*Noth-thing,*" Hunter said, shooting his younger brother a threatening glare.

Dawson turned to Amelia. "I'd like an iced tea, please."

"What?" Confused, she looked from him to the boys, then back at him. Then, "Oh! Of course. Tea. Good. I'll just go and..." She left them and closed the bedroom door behind herself.

Ten minutes later, Dawson rejoined her in the kitchen. He went straight to the glass of tea she had dutifully poured and drained it without taking a breath.

"Well?"

"Well," he said, stretching out the word, "they've both experienced what I assured them was a perfectly normal biological phenomenon."

"Ah. I thought that might be it. I've noticed that *phenomenon* on occasion, but always pretended not to, as any lady would."

"Hunter experienced a rather, uh, stubborn one today. He was afraid it signified something terribly wrong with him, which he wanted to keep from you so you wouldn't worry or get upset."

"That sweetheart."

"Grant was just as considerate of your feelings. He felt you should be told about the affliction in case they both died of it and you found them dead in their beds without knowing what had killed them."

She covered her mouth to smother a laugh.

"I gave them my solemn promise that you couldn't die from it, although," he added in an undertone, "it might sometimes feel like you can. Hunter asked if *it* would ever stop doing *that*, and I told him no. If he's lucky."

The two of them started laughing at once and they laughed for a full minute. "So much for their innocence." Wiping tears of mirth from her eyes, she said, "Lord, it feels good to laugh. Since I've known you, we haven't really laughed together, have we?"

"There's a lot we haven't done together that I've wanted to do."

The mood shifted from lighthearted to serious in the span of a single second. They continued to look at each other, but neither moved to close the short distance between them. Amelia decided to address the issue. "For reasons I can't explain, it seems inappropriate for us to pick up where we left off last night."

Looking pained, he said, "Yeah."

They could hear Hunter and Grant tramping down the staircase. Grant called out, "Dawson, will you play cars with us?"

Amelia said, "But I don't see any harm in you staying for dinner."

He glanced toward the oven. "Something smells good."

"Roast chicken with lemon and rosemary."

"Sold."

The boys came into the kitchen, claiming his attention and ending any chance for a grown-up conversation. But over their heads, he said to her, "After dinner, we have to talk. There's something you need to know, and I want you to hear it from me."

Carl was never without a fallback position. Only a fool would leave himself with just one option, and he hadn't escaped capture this long by being a fool. He'd taken extraordinary measures to keep the cabin from being detected, but if anyone got wise to it, he had the Airstream. It was his personal escape hatch, kept secret from Flora and even from Jeremy. He could retreat to it should the situation ever go to shit.

Which is exactly what had happened.

He'd taken one look at Jeremy's bullet wound and had known immediately that his son wasn't going to make it. It might have been a slow, internal leak, but without surgical repair, he would have eventually been drained dry.

There was no sense in crying over it. It was what it was, and Jeremy knew that as well as he did.

"This place was great so long as nobody was looking for us," Carl had told him. "But now, the heat's on. They're gonna be combing the countryside for us. I've got to get out of here. You know that, don't you?"

Of course Jeremy had recognized the necessity of his retreat. If the head of the snake was chopped off, the snake died. Carl couldn't be captured or killed. If he was, everything he'd stood for, everything he'd done, would have been for naught.

Jeremy didn't argue with his decision or plead with him to stay. He didn't ask to be taken to a hospital where his life might have been saved. No, Jeremy had accepted his fate like a true crusader.

Carl could have done without seeing the tears in his eyes when he'd handed him the revolver loaded with only one bullet. Jeremy had inherited that sentimental streak from his mother. It manifested itself at the worst times, when it was damned inconvenient or impossible to deal with.

Like at Golden Branch. He'd thought Flora would never stop bawling, even after they were safely away. Like that time when he'd cut short their Canadian vacation. Both she and Jeremy had cried then. The last time Jeremy had visited the cabin before she died, the two of them got weepy.

Carl didn't have any patience for tears. Regret? Wasted energy. You did what you had to do. You moved on.

Like he was doing now.

He'd come to the trailer the night he left Saint Nelda's Island. He'd had another car parked in a long-term garage several blocks from where he'd left Bernie's car. At that point, no one was after him. The greatest danger he'd faced had been walking after dark in that part of town, where the crime rate was high. Bernie of the rickety hips would have been easy prey, but he reached the garage without being accosted.

It was an old facility. No cameras, no nosy attendant. He'd reconnected the battery cables, which he'd left disconnected so it wouldn't run down, and the car started without a hitch. He'd crossed the state line into South Carolina singing along with the car radio.

The fifties-era Airstream, sans trailer, was parked not too far as the crow flies from the cabin. It had been there since the day he'd bought it off a commercial fisherman who'd fallen on hard times and was moving to live with his in-laws somewhere in the Midwest.

He'd been happy to unload the Airsteam to the elderly man who had a hearing problem and walked with a cane. The story Carl had spun was that he was escaping the nursing home that his ungrateful children had consigned him to. The fisherman, resentful of Fate himself, sympathized, took his cash, gave him a bill of sale, and never looked back.

Over the years, the aluminum tube had sunk deep into the soil. A thick vine had grown up over the rounded rear of it and over one third of the top. That helped camouflage it, although someone would have had to have ventured deep into the boondocks to spot it in the first place.

What he feared most was that he would return to it after an absence to find that a homeless person, teenagers looking for a hangout, or meth cookers had made themselves at home.

But the trailer was derelict enough to discourage even the most desperate trespassers. The night he'd left Saint Nelda's, he'd found it empty, but musty-smelling. It had been so stifling inside, it was like being in a convection oven. But he'd spent almost twenty-four hours there before reuniting with Jeremy at the cabin.

During that time, he'd prepared his hideout for when it might be needed, which a gut instinct had told him would be soon.

His instinct had proven to be unfailing. Headly's presence in Savannah had represented a turning point in their forty-year-old rivalry. For the first time in their turbulent history together, they were in the same place at the same time.

It had been seventeen years since Carl had been credited with a crime, but the FBI agent hadn't given up the chase, retired, gotten slow and fat. No, Headly was here, and, according to news accounts, he was recovering well from the gunshot.

It seemed to Carl that a long-overdue showdown was inevitable. He looked forward to it. Last night, after bidding Jeremy a final good-bye, he'd come to his hideaway to plan and prepare for it.

He'd provisioned the Airstream with nonperishable food, bottled water, and paper goods. He had changes of clothing to fit various guises. He'd stockpiled items bought over time at hardware and variety stores. One never knew when something would come in handy.

This morning, he'd shaved every hair from his head, using several disposable razors and large amounts of shaving cream in order to make his scalp as slick as a billiard ball. He'd also shaved his eyebrows off. Eyelashes weren't a problem. He didn't have many left anyway.

To his face, he applied a moisturizer with a green tint. It was supposed to reduce ruddiness in a woman's complexion, but what it did for him was give his complexion a yellow-grayish cast.

He dressed himself in oversized clothes and put on a large baseball cap that virtually rocked on top of his skull each time he moved his head. Checking himself in the cracked mirror, he laughed.

He'd achieved the look he was after.

"I apologize for lying to you last night."

Dawson decided to get the apology out of the way first. They'd had their dinner—Amelia was a good cook—followed by ice-cream sundaes and two rounds of Chutes and Ladders.

The boys had gone to bed reluctantly, but finally they were asleep.

He and Amelia had shared the last of the white wine. Since she'd been told to stay indoors, they couldn't go out on the porch, which they would have preferred. Instead they'd taken their wine into the living room and had made themselves comfortable in matching slipcovered chairs.

They'd kept the window shutters open, the lights off. The precaution of semidarkness was taken only in part because of security issues. Actually they were seeking at least the illusion of privacy.

"If you had told me what you had in mind, I would have stopped you."

"You would have *tried*," he said. "I didn't want to fight with you about it. I played it the way I thought best."

He took a sip of wine. She made several revolutions around the rim of her glass with her index finger. The delay tactics ran out.

Looking over at him, she said, "Tell me everything."

"Are you sure you want to know?"

"No," she admitted. "Not at all sure."

"Some of it will be painful for you to hear."

"I realize that. But if you don't tell me, I'll always wonder what he said, and I think that would be worse than knowing the full extent."

He started with how he'd found the property based on Glenda's discovery. "My little covert expedition could have resulted in nothing. But I guess I'll owe Glenda two boxes of candy this Christmas." He then described the cabin. "You knew nothing about it?"

"Nothing."

"Basically it was a dump. I thought at first that no one was there. Then Jeremy told me that he could shoot me through the door. Which turned out not to be true."

"Were you afraid?"

"I won't bullshit you. My heart was in my throat."

"You were crazy to go there. Alone. Unarmed. They could have killed you on sight."

"That crossed my mind," he said, grimly understating. "But I was relying on Carl's ego. I was reasonably sure he couldn't resist talking to me."

"Once before, he confided in a journalist, then killed him afterward."

"Headly told you about that?"

She nodded.

"He shouldn't have."

"He was preparing me for the worst."

He finished his wine and set the empty glass on the end table, signaling that he was getting to the heart of the matter. "He was almost dead when I got there." He described Jeremy's condition in clinical language that spared her the graphic ugliness.

"I called for help, then started asking him questions. He admitted that the house fire was deliberately set to kill the Wessons. He'd been very attached to them, but I guess their usefulness to Carl had expired. He confessed to killing Darlene Strong and Stef. He said to tell you that he was sorry."

"For mistaking her for me?"

"Sorry for wanting you dead." He repeated everything that Jeremy had told him about killing Stef on impulse. "He said that if he'd had time to think about killing you, he wouldn't have been able to."

She absorbed all that, then, her voice thick with emotion, asked, "Anything else?"

"He talked about Hunter and Grant." He related that exchange.

Choking back tears, she said, "He denied himself so much joy."

"His decision. He chose Carl over them. Over you."

"Yes, he made his decision. But unfortunately he's not the only person affected by it." She looked at him imploringly. "How will I tell my children about their father's crimes? About Carl? I must, I know that. But I'm afraid that once they know about their bloodline, it will haunt them and dictate how they live the rest of their lives."

"Yes, it sucks. And, no, it can't be undone. But it can dictate their lives in a positive way. They're made of good stuff, too. Their gene pool also includes you and your father."

Her nod of agreement was thoughtful, made absently, but he regained her attention when he took her wineglass from her hand and set it on the table beside his. Then he clasped both her hands. "Amelia, your dad didn't commit suicide. They killed him."

By the time he had finished telling her what Jeremy had confessed, tears were streaming from her eyes. The tracks of them reflected the meager light coming in through the open shutters, painting wet, silvery streaks on her cheeks.

She pulled her hands from his and placed them over her face, sobbing into them. "How horrible for him. Oh, God, how horrible."

He moved to sit on the arm of her chair and rubbed comforting circles on her back. "You had to be told, and I wanted to be the one to tell you. I knew it would break your heart, but also relieve your mind. Try to forget the horrible part. The last thing your father did was also the best thing he ever did. He demonstrated just how much he loved you."

"He spared my life."

He turned her head to face him and used his thumbs to wipe the tears off her cheeks. "Jeremy could have taken that secret to his grave. Much as I hate giving him credit for anything, that confession is proof that he did care for you. Even loved you, I think. He knew you had agonized over your father's supposed suicide and wanted you to know that he hadn't deserted you. I think Jeremy empathized."

"How so?"

"Floral Stimel is dead. She's buried out there beneath the cabin. They've got a forensic team working to exhume her body now."

He could see the understanding in her expression as she said quietly, "His mother."

"Yeah. For all her misdeeds, Flora was still his mother. It upset him to talk about her. I think he loved her, too."

"How did she die? When?"

"Jeremy's time ran out before he could tell me."

She stared into his eyes as though trying to see into his deepest being. Then her fingertips lightly stroked his eyebrows, his cheekbone, the side of his face down to his jawline. "You were kind to him, weren't you?"

"He was dying." He thought he would end it there, with that simple statement of fact, but she continued to look at him as though knowing there were ambiguities he needed to express.

"I thought if I ever got near him, I'd want to kill him for everything he'd done. Especially to you and those boys. I wanted to hate him. But he was a broken man, Amelia. And, yeah, I felt sorry for him. Because he was a victim, too. Left to the couple who reared him, he probably would have gone a different path.

"But Carl destroyed any chance Jeremy might have had to lead a normal, happy, and productive life. It all goes back to Carl. He's the villain. And I intend to tell him that to his face."

She flinched. "What do you mean?"

"I'm not going to give up on getting a one-on-one with him."

"Once he's captured, you mean."

He left her and, going to stand at the windows, peered through the slats of the shutters. "I wonder where the cowardly bastard scuttled to after leaving his son to slowly bleed to death."

He felt Amelia move up behind him, but he didn't turn around.

"You're not thinking of trying to run him to ground."

"I doubt I'd be that lucky twice."

"Lucky?" She took him by the arm and turned him around with a determination that surprised him. "Why would you consider it lucky to encounter him? Why would you take such a dangerous risk?"

He gnawed his lower lip, searching for words.

"Why, Dawson?" she demanded.

"Because I've been a basket case for long enough. I want to prove that I can hear a loud banging noise without ducking for cover. Or get through a night without pills and liquor, without waking up bathed in a cold sweat, a dying scream in my mouth."

"You want to test your bravery?"

"You could put it that way."

Her chin went up a notch. "Hogwash."

"Pardon me?"

"I don't believe that for a second. You don't need to prove your courage, even to yourself. If you hadn't reacted exactly as you did when Headly was shot, I'd be injured or dead, too. You didn't duck for cover. You took command of the situation.

"You registered the direction the shots came from, even as you pushed me to the ground and then went to attend Headly. You probably don't even remember, but you issued orders to the people who came running, and they did as you said because your response to the emergency was correct.

"So don't try to sell me on the idea that you went to slay a dragon in order to win a badge of courage. To win a Pulitzer maybe. Is that what this is about?"

"What if it is?"

"Would a prize be worth risking your life?"

He pushed his fingers through his hair. "This has nothing to do with a freakin' prize."

"Then what's worth risking your life for?"

He didn't say anything.

"Dawson?"

"What?"

"Tell me."

"What?"

"What is it that you want?"

They stood there, squared off, breathing hard, angry.

Then he pulled her against him and began kissing her with a need so fierce it alarmed him. But not enough to stop. Especially not when she responded in kind. As though pent-up fear, despair, and lust had been unleashed simultaneously and in equal proportions, they kissed ravenously.

But he didn't lose his head completely. Aware of the guards patrolling the beach and keeping a careful watch on the house, he lifted her against him and carried her into a short hallway that would prevent them from being seen. He set her down with her back against the wall and resumed the frantic kissing.

Every primal mating instinct demanded haste and nothing less than total possession. In a matter of seconds, he was pulling her T-shirt over her head. The bra must have been built in, because her breasts were left bare. He cupped them in his hands, reshaping them reflexively, rubbing his lips against her nipple until it beaded, then sucking it deep into his mouth.

She fumbled with the buttons on his fly and then her hand was claiming him, her fingers tightly squeezing, massaging their way up until her thumb was at the tip, pressing—

"Jesus." Gasping with pleasure, he ground his forehead against the wall behind her shoulder in an effort not to come. "Wait, wait."

The fabric of her skirt was as light as air against his hands as he slid them beneath it. He worked his fingers under a wedge of lace. She was soft and warm and wet. He quickly rid her of the underpants so he could luxuriate in the femaleness, the snug, silky, wonderful feel of her.

She pressed down hard on his exploring fingers, moaned his name, whispered, "More."

He lifted her up to straddle his thighs and thrust into her, fully, completely, and without caution. He would have paused then to apologize for his lack of restraint, would have rested there deep inside her, giving them both time to adjust, to breathe.

But she rocked against him and searched for his mouth with hers, whimpering a litany of words that signaled her own urgency.

He fucked her. He gave, took, told her with every stroke what he hadn't been able to convey with words, communicated what he'd felt from the moment he saw her enter the courtroom, and knew, in that instant, that he'd been blessed and doomed in the same heartbeat.

He changed the angle and the tempo to favor her. She clutched handfuls of his hair and squeezed his hips with her thighs. And when her orgasm pulsed around him, he came and came and came.

After half a minute, he regrettably disengaged. Weakly, she slid down the wall to sit on the floor. He lowered himself beside her and gathered her against him. She pressed her open mouth against his throat and murmured his name. She slid her hand inside his shirt and pressed her palm against his heart. The gesture moved him more than a spoken endearment and felt even more intimate than the hard-core sex.

It was time for him to go.

He moved away from her and pulled her skirt down over her bare thighs. He passed her the discarded T-shirt, then stood up and buttoned his jeans. She remained huddled there, looking up at him with perplexity, modestly clutching the T-shirt to her chest. "What are you doing?"

"Leaving."

"Why?"

The dismay behind her voice was almost his undoing. "This shouldn't have happened, Amelia."

"What are you saying?"

"What I've said before. I can't have you."

"You just did."

"You know what I mean."

Her swallow was loud in the silence. "I know you want me."

"Only with every fucking breath."

"Then why are you doing this?"

He backed away from her, moving toward the door into the living room, which would lead him out and away from her. "Because you had one selfish bastard who damn near ruined your life. I won't be the second one."

Chapter 26

Dawson pulled open the door to Headly's hospital room and looked in. The patient was propped up in bed. His chin sprouted a salt-and-pepper beard, and he had bed head, but his color was better. Eva was holding a cup of coffee as he sipped it through a straw. Then he angled his head back and, making a terrible face, complained of it being as "cold as a wedge."

"Be glad you can swallow," she said. "And breathe without a ventilator. If the bullet had affected other vertebrae—"

"I know, I know," he said crossly.

"You're getting meaner," Dawson said as he came in. "A positive sign."

Eva greeted him cheerfully. Headly less so. After an exchange of pleasantries—"How did you sleep?" and so forth—Headly got to the matter of Flora's grave. "I talked to Knutz a few minutes ago. Nothing to report yet. Getting lights in there last night would have been a logistical nightmare, so the team didn't start the exhumation until this morning."

"How long do you think before you hear something?"

"Hard to predict. Until they start excavating, they don't know what they'll find. It's slow-going because they have to be careful not to compromise or destroy evidence. Ascertaining how she died, whether it was of disease or something else, will depend largely on how long she's been buried."

The subject matter apparently distressed Eva. She tried to foist a carton of apple juice on Headly, who reacted as though she'd offered him a cup of hemlock. She returned the carton to his tray, then wheeled the trolley away from his bed. A wheel caught on the tangle of tubes on the floor at his bedside.

Dawson motioned toward it. "Is anybody monitoring what goes where?"

"I hope to God somebody is," Headly groused. "So they don't pump something out that's supposed to be pumped in, or vice versa."

Eva freed the wheel and moved the trolley away from the machines, monitors, and IV paraphernalia. Then she sat down on the edge of the bed and motioned Dawson toward the chair.

"Thanks, but I'm fine standing."

"You're fine?" Headly said. "You're twitching like a man with a rash in his crack."

It was true. He was as restless as he'd been all night. He'd known sleep would be out of the question, but when he returned to his hotel, he'd laid down and had at least tried to rest his weary body.

But within minutes he was up again, moving around his hotel room without aim or purpose except to outdistance his memory of Amelia's disillusionment and the pain he had caused her when he left. He was doing her a favor, but it had entailed humiliating her, and he couldn't stand that.

Headly broke into his disturbing thoughts. "Cough it up. What's the matter?"

Eva laid her hand on her husband's arm, a silent command for him to can it. To Dawson, she said, "You were on your way to see Amelia when you left here yesterday."

"Um-huh."

"How is she holding up?"

"Okay. Ambivalent about Jeremy. She wanted to know everything, but dreaded hearing it all."

"You told her everything?"

"Yes."

"About her father?"

"That was the toughest."

"How'd she take it?"

"Just as I expected. A meltdown over how he'd been tortured. But grateful to have it confirmed that he hadn't taken his own life."

Sadly, Eva said, "Lord, that poor young woman has been put through so much."

Like he wasn't aware of that. Like he wasn't being a goddamn Sir Galahad to spare her from being put through more. He didn't say that, just made a motion with his shoulders to show that he agreed: Amelia had suffered some serious shit.

After giving him time to elaborate, which he didn't do, Eva got up and began straightening things in the room—the stack of fresh towels that an orderly had left near the sink, a bouquet of flowers sent from Headly's office in DC, a sheaf of hospital insurance forms. None of these things needed her attention. She was trying to pretend that she wasn't about to pry, that this was a casual and spontaneous conversation.

Of course Dawson knew better.

"How were the little boys?" she asked.

"Good. Oblivious about their dad. For now. Which is as it should be." In spite of his dark mood, a smile hiked up one corner of his mouth. "I had to give them a lesson in biology." He related the anecdote. Eva and Headly laughed.

"After dinner, Amelia let them make their own sundaes, which were disgusting because they dribbled on everything she set out, including blackberry jam. They made a mess, but I think it was important to her to let them have a good time last night. Considering yesterday's . . . event."

The three were quiet for a moment, then Eva ventured to ask, "Did you explain to her why you went to such lengths to go after Carl and Jeremy?"

"We talked about it some."

They looked at him, expecting more, but he didn't expound.

Eva pressed on, her misty, wistful expression straight out of a greeting-card commercial. "Amelia is an excellent mother."

Dawson cleared his throat. "She is."

"And she's such a sweet-natured person. It was kind of her to stay here with me through that terrible first night."

"Sure was."

"We talked like old friends, not like two women who'd just met."

"Hmm."

"She told me that the boys continually ask about school, because they're aware that it starts next week. She doesn't know how to tell them that they might not be going back when the other children do. They want a house with a yard so they can have a dog."

"I know all this, Eva."

Bickering with Headly was a normal part of their repartee. But he'd never had a cross word with Eva. Taken aback by his testiness, she lapsed into silence. But now that his anger over the situation had been given an opening, it burst of out him.

"I know their circumstances, and they stink, but *I can't fix them*. It would be wrong of me to try. My intrusion would only make their situation worse."

"Amelia wouldn't see your involvement as intrusion."

"How do you know?"

"You make her head spin." He registered surprise. Seeing it, she added, "She told me so. In confidence. Which I just broke."

His heart levitated, then sank. "That's nice to hear, but it doesn't make a difference. The situation is—"

"Subject to change soon."

Headly's mumble arrested Dawson's angry pacing. "Why do you say that?"

Headly looked over at Eva. "Maybe I will have some of that juice, but with ice. Would you please get me some from the machine down the hall?"

She folded her arms over her middle. "Hell, no. I'm staying put. I want to hear why you said that, too."

Headly scowled, but she didn't budge or show any signs of relenting. Headly sighed and looked at Dawson. "Neither of us is getting any younger."

"Meaning you and Carl?"

He nodded. "Always before, when he felt us closing in—even if we weren't—he hightailed it. He's jumped states in a matter of days."

"You think old age has slowed him down?"

"In a manner of speaking. He always had this ragtag bunch of outlaws to aid and abet him. Gun dealers, drug dealers, or petty crooks who were hero worshipers, disciples of his twisted dogma. All willing to do his bidding. Most have either been caught and are serving long sentences, or they've been killed by one of their ilk, or simply died off. By the way, they found the guy who owns the boat."

"The *CandyCane*?"

"He's living in the Keys. But barely. Stage-four lung cancer. He'll die in captivity, but even knowing that, he wouldn't give up any information about Carl." He stared down at his right hand where it lay on his chest and wiggled the fingers experimentally.

Dawson noticed. "The doctor was right."

Headly sneered. "Just to prove how smart he is, last night he stuck a needle, which I'm sure is used to stitch saddles, into my thumb. Hurt like bloody hell."

Eva rolled her eyes. "It was a prick with a straight pin. He howled a profanity that could be heard back in DC. But he's only trying to get off the subject until you two are alone, and I'm not going to let him. Continue, Gary."

He looked at her with exasperation. "Point is, Carl's run out of admirers. Even Jeremy's gone. Carl Wingert is passé, of another era, history that few even know about. He wanted to live in infamy like Bonnie and Clyde, Oswald, Jim Jones, David Koresh. He never achieved those heights. He knows he's a has-been, and that'll eat at him."

"What do you think he'll do?" Dawson asked.

"Stage a spectacular exit for himself. He's got little to lose now except for his inflated self-esteem. He won't care if he doesn't survive, so long as he leaves the rest of us with a lasting impression." He paused. "Knutz has already alerted Homeland Security."

"Excuse me, sir. Can I help you?"

The nurse was young and pretty and eager to be of assistance to such a decrepit older gentleman. Her scrubs were purple. A UGA bulldog snarled from the patch affixed to her breast pocket.

Carl adjusted his baseball cap, as though conscious of his hairlessness, when actually he was tugging down the bill of the cap in order to conceal his face from Dawson Scott, who was at the end of the hallway, talking to an attractive middle-aged woman. Carl assumed she was Headly's wife.

He'd come to scout out the hospital, commit to memory how it was laid out, note where the fire alarms and emergency exits were, plan how he was going to get to Headly and finish their feud once and for all.

Lo and behold, the moment he stepped off the elevator on this floor, the first person he spotted was Dawson Scott. He'd been about to duck back into the elevator and get the hell out of there, but in a millisecond he changed his mind.

He was no longer Bernie. Unless Dawson looked very closely, it was doubtful he would recognize the man who, only a week ago, had been spry enough to fly a kite on the beach. His altered appearance was so realistic, he almost had himself convinced that he was a cancer patient whose prognosis wasn't good.

It was a perfect disguise. After one glance at someone so obviously terminally ill, people tended to look the other way, sometimes out of pity or respect for privacy, often because of an irrational fear of contagion, but always, always with avoidance. In a hospital environment, he would be practically invisible.

He gave the nurse a sheepish smile. "I guess I do look lost. I just realized that I got off the elevator a floor too soon. My friend is on four."

"The elevator usually doesn't take too long." Smiling, she bent down to sniff at the flowers he was carrying. "These should cheer up your friend."

He'd bought the bouquet from a vendor in the first-floor lobby, then taken it into a stall in the men's room. Now besides the flower stems inside the green tissue there was also a six-shot revolver, to be used in case the disguise wasn't as deceiving as he thought. His index finger was on the trigger.

"I like the color combination," he said.

"Very pretty." She patted his shoulder. "Have a nice day."

She was about to move away, when he forestalled her. "Say, isn't that the magazine writer who's been in the news?"

She followed the direction of his pointing chin. "Dawson Scott." Leaning in, she whispered. "All us nurses think he's hot."

Carl chuckled. "I probably would too if I was your age. And a girl, of course."

She laughed.

"What's he doing here?"

"Did you hear about the FBI agent who got shot? Of course you did. Everybody has. Well, Dawson Scott is his godson."

Everything inside Carl went perfectly still for several seconds.

Then his heart began to race with excitement. So, that was it. That was the fishiness that Carl had sensed but couldn't put his finger on. Ever since Dawson Scott had moved in next door to Amelia, he'd thought there was more to him than simply being a writer on the trail of a good story. He and fucking Headly were practically related!

In a stage whisper, he exclaimed, "You'd don't say!"

The naive nurse fell for the act and was all too glad to elaborate. "I've been told that Mr. Scott wasn't too far behind the ambulance that rushed Mr. Headly to the ER. He stayed late into the night, until Mr. Headly was out of surgery. I assumed he'd hung around as a courtesy, on account of he was with Mr. Headly when he was shot.

"But then he showed up last evening and visited for over an hour. After he left, I mentioned to Mrs. Headly—that's her he's talking to—how nice it was of him to follow up. That's when she explained their relationship. They've known him since he was born."

"Huh." It appeared to Carl that the two were disagreeing. She was talking; Scott was shaking his head no. Then she reached out and touched his cheek. He pulled her hand away from his face and kissed the back of it.

The nurse said dreamily, "You can see how close they are."

"Yes, I can. I certainly can. It must be a big comfort to her to have him here."

"She told me as much, but don't let her appearance fool you. She's got a steel backbone. Keeps us all on our toes," she told him around a giggle. "She sticks to Mr. Headly like glue and only leaves the hospital to shower and change clothes. When she leaves, two bodyguards go with her. Like she's J. Lo or somebody."

"Bodyguards?"

"In case the men who tried to kill her husband go after her. Well, *man*, now. It was a father and son, and the son died yesterday. Oh, there's the elevator. Let me grab it for you."

As he hobbled into it, Carl placed his hand at his crotch and winced. She asked if he was all right.

"They cut out my prostate a couple of weeks ago. Still get twinges down there."

Her lips formed a pucker of sympathy. "It gets better."

As the door slid closed, he winked at her. "It already has. And you've been a huge help."

While Dawson was out, the hotel housekeeper had serviced his room. She always turned up the AC thermostat when she left. Every time he came in, he cranked it down again as far as it would go.

He took a four-dollar bottle of water from the minibar and ordered a room-service sandwich. He'd been elevated from Harriet's shit list to star status. The hotel desk had informed him that all his expenses were being covered by *NewsFront*. When he came in last night, a bottle of chilled champagne was waiting for him in his room. The unopened bubbly was turning warm in its bucket of melted ice.

CNN and all the major networks had covered the dramatic story that had unfolded in the ramshackle cabin on the edge of the salt marsh. Dawson had successfully eluded reporters. He'd disconnected his hotel-room phone this morning when the switchboard operator ignored his request and continued to put through calls from correspondents asking for just one sound bite.

Harriet had heard the story about the time he was on the ferry going over to Saint Nelda's. That was when his replacement cell phone—which he'd bought at a supermarket—had begun lighting up with text messages. He regretted having sent her his new number and hadn't bothered to read her texts until after he got back to Savannah. The first few had been gleeful. Overnight, they'd graduated to giddy.

He looked over at his neglected laptop where it sat on the dresser. Last night, after leaving Amelia and returning to this solitary room, he'd planned to write. His best writing always came from scouring emotional wounds that were already raw, which was why he had a love-hate relationship with his craft.

Never had his emotions been as ulcerated as they were last night. Ideally, his impressions and feelings about Jeremy Wesson should be committed to hard disk while they were still fresh. He'd even booted up and placed his fingers on the keyboard, hoping the familiar preparation would jumpstart him.

But he hadn't been able to type a single word. He couldn't think of a turn of phrase that didn't trivialize the thoughts and feelings that went bone-deep, soul-deep. And he realized he never would.

Now he sat down on the edge of the bed and placed the necessary call to Harriet. Before she got completely carried away, she needed to be told.

She answered on the first ring. "Oh my God, *Dawson*!" She practically squealed his name.

"Hello, Harriet."

"I'm having multiple orgasms."

"Congratulations. That has to be a first."

"Go ahead, be your usual insulting self. You're forgiven. You're forgiven every hateful thing you've ever said to me. Tell me, how in the hell did you track them when the FBI had failed? Was it Glenda? Did she help put you there in that cabin? She won't tell me dick, but I suspect it was her. Was it?"

"I'm not writing the story."

When a star collapsed, it didn't create that kind of vacuum. For an interminable amount of time, nothing was said. Then, "This isn't fucking April Fool's Day, Dawson."

"This isn't a joke, either. I can't write the story."

"What are you talking about? You *lived* the story. You *are* the story."

"Which is why I don't want to write it. Why I can't."

"Okay, okay, I'll play along. Why can't you?"

"I'm too close to it."

"You're close to every story. You drive us all nuts with your close-getting. Ordinarily you won't write a story unless you're grafted to it."

"This is different."

"How?"

"It just is."

"Not good enough. How is it different?"

"The man died in my arms, Harriet."

That subdued her, but not for long. However, her voice turned softer. "I know that must've been awful." He imagined her stroking a cat after yelling at it for coughing up a hair ball. "But you've written about soldiers who died of their injuries. Some of them you interviewed hours before they died."

"I wasn't looking into their eyes when the lights went out." He experienced a flashback to working his shirt collar free of Jeremy's grasping hand, and squeezed his eyes shut in an attempt to block it. He propped his elbow on his knee and rested his forehead in his palm. "Look, I don't expect you to understand how this is different. It just is."

"So consider it a unique opportunity. A chance to stretch. It was an awful experience, but you came away from it with a new perspective on life. Share what you learned with your reader." She was going for maternal now. *I know it was a hard knock, but pony up, get on with it. I have every confidence in your ability to overcome this hiccup.*

"It's not an experience I wish to share."

"Maybe not right now. It's still too fresh. Give yourself a few days to mellow. Chill. Take all the time you need." A second or two ticked past. "But if I could have the finished piece by, say, the end of October, I could slip it into—"

"There won't be a story about this, Harriet. Not in October.

Not ever. Not from me anyway. If you want to send someone else—"

"No one else can write it."

"Well, then you're shit out of luck."

He heard her jeweled reading glasses hit her leather desk pad. She was hacked. "Dawson, why are you doing this to me?"

"To *you*?"

"Is this your sick payback for me being promoted over you?"

He laughed. "Don't flatter yourself, Harriet. This has nothing whatsoever to do with you."

"Ohhh, okay. I get it. Duh! You're holding out for perks. Fair enough. I think I can talk management into giving you a bonus for the piece. I can't guarantee it, but I'll try. I can positively guarantee that it'll be the cover story."

"No story."

"From now on, I won't give you assignments."

"You mean I don't have to cover blind balloonists?"

"You can write about whatever your heart desires, and that's a huge concession for me. In exchange, give me thirty-five hundred to four thousand words."

"I'll give you six."

"Six thousand?"

"Six words. Do. You. Want. The. Champagne. Back?"

She hung up on him, which was just as well, because his room-service sandwich had arrived. But when he opened the door, it wasn't the expected roast beef on rye that greeted him.

Chapter 27

I've already made a fool of myself in front of you," Amelia said. "But I'd rather not look like one in front of them." She tipped her head to one side.

Dawson stepped into the hallway. Midway down, two uniformed officers were watching them from the open door of the elevator. He looked back at Amelia. "What's wrong?"

"Nothing, if you invite me in."

He stood aside. She called a thank-you to the deputies, who had insisted on accompanying her when she'd stated her intention of going to Savannah. She pulled the door closed and flipped the bolt, then turned to face Dawson.

He said, "I thought you were room service."

"Disappointed?"

"Surprised. Where are Hunter and Grant?"

"I left them at the beach house in good hands. They and the deputy have bonded."

The conversation died there. She went farther into the room and took a look around. When she saw the ice bucket and champagne, she asked, "What's the occasion?"

Completely baffled, he said, "Amelia, what are you doing here?"

"I suppose it was rude of me not to call first, but—"

"Screw manners," he said impatiently. "Why would you come at all? I thought I would be the last person on earth you'd want to see after last night."

As they stood there looking at each other, the aftershocks of that explosive encounter were still being felt. The demand, the frantic groping, her hands, his mouth, the insistent coupling, the ecstasy of the synchronized climax.

Suddenly he frowned with concern. "I didn't hurt you, did I?"

"No."

"Well, that's good. I didn't exercise much—"

"Control. No, neither did I."

"I was going to say finesse."

"A better word. You're the writer."

Again, the conversation died.

He turned his head aside, looking away from her. "If you're worried about getting pregnant, you won't. I had a vasectomy when I was twenty-two."

That came from so far out of left field, she didn't know how to respond. Eventually she said, "Twenty-two? That was awfully young to make that kind of commitment."

"I don't regret it."

"Then it was the right decision for you."

He looked at her again and seemed annoyed that she hadn't taken issue, that she'd denied him the opportunity to defend his decision. "You still haven't told me why you're here."

"I'm not going to let you get away with your exit line last night."

He gave her a long look, then nodded his head slowly. "Oh, I get what this is about. The morning-after rehash. A must-have for women. I wouldn't have expected something so banal from you."

Her temper flared. "And I wouldn't have expected you to act like a jerk."

He didn't argue the point, which was as good as an admission that a jerk was exactly what he was being. Appearing as ill at ease with himself as much as with her, he ran his hand around the back of his neck. When he lowered his hand to his side and looked at her, his expression was resigned.

"You want me to tell you how good it was? Christ, Amelia, couldn't you tell? Doesn't it go without saying?"

"Then why did you bolt?"

"I told you why."

"You gave me an excuse. But you're withholding the reason."

"In other words, I'm a liar."

"Please don't try to pick a fight to avoid an issue."

"Now I have issues?"

"You've said so yourself!"

"Right," he returned, matching her tone. "I do. So you should heed the warning and stay away from me."

"Why, Dawson? Why do you say you want me with every breath, then push me away? I want to know. Tell me now. *Why?*"

"Because Jeremy put you and your kids through hell. I won't do that to them or to you."

"I've come to think that Jeremy didn't have post-traumatic stress."

"Maybe. But I'm not faking *my* nightmares."

"I'm willing to help you through—"

"Thanks, but *I'm* not willing for you to."

"Isn't that my decision to make?"

"No."

She paused to catch her breath. As she did so, she noticed his determination not to look directly at her. "Your nightmares aren't the reason, are they? That's just another excuse. Like the loner thing."

"Loner thing?"

"Headly said you—"

"Oh, Headly said. You've talked about me with Headly?"

"You've assumed a loner outlook, when actually it goes against your nature."

"What the fuck? Headly's an expert on my *nature*?"

"I think there's something to what he said."

"What makes you think so?"

"A vasectomy at twenty-two for one thing."

"That has nothing to do with what we're talking about."

"It has everything to do with it."

"You're wrong."

"No, I'm not. If there weren't some truth to what Headly said, you wouldn't be shouting."

Seething, he turned his back to her and switched from shouting to muttering.

"Where's your story?"

He jerked himself back around to face her. "What?"

"Another excuse has been your heedless pursuit of a story. Nothing matters like the story. You'll go to any lengths, take insane, life-threatening risks to get the story. So..." She gestured toward his sleeping laptop. "Where is it?"

"I haven't written it yet."

"Have you even started?"

"No."

"Why?"

"It hasn't gelled. I haven't decided on the direction I want to take it. Besides, the ending can't be Jeremy dying alone in that cabin. The story won't end until Carl is captured or killed."

"That's what you're waiting on."

"Exactly. That's the only reason I'm still here."

"Oh. You've hung around this long only to get the story."

"That's right."

"Your involvement with me, the boys, only a means to an end?"

"The truth?"

"A yes-or-no will do."

"Don't make me hurt and embarrass you."

"So that's a yes."

He didn't say anything.

"You were only working an angle. Getting to us to get your story."

After a beat, he bobbed his head once.

She held his stare for a long moment, then said softly, "You're lying, Dawson."

"You've repeatedly accused me of doing just that."

"And you've vehemently denied it. You'll never make me believe otherwise now."

"Oh, yeah? Bet I can. You want to know how far I'll go to get a story? I'll tell you. But you may want to sit down first."

She backed into a chair and sat.

His motions were angry and abrupt as he began to pace the width of the bed. "I had gotten some good material in Afghanistan. The stories had generated a lot of hype, notice. But it wasn't enough. I wanted more. The real nitty-gritty.

"So I talked some army brass into letting me go to a combat outpost near the Pakistani border. A dark base. When the sun goes down, it's dark until it comes up again. No lights. To move from building to building, personnel walk around with red flashlights. That kind of place. High alert twenty-four/seven.

"Stationed there was this platoon. They were set apart. Not much interaction with other service members. Tough guys. Small, wiry, lean and buff. When they weren't on a mission, they worked out. Wrestled with each other. Everything they did was very physical, combative, and they did everything together. Like a wolf pack of trained fighters.

"They were great subject matter, what I'd been hoping for. I wanted to live with them, get to know them, learn what they were about. What made them good soldiers? Were they patriots?

Or were they ruffians looking for a fight, and this was the best—or worst—to be found?

"They liked me but couldn't understand why I was there when I could be somewhere else, anywhere else in the world, where there were women and booze, movie theaters, bars, normal life. I impressed upon them that the creature-comfort sacrifices were worth the story I would come away with.

"I slept in their barracks, talked smack with them, played poker. I couldn't accompany them on their missions, because those involved finding enemy targets and taking them out.

"They'd be gone for days at a time and would return dirty, tired, hungry for hot meals, but always pumped. Mission accomplished. One less terrorist in the world. They'd talk. And talk. Eager to tell me about the most recent firefight. Talking over one another, outdoing one another with the foul language. 'Get this down, Dawson.' 'You can quote me on this.' 'Don't believe his bullshit. You want to know how it went down, talk to me.' I'd won their confidence. They wanted me to tell their story."

He stopped pacing and sat down on the end of the bed, facing her. "Then in May, they went out and were gone for longer than usual. The brass wouldn't tell me anything. I didn't expect them to. The mission was classified, of course, but this time there was a palpable tension behind the secrecy. With good reason, I found out later.

"An America chopper had crashed. The two pilots were injured, but they'd survived. The area had seen a lot of action, and the fighting was too hot for the pilots to be immediately rescued by air.

"Near the crash site was a village. One of those built into the mountain face. Most of the dwellings are caves. The people are tribal, steeped in their traditions and religion, for the most part shut off from the rest of the world. But the villagers harbored the pilots. My platoon was sent there to provide protection until a rescue could be planned.

"But Afghani rebels with Taliban ties got wind of it and reached the village ahead of the platoon. They killed the two pilots execution-style, then began punishing the villagers for sheltering them.

"For days the platoon, who'd had to take up a position on a lower plateau, hammered them relentlessly, but they were dug in deep. And when they did come out from cover, it was to kill a civilian where our guys could do nothing except watch helplessly. They murdered them singly, sometimes two or three at a time. The lucky ones, they shot. Some weren't let off that easily. Old men. Kids. Women, who were..." He paused to clear his throat. "What they did to them is unspeakable.

"Our guys finally got air support and stormed the place, but it was literally an uphill and bloody battle. They took out a few of the enemy, but many got away. The carnage they found in the village was unimaginable."

He spread his knees wide and stared at the serviceable but ugly carpet between his boots. "When they returned to the outpost, they were whipped. Casualties had been heavy. Six men dead. Five seriously wounded. Those were helicoptered to the hospital at Bagram. One of them died en route. The rest of them took these losses hard.

"In the barracks the mood wasn't boisterous. No one was pumped. They didn't joke or swap insults or play grab-ass. They didn't talk except when necessary. They barely made eye contact with each other. They had seen the ugliest face of war, and it had changed them. They'd had an up-close-and-personal experience with it, and it wasn't glorious.

"That was going to be the hook for my story. What happens to the warrior when war ceases to be noble and deteriorates into savagery? Not especially an original theme, but I figured I could write it with fresh insight. *If* I could get them to talk about the experience."

He continued to stare at the floor. "Gradually, with some gentle prodding, a few of them began to open up to me. They told me that some of the villagers had been used as human shields. They were having a hard time dealing with the fact that it was actually their bullets that had ripped apart the bodies of grandmothers, boys, girls barely past puberty, a woman heavy with pregnancy."

He stopped speaking, and for a moment, Amelia believed he was finished. When he resumed, his voice was husky and uneven.

"One of the men I hoped to interview was a corporal named Hawkins. Good-looking ranching kid from North Dakota. Smart. Natural leader. Everybody's friend. He'd come through the mission without a scratch. He'd consoled those who'd lost a particularly close buddy. He wrote letters to the kin of those who'd died, commending their valor.

"One morning, I was on my way back to the barracks after breakfast. Hawkins was sitting on the crest of this rise, his back to the mountains, which were about two miles away. The sun had just topped them. He was in silhouette, and I had to shade my eyes to see who had called out to me.

"He said if I wanted a story, to come up and join him. I started up. But the ground was loose sand and rock—I mean, this is the most desolate, lifeless, godforsaken place on the planet. The climb was a struggle. I kept losing purchase and slipping back down. He was laughing, deriding me, telling me to hurry my ass along."

He clasped his hands between his knees and studied the ridge of his knuckles. "I finally made it to the top. The sun was blinding. Sweat was stinging my eyes. I shaded them so I could see Hawkins against the glare. He gave me his homespun smile.

"'Want a story, Dawson?' I said, 'That's what I'm here for.' God's truth, I can feel how idiotic my grin must have looked. I was blinking sweat out of my eyes, wishing he'd given me time to get my laptop, fishing in the pocket of my vest for a pencil and pad."

He placed his elbows on his knees, bent from the waist, and pressed his thumbs into his eye sockets. "Hawkins put a pistol in his mouth and pulled the trigger."

Overwhelmed with sorrow for him, Amelia remained unmoving until he lowered his hands from his face and looked across at her. His lips formed a bitter line. "I got my story."

Quietly she said, "That's your nightmare."

"Last thing I hear before my own scream is the gunshot."

Mournfully, she whispered his name.

"Don't feel sorry for me."

She left the chair and walked toward him. "You're pushing me away again. Or trying to." When she got closer, she reached out to stroke his cheek.

He yanked his head away from her touch. "Thanks anyway, but a pity fuck isn't going to rid me of the nightmare."

"Another push, that one more like a hard shove." She moved between his wide-spread legs. "But not hard enough, Dawson. I'm still here."

He placed his hands on her hips as though to forcibly push her away. But upon contact, his fingers reflexively curled inward, digging in to hold her tighter. One heartbeat later, his head dropped forward. Grinding the crown of it into her middle, he rasped, "Yes, you are."

She held his head close, her fingers moving through his hair. "Thank you for telling me."

He looked up at her. "You're thanking me?"

"Who else has heard that story?"

"No one."

"Headly?"

"No one."

"But you entrusted me with it. That makes me special."

"You were already special," he said gruffly.

"Don't push me away again."

He rubbed his face against her breasts. "I don't want to, God knows."

She tipped his head up. "Then why do you? The reason this time."

Before he could speak, there was a knock on the door.

She threw a glance toward it. "Room service."

"About bloody time."

Another knock. "Mr. Scott?"

She sighed. "Bad bloody time, but I don't think he's going away."

Dawson made to get up, but she told him to stay put. She walked the short hallway, released the bolt, and opened the door. Anticipating a room-service waiter bearing a tray, she was momentarily puzzled by the funny-looking man holding a wilting bouquet of flowers.

Which he immediately threw to the floor, leaving only a pistol in his hand. He jammed it against her ribs as he pushed her backward into the room.

She turned and cried out to Dawson. He bounded off the bed, but drew up short when Carl caught her around the throat from behind and placed the barrel of the handgun against her temple.

"Well, how about this? A little reunion with my beach friends."

Dawson's hands balled into fists at his sides. Enunciating each word, he said, "Let her go."

"Now, why would I do that?"

"Because if you hurt her, I'll kill you."

"You've got it wrong. I'm killing you." He swung the pistol away from her and aimed it at Dawson.

Chapter 28

"I'm about done for the day. Before I sign you over to the evening shift, is there anything I can get you?"

The nurse was one of Headly's favorites. Even so, he replied grumpily. "Cheeseburger and fries."

"Don't ask for what I can't deliver. You're still on a restricted diet."

"He knows," Eva said from the chair where she was thumbing through a magazine. "He's just being ornery."

The nurse wrapped the blood pressure cuff around his biceps. "How about some skim milk?"

"How about a stiff bourbon?"

She swatted his arm. "BP's lowered. That's good." As she noted it on the chart, she asked Eva if she was staying overnight again. "That foldout can't be comfortable."

"It's not bad. The patient, however, is a pain in the butt."

"Stop talking about me like I'm not here."

The nurse chuckled. "I know what a grouch he can be, so I think it's sweet of you to stay with him, Mrs. Headly. In fact, your ears should have been burning earlier today."

"Oh? Why's that?"

"I was bragging on you."

"To whom?"

"This little old man who was waiting on the elevator. He saw you in the hall talking to Mr. Scott and recognized him. I confess the conversation got gossipy. I told him how y'all had known Mr. Scott since birth, that he was your godson, but mostly I bragged on you for staying here in Mr. Headly's room, taking very few breaks. Like everyone else, he was impressed." She made one final adjustment to Headly's IV drip. "Changed your mind about the milk?"

"No, thanks."

"Well then, I'm out of here. Rest easy. See y'all tomorrow."

As the door closed behind her, Eva remarked, "Sweet girl."

"Hmm." Headly worked his head deeper into the pillow and closed his eyes. He was more tired than he let on. A physical therapist had been in earlier doling out wisecracks, bonhomie, and sheer torture. By the time the fifteen minutes was up, Headly's hands and arms were tingling. Which was a relief, but still.

As though reading his mind, Eva said, "You should be doing the exercises the therapist showed you."

"Give me ten minutes' rest."

"He said—"

"Ten minutes and I will."

"Gary."

"Eva. Just because you're the most popular girl on the third floor, don't think you can boss me."

"I do have my admirers, it seems."

"A little old man? Humph. You've already got one."

She sighed. "You're right. I guess I'm stuck with you. Besides, it sounded like he was as interested in Dawson as he was in me."

Headly was about to make a wisecrack about that when suddenly it felt as though an electrical charge had shot through him, jolting his brain and body out of lassitude. "Eva!"

She tossed her magazine aside, lunged from her chair, and was at his side in a blink. "What? Are you in pain?"

"Get her back."

"What?"

"The nurse, get her back in here!"

She didn't waste time on questions but dashed from the room and, within seconds, was propelling the startled young woman back through the door. Headly said, "What did he look like?"

She just gaped at him.

"The man. The little old man you were talking to about Eva and Dawson. He asked questions about them?"

She nodded, swallowed. "He recognized Mr. Scott."

"What did he look like? Describe him."

"He was a little old man," she said in a helpless tone. "A cancer patient."

To Eva, Headly said, "Get Knutz on the phone." Going back to the nurse, he asked her the man's approximate height and weight, age, what he'd been wearing. By the time Knutz answered, Headly had a description.

Eva held the phone to his ear as he rattled off information. "Carl's disguised himself as a cancer patient. Shaved head. No eyebrows. Baggy clothes and a blue baseball cap. He was in the hospital, on this floor, around ten thirty or eleven this morning. Check the security cameras."

Knutz began putting up a reasonable argument, but Headly cut him off. "Goddammit, of course it could've been a little old man with cancer," he shouted. "But this is like something Carl Wingert would do, and I fucking know it was him. It *feels* like him. Yeah, yeah, I'll hold."

He secured the phone between his ear and shoulder and said to Eva, "Call Dawson. You have his new number?" She fished her phone from her handbag and called the number Dawson himself had programmed into her speed dial. Headly added, "Tell him to take this as a serious threat. Not to be macho and blow it off."

The nurse was crying and wringing her hands. "If I did something wrong, I'm sorry. We were just talking."

"Don't be sorry," Headly said. She was about to lose it, and he knew that if he applied the pressure he wanted to, she would probably collapse and he'd get nothing more from her. Gentling his tone, he said, "Did you get his name?"

She shook her head.

"Did he tell you where he lived?"

"No."

"Where he was going?"

"He... he was taking flowers to a sick friend and had gotten off on the wrong floor."

Like hell a sick friend, Headly thought. He'd been reconnoitering the hospital. "You're doing great, sweetheart. Now, start at the beginning and tell me exactly what you said, what he said, as best as you can remember."

She recounted the conversation in stops and starts but without folding completely. "He... I don't know how to describe it."

Headly pounced on her hesitancy. "Describe what? He what?"

"He perked up some when I told him that Dawson Scott was your godson. You know? Like a light came on."

Headly shot a glance toward Eva, who was holding out her phone, looking as gut sick and every bit as fearful as Headly felt. "Straight to voice mail."

"What a disappointment." As Dawson spoke, he was looking into Amelia's face, wanting it to be the last thing he saw before he died, not Carl Wingert's gloating sneer.

But Carl didn't pull the trigger. Dawson's remark had piqued his curiosity just as he'd hoped it would. "Disappointment?"

Dawson shifted his gaze to the criminal. "I'm not sure you're worth writing about, after all."

"That's why you went to the cabin? Hoping to get an interview with me?"

Dawson could tell the idea appealed to him. "With the famed Carl Wingert. I had to settle for an interview with Jeremy instead. Now I'm thinking maybe he was the better subject."

"Awww. You're hurting my feelings."

"You're just not that glamorous anymore, Carl. Killing me, killing Amelia. That's your grand finale? Hate to tell you, but that's a lame ending to your illustrious outlaw career."

Without his white hair and bushy eyebrows to give him a benign mien, Carl's smile was one of unmitigated evil. "Who says killing you will be my finale?"

"You think you'll be able to shoot both of us, then waltz out of here?"

"Yep. The same way I waltzed in, while her guards were chatting up the girls working the desk. Nobody pays attention to an ailing senior citizen."

"Clever disguise."

"Don't I know it."

"But hardly razzle-dazzle."

"I have other plans that don't include you."

"Hunter and Grant?" Speaking for the first time, Amelia asked tearfully, "Will you take them?"

"Hell, no. What would I want with a pair of kids?"

"But…but I thought that's what all this was about. You and Jeremy staged his death so you could get the boys and no one would ever dream that their father had taken them."

"That was Jeremy's goal, not mine."

"He'd have to love his grandsons to want them, Amelia," Dawson said. "And he doesn't love anybody."

"I've got nothing against the boys." He nudged Amelia. "Nothing personally against you, either."

Dawson jumped on that. "Because her marriage to Jeremy,

his faked PTSD, their divorce, were essential to the setup, right?" *Keep him talking. Keep him distracted. Stoke his ego. Pray for a miracle.*

"Right. You, Amelia dear, were instrumental at several stages. But I no longer need you. Thanks to Jeremy's deathbed confession, that white-trash cretin has been exonerated."

Dawson said, "If all had gone well, if the cop hadn't shot Jeremy and Willard had gone to death row, you and Jeremy would have been free to wreak havoc. Was that the plan, Carl?"

"Point's moot."

"Yes, but just so I'm clear, how was it going to work exactly? Your eyesight is dicey, your hips are shot. My guess is that you would have stayed in the background and thought up ways to rob, destroy, and kill while Jeremy actually did all the work and took the risks. Am I warm?"

"What risks? It was perfect," he boasted. "No one would have suspected a dead man of, say, blowing up a bus full of troops."

"Hmm." Dawson nodded his understanding of the concept. "But things got royally fouled up when Jeremy got antsy, overanxious, killed Stef, and left a fingerprint. That was a major uh-oh. Suddenly Jeremy Wesson isn't dead anymore."

Carl said nothing to that, but Dawson could tell he'd struck a nerve. Carl's trigger finger was twitching.

Talk fast. "Jeremy didn't have your smarts, Carl. He tried to be as ruthless as you, too, but in the end he developed a conscience. He died talking about his children. Lamenting the way he'd treated Amelia. With his last breath, he was crying over his mother." Dawson watched Carl's eyes. They remained implacable, the reptilian lids unblinking. "You killed her, didn't you?"

"Too bad you didn't write mysteries. You seem to have a flair for them."

"How did she die, Carl?"

He replied querulously. "Pneumonia. If I was guessing. She had a cough that wouldn't go away. Got worse. She was hacking up disgusting stuff. Complained of her chest hurting."

"You wouldn't let her get medical treatment."

"She always had weak lungs. She'd recovered before."

"But not this time. So you killed her."

"I didn't raise a hand to her. The disease killed her."

"But you left her there, didn't you? Left her in that cabin to die alone."

"I had to go get supplies. I didn't know she was going to be dead when I got back."

"Sure you did, you gutless son of a bitch. Abandonment is your specialty. When the going gets tough, you run."

He'd struck another nerve. Carl's expression turned even harder, colder. And something else: defensive.

"I never left anybody who could have made it."

"Jeremy could have. Flora could have."

"You through?"

"One more question. Why us?"

"What?"

"Why kill us? Why aren't you out blowing up a bus full of troops? My guess is that you've run out of steam. Without Jeremy, you've got no muscle. You're all talk."

"Is that your guess?" His malicious grin made Dawson's blood run cold. "Well, you're wrong. This is perfect. See? I kill you, I crush Headly."

Dawson's heart constricted. He thought, *We're dead*, but he brazened it out. "Gary Headly? The FBI agent that Jeremy shot?"

Carl snickered at Dawson's feigned indifference. "I thought about taking out that pretty wife of his, but that's so predictable. Headly would expect that, which is why she's guarded." Again that chilling grin. "This is much better. His *godson*. I kill you, he'll never get over it."

"You're right, if you kill me, Headly will grieve his heart out. But he'll also have the last laugh on you."

"Just for shits and giggles, what makes you think so?"

"Headly knows you inside and out, Carl."

"I doubt it."

"Close enough. He's made studying you his life's work. But to nail your character he actually needed only one day. The day before Thanksgiving 1976."

Carl glared at him.

"Yeah, I thought that would ring a bell. Headly's been on to you since Golden Branch. On that day, you revealed the caliber of man you are, and Headly's opinion of you hasn't wavered."

"Like I care about his, or anyone's, opinion of me."

"How many bullets did that man take for you while you were running for your damn life?"

"He was going to die anyway."

"We'll never know."

"*He* knew. He had a hole in his head, for chrissake. He volunteered to hold them off."

"While you ran. How hard did Flora have to beg for you not to leave her and Jeremy behind?"

"I didn't leave them though, did I?"

"But you wanted to."

"She could barely walk. Blood all over the damn place. I had to bind her up in a sheet, and even then she left a trail."

Like a potent narcotic, a slow rage was seeping through Dawson. He embraced it. He wanted it to saturate every cell. "During the standoff, and while you were escaping through the woods, how did you keep Jeremy from crying?"

"Doped him. Only way to shut him up."

"You doped your son. How old was he?"

"Eleven months."

Amelia started with surprise. Her lips parted in a silent exclamation.

Dawson registered her stunned reaction, but his gaze never flickered off Carl. "The newborn never made a sound."

Carl snorted with contempt. "So they found it?"

"Headly did."

"Figures."

"When did Flora go into labor?"

"Around midnight. She was still at it when the cops showed up. It was a nasty business. Thought I was never going to get the thing out of her."

"But you finally did."

"Had to cram a towel in her mouth to keep her from screaming."

"As soon as the baby was born, you stuffed it down through a hole in the floor."

"First time I've thought about it since."

His blasé dismissal of what he'd done was as shocking as the barbarous act itself.

Dawson swallowed bile and had to force himself to continue. "As they were searching the house—"

"They didn't find me," he said in singsong.

"But Headly found the baby in the crawl space."

"What a frigging Boy Scout."

"Barely alive. Still attached to the placenta."

"You're breaking my heart."

"That's when he knew you are an irredeemable sack of shit."

"Who's gonna kill you now."

Carl pulled the trigger, but Dawson had anticipated it and dropped. The bullet missed him. Carl roared in outrage and flung Amelia out of his way as though she were a rag doll.

That was his undoing. She was the only reason the SWAT-team snipers on the neighboring roof hadn't fired before then. Now they had a clear target. As the gunfire erupted, shattering window glass, Dawson lunged forward to cover her and keep her down. SWAT officers barged through the door.

It happened within seconds.

"Are you hit?" Dawson asked Amelia.

Dumbly she shook her head.

As the room filled with SWAT officers, he crab-walked over to Carl, who lay on his back staring at the ceiling, his eyes open, his slack features forming an incredulous expression. Dawson grabbed the front of his bloody shirt and yanked him into a sitting position. The man's bald head wobbled on his neck.

Dawson shook him until his unfocused eyes found him. Teeth clenched, he said, "Look at me, old man. While you're burning in hell, remember my face. I'm the other son you left to die."

Diary of Flora Stimel—November 27, 1977

He would be a year old today. I woke up remembering what the date was, and it's kept me sobbing all day.

Carl asked me what the hell was the matter, and when I reminded him that this was the anniversary of Golden Branch, I thought he was going take my head off. He got so mad, he stormed out of the room. (We're in some crappy motel in Colorado that has a dusty cow head on the wall.)

It's okay with me that Carl left. Jeremy's been acting up. I guess what they say about the twos is right. They can be terrible. Jeremy was being noisy and restless, jumping on the bed, and getting on Carl's nerves. My crying was aggravating him. So it's just as well that he went somewhere to cool off. While he's gone, I have a chance to write in this diary. I'm way behind.

This seems like a good day to pour my heart out. My heart that's broken. Broken hearts truly do hurt. I didn't know that for a fact until I had to leave my baby in that awful old house up in Oregon. Carl told me he was born dead. I'm not sure I believe him, but I never heard the baby cry, and I sorta hope it's true, because then I don't have to feel so guilty for running off and leaving him. I'd burn in hell for sure if I'd left him there still alive. I think about that all the time. I guess you could say it haunts me.

And I wonder sometimes, what if Carl was wrong (or lied), and the baby *was* alive when we escaped, and some cop found him? Where is he now? Would he be in an orphanage or something? Or was he given away to a good family?

What if we crossed paths someday and didn't even know each other? Maybe I would recognize him if he looked anything like Jeremy. Or he could have blond hair like mine. What color would his eyes be?

Why do I do this to myself? It's torture to think about what he would look like and what he'd grow up to be.

Of course I look at Jeremy and wonder that, too. What kind of life is this for a child? I chose Carl. I chose this life. Poor little Jeremy has no choice except to go along. I guess if that other baby boy had lived, he would have gone along with our way of life, too. That's a sad thought. Almost as sad as knowing that he died before taking his first breath.

And I'm sure that's what happened. Carl wouldn't be so mean as to tell me that the baby was dead if he wasn't.

Wherever my other little boy is, I hope his soul is at peace.

Mine isn't. It never will be. Not over this.

Chapter 29

I'm going to have a drink. Want one?"

"Please."

"Anything you want, it's on the house." Dawson poured two minibar bottles of bourbon into glasses. "Somebody gets shot in your room, hotel management goes all out to make up for it. To say nothing of how bad they felt about my overlooked room-service order."

After Carl was taken away, they had been questioned extensively by Knutz. Acting on Headly's telephone call from his hospital bed, the FBI agent had assigned men the job of checking hospital security cameras. Others were sent to warn Dawson. He didn't answer his cell phone or his room phone, but sheriff's deputies, waiting in the lobby for their charge, verified that he was in his room and that Amelia Nolan was with him.

Knutz had been hesitant to bust in on a romantic rendezvous, but when a desk clerk remarked on an elderly man with a bouquet of flowers entering the hotel and going up in the elevator, Knutz mobilized a SWAT team from Savannah Metro.

Meanwhile, a silent evacuation of that floor of the hotel was conducted while agents in the room next door to Dawson's, using listening devices, confirmed a hostage situation. Snipers took up positions on the roof of a neighboring building that afforded them a view into the room through a window. When Carl pushed Amelia aside, they were ready.

After all the officials finally had cleared out, Dawson was informed by a nervous manager that he was being moved to the hotel's best suite. It didn't rate five stars, but it had a living area separated from the bedroom by a pair of French doors and was better appointed than his previous room.

Now he passed Amelia her drink. She was curled into the corner of the sofa. He took one of the easy chairs and raised his glass in a mock toast. "Cheers." He shot his drink and set the empty glass on the coffee table. He looked across at her, knowing the time had come for the inevitable denouement. "Well, now you know the *reason*."

She nodded.

"Can't say you weren't forewarned to keep your distance."

He got up and walked over to the windows. From this perspective on the top floor, he could see that there were still a few patrol cars parked in front of the hotel. The media vans had come and gone, following Carl to the hospital's trauma center. His condition was reported as "serious."

The man wanted for decades by the FBI had been nabbed. He was the story now. No doubt national news crews were keeping the airlines into Savannah oversold. Dawson Scott, magazine journalist, would be a footnote in the news coverage, and he hoped he remained so. None of the SWAT officers swarming the hotel room had overheard his declaration. He hadn't told Knutz about his relationship to Carl. Outside the Headlys and Amelia, no one knew. Well, except for Carl himself.

"They'll be pulling off the guards on Saint Nelda's if they haven't already," he said. "You and the boys will be safe."

"Tucker is going to leave several deputies out there to discourage the media. Just until the hubbub dies down. A few days."

"That's good. Kids all right?"

"I talked to both of them on the phone. They're as happy as little clams. The deputy is spoiling them. She told me there was no need to come back tonight, since it would be such a short turnaround."

Knutz had asked that they meet with him at nine o'clock the following morning to "wrap up."

Dawson turned back into the room. He looked at her for a moment, then spread his arms out to his sides. "The secret's out. Any questions?"

She took a deep breath and exhaled slowly. "How old were you when you found out?"

"Thirty-seven."

She looked at him with stupefaction. "You haven't known until now?"

He returned to the chair and sat down. "To be precise, it was eight, no, nine days ago, that I learned the fate of my brother. I knew all about the standoff in Golden Branch and how I came to be. Carl, Flora, all that.

"My parents—adoptive parents—never hid my origins from me. I grew up knowing how Headly had found me, nearly dead but miraculously still breathing. I spent a couple months in a neonatal ICU, then was released with a clean bill of health.

"The authorities kept my existence a secret from the press, one of those things they hold in abeyance for crime-solving purposes. Headly and the agent in charge that day also kept a lid on it to protect me, my identity.

"I, Flora's newborn, was the only baby found inside the house. But it wasn't my DNA on the baby blanket. For thirty-seven years, that remained a mystery. The DNA had been tested, and it was confirmed that Flora was the mother of whoever it belonged to, but where was the child? Who was the child? What had happened to it? Carl and Flora had never been spotted with a child, not even while under surveillance in Golden Branch. He remained the mystery baby.

"Then," he said after pausing for breath, "nine days ago, Headly sent me a text, told me to get over to his house ASAP. I went. He told me about a murder trial in Savannah. The shocker—the presumed victim's DNA matched that anonymous sample. My brother, who, according to Carl, was eleven months older, had been found. Apparently when Carl and Flora ran for their lives, they took him. Left me."

He picked up his empty glass and swirled it, wishing for a drop in the bottom of it. When one didn't appear, he replaced the glass on the coffee table and looked across at Amelia.

"When you were growing up, did it bother you, knowing that you had been abandoned?"

"There was no reason to be bothered by it. After all, my birth parents were despicable characters. I had got the best deal. Headly knew how badly his childless friends wanted a baby. He engineered the adoption as soon as I was released from the hospital. My parents loved me. I loved them. I couldn't have asked for a more loving, stable home and family life."

"However?"

"However," he said slowly, "as I got older and realized the importance of bloodlines, I determined not to subject anyone else to mine. Especially not a woman who had the misfortune of falling in love with me."

"You made certain that didn't happen. No long-term relationships that could lead to marriage. No children."

He left that alone. He didn't tell her about the vials of semen the doctor had insisted on retrieving and freezing before he would perform the sterilization procedure on a patient so young. At this juncture, it was pointless for her to know they remained in a sperm bank... in case he ever changed his mind.

She said, "This explains everything."

"Right. Which is why we don't need to talk about it anymore. The situation won't improve with discussion. There's nothing to be worked out. It just *is*, and it won't ever change. I was sired by Carl Wingert, criminal of renown. Jeremy, my brother, was your husband."

"Hunter and Grant are your nephews."

"Yeah." Mention of them caused him to smile spontaneously, in spite of himself. "And they're great. God, there were times when—" Realizing what he was about to say, he broke off.

She tilted her head inquisitively. "When what?"

"Nothing."

"When what?"

He chewed his bottom lip, but then decided, *The hell with it.* "When I wanted to hug them and hold on. They were the first blood relatives I'd ever met."

Her chest rose with a sudden swell of emotion. "You can hug them any time you want."

"Not gonna happen."

"Why?"

"Those boys are going to have enough to deal with just living down their heritage. Having me in their lives would only make the issue muddier."

Besides, he added to himself, he couldn't be around them without being around Amelia, and he couldn't be around her without wanting her, and wanting her without having her was already killing him.

"I'm your sister-in-law."

"I'm fully aware of that," he said tightly. "I was aware of it when you walked into the courtroom and things went haywire."

"What things?"

"Things. Everything. I was sitting there wishing for a drink, a pill, cursing Headly for sending me down here, telling myself that I didn't care about the fate of a brother I'd never known.

Wishing my ass was anywhere else except growing numb on that hard bench in the courtroom.

"Then the doors at the back of it were opened, you walked past me, and all of a sudden I'm being sucked in. By you. Jeremy. Lust. Despair."

"What do you feel toward him now?"

"Hell, I don't know. I hate him for what he became, what he did, but..." He turned his hands palms up and extended them toward her. "I was holding his head, looking into his eyes when he died, Amelia. My brother. First time I set eyes on him, and he *dies*." He gave a bitter laugh over the cruel irony of it.

"Did you tell him?"

He shook his head. "But there was a moment, no an *instant*, of recognition. Connection. Something. Or maybe I just imagined it because I wanted to see it. Doesn't matter now, though, does it?"

"Not to Jeremy. I think it matters greatly to you."

"I was right not to tell him. He was better off not knowing that the stranger moving in on his family was his brother."

"Dawson," she said softly, "when you and I met, I hadn't been Jeremy's wife for a long time. I'd believed him dead for more than a year. Does it bother you that much to know that he and I... That—"

"That he had you first? Yeah. It bothers me some. But not in the way you're thinking."

"What am I thinking?"

"That it's a sexual competition, that I'm afraid you're making comparisons. It's not that."

"Then what is it?"

"It's that I wanted you in the first place."

"When I should have been off-limits."

"Something like that."

"I think we can forgive ourselves for our mutual attraction."

"You can forgive yourself because you didn't know about the

relationship. I did." He'd said they weren't going to discuss this, but they were. He made an impatient gesture. "Jeremy was a minor obstacle compared with the other one."

"Your bloodline."

"Which is poison."

"Hmm." She pursed her lips thoughtfully. "I suppose I'll have to throw the boys back, too."

"What?"

"Well, they're your blood relatives, remember? Doesn't that make them just as toxic as you? If I reject you because of that taint, then it only follows—"

"Stop being ridiculous."

"You took the words right out of my mouth."

She stood up, rounded the coffee table, and came to kneel in front of his chair. He tried to stand up, but she angrily pushed him back into the seat. "I'm going to have my say. Then you can do what you want, but I'm not going to let you sail out of my life and forever regret that I didn't say this and wonder what would have happened if I had."

She placed her hands on his chest as though to impress upon him her earnestness. "For months during and after my marriage, I couldn't even fathom myself being in another relationship. Ever. I couldn't imagine a man's—any man's—touch being something I would invite. I couldn't see myself ever feeling anything like desire again.

"After some distance from it, when the wounds were no longer fresh and even my sons couldn't fill a particular loneliness, I began to realize how unrealistic it was to think that I'd live the rest of my life alone. I'm not programmed for a lifetime of abstinence. I'm not talking only about sex but about emotional intimacy. I began to want that again. Need it.

"Gradually, I accepted the probability that one day a man would enter my life and rekindle me, that he and I would share what I'd wanted with Jeremy but hadn't had. I anticipated his arrival, but was in no particular hurry. I wasn't going to seek him. I was content to wait and let him find me.

"I didn't know what he would do professionally, or what his interests would be, the nature of his personality. I didn't know what he would look like . . . until I saw you." She touched his lips, following their shape with the tip of her index finger. "I was afraid of you and absolutely furious at you, but all the while I was railing at you for spying on me, I was thinking, 'This is him. He's here. And he's way more than I dared hope for.'" She gave a self-conscious little shrug. "That's it. That's my say."

He took a strand of her hair between his fingers and rubbed it thoughtfully, for a moment too emotional to speak. Then he said, "No one's ever talked to me that candidly. About anything, but certainly nothing that personal. And I think you're incredible."

"It sounds like there's a *but*."

"No *but*. An *and*." He pulled her to her feet as he stood up. "You're incredible *and*, this time, all clothes come off."

In the bedroom, he flung back the bedcovering, then turned to her and quickly unbuttoned her blouse and pulled it off. He fumbled behind her back for her bra strap while she hastily undid his shirt buttons. Skin to skin they hugged. Just that. They held each other and savored the closeness, the various sensations, the arousing contrasts of their bodies.

Finally he murmured, "I hope you don't mind chest hair."

"Mind?" She rubbed her face in it.

He hadn't realized biceps could be an erogenous zone until she took a love bite out of his. Reaching behind her, he undid the fastening of her skirt. It dropped to the floor. She unbuttoned his jeans and slid them down along with his underwear past his hips, her hands firm against his ass.

He nudged her middle with his erection and smiled. "I know you're a lady, but feel free to notice."

She did considerably more than notice. He stopped her from

taking more than the head, but the attention she lavished on it was almost more than he could endure. After several minutes, swearing and praying at the same time, he brought her up to standing and plunged his tongue into her mouth that had treated him to such hot, wet bliss.

They got onto the bed. Lying face-to-face, he lowered his head to her breasts. "Remarkable."

"What?"

He used his tongue to illustrate their sensitivity. "That first day on the beach—"

She groaned. "I knew you noticed."

"I knew you knew I'd noticed, but I couldn't help myself. Each time the breeze kicked up, I went a little crazy with wanting to see them like this." His lips tugged on her nipple.

"I was trying to be modest."

"I was praying for a gale wind and fantasizing this." He continued the love play until it was unclear whether he was doing it to tantalize her or himself. It was working on both. Easing her onto her back, he kissed his way down her center, then angled himself away in order to take a look. "Beautiful terrain." His hand skimmed past her navel.

"Thank you."

Finding a faint white stretch mark on the outside of her hip, he followed it with his fingertip. "Which one gave you this?"

"Grant."

"And this one?" he asked, finding another in the hollow where belly met thigh.

"Grant."

He grinned. "Why am I not surprised?" Next he traced the slender white scar that was barely discernible under the soft hair. "Which one?"

"Both. Hunter had to be Cesarean, and after one…"

Her words dwindled to a soft moan when he dipped his head to nuzzle lower and his tongue began gently exploring the furrow. She responded exactly as he'd hoped. Parting her thighs, she clutched his hair, arched up against his mouth, responded to the guidance of his hands as they repositioned her, and gasped his name as the spot, the tempo of his stroking tongue, and the pressure he applied coalesced into a melting orgasm.

He levered himself above her and watched her face as she slowly came down from it. She opened her eyes and gave him a drowsy smile, which he covered with a soft kiss. "Can I make a confession?"

She nodded.

"I've fantasized doing that to you."

"I can't be less than honest." Lifting her head, she whispered directly into his ear, "I fantasized you doing it, too."

They smiled at each other as he settled between her thighs, pushing into her only a little, but enough to cause him to groan softly. "God that feels good."

"What else have you fantasized?" she asked.

"Hard and fast against a wall. No, wait. We did that for real. It just seemed like a fantasy." He felt her soft laugh all the way to the base of his cock, and it caused him to grimace with the effort of withholding himself from sinking into her completely.

She trailed her fingers down his spine to the cleft of his butt. His breath caught. "Anything else?" Her voice was as sexy as the feathering motions of her fingertips.

"You taking me in your beautiful mouth. Oh, you did that, too. Or was I hallucinating?"

"If you were, so was I."

"That's a fantasy that bears acting out again, don't you think?"

"Oh, absolutely. Often."

He gave her a wicked smile, which she matched.

"So, is that it?" she purred. "Have we run out of fantasies?"

"Hell, we're just getting started." Sliding his hand beneath her bottom, he tilted her up. "Going real slow, like now." He kissed her, his tongue sliding into her mouth with the controlled intensity with which he was pushing into her. He pulled out, almost entirely, before sinking into her a little deeper than before. And again.

She made a small, wanting sound and breathed his name. "What exactly do you call this particular fantasy?"

He buried himself inside her fully and, just as he kissed her again, whispered, "Making love."

She lay on her side, facing away from him. Replete. Happier than she remembered feeling in . . . Possibly ever. She slid her foot up the length of his shin.

"Know what first attracted me?"

He pushed his penis against her bottom. "It is impressive. Sometimes embarrassingly so."

She laughed. "That wasn't it."

"Oh."

She laughed again over how crestfallen he sounded. "It was your crooked tooth."

"The one that defied orthodontia?"

"It's very sexy."

"Glad you think so."

"And your hands."

"They're sexy?"

"They're large and masculine and capable. And sexy." She sighed as one closed around her breast possessively. "Will you be able to sleep tonight?"

"Well, if my recent exertion didn't wear me out enough to sleep, I can't imagine what would." He bit her lightly on the shoulder. "Who knew you'd be so insatiable."

She bumped his ribs with her elbow, but, unwilling to leave the subject of his nightmare, repeated her question.

"Sleep? Maybe," he said.

"Surely talking about it lanced the wound."

"We'll see." His arm tightened around her. "Lying with you is bound to help."

Contentedly, sleepily, she mumbled, "Notch up another fantasy fulfilled. I've been longing to sleep with you."

"You will."

"Will?"

"Just not quite yet."

His hands, with their tender touch but masterful guidance, drew her back and up and open for him. He secured himself inside her with his hand on her front, planted firmly between her thighs.

With very little movement, he pumped into her rhythmically while in shockingly coarse terms he described how it felt to be enveloped by her and the pleasure his fingers and mouth derived from pleasuring her. Soon his lyrics changed to those of poets, but the subtext was as erotically charged.

When both were on the brink of implosion, his voice became rough with emotion. His breaths became bursts of air against the back of her neck. In the language of raw need, he gasped, "Squeeze me. Tighter." His body strained, and each shudder was marked with the harsh, choppy cry of a man in the throes of release that went beyond the physical. Finally, as his body relaxed and enfolded hers, he sighed her name like a benediction.

She fell asleep with all those wonderful words echoing in her heart.

Hours later when she woke, she instantly missed his warmth, his scent and breath, the weight of his arm across her waist. Alarmed, she sat up. "Dawson?"

He was gone.

Chapter 30

Headly had persuaded Eva to go to the hotel. His condition continued to improve. Carl Wingert was no longer a threat. It was unnecessary for her to spend another uncomfortable night on the foldout chair in his hospital room.

"But you know the real reason I didn't want her here," he said to Dawson after explaining Eva's absence.

"Same reason I came now, in the wee hours, when few people are around."

Standing behind the chair in Headly's room, he braced his hands on the back of it and looked meaningfully at his godfather. "I assume you gave them orders not to kill him."

"If it could be avoided."

"He was bleeding pretty bad."

"One bullet went through his right shoulder, grazed a lung, causing partial but significant collapse. They put in a chest tube. He caught another bullet in the back of his knee. His age is a factor, of course, but I'm told he came through the surgery fine. When he's well enough, he'll be turned over to the judicial system."

Seconds ticked by as they held each other's stare.

Finally Dawson said, "We can't leave it at that."

"You can. I can't."

"I can't either."

"Dawson—"

"Let me rephrase. I *won't*."

He must have sensed Dawson's resolve, because he said, "I've been trying to figure out how we can do it. He's got marshals guarding him. They're not going to let us in there with a weapon. But I have an idea."

Dawson listened while Headly laid it out. He nodded somberly. "I can do that."

"We won't get away with it, you know."

"Probably not."

Headly studied him for several long moments, then, mind made up, looked down at the IV taped to the back of his hand. "First thing you gotta do is pull this friggin' thing out."

Five minutes later, Dawson pushed the wheelchair into the elevator. He had successfully gotten Headly disconnected from the IV, out of the bed, and into the wheelchair, but it hadn't been easy. Headly was rapidly regaining sensation and some muscle control in his arms, shoulders, and hands, but for all practical purposes, they were useless.

In the confines of the elevator his breathing sounded labored and uneven. He looked pale beneath the fluorescent glare, and his face was moist with sweat. Dawson asked if he was in pain.

"I'm fine."

"We could wait."

"I don't know when they'll move him. We may not have another chance."

The elevator doors opened onto a dimly lighted hallway. "Leave the marshals to me."

The two, seated outside Carl's room, looked at them curiously as they approached. "Evening, gentlemen," Headly said in his most authoritative tone. "I'm Special Agent Gary Headly, here to question the prisoner."

The two marshals looked at each other, then at Dawson, finally back to Headly. One said, "He's still in serious condition."

"Right. He could die. Which is precisely why I need to question him now."

"Where's Agent Knutz?"

"Probably up to his earlobes in paperwork, which is why I'm handling this interrogation."

"With all due respect, sir, you don't look all that well. Are you up to it?"

Headly glowered.

The marshal, discomfited, cleared his throat and gave a nod toward Dawson. "What about him?"

"This is Dawson Scott. He's the one Wingert held at gunpoint yesterday afternoon."

"I know who he is. Why's he here?"

"To dispel any of Wingert's bullshit."

The two marshals exchanged another uneasy glance, then one worked up enough courage to challenge him. "Sorry, sir. I can't let you go in without—"

"Authorization?"

"Yes, sir."

"Fine." His cell phone was lying in his lap. He nodded down to it. "The AG's number is programmed under the numeral eight. Wake up our boss and tell him that you're denying me access to a fugitive that I and the entire Department of Justice have been chasing down for nearly forty years." Smiling benignly, he added, "He'll probably be tickled to hear from you."

It took the marshal about three seconds to decide. He left the phone where it was. "Are you armed, sir?"

"Yes. With a catheter up my dick and the bag into which my bladder is draining. You're welcome to check." Again he nodded down at his lap, covered only by the flimsy hospital gown.

The marshal said, "I don't think that will be necessary."

"Son, even if I had a weapon, I can't move my hands."

Meanwhile the other marshal had been patting down Dawson. "He's good."

One of them held open the door as Dawson wheeled Headly into the room where Carl Wingert was strapped to the bed not only by restraints but also by a network of medical paraphernalia.

Dawson pushed the wheelchair to the bedside. Carl's eyes were closed. Headly said his name, and when he failed to respond, he told Dawson to poke him. None too gently, Dawson prodded Carl's elevated bandaged leg. Groaning, he opened his eyes to slits. They flared wide when he saw the two of them.

Being this close to him again, Dawson suddenly felt claustrophobic. The sound of a thousand bees buzzed inside his head, their racket underscoring the blips and beeps of the various machines and IV drips that Carl was hooked up to. Their tubing created the same tangle at the side of the bed that Dawson had remarked on in Headly's room.

Carl was the first to speak. "Well, well," he said to Headly. "At last we meet." He took note of the wheelchair. "In the flesh, you don't look so tough."

"You don't either."

"I've had better days."

Headly shot him a grin. "I haven't."

"Chalk one up for you. You figured me out today."

"You're getting old, Carl. No longer as smart as you think."

"Oh, I don't know about that." He spoke in a musical, disarming tone reminiscent of Bernie.

"Do you hurt?"

"All over."

"Good."

"Why didn't they kill me?"

"Because I ordered them not to."

"I wonder why?" Again, another sly smile, then he focused on Dawson. "Tell me, boy, how does it feel?"

Dawson had been following their exchange, but also studying the nest of plastic tubing at Carl's bedside. Now he looked at the man. "How does what feel?"

"Fucking your dead brother's wife."

It took incredible control for him not to lunge at the man and wrap his fingers around his throat. Instead, he leaned down until his face was within inches of Carl's. "You left me to die."

"Well, I sure as hell didn't want you. You were an ugly little monkey, and I'd been up all night trying to squeeze you out of her. I hated you before I ever laid eyes on you. Flora was carrying on like a madwoman."

"You took her newborn from her."

"Wrong. I told her you were born dead, told her it would be better if she never even saw you. I just scooped you up like so much fish guts and dumped you down that hole in the floor, hoping to hell you wouldn't take a breath and start crying."

Even now, knowing everything he did about this man, it was inconceivable to Dawson how any human being could be that cold and heartless. "How could you do that?"

"How could I?" His low chuckle was rife with menace. "You said today that Headly would get the last laugh on me, but you're wrong. The last laugh is on *you*." He looked Dawson up and down with scorn. "You're no kid of mine."

Dawson stopped breathing for several seconds, then he wheezed, "What?"

"You heard me. You came from someone else's slime. Don't know whose. Could've been any number of men."

"You're lying," Headly said. "I studied Flora as thoroughly as I studied you. For whatever warped reason, she loved you and would have followed you into hell. She would never have slept with another man."

"Not unless I told her to."

The two of them stared at him, stunned by the flippant statement and its significance. "Jesus," Headly hissed.

Dawson had no words. Reeling from the shock, he wasn't sure if he should feel elation or revulsion, if he should shout with joy or weep over the misery and humiliation that the woman who'd borne him had been forced to endure.

"Sometimes I let guys use her to blow off steam. Or as a reward. She got pregnant with you on just such an occasion when three or four of them—"

"Shut up."

Dawson's wrath seemed only to amuse him. "Maybe Flora knew which one *took*, but I doubt it. If she did, maybe she wrote his name down in that diary of hers."

Dawson flinched. "Diary?"

"The sneaky bitch," he snarled. "I guess she'd been writing in it for years. She died with it clutched to her bosom. You're digging her up, right?" he asked of Headly. "I tossed the book in with her. Should be a real entertaining read. Or maybe not. She was so damned ignorant."

It was obvious that Carl was enjoying himself. He was deliberately goading them, watching closely and hoping for a volatile reaction. Dawson refused to gratify him.

Instead, he looked down at Headly. "I've heard all I can stomach. You?"

"He was too much for me to stomach at Golden Branch."

Dawson had been fiddling with the network of tubes and had isolated one from the rest. "You have enough control to do it?"

"Left hand. Thumb and index finger."

Dawson carefully looped a section of the tube around those fingers twice, so that Headly could get a good grip.

Rather than being alarmed, Carl cackled. "Headly, you always did play right into my plan."

"How's that, Carl?"

"I knew you wouldn't rest until you saw me dead. I knew

you'd come to finish me off yourself. And here you are." Carl raised his head as far as his bandaged shoulder would allow and blew Headly a kiss. "Thank you."

"My pleasure."

Just as Headly gave the tube a yank that snapped it free of a machine, the door burst open. The marshals were the first into the room. One shouted Headly's name. Amelia rushed in behind them, her gaze wild and fearful. "Dawson, don't!"

The three drew up short and took in the scene.

Carl was gaping at the end of the tube dangling from Headly's hand, his lips working wordlessly. Finally he said stupidly, "Nothing happened."

"Of course not." Dawson took the tube from Headly's left hand and, slowly winding it around his fist, pulled the other end free from the tangle of tubes on the floor. "It's not attached to anything. See?" He dangled the two loose ends inches away from Carl's face. "They really should remove these once they're no longer in use. What if somebody pulled out your chest tube by mistake?"

Carl looked in stunned horror at Headly, who smiled. "Carl, Carl, did you actually think I came in here to kill you? And by doing so deny myself the pleasure of watching you rot in chains for the rest of your goddamned life?" Headly shook his head. "No way in hell, Carl. No way in hell."

Epilogue

He drove with the car windows down. The salt air was soft, the surf calm as it sometimes was just after daybreak. As he neared Amelia's beach house, his eyes were inexorably drawn to the one where Carl Wingert had spent summers as Bernie.

That was the only thought Dawson gave the man, and it was more consideration than the reprobate deserved.

He didn't expect Amelia or the boys to be up yet, but as he alighted, he spotted her on the beach. She was walking near the waterline, a pair of flip-flops dangling from her fingers. She was dressed in roomy, thin cotton pants and a tank top, which she'd probably slept in. Her hair was in a messy topknot. She'd never looked so good to him.

He had covered over half the distance between them before she saw him. She dropped her sandals and met him at a full run. He caught her against him and they kissed hungrily. They didn't come up for air for several minutes, and when they did, they continued to hold each other as though to assure themselves that they were together again after a ten-day separation.

She leaned back into the firm circle of his arms so she could look up into his face. "How was it?"

"North Dakota can be cold even in September. Around freezing one morning I was there."

She brushed a windblown strand of hair off his scruffy cheek, then laid both palms on his chest. In a softer voice, she asked, "How was it?"

"It was good," he replied, matching her serious tone. "They're wonderful people. Salt of the earth. American flag flying proudly from the eaves of the house. Pot roast for dinner. There were pictures of Hawkins all over the house. They wanted to hear everything."

Shortly after Dawson's return from Afghanistan, he'd received a letter from Corporal Hawkins's parents, asking him to please call them. They expressed an earnest wish to talk to him about their son and his last few days. They repeated the request in voice mails, e-mails, and additional letters. "He thought so highly of you, Mr. Scott. Please call us."

He hadn't been able to bring himself to make that call.

But talking through the incident with Amelia had been the catharsis he'd needed. Once the ban on the topic of Hawkins had been lifted, he could think about him without cringing inside. As soon as he had accompanied Headly home to DC, he booked a flight to North Dakota.

"They told me everything about him. I met his brother, two sisters, six nieces and nephews. I was shown his baseball trophies and high school prom pictures. Our talks were heartrending, but healing for them as well as for me."

"I want to hear all about it whenever you're ready to tell me." She stood on tiptoe and kissed him. "Sleeping better?"

"Two nights in a row without the nightmare."

"Definite progress."

"Thanks to you."

Several sessions with a therapist in DC had helped enormously, too, although he still gave more credit to Amelia than to the man with all the framed degrees on his office wall.

"How are Headly and Eva?" she asked.

"He gets better every day. The Bureau urged him to reactivate until Carl's case is closed. But that'll take a while, so he declined."

"I'm surprised by that."

"I was, too. But he explained that nothing could top that dramatic ending in the hospital, with Carl screaming invectives and begging for somebody to kill him."

She dropped her forehead against his chest. "When I woke up, and you weren't there, I thought—"

"Carl thought so, too. That was the point. But no such luck for him. Headly wanted a face-off. I helped because I knew how important it was for him to confront his enemy. He would never have been satisfied with less."

"Nor would you."

"You know me well."

She pressed a kiss to his throat, and when she pulled away, she said, "So, it was easy for Headly to turn down the Bureau's request that he stay on?"

"Made much easier by Eva. She told him if he returned to work, she was going to grind up Viagra in his food and then withhold sexual favors."

"She'd do it, too."

"You bet your life. By the way, she invited us up for Thanksgiving." He stroked her hair. "How was your trip to Kansas?"

"Quick, but I didn't want to leave the boys with the Metcalfs for more than one night. The memorial service was terribly sad."

"I'm sure Stef's parents were touched that you went."

"They said as much. At least they were relieved of having to go through a trial. Jeremy's dying spared them that." She hesitated for a moment, then added, "I saw to his cremation."

He held her face between his hands and searched her eyes. "We've got a lot of forgetting to do, Amelia."

"I know."

"I can't wait to get started."

"Me, either." And for a long moment they just looked at each other with full understanding.

After a time, she nodded toward the house that Bernie had occupied. "I'm happy to report that it's been sold. The realtor who brokered the deal was out here yesterday with a contractor. The new owner is having it torn down and plans to replace it with a larger, more contemporary house that he'll rent long-term.

"It can't be razed fast enough, as far as I'm concerned," she continued. "Every time I glance in that direction…" She trailed off and tilted her head in puzzlement. "You don't seem at all surprised by this news." She stared at him for seconds more, then realization dawned in her eyes. "You bought it."

"You could never sell this house. It means too much to you. The only solution was to get rid of that one."

"I can't let you do that," she exclaimed.

"I have a trust from my folks that I've never touched. It seemed fitting to do this with some of the money. Carl didn't sire me, but he tortured my mother and left me to die. I don't want any reminders of him around when we're here." She was about to protest further, but he stopped her. "It's done."

She relented, asking quietly, "Did they find Flora's diary?"

"Yes. Mostly intact. Headly's read some of it. He's having the contents transcribed for me."

She looked at him expectantly.

He raised one shoulder. "I don't know that I'll ever read it. Maybe. Right now, I need a break from all that."

"Will you ever want to know who your father was?"

"No. It's enough—more than enough—to know it wasn't Carl. My quarrel with him wasn't fathering me, it was abandoning me. My DNA ruled out that any of the men who died in Golden Branch had sired me. I don't see the point of continuing the saga."

Her arms tightened around his waist. She rested her cheek on his chest. "Will you write the story?"

"Harriet's bugging me to, but I've told her no. I couldn't write it without including you and the boys. I won't do that." He pushed his hand under her tank top and stroked her back, marveling over how familiar and wonderful the feel of her skin was, shuddering to think how close he came to foolishly denying himself this woman.

"I've considered writing about Hawkins. His parents endorsed the idea. Military suicides are at an all-time high. It speaks volumes that a young man with a background as solid as his could sink to that depth of despair. The theme would be the effects of combat even on those with the strongest fiber. It could be a worthwhile piece."

"Written by the best."

"Awww," he drawled and eased her cheek off his chest so he could whisk a kiss across it. But when he tried to kiss her in earnest, she resisted. "What?"

"You said of this house 'when *we're* here,' and that Eva had invited *us* for Thanksgiving. Come Thanksgiving, will we still be an us?"

"I'm counting on it. You're not?"

"Yes. *Yes*. Definitely."

"Good to know."

"But how will it work? The boys went back to school this week. I was planning to buy a house with a yard and a dog. George embraced the idea of having a room at the museum devoted to PTSD. If we get it past the board, I want to oversee the project. I'll want to be involved if Daddy's house is enshrined." She looked at him ruefully. "And you live in Virginia."

"Right. We've got some stuff to sort out, but they're practical matters. Nothing insurmountable. So long as I meet deadlines and attend an occasional editorial meeting, my job is more or less portable.

"I may read Flora's diary, or not. I'll draft a story about Hawkins and then decide if I want it to be published. If not, I'll write about something else. And when the boys get old enough to learn about their lineage, we'll explain it. They'll come to terms with it just as I have. We'll help them with whatever problems arise. The point is, we don't have to figure it all out today. We *can't* figure it all out today."

Placing his lips against hers, he whispered, "We're past the heavy stuff, Amelia. By comparison, the rest of it will be a breeze. Let's let up on ourselves for a while. We'll make decisions on an as-needed basis, love each other like crazy, and live one day at a time."

She smiled against his lips. "Sounds like a plan. I'm especially fond of the part about loving each other like crazy."

"Yeah, I like that part, too."

He cupped the back of her head and was settling in for a long, deep kiss, when she groaned, "We've got company."

Hunter and Grant, still in pajamas, were racing toward them, their bare feet thudding on the boardwalk.

Amelia yelled at them to be careful of splinters but the caution didn't slow them down. Gleefully shouting his name, they ran pell-mell toward them.

She gave him a dubious smile. "Are you sure you want to take them on?"

"That's one decision already made."

He wrapped his arms around her waist, so that when the boys tackled him into the sand, she went with him.